SUNSET BRIDGE

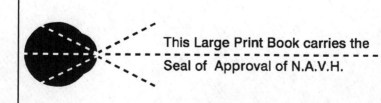

This Large Print Book carries the
Seal of Approval of N.A.V.H.

A HAPPINESS KEY NOVEL

Sunset Bridge

Emilie Richards

THORNDIKE PRESS
A part of Gale, Cengage Learning

GALE
CENGAGE Learning™

Detroit • New York • San Francisco • New Haven, Conn • Waterville, Maine • London

GALE
CENGAGE Learning

Copyright © 2011 by Emilie Richards McGee.
A Happiness Key Novel Series.
Thorndike Press, a part of Gale, Cengage Learning.

Thorndike Press® Large Print Core.
The text of this Large Print edition is unabridged.
Other aspects of the book may vary from the original edition.
Set in 16 pt. Plantin.

LIBRARY OF CONGRESS CATALOGING-IN-PUBLICATION DATA

Richards, Emilie, 1948–
   Sunset bridge / by Emilie Richards. — Large print ed.
    p. cm. — (A Happiness key novel series) (Thorndike Press large print core)
   ISBN-13: 978-1-4104-4145-4
   ISBN-10: 1-4104-4145-8
   1. Large type books. 2. Female friendship—Fiction. 3. Florida—Fiction. I. Title.
PS3568.I31526S86 2011
813'.54—dc23   2011024582

Published in 2011 by arrangement with Harlequin Books S.A.

Printed in the United States of America
1 2 3 4 5 6 7 15 14 13 12 11

With thanks to the art department at the original publisher, MIRA Books, whose gorgeous covers for their versions of the Happiness Key novels have been the next best thing to a Florida beach vacation.

CHAPTER ONE

On Thursday afternoon, the first day of her Everglades canoe trip with her lover, Marsh Egan, Tracy Deloche fell overboard into rotten egg–scented water. Unfortunately, her paddle lodged in a mangrove root. She stayed with the paddle, and Marsh stayed with the canoe.

On Thursday *evening* of their Everglades canoe trip, she discovered that their campground was a chickee, an elevated wooden platform above a channel that had turned to mudflats, and that the chickee came with no water, although it *did* come with two whining children and one portable toilet. The cheerful mom explained that this was a homeschooling field trip, and the children would be up and down all night recording observations in their journals.

Next to sleeping on a deflating air mattress, the children were no problem at all.

By Friday evening of their Everglades canoe trip, Tracy Deloche was pretty sure she and

Marsh were not meant to spend their lives together.

"Don't tell *me* about chiggers and no-see-ums! You think I need a biology lecture?" Tracy, perched on a fallen tree, was rolling up the legs of her jeans and spraying her calves with repellent as she spat out the words. Her ankles already felt like smoldering logs. Her arms ached from canoeing for hours through mazes of mangrove-lined creeks. Her head throbbed from wood smoke billowing up her nostrils.

"Here's the deal, hotshot, unless you *also* want chiggers in places only I ever see, you'd better move over there." Marsh pointed to one of two plastic coolers on the other side of the campfire, where an armload of salt-crusted driftwood was ramping up the smolder factor. "Chiggers thrive in dead wood."

Tracy leaped to her feet, which were — not surprisingly — bare, since that morning she'd found a scorpion in the toe of her water shoes, and found it the hard way. Earlier she'd taken her chances with flip-flops, since her big toe had swollen to twice its normal size, but now even the flip-flops had run for cover.

"You know, we're supposed to be having fun here," Marsh said. "That's why I'm with *you* instead of the rest of the Wild Florida gang. That's why you're with *me* instead of back at Happiness Key fixing up a cottage

8

for Wanda's daughter. Something going on I should know about? This whole weekend you've been wound tighter than a banjo string. The least little thing sends you screeching."

"Little?" Tracy pointed to her legs, peppered with scarlet dots. "Is *little* redneckspeak for miserable?"

He squatted to take a closer look, running a finger along her shin before he looked up and smiled. "We'll smear your legs with petroleum jelly. You'll feel better, and I'll get a little thrill."

"And it's the only thrill you're likely to get on this trip, too."

Marsh looked as if he was debating what to say to that. As always, he was dressed a lot more like the Florida Cracker he claimed to be than the pit-bull attorney who was director of one of Florida's most effective environmental organizations. His sandy hair was pulled back at the nape in a short ponytail, and he needed a shave. His faded green T-shirt was ripped under one arm. His cutoffs needed a good trim, and his feet were happily bare. In fact, he looked like the embodiment of Wild Florida, whose success at stopping a wetlands shopping mall had been the motivation for this celebratory camping trip. Marsh was in his element.

Tracy was not.

"You said you wanted to come." He sprang

back to his feet without using his hands. "I told you it would be rugged."

Tracy struggled to be fair. Knowing full well that this was not going to be a weekend at the Four Seasons, she had agreed to come along while Bay, Marsh's ten-year-old son, spent a long weekend in California with his mother, Marsh's ex. Some of Marsh's staff were doing a more grueling version of the trip, but Marsh had given that up to plan this shorter one with Tracy.

Tracy had come a long way in the year-plus that she'd lived in Florida, from spoiled Southern California socialite to a woman who held her own in almost any setting. Only not this one. Apparently the Wilderness Waterway of the Everglades was just a tad beyond her capabilities, or maybe the problem was everything else in her life, rolled into one giant, torturous sandspur of complications.

Tears sprang to her eyes, so unusual that she immediately credited the campfire. She might be a lot of things, but never a crybaby. She hadn't shed tears on the day that her husband, CJ Craimer, told her that life as she knew it had ended and she was about to become the wife of a felon. Ex-wife, as it turned out, in a divorce she hadn't cried over, either.

Marsh looked perplexed, as if this Tracy

10

Deloche was someone he didn't know or care to.

"Look . . ." She sniffed. "I'm trying. Okay? So, you warned me. I thought I'd be fine. Just give me a moment to be miserable."

He raised a brow. "I'm going fishing. We could use more firewood."

She heard him. Go in search of mangrove and buttonwood debris for the campfire, and while she was gone, please get her act together.

Even more annoyed, she debated. All she really wanted was to crawl into the tent and pull the sleeping bag over her head, only it was too hot. They hadn't waited until winter, when everyone else paddled the Wilderness Waterway. No, they'd come while the air was still warm and the bugs were frenzied, instead of simply omnipresent.

"I've got a great dinner planned," Marsh added, as if taking pity on her. "You'll feel better afterward."

She supposed he was trying. Last night they had eaten sandwiches and shared an apple, so how petty would it be to point out that not even rack of lamb or crème brûlée was going to lighten her spirits, much less the chicken breasts marinating in a plastic bag in one of the coolers? She knew the menu because she'd peeked yesterday before they even slid the canoe into the water.

Yesterday, when she was still young, eager

11

and looking forward to camping together.

"Has it ever occurred to you," she asked instead, "that the only time we're together, we could be mistaken for two good ol' boys swilling beer after an afternoon of cleaning spark plugs? When was the last time we did something that required a dress?"

"I don't look that good in ruffles." He leaned over and kissed her. "Don't stray far. Those dark clouds don't mean night's coming earlier, but hopefully they'll pass. Get a whole armload of wood, okay? If we can keep a good fire going, it will help with the bugs."

"Bugs." She shook her head so hard her ponytail flicked her cheek. "And I was *so* looking forward to more."

She started down the beach and around the end of the tiny key where they'd made their new campsite. She supposed she ought to be glad that tonight Marsh had chosen a beach and not a Calusa Indian mound in the middle of the mangroves, or yet another platform. This site allowed campfires, and it had a portable toilet down the beach from their tent, while many sites only had instructions for waste management. Just for her, she supposed. Considerate to a fault.

She determined not to go back until her mood improved. Sure, she could make a case for ruining the evening, but the thought gave her no pleasure. She had come on this trip because she wanted to spend time with

12

Marsh. As much as she enjoyed Bay, hours alone with his father were rare, and when the three of them were together, she and Marsh still promoted the illusion that Tracy was just a friend, despite their being lovers for two months.

Chalk up another problem.

Tracy was still barefoot, so she decided to stay close to the water. The sun was sinking fast, and already the sky was layered with violet and amber. Although dark clouds were moving in, the Gulf of Mexico was still relatively calm. Normally she was a fan of evenings on the beach, and normally she was able to tolerate a little discomfort as payment. But since the moment she had helped Marsh drag the canoe into the water near Everglades City, she'd been out of sorts and miserable. She almost felt sorry for him.

Almost.

She had dragged more than a canoe on this trip. She'd dragged problems that weren't going away. She'd been feeling tired and out of sorts for weeks, unable to concentrate. Wanda Gray, who lived in one of the five cottages Tracy owned in a shabby development called Happiness Key, had warned her this might be the start of menopause, even though Tracy was only thirty-five. Her periods had become increasingly spotty and erratic, although at her last checkup, doctor had blamed her condition on a prescribed break from birth

control pills. Thirty-five was young for menopause, but not unheard of. She had made
another doctor's appointment for next week,
but she wasn't looking forward to the diagnosis.

She had never really yearned for a baby,
and she wasn't sure she had much to offer
one. Still, having the decision taken away
from her by a whacked-out biological clock
didn't seem fair. Night sweats, facial hair, a
libido on holiday? None of it appealed to her.
Change of life? She had just begun to like the
one she had, thank you very much.

When she'd called her mother, to see if
such a thing ran in the family, Denise Deloche, with her usual level of maternal support, had cackled that maybe now Tracy
would understand what it felt like to be over
the hill *and* poor. Good old Mom had never
gotten over the fact that Tracy's ex had taken
everyone in the family down on his way to
prison for financial hanky-panky. Never mind
that Tracy herself had lost everything along
the way.

Well, almost everything. She *had* ended up
with Happiness Key. Which was yet another
problem.

Fifteen minutes later, hauling branches
behind her, she was back at the tent.
Charcoal-hued clouds blanketed the horizon
so thoroughly that if the sun had already
slipped behind it, she was none the wiser.

But darkness was falling quickly, and Marsh's fire had already petered out.

In the distance, she could see him about ten yards from shore, submersed up to his hips, contentedly casting a line into water that was growing choppier as she watched.

She was filthy. She could wade out and splash off the worst of the dirt and sweat, but Marsh wouldn't appreciate her scaring away all hope of a catch. Instead, she decided to fill a bowl and take a sponge bath with some of their limited store of water. Marsh had assured her he'd brought enough for that along with cooking and drinking.

The guy was all heart.

She dug a metal bowl and hand towel from a pile of supplies by the tent flap, and found a bar of soap in her own small day pack, the only thing she'd been allowed to bring in the crowded canoe. The pack contained little more than a few clothes and some toiletries, but she'd hidden her secret stash of power bars and chocolate inside her sleeping bag. Just in case Marsh got lost in the maze of mangrove trails, and their three-day trip morphed into a spectacular rescue.

She decided to change her T-shirt after she washed. Maybe a clean T-shirt wasn't exactly dressing for dinner, but she probably owed Marsh that much. Soap, water and a fresh coat of bug spray. She might feel almost human again.

Squatting, she threw open the tent flap and leaned forward to grab her shirt. From inside the tent a hissing ball of fur launched itself in her direction.

By the time Marsh got to shore, Tracy's screams had dwindled to whimpers.

"How're you doing?" Marsh asked an hour later, approaching Tracy warily, as if he fully expected her to propel herself at his throat, hands squeezing in anticipation. She was sitting beside the fire, staring at the flames, and for a moment she didn't look up.

"I'm fine. I really am. It's just . . . I just wasn't expecting a raccoon scrambling over my chest to freedom."

"That's why we don't leave food in the tent. They'll steal anything that's not tied down, even eat right through water jugs. That's why I slung ours from that tree a little while ago." He inclined his head toward a spot just above their tent. "We don't want to encourage them. They steal eggs from nests and generally wreak havoc on bird life."

She crooked a brow and hoped the message wasn't too subtle. If Marsh continued the lecture, she was going to kill him, or swim back to Everglades City and take her chances with gators and sharks.

"I guess you don't need to hear that right now, huh?" He smiled a little. "You need some cheering up?"

16

"I'm supervisor at the rec center, remember? I don't sit at a desk all day. I took the older kids camping in June. I'm not some kind of lightweight prima donna. I can build a fire, erect a tent, even lead a rousing chorus of 'Kumbaya' if I'm forced to."

"Let's hear it."

She glared at him.

"Or not," he said quickly. "Okay, I'll admit this trip's a little more grueling than I let on."

"Yeah, about that . . ."

"I just wanted to get you to myself, Trace."

She sighed. How could she stay angry? Marsh had only recently begun calling her Trace, as if he was welcoming her into his little family with its cute geographical nicknames. Marsh and Bay, now Trace. He'd explained that a "trace" was a path through uncharted territory, which, to her, seemed a fitting description.

"And I wanted you to *my*self, too," she said. "I'm just not at my most adaptable right now."

"Let me get you some wine. And I've got something special to go with it."

Now she was sure she was stressed, because a glass of wine really didn't sound good. Her stomach was still roiling from the raccoon encounter. Nevertheless, the man had hauled a bottle of wine in the crowded canoe just for this moment. She'd disappointed him enough

17

for one trip.

"Great," she said. "Need help?"

"Let me take care of you."

She smiled in thanks and relaxed a little. The clouds hadn't yet produced rain, and there was enough sky still visible to enjoy the few stars willing to shine. Best of all, a strong breeze was blowing off the Gulf, and between breeze and campfire, a percentage of mosquitoes had zoomed off to find easier prey. She had managed to wash up, and except for paw prints, her T-shirt was clean. Surely she would survive.

He came back with a glass, which she cradled in her palms; then he left for a minute and returned with a plastic plate and held it out to her. At first, by the flickering light of the campfire, she wasn't sure what he was offering. Then her stomach dived to her toes.

"Oysters," she said. "Wow. Raw oysters on the half shell. You got these out there?" She nodded toward the water.

"No, although they're actually creating oyster reefs not far away, but —" He stopped himself, as if realizing another environmental lecture wasn't going to go over well. "These are from the panhandle, flown in yesterday morning to that little general store where we parked my pickup."

"Oh . . ." She was thinking fast. "And you bought them without me even noticing."

"You were off having your last encounter

18

with gen-*u*-ine plumbing."

She'd used up her pathetic store of chatter. She grinned wanly. "Thing is, Marsh? I don't eat raw oysters. Smoked, sure. Fried and roasted, uh-huh. But I've never been able to, you know, swallow one that looks like that."

"You're kidding."

"Um . . . nope."

"All this time we've been together and I didn't know that?"

"Why, would that be a deal breaker?"

"We made some kind of deal?"

He was joking, but the question hurt. They had never discussed their relationship or the way they felt about each other. Marsh, who was open about many things, was zipped up tight when it came to feelings.

"You've ordered them when we've eaten out," she said. "I guess you just never noticed I ordered other things."

"Guess not."

"So you understand?"

"I understand nobody's ever showed you how to eat one. You're a foodie. You love everything. You'll love these."

He had gone to a lot of trouble, that was clear. Buying them, sneaking them on board, probably prying them open a little earlier, while she was recovering. The oysters were a gift, and he was proud of himself.

"I bet they'd be fabulous roasted in the campfire." She batted her eyes at him, but he

19

didn't buy it.

"There's nothing like a *raw* oyster."

"I think we could agree on that."

"You eat snails."

She could see this mattered. "Not raw." Still, as ornery as she felt, she didn't want to spoil the dinner for him. "Tell you what. I'll try one just for you. To show what a good sport I am and how much I appreciate the effort."

"Great." He headed off in the direction of the tent.

She'd hoped agreeing would be good enough, but clearly that was not to be. He returned with a miniature bottle of Tabasco and a pack of soda crackers.

"You can do it a couple of ways. Just stick the shell against your lip and slurp it down. Some people chew and some don't. Swallowing it whole makes no sense to me, because where's the taste?"

She didn't bother explaining that she was going to be a swallow-it-whole kind of gal.

"And the other way to do it?" she asked, hoping for something that involved tossing it over her shoulder for good luck.

"Shake some Tabasco on it. Throw it on a soda cracker and nibble away. Your choice."

"I'll take mine straight." She sent him a glorious smile, as if she was planning to enjoy herself. If she had to do this, she might as well achieve maximum benefit.

20

"Attagirl."

She was still smiling when he offered the plate so she could make her choice. She looked for the one most likely to slide down fast, because just looking at the platter made her throat threaten to close up shop.

She took what appeared to be the smallest.

"Hold it this way." He showed her. "Now put it up to your lips and slurp it down."

She remembered childhood and a nasty pink liquid she'd had to take for an ear infection. The family maid had sat on her feet and imprisoned her hands, and her mother had poured the liquid straight down her throat. She remembered gagging and retching and —

"Okay, here goes," she said brightly. She tilted the shell, and something wet, cool and slimy passed over her lips and crossed her tongue. She was drowning. She was going to choke.

She was *finished*. Thankfully, she realized that the oyster was finally slithering somewhere between her vocal cords and her bowels, and she was still breathing.

She opened her eyes and licked her lips. The taste reminded her of putrefying bait at Randall's, her local grocery.

"So what do you think?" Marsh asked.

She tried to come up with something that didn't begin with profanity. She nodded slowly. "I think . . . I think maybe it's not my thing." She nodded again, more emphatically.

"Oh, you'll learn to love them. Next time we'll try just a drop of Tabasco."

She held out her hand. "Now."

"Now?"

She curled her fingers and flexed them. "Now, please."

He handed her the bottle, and she shook a fair measure into her palm and licked it clean.

"I've never seen anybody do that," he said.

Thankfully, the worst of the taste was now gone, even if part of her tongue seemed to have gone with it. "I wanted the whole experience." She had problems shaping the words.

"I'll stick the rest of your oysters along the edge of the fire to roast."

"Right."

"You're a trouper." He bent over and kissed her forehead.

She hadn't wanted the wine, but now she sipped a little anyway, to keep her tongue from swelling to twice its size and to rid herself of the last vestiges of oyster slime. Her stomach was performing circus tricks, and she struggled not to reverse the oyster escapade. She breathed deeply and swallowed hard.

Marsh hummed as he cooked. He was a marvel in the kitchen, and apparently at the campfire, too. He slung a grate over coals that had burned down, propping it on three logs he'd nestled in the sand. He grilled chicken

22

breasts, sliced eggplant and zucchini and buried prebaked sweet potatoes in the ashes.

While he cooked he chatted, and if he realized how little she was contributing, he seemed to understand.

By the time she had eaten a little cooked food and they had cleaned up, she felt better. The air had cooled considerably, and the oyster was history. Marsh gauged her lightening mood and suggested a walk.

"Not a long one, though," he added. "It's about to rain."

"Maybe you'll be wrong."

"I prepared. We'll stay dry. Ground cloth, trench, whole nine yards." He took her hand. "Besides, I like the idea of cuddling and listening to raindrops pattering on the roof. We can zip our bags together. What do you say?"

"You're such a romantic guy."

"Just with you."

They strolled hand in hand along the water's edge. They had seen other boats, but no one else was camping on the key tonight. She thought she glimpsed lights halfway to the horizon and envied the sailors in their comfortable berths. Exhaustion? Anxiety? Hormones? Everything seemed to be pooling under her feet and sucking her down.

"You want to tell me what's been bothering you?" he asked. "Something's going on."

She was not about to discuss the possible

23

onset of menopause with Marsh. Nor was she going to ask how he felt about her and where their relationship was going. That took courage and patience, both of which seemed in short supply this weekend.

She settled on the third concern that had been gnawing at her. "I had bad news right before we left."

He stopped and faced her. "You didn't say anything."

"There's not much to say. Seems both the water system and the septic system at Happiness Key have to be replaced in the near future. And with all the changes in the laws since they went in originally, plus the environmental considerations, the cost is going to be enormous."

He whistled softly. "I knew it was coming, just not so soon."

"You knew?"

"We did have to check out the property before we agreed to the easement."

"We" was Wild Florida, who had convinced Tracy to agree to a conservation easement on her property, for which she received tax and other benefits. In return, Wild Florida received assurances that another piece of Florida would be protected from extensive development. Happiness Key might be a small community of five shabby cottages on twenty-five acres, but it was in a strategic location surrounded by other protected

24

properties. She'd met Marsh because of that.

"I don't know how I'm going to pay for it unless I take out a mortgage. And who knows if I can get one?"

"I could help," he said without hesitation.

Tracy had known he would offer, but her mind was made up. She'd spent the first decades of her life letting other people take care of her. That wasn't the way she planned to spend the rest of it.

She squeezed his hand. "Thanks, but this is my problem." She debated whether or not to tell him the rest, then forged ahead. "The contractor who made the evaluation offered to take the whole place off my hands."

"Does he know about the easement?"

"Sure. According to the documents, he can build on the foundations of the old cottages and renovate the ones that are still standing. CJ drew up some plans, remember? This guy thinks people will pay big bucks to live there, even without a lot of square footage."

Marsh was silent. She knew what he was thinking. Wild Florida had been generous in their terms, and now he was probably sorry. He didn't want to see anything done to the property except maybe send the whole place back to a time when nothing had stood on it but trees and Florida wildlife.

"I know how you feel," she said. "And I have my own issues. What would I tell the others?"

The others in question were her renters, three women she'd grown surprisingly close to since she'd moved to Florida. How would she tell them she was booting them out so she could avoid a mortgage?

"So that's why you've been so —"

"Don't go there, okay?"

"Look, we'll talk this over another time. Right now you're too wiped. Let's get you to bed. It's been a big day, and I can hear you falling asleep on your feet."

She let him lead her back to their campsite and was glad she had when rain began to fall. She brushed her teeth quickly in water he poured for her, then splashed a little on her face, forgoing anything more extensive.

When she got inside the tent, she saw that while she'd readied herself for bed, he had zipped their bags together.

"Crafty, aren't we?" she asked when he came back a few minutes later. "You think you're getting lucky tonight?"

"Nah, I think you might need a good back rub and a warm body next to yours."

She was touched. Tears actually sprang to her eyes again, and all her insecurities flooded back. She cleared her throat. "If the tent starts to flood, I'm sleeping on top of you."

"I'll leave the flap up and live in hope."

Despite his words, he zipped up the flap, adjusted the zipper, then crawled in with her. With the flap closed, the tent was dark, but it

26

was a backpacker special, and the space was so small, he was beside her in two seconds. His arms went around her, and he pulled her close.

"We'll take it easier tomorrow," he said softly. "I didn't mean to wear you out. You're such an athlete, I figured you'd love it here as much as I do. But you don't have to. I just appreciate that you tried."

She turned over so she was facing him. She could smell soap and toothpaste, and she reached up to stroke his stubbly cheek.

"It's beautiful. I mean that. Really. It's just . . . I'm, you know, just out of sorts."

"Been there, done that, every single month of my marriage."

She laughed a little and hoped he was right. "Maybe that's it."

"Can I do anything to make you feel better?"

She found his lips in the dark and kissed him. "Just forget I fell in the water, and complained about the chiggers and the no-see-ums and stubbed my toe on a scorpion —"

"Your secrets will be safe with me."

"Am *I* safe with you?"

"No question." His arms tightened around her. "Now, go to sleep, okay? And don't keep wiggling like that, or I can't guarantee what'll happen next."

"Let's conduct an experiment."

27

"Trace, you realize what you're doing?"

"We've still got a few hours until this day's over. Let's end on a better note, okay?"

"I guess, if it makes you happy, I could oblige." He kissed her, missing her lips and finding her chin instead, then moving lower.

"You can always . . . be counted on . . . to do what's right, can't you?"

This time he found her lips, and for a long time there was no need to say anything. Sure this wasn't in the cards, she hadn't bothered with her diaphragm, but Marsh, ever hopeful, took care of the birth-control angle. Wrapped in his arms, the rain falling faster on the tent top, she forgot everything else and let him take her to a place where there were no more questions.

Afterward, he pulled her close and rested his head against her hair. "I'm not sure which was better. That, or fishing you out of the water this morning without tipping the canoe."

She tried to laugh, was willing to, but suddenly the tent whirled and undulated, and since they'd just indulged themselves, she knew the sensation was not pent-up passion. Tracy tried to sit up, but for a moment, she was so disoriented, she wasn't sure which direction to try.

"Marsh . . ." She swallowed hard and managed to claw her way out of the sleeping bag and his arms.

28

"What's wrong? Need a bathroom trip?"

She was very afraid that what was wrong wasn't going to wait for the hike to the Porta Potty. She pitched forward and began to crawl toward the flap — at least she hoped that was where she was headed.

"Trace?" He sat up, too. "What's the problem?"

She couldn't speak. Wildly, she felt along the tent flap, praying she could find the zipper pull. Just as she was about to despair, she found it and managed to inch it up until air poured in, along with cool splashes of rain. She continued crawling until she was out and up on her feet. Then, bent over and clutching her abdomen, she stumbled toward the water.

She made it just in time. The entire night's meal vanished into the waves.

She was still heaving and gulping air when Marsh joined her. "Here." He held out a towel, although it wasn't much help. Rain was falling steadily, and she was soaked.

"I'm . . . sorry," she gasped. "That oyster!"

"You think it was the oysters?" He sounded incredulous.

"That raw one tasted . . . awful. Maybe I got a bad one."

"*I* feel fine."

"Maybe you got all the good ones." She held the towel to her face anyway. "Or maybe I'm coming down with something. There's been some kind of virus going through the

29

center. A . . . lot of kids have been sick. I . . ."
She buried her face again. She was shivering now, after a whole day of steaming in the heat.

"Are you okay? Do you need to stay here a little longer?"

She could hardly think. She no longer felt nauseous, but that might not last. "You go back. I'll join you in a minute. I'm okay. Really. I just want to wait here by myself to be sure. Go."

He hesitated, but she reached out and pushed his shoulder. "Go, please."

He shook his head and left her. She waited until the darkness swallowed him. Then she buried her face in the towel and bent over, rain sluicing down her back. But the rain was nothing compared to the revelation.

There was no mysterious virus making the rec center rounds, and even if there had been, she would not have succumbed. She was known for her cast-iron stomach.

She was not going through the change of life, although her life was certainly about to change forever. The problem was hormones, all right, but not their absence. In fact, if she was right, she was suffering from an overabundance. All the evidence had finally fallen into place and revealed an answer so ludicrous, it was no wonder it had eluded her.

She hadn't been poisoned by oysters, raw or roasted, but she did have something in common with the bivalves. She, too, could harbor something infinitely precious and priceless inside her.

Not a pearl, but a baby.

Tracy was almost certain she was pregnant.

CHAPTER TWO

"Last time I decorated a place for Maggie, she was moving out of the nursery into a big-girl bed, so the baby-to-be could sleep in her crib. I painted her new room pink, and not that beigey pink that looks like a bad sunburn, but the real deal. Like my mama's favorite roses. Pink walls, pink bedspread and curtains, even a little pink rug. And you know what that girl told me?"

Wanda Gray stopped the narrative and looked at Janya Kapur, who was rolling ivory paint onto the largest wall in the cottage Maggie would be moving into that afternoon.

Janya, who knew a cue when she heard one, turned her head. "What did she tell you?"

"She said she wanted to sleep with her daddy and me 'cause her room looked like a strawberry ice-cream cone, and it made her tummy hurt."

"Children say clever things."

"She meant it, too. We tried to make her happy, but Maggie always knew exactly what

she wanted. Once she made up her mind
. . . ? There was no changing it." Wanda shook
her head.

Before she went back to rolling paint, Janya
patted her friend's shoulder. "And, of course,
there is no one else in your family who acts
this way."

"Oh, please. Me? Nothing like it. Maggie
and me, we're as different as a palm tree and
an oak. I had to go back into that room, me
expecting a baby in a month, you understand,
me as big as that Statler mansion where you
fell into the swimming pool —"

"It would be polite not to remember that
afternoon out loud."

Wanda was always glad to get a rise out of
her young friend. "I still think of you, drip-
ping wet and that pretty Indian thing you
were wearing all clinging to you, and those
men staring at you like you were some kind
of water goddess come to earth."

Janya was only in her twenties, with long
black hair and a body men noticed even when
it wasn't so perfectly revealed. " 'Course,"
Wanda continued, "you fell in to help me out
of a jam, so I'll just pretend I don't remember. But anyway, there I was, at least as big as
that Statler place or more, having to go back
to that beautiful room I'd already painted
once, and paint the walls pale green. She
picked out that color herself, and her hardly
even three. To me, that room looked like a

33

head of iceberg lettuce, but Maggie, she was happy."

"She will be happy with *this* color? It is very soft, like morning light."

"She's not happy, she can paint it herself."

"She will be bringing some of her own things to make it her home?"

Wanda didn't know what her daughter would be bringing with her. She was still amazed Maggie was coming to Happiness Key to live. Maggie, the unemployed cop and jilted lover. Maggie, who until now had always known exactly where she was going and how to get there.

"I doubt she took much when she walked out on her job and Felo," Wanda said.

"Felo? This is an American name?"

"Short for Rafael. Spanish. Rafael Estrada. Family's from Cuba. He's third-generation here on American soil. Grandparents on both sides came right after the revolution — theirs, not ours. One side were dentists or something like that, but couldn't be dentists here, on account of different rules and such. I guess it was hard, the way things changed for his family. One minute you're a hotshot, the next you're sweeping floors and washing windows. Rafael's grandmother had to live with an aunt when she came over 'cause her parents never got out at all. Sad story, huh?"

"Very sad, yes. And this Felo? He had problems? This is why Maggie walked away from him?"

Wanda didn't know how to answer that. She had always liked Felo Estrada. Oh, sure, at first she'd been surprised Maggie'd chosen somebody from a different culture. Then Maggie and Felo moved in together, into a house in Little Havana, which was, in Wanda's view, as strange as moving to Argentina or Peru, although not like moving to Cuba, since the people in Little Havana weren't all that fond of Castro. Still, Maggie had been happy there in the tidy bungalow with a lanai looking over a postage-stamp pond Felo had put in all by himself. Their neighbors came from different places. Some from Cuba, of course, but some from Haiti and Nicaragua, or maybe it was El Salvador — Wanda could never keep those Latin countries straight. Maggie was fluent in Spanish and chatted with anybody in the neighborhood — or arrested them, if it came to that. She'd fit right in.

"I don't know as you could say Felo has problems," Wanda said. "He's a cop, just like she used to be. He's as handsome as sin and just as enticing, you know what I mean? He attracts women the way orange blossoms attract honeybees. Maggie said even the old ladies on her street used to flirt with him."

"I know this kind of man."

Wanda shrugged. "Maybe, and maybe not. I like Felo, and so does Ken." Ken was

Wanda's husband, a police officer himself and the best judge of people Wanda knew. "Seemed to me Felo always made women feel good about themselves, while he kept just enough distance to let them know he was taken."

Janya made one more stroke down the wall, then she stepped back. "But not taken now?"

"I don't know for sure what went wrong. I just know Maggie left the force, then she left him. She's been off camping for six whole weeks. Half the time we didn't know where she was. Then the last time we talked and I told her how sick I was of the assistants parading through my shop who don't know lard from butter, she said she'd come and help out for a while."

"It's good she's moving here. You will like having her so close."

Wanda hoped that was true. She and her daughter were so different. Wanda was never quite sure what to say to Maggie. Maggie kept her thoughts to herself, but Wanda was just about sure she didn't approve of her mother. Loved her, sure. But approve? Not so Wanda could measure.

"What else do you think we should do in here?" Wanda asked. "I wish Ms. Deloche had seen fit to stay behind and give us an idea or two."

"There was no reason for Tracy to miss the camping trip, and I can be here when Maggie comes." Janya glanced at Wanda. "Would you like that?"

Wanda realized she hadn't fooled her friend. That was what she and Janya were, of course, even if Janya was younger than her own daughter. They were friends, no mistaking it. All the women at Happiness Key were friends, even if they'd gotten off to a rocky start.

"It wouldn't hurt," she said. "I can introduce you that way."

"The kitchen's clean, and there is so much food in the refrigerator, she won't have to shop for a month. You put in the new shower curtain?"

Wanda nodded. "And I made up Lizzie's bed. Only it's not Lizzie's anymore, is it? I still can't get used to her and Dana being gone for good."

Dana Turner had been the last tenant of this cottage, and she and her daughter, Lizzie, had become part of the Happiness Key family until an abrupt and lamented departure. Dana had also been the only decent assistant Wanda had so far been able to hire for Wanda's Wonderful Pies, her pie shop and café. The women received postcards now and then, but so far no one knew exactly where the two had gone. Or Pete, the man who had disappeared with them.

"The new slipcovers and pillows look cheerful and bright," Janya said. "Maggie will

37

be happy here."

Wanda straightened the edge of a throw rug she'd bought to set in front of the sofa. "I always got along better with Junior. He's more like me. Maggie, she's like Ken. She won't tolerate a fool, not Maggie. That's how come she's not a detective anymore."

"She got in trouble?"

"Anybody would have, doing what she did. See, she was assigned to the crime-suppression unit — drug stuff mostly. She worked on this big case for most of a year. There was this dealer, headed a whole ring of dealers, kind of a CEO, if you want to call him that, or a kingpin. She and her partner laid up enough evidence against him to build him a jail cell for the rest of his life.

"Only the state's attorney, a guy named Paul Smythe, declined to prosecute him. Just up and said, 'Nope, what you brought me isn't good enough. So go work on something else, 'cause this case is going away.' "

"A year?" Although she hadn't been in the country for long, Janya seemed to understand the significance.

"A year. And everybody was mad about it, you bet. But her superiors told her to let it go. Felo told her to let it go, too, and the thing was . . . ? That drug dealer . . . ? He was a Cuban American, just like Felo. Even worse, Felo's best friend, who's a hotshot in one of the big sugar companies, knew him

38

real well, even partied with him sometimes."

"Did Maggie believe there was a connection?"

"She must have. Why else would she walk out on him the way she did? The day Felo told her to back off, she walked into a press conference Paul Smythe was giving, took off her badge, laid down her gun and in front of all those reporters, said she was quitting the police force because the real criminals were wearing suits and giving press conferences, and she didn't want any part of that. Then she went home and packed."

Janya was silent a moment. "She will not be going back to him," she said at last. "This is a hurt she cannot heal."

"Maybe, maybe not. He's been calling me, you know. For the past six weeks, ever since it happened. Calling to find out where she is. I told him it wouldn't do any good, but he calls anyway. Called two days ago, as a matter of fact, and he knows I hate being in the middle like this."

Janya wiped her hands with a wet rag; then she put her arm around Wanda's waist. "We will do one more tour of the cottage, just to be sure. But your daughter will feel welcome here. All of us will welcome her."

Wanda put her arm around Janya, too. "I can count on you. I know that. But I might need some advice, you being closer to Maggie's age and all."

39

"Tracy and I will do what we can. And Alice can be her grandmother, if she needs one."

Wanda wasn't sure what her daughter was going to need, but she figured that whatever it was, Maggie was coming to the right place to find it. Even if Wanda herself couldn't provide the answers.

"Okay, I know you didn't like staying with Mrs. Sanchez," Maggie Gray told the yowling cat in the travel carrier beside her. "Even if she did feed you fresh chicken twice a week. But your memory's short, right? You're a cat, Rumba, despite what Felo told you. And sometimes cats just have to go along with whatever life throws at them."

Rumba, sleek and white, with eyes the color of duckweed, continued to glare at her, although the yowling dropped a decibel.

Maggie hadn't wanted to leave Rumba with a stranger. Six weeks ago, when she packed her suitcases and loaded her car, she had considered leaving Rumba with Felo, in the cat's familiar home, until she was settled somewhere. But Felo, whom Rumba adored, might have refused to give her back. Instead, Maggie had left Rumba with the mother of a friend, who liked cats, but liked to travel, too. Mrs. Sanchez had been glad for a temporary companion.

The cat was clearly Maggie's. A year before she and Felo moved in together, Maggie had

40

found Rumba, a pathetic tuft of white fur, in the burned-out shell of a drug house and nursed her back to health with an eyedropper and unstinting devotion. But in the four years she and Felo had shared a home, Rumba had extended her aloof feline affection to him, as well. Maggie supposed once she and Felo were able to have a civil conversation, she would grant him visiting rights. It seemed cruel to remove the cat from his life the way she had removed herself.

"You'll like living near the beach," Maggie said, although she had no plans to let Rumba out of the house to chase seagulls. "And my mother will probably bake you a pie, something with tuna and hard-boiled eggs. She'll come up with a winner."

Maggie smiled just a little at that. During her childhood, any disaster had rated one of Wanda's pies. Maggie's mother was a practitioner of pie therapy. Strawberry pie on the day Maggie came home from school with a sprained ankle. Chocolate meringue the day Junior was sent home with lice — but only after Wanda had fiercely scrubbed his head, of course, and given him a crew cut. In the years that followed, every time her scalp itched, Maggie had been terrified her own auburn hair would be quickly reduced to stubble.

"We had key lime pie for the most special occasions," she said out loud, because the cat

41

had started yowling again. "Sweet potato pecan or walnut chocolate chip when family got together on holidays. Lemon pie as light as clouds, anchored by slices of candied lemon. Luscious Lemon. That one's still my favorite."

Maggie realized how silly all this must sound. She could hardly believe she had been reduced to discussing pie with a cat. She'd never imagined that someday her mother would own her very own pie shop. And she had certainly never imagined that she would become Wanda's assistant.

"You've met my mother," she told Rumba. "Maybe you didn't notice she and I are related, but we are. She's a character, and she'll take some getting used to. She has a dog, a greyhound named Chase. She rescued him, the way I rescued you. Maybe you two can be friends.

"And you already like my father," she went on. "You sat on his lap last time he visited. Felo and I were surprised."

She could think his name, but saying it out loud? Harder. Much harder.

"I don't know how long we'll be staying," she said, starting a new topic. "Mom needs an assistant, and Lord knows, nobody else would know better how to work with her. We'll get things stabilized there, then I'll look for something more up my alley."

The problem, of course, was that she had

no idea what that might be, which was why she had volunteered to help her mother for a while.

She had always wanted to be a cop. From the moment she understood what her father did to support his little family, she had wanted to follow suit. Her mother had discouraged her, believing one cop in a family was plenty. Maggie had understood her mother's fears, even as she quietly worked around them.

At the University of Miami she had taken a double major in criminology and psychology, all the while knowing that both would serve her well when she applied for the force. She had also been a competitive swimmer, to stay fit and ready. She had talked to her father's friends, sought relevant summer jobs, made contacts.

After graduation, she had gone straight to the police academy; then, with few choices because of hiring freezes, she had started her career in central Florida, in a sheriff's department with a record of treating women poorly. She had been warned away by professors and family alike, but she had taken "That which does not kill me only makes me stronger" as her motto, and survived two miserable years of discrimination and harassment. She had come away with survival skills, a strong aversion to male bonding, faith in her own good

43

judgment and a well-deserved reputation as a loner.

Homesick for the city of her birth, she had applied repeatedly to the City of Miami Police Department so that she wouldn't be in her father's shadow in the larger Miami-Dade police force, and once a job was finally available, she had never looked back.

Not until now.

"I don't know where we'll go or what we'll do after this," she said. "Maybe some state with four seasons. You'd like snow. I could put you outside in a snowdrift and never see you until spring. Maybe I'll find a job doing security. Or maybe I'll get a job as some kind of private dick and follow cheating husbands around with a camera."

Even the suggestion made her feel sick. She'd been a real cop, not a wannabe. The cat curled up in a ball and closed her eyes, but now Maggie was feeling worse by the second.

How had everything come to this? Three months ago she'd thought she had it all. Now she was heading home, tail between her legs. Not that Palmetto Grove or the preposterously named Happiness Key had ever been home to her. But that was where her parents lived now. Her mother had developed a close circle of friends, and was happy with them and her new profession. Her father liked being a cop on a smaller force, a bigger fish in a smaller pond.

Maggie herself would just be a fish out of water. Job gone. Profession gone. Lover . . .

Gone.

She realized that while she'd been soul searching and placating her cat, she had reached Palmetto Grove. She drove past the city-limits sign, and the area began to look familiar. Maggie had been here over Easter. Her parents had rented a spacious gulfside motel suite for a weekend, and the whole gang had come. Junior, his wife and two children, Maggie and Felo. She and Junior had driven across the bridge to view their parents' new quarters. The house was weathered and basic, but the problems that had haunted the Grays' marriage during their final year in Miami had been noticeably absent.

For that, if for nothing else, Maggie was glad they had moved here.

But how would it work for her?

Palmetto Grove was unremarkable except that it seemed to lack the worst problems of Florida's east coast cities. The landscape was familiar, as were the noises and the salt smell of the air. Still, she immediately missed the bustle, the energy, of Miami, particularly Little Havana, with old men playing dominoes under palm trees, the fragrances of cigar smoke and Cuban coffee, the lilt of Latin music that permeated their lives.

45

She waited at one traffic light, then another, before she had a clear shot at the bridge that would take her to the key. She passed a sign announcing the erection of a new span in December, and a list of local officials who had appropriated all the credit. She wondered if the construction noise would reach as far as her new house.

Once she crossed over, she took her time. The bridge end of the key was the most settled, although she remembered her mother saying that beyond this first sparse cluster of pricey houses, much of the rest of the island was protected from development. Maggie was a fan of all things wild and natural, so this was a plus. No one had come here, as they had on other Gulf Coast islands, and denuded it to build high-rise condos and hotels, or replaced native foliage with water-guzzling, fertilizer-hogging exotics.

"Almost there," she told the sleeping cat, although there was no joy in her voice. She was thirty years old. Once she had moved to Miami, she had made detective in record time. She had commendations on her record. And now she was going home to live with Mommy and Daddy while she put her life back together.

She could still turn around. She hadn't spoken to Felo, but in a moment of weakness she had listened to one of his messages, although she had deleted the rest. He wanted her back. He was angry, yes, but he wanted her to come home. Her job would *not* be waiting, of course, but Miami was a big city, and there would be other opportunities.

For just seconds, her foot eased up on the gas pedal. Then she gripped the wheel until she saw the first battered cottage of Happiness Key appear. She came to a halt at the end of the community, lined with similar concrete-block cottages.

Wanda was sitting on a wooden bench in the house's shadow. Her copper-colored hair was lacquered into curls on top of her head. Her black-rimmed glasses tilted at the corners like the Cheshire cat's smile. She wore purple spandex capris and a lime-green blouse, which somehow managed to look okay. Beside her was a gorgeous young woman with dark skin and hair. Although all the neighbors had been gone during Maggie's brief visit, she knew from her mother's stories that this must be Janya.

Wanda had become a mother at twenty-three, but she had been more than ready for the job. She'd been the go-to mom on the block, the one who always had homemade cookies in a jar, who set up the sprinkler for games of tag on hot summer nights, who didn't complain when wet bathing suits left spots on her succession of flowered sofas.

She had fought for her children when necessary, let them wallow in their own mistakes when *that* was necessary, too. She was loud, opinionated, insensitive — and fiercely loyal to everybody she loved. She was Mom, but she and Maggie had never found the same frequency so they could really be intimate.

Now, seeing her on the bench with her friend, just waiting for the opportunity to jump back into Maggie's life, made Maggie question every decision she had made.

It was too late to drive away. For better or worse, she and Wanda needed each other. She needed a place to recover. Wanda needed someone to help as her business grew. And Maggie had a chance to give something back to the woman who had raised, educated and supported her.

She opened the driver's-side door and swung her legs over the seat. Rumba awoke and began to lick a paw as Maggie got out. She'd fully expected her mother to rise and hurry down to help unload, but Wanda didn't move.

Maggie lifted a hand in greeting. Wanda lifted one, too. For just a moment they stared at each other. For once Maggie understood exactly what her mother was thinking.

Wanda was worried, as well. Maggie's breath caught. They were trapped in this decision now, but for the first time they had everything in common. They were afraid that the distance between them would finally be

48

revealed, that the surface peace and intimacy they had found would be exposed as a sham.

Her life was in turmoil, and everything she had wanted was suddenly gone, but if Maggie had needed proof that she was standing on a precipice, here it was.

She couldn't see her mother's eyes, but she knew what was in them. Fear that she would fail Maggie. Concern that their relationship would not survive this challenge. And the endless, aching love of a mother for her daughter.

Maggie lifted her hand higher. "Hey, Mom, come get Rumba, would you? She needs you to talk some sense into her."

Wanda got to her feet. "Nobody better equipped to do it."

Maggie smiled at last, and Wanda smiled, too.

CHAPTER THREE

"I have done something you will not appreciate."

Janya looked up at those words and gazed steadily at her husband over the remnants of a late lunch. Perhaps Rishi was not a handsome man, but the new absence of a bristly mustache and a more attractive haircut had done wonders for his face. Or perhaps she was simply a wife falling in love with the stranger she had married.

She considered this conversation opener. Often the only time they had to talk was while they were eating. Although they had not yet been blessed with children, their lives were still busy, even on weekends. She had left the house early to help Wanda paint; then he had left to get his hair cut before she returned. They were finally in the same room.

She smiled encouragement. "Really?" she said, hoping for more.

"I have invited guests to visit this afternoon."

50

"Today?"

He nodded sheepishly. "Soon. I told you about Harit, my barber, and his wife, Kanira? I invited them to come. It happened before I even knew I was speaking."

"And you didn't think to telephone and warn me?"

"I expected to be home earlier, to tell you in person. Then I remembered another errand and forgot to call." He paused, fork to mouth. "I am sorry, Janya."

Rishi was a brilliant software designer, thought by many to be a genius. He was also a good businessman and loving husband. But while he could remember the smallest technical details, more often than not simple day-to-day matters slipped right by him.

"You have wanted to invite them for some time," she said graciously.

Rishi had met Harit at the shop where Harit worked part-time. He and his wife were from India, too, although they were from Kolkata, in the east. Still, in Palmetto Grove, where few Indians had yet to gather, the region mattered less than the country. Rishi had been delighted to find a new friend with whom he had much in common.

He was clearly relieved. "I would like to know them better. And Harit says Kanira is lonely for other Indian women and will be glad to meet you. They will not be here for a meal, because the children go to sleep early.

51

But they can run and play on the beach for a little while."

"Children?"

"They have two, a boy and a girl. Little children." He sounded wistful.

Janya didn't say anything to that, but her heart went out to her husband. Rishi had discovered that the lack of children in their lives was due to him, and while he had undergone surgery that might help increase his chances of fatherhood, so far, no pregnancy had resulted. While she had assured him this was not a question of fault, and that they would find a solution together with the doctor's help, he still felt guilty.

Janya was glad she had cleaned the house thoroughly yesterday. When they had first come to live in the cottage just a bit more than a year ago, she'd had little to do except clean. Now she was busy at least several days a week painting murals of forest animals or underwater scenes on nursery walls. Last week she'd spent four long days on the entryway of a home in a lavish gated development. The owners had asked for a vivid depiction of the legend of Tsarevich Ivan and the Fire Bird to greet their visitors. They had paid her so much on completion that she still expected someone to appear and demand she return the bonus.

"I will be glad to welcome them," she said.

"You are good to me." He reached across

to take her hand.

She squeezed it. "I will make lemonade, and tea. And you will drive down to Randall's, and buy doughnuts and cookies."

"I'm glad you're not angry." Rishi rose and began to clear the table. "I will sweep the patio when I come back from the store."

She thought, as she often did now, that she had married well.

Rishi's friends arrived an hour later. Janya watched the family emerge from an economy sedan that reminded her of the one Rishi had bought for her after she'd passed her driving test last year. Only, this car was older, much older.

She and Rishi went outside to greet their guests. Harit was shorter than Rishi, and thinner, with straight black hair parted in the middle and swept behind his ears. In his black T-shirt, Janya thought he resembled a pirate from one of the novels Wanda loved so well. Kanira was even shorter, probably not quite five feet, with hair that was just a few inches longer than her husband's and dangling gold earrings. She wore a dark red dress that trailed nearly to her ankles, but no smile.

The children were younger than Janya had imagined. Kanira carried the youngest, a tiny girl in a ruffled white dress, with a fluff of dark hair fluttering like dandelion down in the breeze. A little boy of about four walked beside his father, whom he resembled.

53

Rishi moved forward. "Harit, Kanira, welcome."

Harit and Rishi clasped hands and exchanged courtesies. Kanira nodded a silent hello to Rishi as she fussed with the baby's dress. She did not look happy to have come. Perhaps she had not been happy even to leave home. She looked tired and hot, and Janya immediately stepped off the stoop to introduce herself.

Kanira gave a wan smile in response. Harit was more enthusiastic and thanked her for the invitation. He introduced the children.

"My son, Vijay."

Kanira spoke up immediately. "But *we* call him Jay because he is an *American* child."

Harit ignored her. "My daughter is Lily, and we call her *Lily.*"

Janya heard the tension and tried to defuse it. She gestured toward the house. "It must be difficult to travel even a short distance with small children. Come sit inside, where it is cool. I will get you something to drink."

"I have asked and asked Harit to have the air conditioner in our car repaired, but he does not listen."

Janya glanced at her husband and Harit, who were deep in conversation. If Harit had heard, he didn't seem concerned.

"Would you like me to carry the baby?" Janya asked.

Kanira ignored the fact that the child was

reaching for Janya's gold necklace and squirming to get closer to her. "She doesn't like strangers."

"Let's settle you inside, then. We'll visit the beach once you've rested."

"I told Harit. The children are too young to enjoy a beach. But how would he know what is good for them? He is always locked away, writing his books." Kanira followed Janya, while Harit stayed behind to finish his conversation with Rishi. Or to avoid his wife. Vijay stayed with his father.

Inside, Janya settled Kanira and the baby on the sofa. "Books? Harit is a writer? What a gift he must have."

"*He* is no gift. That I can tell you. There are many things he could do to make a better living for us, but Harit is determined to write novels."

"Does he not work at the barbershop?"

"Yes, he cuts hair in the afternoons, then in the mornings and evenings he finds a quiet place outside our home and writes. He makes just enough money from the shop and a small literary grant to feed us, but little more."

Janya didn't know what to say. Kanira was a stranger, but she was already telling Janya secrets she didn't want to hear.

She offered her guest lemonade, but Kanira shook her head. "I am too upset to eat or drink. I am wasting away." She began to fuss with the little girl's dress again, and Lily began to whimper.

Janya lowered herself to the sofa beside them and, without asking, took the baby off Kanira's lap. The little girl snuggled sleepily against her and reached out to play with her chain. "Rishi has been so pleased to find another Indian family to visit with," Janya said.

"Rishi has his own business?"

"He designs and packages software. For computers."

"Now, *that* is a job to be proud of. And he does well?"

"Well enough. He will do better in time."

"You have no children?"

"Not yet."

"Well, I'm sorry I do."

This time Janya couldn't think of one word to say.

Kanira didn't notice, because she'd already continued. "I hoped that children would convince Harit he must stop playing at being a writer and start providing for us. He graduated from Princeton on scholarship. Princeton! For a boy from his village and caste? He was extraordinary. He could have gone on, become a doctor, an engineer, anything. Instead, he decided to become a writer. I thought children would make him responsible, but now I know nothing will do that. I should have realized it before I said I would marry him. I was blinded by love."

"Then you chose each other? He was your own choice?"

Kanira made a face, as if that fact only made things worse. "Wasn't I the fool?"

Once she and Marsh were parked outside her house, Tracy leaned over and kissed him on the cheek. "Don't get out. I'll just grab my backpack and head inside."

"You're sure you don't want me to come in and make certain you have enough chicken soup for dinner?"

"I told you, I feel a lot better today. Whatever hit me last night is working its way through my system."

And if she was correct, it would work its way out in something just short of nine months.

Marsh looked relieved he wasn't going to be called on as a nurse. "Take it easy. And call the doctor if you don't feel better by Monday."

"I'm really sorry we had to cut the trip short."

Tracy figured as lies went, that was a small one. The larger one, the possible pregnancy, was the whopper. Of course, this evening she was not as convinced her diagnosis was correct. She'd felt nauseated in the morning, and a breakfast of instant oatmeal and powdered milk hadn't helped. But as the day wore on, her stomach had settled. So what if

57

she was experiencing every pregnancy symptom she'd heard women complain about? Surely it could be something else.

Maybe it was something easier to deal with, like a life-threatening illness.

"You'll call if you need help?" he asked.

"I'm surrounded by women who'll come over and hold my hand. Call me before you go to bed, and I'll sing you to sleep."

"I'll call if you promise not to."

"Coward." She tossed him a smile, got out and reached into the back of the pickup cab for her pack. Stepping back, she waved goodbye, and he finally pulled away.

When she was sure he was gone, she dropped the cheerful act, rummaged through her purse for her keys and took off for her Bimmer.

In just minutes she was at Randall's, the only store on Palmetto Grove Key. She had forced herself to drive slowly enough not to overtake Marsh, but now she pulled into a parking slot so fast she slid on loose gravel. She cut the engine and took a deep breath.

So Randall's wasn't a drugstore. The wooden building with a vintage Coca-Cola chest on the porch was an odd cross between a gourmet food and bait shop, where chicken gizzards nestled next to prime Angus steaks, and fishing lures winked at French-press pots and bamboo steamers. Surely somewhere on the crowded, chaotic shelves she would find a pregnancy-test kit. She didn't have the patience to drive into town.

Inside, she scanned the aisles, just to be sure no one she knew was nearby. Satisfied, she went in search. Ten minutes of digging through dusty boxes in the pharmacy aisle turned up nothing. Finally she cornered a clerk, a scrawny post-adolescent with a goatee and one gold hoop in his earlobe.

"I need a pregnancy test for a friend." She had no idea why she was lying to the young man, but it glided across her tongue like extra-virgin olive oil. "I don't see any."

"I'll see what I can find out." He ambled off so slowly that at first she wasn't certain he was moving.

She looked around for something to do while she waited. Settling at the magazine rack, she was paging through the newest *People* magazine, counting the faces she had seen at parties when she was still married to CJ, when she heard a familiar voice call her name.

"Tracy!"

Startled, she dropped the magazine, but she recovered as she picked it up and was smiling brightly by the time Olivia Symington came skipping toward her.

"Well, hey there!" Tracy made herself look pleased to see the girl, although for once, she really wasn't.

"We're getting ice cream. My soccer team won."

"Congratulations." They high-fived. Eleven-year-old Olivia was one of Tracy's favorite people. Pretty, with brown hair, clear skin and startlingly blue eyes, she was already showing the promise of greater beauty. She and Alice, who was now coming up behind the girl, were Tracy's neighbors. Alice had custody of Olivia, her late daughter's child, while Olivia's father, Lee, was in prison. Olivia would be grown by the time Lee emerged — *if* Lee emerged — something for which all the neighbors were grateful.

"I hear your granddaughter's team is tops," Tracy told Alice, once the older woman joined them.

Alice looked tired. She was in her late seventies, and she had already suffered one stroke. As devoted as she was to Olivia, at her age, raising a preteen with an active schedule wasn't easy.

"She was marvelous," Alice said, resting a hand on Olivia's shoulder.

Tracy wasn't sure whether the hand was there for affection or support, but she didn't have time to worry about it. She scanned the store, looking for the young man who might at any moment plod over and flash a pregnancy-test kit at the little group, or tell her in no uncertain terms that they didn't have one in the store. She was not ready to

60

explain this situation to Alice, and particularly not in front of Olivia.

"Well, I won't keep you from your ice cream," she said brightly.

"Would you like a cone?" Alice asked. "Our treat?"

Tracy's stomach flip-flopped, and just that easily, she was certain, once again, what the pregnancy test would prove.

"No, no, thanks. Still watching my weight, and I haven't had dinner. You two go ahead. I'll see you soon. Aren't we coming to your house Thursday night?"

Alice looked surprised, but she covered it quickly. Tracy wondered if she had forgotten, or if the thought of the work involved was an unpleasant reminder.

"Listen, don't overdo," Tracy said. "Randall's rotisserie chicken is great. Wanda will bring a pie, and we'll get Janya to make something with rice. I'll bring wine."

"I'll be fine, dear." Alice smiled gamely. Then, after Olivia gave Tracy a spontaneous hug, grandmother and granddaughter crossed to the ice-cream counter.

Just in time.

"This what you're looking for?" a voice said behind her. Tracy whirled to find the young man holding out a battered box picturing a mother and father with a fat pink baby.

"Holy crap," she said. "Where did *you* come from?"

He looked as if he was taking the question seriously. She was afraid if she didn't cut him off, he would begin with the moment of *his* conception.

"Look, thanks. I appreciate you finding it for me," she said, grabbing the package from his hands.

He gave a vacant-eyed nod and wandered off again. Clutching the box, Tracy wandered aisles, ready to shove it behind cold medicine or canned peas until she was sure Alice and Olivia had gone. Once she saw them walking out the door, she took off for the cash register before anybody else she knew arrived.

The trip home was just long enough for Tracy to ask herself how she would feel once she was standing in her bathroom viewing the test strip, though she'd thought of little else since the truth had washed over her on the beach last night.

She and Marsh had only been a "couple" for a few months. They'd moved slowly into a relationship, with too many obstacles blocking an easier passage. From the moment they had finally given in to their obvious attraction and slept together, they had been nearly inseparable. When Marsh was cooking, she went to dinner. When he and Bay craved beach time, they came to Happiness Key to enjoy it with her. She sat in the audience when Bay's class presented a program, and went with Marsh to meet Bay's teachers.

When something important was happening at the rec center, the two Egan guys showed up to support her. She had even walked a Wild Florida picket line when the wetlands mall was still a possibility.

She, Tracy Deloche, had walked a picket line! What more did she have to know about her relationship with Marsh? Before him, "protest" was something she did when her favorite spa discontinued a shade of nail polish.

So maybe things had deepened. Maybe she was happiest when they were together. Maybe eventually the man would admit he needed her, even loved her. But they weren't there yet. They'd both weathered bad marriages. They had only just begun to weather their differences and find common ground. But a severe thunderstorm like an unplanned pregnancy? Possibly too much weather to weather. She just didn't know.

And that was only the Marsh part of this cataclysm. What about the Tracy part? She, who had passed on having children the way she passed on having a second martini if she knew she had to drive.

With relief she saw she was home. At top speed she wheeled into her driveway, got out and grabbed the Randall's bag. She didn't even bother with her backpack.

Inside, when the door didn't click shut behind her, she didn't bother going back. By the time she crossed the living room, she had unbuttoned her jeans, opened the box, removed the contents and tossed the container in the garbage can by the kitchen doorway.

In the bathroom she stood at the sink and ran the water until it was hot enough to wash her hands, then she unfolded the directions, read them and laid them on the counter. Finally she took out the test strip. For a moment she froze. How could she do this if she didn't even know what to hope for? Surely she had to hope she wasn't pregnant, that her life wasn't about to be altered forever?

Except she couldn't say that. Not quite. Not yet.

Reminding herself that the results would be the same no matter how she felt, she perched on the toilet seat and followed the directions. When she had finished, she waved the test strip in the air while she grabbed for toilet paper. Then she pulled up her pants and zipped.

She was afraid to look at the test strip. This was not the newest kit on the block. The directions said that five minutes was a definite, but that she might have an answer as soon as forty seconds.

"One Mississippi. Two Mississippi —"

"Hey, Ms. Deloche, you home? We saw your car, and your door was wide open. You okay?"

Tracy closed her eyes. Wanda. Wanda who was part of a mysterious "we." For a moment

Tracy wondered if she could ignore her and whoever else was out there, but it would be just like her brash friend to come charging into the bathroom to check on her.

"Just a minute," she called. She opened the top drawer beside the sink, cleared a little spot for the test strip and the instructions, and set them inside.

As she washed her hands, she considered taking her time and peeking at the strip in a minute, but she knew Wanda was perfectly capable of pounding on the door if she was in here too long.

After quickly wiping her hands on a towel, she strode down the hall and saw that "we" included Janya.

"You must have been in some kind of hurry," Wanda said, "leaving your door open like that. And aren't you supposed to be off camping with that man of yours? Just the two of you cozying up in the Everglades with the mosquitoes and gators for another couple of nights?"

"Got tired of Porta Potties, so I waited until I got home to go, and I really had to."

"Really? I saw you come back in Marsh's truck a little while ago, then leave again."

"Okay, so I forgot to go the first time. Good grief, Wanda! Isn't anything private around here?"

Wanda lifted an eyebrow. "Something happen out there? You look like something ugly and mean drug you through the —"

Janya interrupted, always a good idea before Wanda *really* got started. "We were just worried, since we didn't expect to see you so soon. And the door . . ." Her voice trailed off.

"I'm fine. Really." Tracy wondered about that, but the answer was still out of reach in a bathroom drawer. "The trip was a lot more grueling than I expected, and we just called it quits a little early, that's all."

"You and Marsh fighting again?"

"No!" Tracy took a deep breath. "I just needed a quiet night in a comfortable bed. My own bed." She nodded in emphasis, hoping Wanda would get the point. "I'm worn out."

"Well, I wanted you to know Maggie got in okay, and she's settling in fine. I told her you'd go down and see her once you got home. But there's no hurry."

Janya stepped forward, and Tracy realized she was carrying a plastic bag. "In case you didn't stop for dinner."

Tracy peeked inside and saw her friend had packed containers of the meal she had probably served at home that evening. Without thinking, Tracy lifted a lid to inhale. She was a fan of Indian food and had gratefully enjoyed all Janya's aromatic native dishes. But the moment the top came off the container, her stomach turned inside out.

She could feel herself going pale, the blood draining to her feet. She thrust the bag back into Janya's arms and took off for the bathroom.

And not to check the test strip.

Janya was standing beside her with a wet washcloth when Tracy was finally able to stand again.

She took the cloth and looked beyond her friend to Wanda, who was lounging in the doorway.

The older woman held out the test-kit box and shook her head.

"Did you really need this?" she asked. "I could tell you what's wrong with you."

Tracy was too weak to protest the invasion of privacy.

"So what'd it say?" Wanda asked.

"I haven't had a chance to look. I've been entertaining my neighbors."

"Well, go ahead and look now. Just to shore up what we already know."

Tracy went through the motions. She opened the drawer and stared at the strip. There were two lines where one would have been before she and Marsh began making love two months ago. She shook her head. "Man . . ."

She looked up and saw Janya's expression. "I'm sorry, Janya. I know this moment should belong to you."

Janya rested her hand on Tracy's shoulder.

"No one decreed there will be only one baby at Happiness Key. You have taken nothing from me."

"I know, but here I am pregnant, without even trying." Tears filled Tracy's eyes, and she blinked them away.

"Well, you must have done *something* to make this happen," Wanda said. "You need a little education?"

Tracy took a deep breath. "No . . . but I need one thing. From both of you. Promise you won't tell anybody. I don't want anybody else to know. For now it'll be our secret, okay?"

"What about Marsh?" Janya asked. "You will tell him, of course?"

"Marsh Egan is the last person I'm about to tell. Not until I've had time to think this through."

Wanda's eyes narrowed. "You're saying you don't want the baby's father to know? Or you're saying you don't know the baby's father?"

"Wanda!" Janya was clearly shocked. "As if that is our business."

Tracy held up a hand. "Just stop right there. There's no question whose baby this is."

"Well, that ex of yours was sleeping in this house for a while."

CJ, who had gotten out of prison on a technicality, had been a guest in Tracy's house during the summer, but she repeated

68

what she'd already told Wanda months ago. "I told you then, and I'm telling you now . . . CJ was sleeping on my *sofa*. He was not sleeping with *me.* This is Marsh's baby or it's an immaculate conception, and I doubt I'd be first pick for that."

"Then why aren't you telling the man?" Wanda demanded. "You think he doesn't have a right to know?"

The reasons were too long, complicated and confusing, and Tracy just shook her head. "I've known I'm pregnant for what, a full minute, Wanda? Give me a break. Be a friend, and just this once, back off. Okay?"

Wanda chewed her lip. She wanted to say more. That was perfectly clear. But finally she gave a curt nod. "You need a good talk, you come to me, you hear?"

"I know where to find you."

Janya grabbed Wanda's arm and tugged, but Wanda didn't take the hint. She stared at Tracy for a moment; then she stepped forward, pulled her off balance and gave her a squeeze. Afterward, she and Janya left together.

Tracy listened to the sound of their footsteps retreating and, finally, the door closing behind them.

She bowed her head. She didn't know whether to laugh or cry. So she just stood there and thought about all the ways her life was about to change.

CHAPTER FOUR

"You doing okay back there, honey?" Wanda called.

"Feels like old times." Maggie's voice floated to the front of Wanda's Wonderful Pies.

"You just let me know you need anything." Wanda waited, then realized that was going to be the sum total of their conversation. She sighed.

Maggie was busy in the back of the shop, cranking out piecrust. Wanda had resisted treating her any differently than she'd treated Dana, the only other assistant she'd had who was worth her salt. So this morning early she'd put her right to work. Maggie had grown up making pies, so after a quick tour of the kitchen, and an explanation of what she needed and how best to produce it in bulk, Wanda had left her daughter alone.

She thought Maggie looked particularly nice today, even though she'd been elbow deep in flour and butter for a couple of hours.

Her shoulder-length hair was braided tightly against her head, tucked in at the nape and pinned, the way she wore it when she was in uniform. The look suited her. Feminine yet spare, with only tiny gold hoops and a few escaping tendrils softening the effect. She wore jeans and a forest-green shirt, which were covered now by one of the striped logo aprons Wanda had bought for the shop.

She'd always thought her daughter was a pretty woman who missed being prettier by a thin nose and a rectangular face that was a little long, a little somber. She had golden-brown, Bette Davis eyes that were heavy-lidded and sultry, and hair the color of Maureen O'Hara's in *The Parent Trap*. Both attributes had come from Wanda's mother, who had been a Scots-Irish beauty. Wanda's natural hair color was mousier, but red enough to convince her that the baby they'd placed in her arms in the hospital thirty years ago was her own.

In the past twenty-four hours, she had struck out completely with both her daughter and her landlady. When questioned, Maggie had pointed out that Wanda knew the facts about her life and there was little more to tell. Tracy had also outlined the facts of her situation, but neither woman had been willing to talk about feelings. Maggie had always kept hers to herself, but after those two rotten years of abuse in the sheriff's department,

71

she had become even less likely to share.

Wanda felt like a kid with her face pressed against the plate-glass window of a candy store.

Feeling surprisingly lonely, she was busy setting red carnations in vases on the tables when the doorbell tinkled and a man walked in. She glanced up and smiled, although she didn't much feel like it.

"I like a man who wants pie at this hour of the morning," she said.

He was overweight, but not morbidly so, more like somebody who just enjoyed eating and indulged himself more often than he should. His complexion was ruddy, his hair fair and beginning to recede. She thought he might be pushing forty.

"I'm looking for Wanda Gray," he said. "Have I found her?"

Wanda was interested. People always guessed she might be the Wanda on the sign, but rarely did they care about last names.

"You're not from the IRS, are you?"

The man approached and extended his hand. "I'm Phillip Callander, and I've got good news for you."

Wanda tried to remember if she'd entered any contests lately. She'd always wanted to open her door and find half a dozen people with red roses and balloons announcing that she'd won a trip to Las Vegas or a summerhouse in the mountains.

"I like good news," she said, shaking the proffered hand.

"How's this? You remember Gaylord's?"

Her eyes narrowed to slits. Before beginning her career as a baker of pies, she'd waited on tables at a restaurant called the Dancing Shrimp, a well-known, well-loved historic seafood joint on the water. Despite being a favorite among customers, she had been given the ax when a young couple from Manhattan bought the business, changed the name to Gaylord's and turned it into a tapas bar.

Of course, losing that job had been the push she'd needed to open this shop.

"I know about Gaylord's," she said. "Did you eat there and get food poisoning? That would be good news. Although, not so much for you."

He laughed. It was a deep, musical belly laugh, and Wanda quickly warmed to him.

"I *never* ate there," he said, screwing his face into folds. "The food they tried to pawn off on people? Di-*sas*-ter!"

"Tried?" She knew she sounded hopeful, but she couldn't help herself. "Past tense?"

"You know how long most new restaurants last? Ten to fifteen percent close every single year, and most of those have only been in business for three years or less."

She hoped those statistics didn't include pie shops. "You're saying they closed?"

73

"Six weeks into it. Gone. Just like that. Didn't know the first thing about running a business and couldn't even hire a decent chef. And you know the worst thing?"

She was leaning forward, trying not to crow with delight. "Nooo . . ."

"They didn't have a clue what people *here* like to eat." He paused. "But I do. So I'm bringing back the Dancing Shrimp."

Now she crowed unreservedly.

"I can see we're on the same menu page," Phillip Callander said with a grin. "We're deep into renovations. They paneled the whole place, painted everything that wasn't moving black, even put in windows so narrow no light can shine through. They were right on the water, and they shut out the view."

"They also got rid of all their good servers, but we won't go into that," Wanda said. "So you're putting it back the way it was?"

"Close. It'll be a tad more upscale, but comfortable, the way the old place was. I'll bring back the most popular items on the menu, but add others with more complexity. I'll sure keep those shrimp-stuffed hush puppies, and I won't be serving them with hoisin sauce, either."

Wanda thought she might be in love with this man. The Dancing Shrimp might be getting some new duds, but it sounded like the same old gal.

"And along with being the owner, I'm also the chef. That's why I'm here."

Wanda held up her hands. "Sorry, but I've got my own gig now. I'm not going back to serving. If you want help recreating the menu, I could think about it."

"No, no, I've got menus, recipes. The original owner was delighted to part with them. No, what I need only you can give me."

She waited, charmed.

"Pies," he said, drawing out the word as if savoring it. "Dancing Shrimp pies. Signature pies only we serve. Pies *you've* created for us. What do you say?"

"Me?"

"Who better?" he asked. "I've been sampling on the sly for a couple of weeks now. And your pies are the best I've ever eaten. Pie goes with my menu like fish with fries, lemon with sweet tea. But I don't like baking, and I'm not half as good as you are anyway. So why hire a pastry chef when I can buy pies from you? A standing order. We'll even pick them up in the morning to save you delivery costs."

"I'll be!"

"And you know what? I want a chatty, happy menu. Stories, not just descriptions, so there'll be something on the menu about you, and how you used to work at the Dancing Shrimp until you became a famous pie baker. What do you say?"

Wanda didn't know what to say. This was better than red roses and balloons, if not quite as good as a summerhouse. This was a standing order, one she could count on almost every single day. And the publicity? The publicity would be fabulous.

"Darned tootin'," she said. "How many kinds, and how many pies a day?"

"Come up with some ideas and we'll talk details. Something decadent and chocolaty, for sure. Something citrus, but not plain old Key lime. Everybody in Florida has plain old, plain old."

Her mind was whirling. "About when will this happen?"

"I'm hoping to open up in six months at the earliest. Eight at the latest."

"Now, that's a shame."

"Tell me about it." Despite his words, he was still smiling. "But there's more good news. I've got another proposition for you, and I don't think you'll want to turn this one down, either."

Wanda had a strange desire to pull out one of her chairs and flop into it. Good news was exhausting. "What?" she asked. "You want me to make pies for the governor?"

His grin widened. "Dream bigger, Wanda. That's what dreams are for."

Maggie liked her new home well enough. The cottage was small and nothing special, a concrete block like all the houses in the tiny development, clean, but still with the required tinge of Florida mildew. All in all it suited her fine. There was even an extra room off the bathroom, in case somebody came to visit. Not that she was passing out her address to old friends. Eventually Felo would find her, but she was happy to delay the inevitable.

The kitchen was well equipped. Maggie could make almost anything she wanted in it, although most of the time when she was alone, she cooked simple things, if she cooked at all. When gourmet was called for, Felo had been their chef, creating mouthwatering Cuban specialties like stuffed pork or arroz con pollo, which was nothing like the more anemic farm-table version. His black beans were redolent of garlic, pork and chili powder, and his picadillo was served over rice that was fluffy enough to stuff a pillow. Unless she had baked a pie, Felo usually ended with a coconut-rum flan that was sexy enough to make any woman love him.

And many probably had.

She didn't want to think about Felo.

After being on her feet all day, Maggie was tired tonight. She had put a lot of energy into rolling out crusts, grinding and chopping fruit, scrubbing and rescrubbing the kitchen. Her mother had done the serving, schmoozing and selling, but Maggie knew she would graduate to that, as well.

She still couldn't believe she was doing any of it.

She didn't want to think about *that,* either.

A soft knock at the door saved her from unwelcome introspection. She expected to see her mother ferrying leftovers, but the woman on the doorstep was a contemporary, with dark shoulder-length hair and a million-dollar smile. The stranger's eyes were gray in the twilight, and for someone who lived on the beach, she was pale. Maggie decided this was a woman who knew how to take care of her skin, and that she, like Maggie herself, had to use sunscreen frequently to keep from burning.

"Tracy Deloche," the woman said, and held out a basket.

Maggie had already correctly guessed Tracy's identity. She took the basket and stepped aside to let her inside. "What have we here?" she asked as Tracy moved past her.

"Some dinner things to get you through while you settle in. Some mixes, soups, nothing that takes more than five minutes to prepare."

"You must know all about me. I bet Mom's been pumping you full of information."

"No, but I think you've led a busy life, and it probably never lent itself to leisurely sessions in the kitchen after work."

Maggie smiled her thanks. "I appreciate

this. I'd like to stay out of fast-food lanes if I can."

"Tell me about it. I just spent the summer losing fast-food weight." Tracy hesitated, then said something that made no sense to Maggie. "Of course, what difference does that make now?"

"I'm sorry?"

Tracy looked at her. "Um . . ." Then she shrugged. "I'm muttering to myself."

"Now I have to guess. You just broke up with a guy, the reason you wanted to look slim and perfect?"

"Not exactly." Tracy took in the decor. "I like the new slipcovers. Your mom must have bought them. The sofa's comfortable, but worn, so that's a huge improvement. Although this isn't exactly Wanda's taste, is it?"

"You mean it's not bright enough?" Maggie examined the subdued beige-and-white-striped fabric covering a chair and sofa. The pillows were floral, but not the eye-popping prints Wanda always chose for herself.

"I ask myself why, but I like the colors your mother's used at her place. Those orchid walls always give me a jolt, then I start to feel right at home."

"Mom always says paint's cheap and life's short."

"I can't imagine growing up with Wanda."

Maggie didn't feel insulted, because who *could* imagine it?

"It must have been so much fun," Tracy finished, surprising her.

Maggie thought she was going to like her landlady. "Let me put this in the kitchen," she said, nodding at the basket. "Would you like a drink?"

Tracy followed and stood in the doorway. "Would I like one? No question. Will I have one? Water will do."

Maggie turned. "Not drinking tonight? Or not drinking ever?" She'd seen her share of alcoholic cops and didn't feel shy about asking. Recovering alcoholics were usually only too happy to get that secret out in the open so they didn't have to field frequent invitations to fall off the wagon.

"Not drinking for nine months," Tracy said.

Maggie stopped, hand halfway to the cabinet to get a glass for ice water. "Oh."

"Not telling people, either, but your mother knows, and if Wanda knows, you will, too, even if she doesn't plan it that way."

"So that explains why a diet seems futile now."

"This wasn't on my mind at the time." Tracy patted her flat tummy. "In fact, it was never on my mind." She looked up. "That probably sounds awful."

"Not to me. It wasn't on my mind, either. My . . ." Maggie lifted her hands in question. "What do we call the men in our lives? Partner was the detective I worked with every day. Significant other? Too cumbersome. Lover? Too much information. Boyfriend? Too adolescent."

"How about guy? Not so much baggage."

"In my case, my *former* guy, Felo — that's his name — wanted children. I wasn't ready."

"I didn't spend a lot of time thinking about babies, and I don't know the slightest thing about taking care of one. Besides, my ex-husband would have been a horrifying father. And the guy I'm with now? Has a kid already and doesn't know he's about to have another."

"Did you just find out?"

"Yesterday. I'm still trying to wrap my head around it."

At that moment Rumba streaked by on her way from the bedroom to her new favorite perch on the back of the sofa.

"Meet Rumba," Maggie said. "Mom told you I'd be bringing her, right?"

"No problem. I've thought about getting a cat, only I never liked being pinned down. I don't even keep houseplants. I tried a few, but I had to give them back to Janya when I forgot to water them. She's the gardener around here. She's also the one who wanted a baby. And look who got pregnant."

Maggie filled two glasses with ice and water, and handed one to Tracy. "Want to sit outside? The evening seems cool enough."

"Don't you have to unpack?"

"I'm all done. I didn't bring that much, just whatever I could stuff in the car with my camping equipment." They walked to the door and settled themselves on the bench beside the entryway. Maggie had the odd feeling they had been friends for years.

"Camping equipment?" Tracy said. "I just went camping in the Everglades."

"Ooh, too bad. Next month will be nicer."

"I'll pass. Where were you? Your mom didn't say."

"Backpacking in the Blue Ridge. Georgia all the way up into Virginia. Anywhere there was a lake I could swim in and a skyful of stars."

"Did it help?"

"Not as much as I hoped."

Tracy sipped her water, and they both stared in the direction of the Gulf, which was too far away to see. Still, Maggie could hear distant waves, and the salt-tinged air wafting through palm fronds smelled like home.

"Your mother's worried about you," Tracy said at last. "I know a little about what happened."

"That I quit the only job I ever wanted and left the only man I ever loved?"

"You don't get over that quickly, do you?"

"You sound like you know something about it."

"I was married to the wealthy man I'd been trained to catch and shackle. I even convinced myself I loved him. Then one day we lost everything. All our money. Our dignity. All our friends. He's a con man of the worst sort."

"What sort is that?"

"The kind who could bottle a mud puddle and claim it's fifty-year-old scotch. Worse yet, you would swear it was the best you'd ever had."

"Did he get what was coming to him?"

"He went to prison for a while, got out on a technicality, came to visit while he waited for a new trial, then . . ." She glanced at Maggie. "More or less disappeared."

"More or less?"

"I think he's living someplace south of the border with no extradition treaty and lots of cheap labor, so he doesn't have to mix his own drinks or press his own pants. Last time I saw him, he as much as said that's what he was planning. I've passed that on to the authorities, but it's not much help. CJ lands on his feet. Some people always do."

"Right, like the guy I built a case against in Miami, who was never brought to trial."

"Your mother told me the story. You worked on the case for almost a year, gathered a ton of information, and then the prosecutor refused to indict him."

"Paul Smythe, the state's attorney, is as crooked as a trail through a mangrove swamp. And nobody would do a thing about it."

83

"You didn't know that going in?"

Maggie wondered. What had she known exactly? And what had she continued to believe in spite of that? That if she did everything exactly by the book, nobody could dispute her case? That if she worked hard enough, she could overcome corruption at the highest levels? That if she believed in miracles, somebody would wave a magic wand and make sure she got one of her own?

"I should have known," she said. "If anybody should have known, it was me."

"Why?"

"My early years in police work should have been a warning."

"I hear it can be tough for women, even now."

"Tough? Right. There was the subtle harassment. Like my first day on the job when somebody went through my locker, and I found a little message on my desk spelled out in my own tampons." Maggie shook her head. " 'Get Out.' Cute, huh?"

"The kids I work with have a similar level of maturity."

"These weren't kids. I'd have been okay with the little stuff, even though it kept coming and coming. I thought maybe they were just testing me, to see if I cried easily or couldn't take a joke. But it was more than that." She stopped, not sure whether she wanted to go on.

84

"Wasn't that bad enough?" Tracy sounded genuinely interested.

Maggie wondered why she was telling a stranger the story she'd never even told her parents. But the answer was simple. Her father would have pulled every string, gone to every official he'd met in all his years on the force, to get justice for her. Maggie hadn't wanted to be daddy's little girl. And her father's fury would have played right into the hands of her tormentors. Even after the fact, she'd never told Felo the story, for the same reason, but Tracy had just shared hers. Maggie thought she, of all people, would understand.

"That was the first time they went after me, a warning of sorts. But I'm not good with threats." Even thinking about it made Maggie's throat tighten. "I started out in public relations, stuff they thought a woman should do. But by the end of my second year, when I was still sitting at a desk, I started talking about a lawsuit. That department had already been in trouble, so rather than chance another investigation, they put me in a car with another cop, a guy who'd never given me any problems — one of the few — and sent me out on patrol to learn the ropes.

"The first couple of nights went fine. Nothing much happened, and even though my partner hardly spoke, I figured things would improve once he saw I was holding up my end. We got a call, domestic violence in a housing development where it wasn't uncommon. Too many hopeless people crowded together, with too much anger. It was a two-story building, two apartments up, two down, little courtyards separating them. We went to the door together, and we could hear shouting, so of course nobody answered when we pounded on the door. My partner told me he was going around back to make sure nobody left that way. I was supposed to stay at the front and keep pounding on the door until somebody answered."

"Somebody did," Tracy guessed.

"Yeah, a big guy, maybe two hundred forty, fifty pounds? With a baseball bat." Maggie turned to her. "My partner didn't come back, even though I know he heard the guy screaming at me. He could have killed me. He was hopped up on something, out of his mind with rage. He came after me swinging. I managed to evade him, but I couldn't get close enough to stop him, and I probably wouldn't have been able to restrain him, even if I could have gotten my hands on him. No time to pull a weapon. I knew for sure two of us could have taken him down, but me alone . . . ?"

Maggie remembered, as she did every time she relived that moment in her all-too-frequent nightmares, how terrified she had been. She had expected to die, simply because she was a woman trying to break into a department that didn't want her.

"That's an awful story." Tracy sounded outraged. "I can't believe that goes on."

"Believe it."

"What happened?"

"A miracle, really. The guy's neighbor came out and tackled him. I don't know what would have happened otherwise. He dropped the bat, and I managed to cuff him. Then, when it was all over, my partner came strolling around the side of the house. I can still see his grin. In the car he asked how I liked my first encounter with real police work. Then he told me I might as well prepare for more of the same and not waste my time whining, because nobody was going to believe my version of anything."

She paused. "And, of course, he was right. From that point on until I moved over to Miami City, nobody had my back. No matter what went down, I was alone out there, worse than alone, because the people who were supposed to be there for me were out to get me, too."

"Things were better in Miami?"

"I thought so, until recently."

"But you stayed in police work after all that. Why would you?" Tracy sounded genuinely perplexed, and Maggie figured her confusion made sense.

"Even after everything, I still believed I was

better than the bad guys. All of them. In the end, as it turns out, they might not be *better,* but they're stronger and have better connections. When the investigation Mom told you about was tabled, I was pretty sure I was slated to be taken out of crime suppression and moved to something really important, like community relations again. Wasn't ready to repeat."

"Bummer."

"Well said."

"So, two of us, looking at our futures, without any real idea what they're going to hold. I think maybe you and I have a lot in common, Maggie Gray." Tracy held out her water, as if in toast.

Maggie toasted her right back, and their glasses clinked.

Maggie wasn't sure about a lot of things in her life, but she was sure she had just made a friend.

CHAPTER FIVE

The women of Happiness Key met every Thursday evening for dinner, alternating houses so nobody would bear too much of the burden. If grouper was fresh, Wanda grilled and slathered it with lime butter, always careful to have plenty of vegetables for vegetarian Janya, too. On Janya's night she re-created the succulent dishes of her native Mumbai, and nobody missed meat. When it was her turn, Tracy usually picked up deli salads and fresh rolls. Alice specialized in casseroles filled with rich sauces and tender vegetables.

Tonight Alice had prepared her special four-cheese macaroni, laden with mushrooms, tomatoes and onions. Except for accepting one of Wanda's pies for dessert, she had refused all offers of help. No matter where they ate, Wanda's pies capped the meal.

They'd begun with a toast to Maggie and welcomed her to their ritual dinner. Now Tracy waited until Alice joined them before she reached for a complicated layered salad served in a cut-glass bowl. She wondered how long the salad had taken to prepare, and what she could say to convince Alice that next time, she didn't have to work so hard. Alice's age had never been more apparent than tonight. She looked exhausted.

Tracy passed the bowl to Maggie beside her. Maggie's hair was down, and she wore a simple scoop-neck blouse of pale gold over faded jeans. She really didn't look like her mother, but there was a hint of resemblance around her lips, and she definitely had Wanda's stubborn chin.

"Alice," Tracy said, reaching for the casserole. "You worked so hard tonight. Everything looks fabulous."

"I like to cook . . ." She hesitated, as she sometimes did, while she waited for the words to form. ". . . for all of you."

No one rushed Alice. The halting speech was left over from the stroke she had suffered several years ago. The gap had closed considerably, and now it was more like a missing beat or a hiccup, but Tracy was afraid it was going to get worse if Alice kept pushing herself.

"Why don't you tell us what you've been doing," Tracy said. "It's your house, you ought to start."

Across the table, Wanda had dished up applesauce, and now the bowl reached Alice, who took some before she spoke again, as if she was too fatigued to do two things at once.

"Olivia . . . is very busy, and I've been busy . . . keeping up with her."

"I remember when Maggie was that age," Wanda said. "I told Ken I was going to need a chauffeur's license and a spiffy black cap. Then Junior made the travel soccer team, and I pretty much lived in the car for three years."

"I know how busy Bay can be," Tracy said. "Coming and going from the key a couple of times a day must be exhausting."

"We manage," Alice said. "It's good for . . . Olivia."

And it was. Tracy knew that. The girl, who was studying with a friend tonight, had suffered so many losses, but she had managed to overcome the worst and move forward. She had been voted most congenial at the rec center youth camp this past summer, and she was vice president of her class at middle school.

"Isn't middle school a lot harder to manage?" Tracy asked.

Alice nodded. "And she's in a youth group . . . at our church. So Sunday nights now . . ." She didn't bother to finish.

"We can all help out, you need us," Wanda said. "Olivia could come to the shop after school — there's a city bus stop at the end of the block. Do her homework at one of the tables, and I'd take her home, or Maggie would, once we finished for the day."

"Or she can always come to the rec center," Tracy said. "She's no trouble. She could join the after-school program."

"She likes to work on murals with me," Janya said. "I could help, too."

Tracy expected Alice to refuse. Olivia was her only grandchild, and they were particularly close. But Alice nodded, as if she might think about it.

"Good," Wanda said, when nothing followed. "We'll expect you to let us know, and we'll say no if we can't help."

"That's settled, then," Tracy said, watching Alice's expression. "Anything else going on, Alice? How's your bridge club?"

"I . . ." Alice shook her head. The message was clear. She had dropped out, and nobody had to be told why.

Tracy knew they were going to have to keep track of this. She had enough problems to keep herself occupied for, oh, the next twenty-one years? But she was more than fond of both Alice and Olivia. She wasn't going to let a problem go long term.

As unofficial facilitator, she turned to Janya. "What's up with you, Janya?"

"Very little. Rishi invited Indian friends to visit on Saturday. The woman, Kanira, is so unhappy, and she makes everyone else unhappy along with her. I want to help and have no idea how. Rishi says we should just be there if they need us."

"Why's she unhappy?" Wanda asked. "Is it one of those arranged marriages again? I never did understand that whole notion, but then, I never did understand why normal marriages don't work, either. I'm not sure any of us are meant to spend our whole lives with a man."

"Your *normal* marriages fail because romance is not the only part of marriage leading to success. Family ties and culture are important, too," Janya said.

"Your family's far away," Wanda pointed out. "And you and Rishi get along just dandy."

Janya smiled. "I think sometimes Rishi and I get along *because* my family is far away."

"Your new friends . . . have children?" Alice asked.

"Two, and the sweetest children you could ever meet. I hope for their sakes the parents will learn to make a happy home together."

"Or split up," Wanda said. "Sometimes that's best for everybody. Better than fighting all the time."

"That doesn't sound like you, Mom," Maggie said. "Who liberated you? It used to be all 'till death do us part.' The first time I went steady, you preached a whole sermon on being loyal and supportive of my man. I was twelve."

"She exaggerates," Wanda told the other

women. "Pay her no mind."

"I exaggerate only a little." Maggie was clearly feeling at home with the group.

"What else is going on?" Tracy asked Janya.

"Murals. Two lined up for next month. I will be busy." She paused. "Which is good, because there is no baby coming to bless us. Not yet."

Everyone made sympathetic noises.

With no real experience in theater, Tracy still knew a cue when she heard one. "Alice, you're the only one here who hasn't heard my news. There is a baby coming to bless *me* — and Marsh, too, only he doesn't know it yet, and I don't want anybody to tell him. So, please keep this a secret. Let's not tell Olivia, okay?"

Alice looked stunned. "You're . . . pregnant?"

"Symptoms, test results, the whole nine yards."

"You were planning . . . ?"

Tracy shook her head. "And we've been so careful about birth control. I'm never careless . . . except, well, once. The first time we, you know, did it. It was the evening of Bay's birthday party. Marsh and I had been keeping our distance. I went to drop off a present, and Bay wanted me to stay. Afterward, Marsh and I made up big-time. I didn't have my . . . anything with me to prevent pregnancy, and we just kind of fell into bed — actually the floor — before either of us thought that far ahead. But it was just that once. Man, who'd have thought just once would do it?"

"Anybody who's ever had a sex-ed class," Maggie said, fork halfway to her mouth.

"Oh, great, another wiseass at Happiness Key." Tracy tried a bite of the macaroni and waited to see if her stomach would rebel. It didn't. She took another.

"So, there's got to be a good reason you aren't acquainting the baby's own father with the situation," Wanda said. "Let's have it."

Tracy ate another three bites quickly, more because she wanted to strike while the iron was hot than because she wanted to avoid answering. She wondered if that was how the entire pregnancy would go. She would eat during the brief moments when her stomach was behaving, and the other twenty-three and a half hours each day she would avoid food and any mention of it.

"That casserole's not going anywhere," Wanda said. "Spill, and I don't mean maca-roni."

"It's complicated, and this is the first thing I've eaten since noon that's stayed put."

"Then talk with your mouth full."

"You can't let Mom bully you," Maggie said. "Give her an inch . . ."

"You think they don't know that?" Wanda said. "We been neighbors more than a year now. They're still standing, aren't they?"

Tracy thought if everybody had been sentimental, touchy-feely about her announcement, she probably couldn't have said another word. But she felt reassured, somehow,
by Wanda's matter-of-fact digging.

"You're not sure you're going through with
this pregnancy?" Wanda said, turning back to
Tracy. "That's why you don't want Marsh to
know?"

Tracy couldn't say that the idea of *not* going through with it hadn't occurred to her. A
woman carrying a baby she hadn't planned
for had legal options, and she wasn't naive.
Still, she felt those options existed for circumstances decidedly different than hers.

"I'm glad women have choices," she said,
"but I don't think that's one of mine. And I
would never leave Marsh out of a decision
like that, either."

Wanda didn't look surprised. "I figured. I
only wanted to get you talking."

"Marsh and I were just getting started."
Tracy looked around the table. "We finally
got past all the garbage, and we were starting
to figure each other out. Now, how will I
know what he really feels? Whatever he does
will always be mixed up with this baby. I'll
never know if we were falling in love big-time,
you know? It's all going to be about custody,
and whether we live together for the sake of
the kid, and who gets him or her when and

96

for how long. Not about *us,* but about *all* o
us."

"You could always ask him and get it over
with," Wanda said.

"The man's never even told me he loves
me. I might ask and get silence, because I
don't think Marsh knows how he feels."

No one seemed to know what to say to that,
until finally Janya broke the silence. "Some
men don't know how to admit such a private
thing."

"Marsh had a bad marriage. Maybe it
soured him on saying the love *word,*" Wanda
said. "Maybe he said it the first time, then
things didn't turn out so hot. Maybe he's
afraid he'll jinx what you have."

"Or maybe he's just not that into me,"
Tracy said. "It happens."

"You spend every waking minute with that
man, and some not-so-waking ones." Wanda
dished more macaroni and cheese onto Tracy's plate. "A man doesn't spend all that time
with a woman he's not into."

"Maybe not, but I think I need some time
without the baby in the middle making all
our decisions. I need to gauge what's going
on before I tell him he's going to be a father
again. Then I can tell him, and maybe I'll
have some idea how to break the news. He
has a child. Who's to say he wants another?"

"You could tell him tonight and watch his
expression," Wanda said. "Either he'll be as

happy as a chick in a bug patch, or he'll be figuring out how fast he can pack."

"Tracy should . . . do what she wants," Alice said. "If she needs time, she should take it."

"She's right," Maggie said. "I know I'm new here, but I just got out of a relationship, and I wish I'd taken some time to pay attention to what was happening around me before things fell apart. That's all Tracy's trying to do. She wants to pay attention, without distractions."

"A baby is not a distraction," Wanda told her daughter. "A baby is a human being with needs and feelings. Some of them even come into the world with colic. Like certain people I know."

Maggie ignored her. "Once Tracy has to consider the baby's needs and feelings, her window of opportunity to observe the baby's father will be over."

"Is this a test?" Janya asked Tracy. "And if it is, will you know when to give Marsh a passing or failing grade?" When Tracy didn't answer, she added, "Perhaps it's not only Marsh who is unsure how he feels? Perhaps the baby's mother is also wondering."

The table went silent, then Wanda pushed her chair back.

"Let the unwed mother eat her macaroni. I've got news to share."

Tracy had never been more grateful to be

out of the limelight. As pushy as she was, Wanda never shoved anybody over the edge.

Well, okay she did, but rarely.

"I'll be baking pies for the new Dancing Shrimp," Wanda said. "Gaylord's is gone, and the Dancing Shrimp is back, only the dessert menu will be featuring my pies." She explained how the pie order had come about, and everybody applauded spontaneously.

"So I brought a new one tonight for you to try," Wanda said. "I'm calling it Citrus Sunrise. But not only that, while the restaurant's being renovated, Phillip Callander is going to be doing a little catering. And guess who it's for? For Derek Forbes and his film production company from Hollywood! They're going to be working on location right here in Palmetto Grove and staying in the Statler mansion where Janya fell in the pool. And guess who's going to be baking pies for the cast and crew?" She hitched a thumb toward her ample breasts. "Little ol' *moi.*"

Maggie departed first, claiming she needed a good night's sleep before another day at the pie shop. Wanda followed soon after; then Janya shooed Tracy out the door, promising that *she* would help Alice with the rest of the cleanup. Now, as she neared her own cottage, Tracy realized how tired she was when she found herself nearly on top of Marsh's pickup before she realized what its presence signaled.

99

As Alice might say, she had a gentleman caller.

Marsh was sitting on the stoop, lolling on his elbows and gazing at the stars. His tan skin was burnished by the moonlight, and the golden highlights in his hair were luminous. She thought of everything she had told her friends, and all the insecurities she hadn't fully admitted to. Then she steeled herself.

"Did I know you were coming?" she asked.

"You've been dodging my calls. I thought I'd better find out why."

Tracy's heart picked up speed, but she managed a smile. "I haven't been dodging anything. I left you a message. Didn't you get it?"

The message had been timed to coincide with Bay's morning trip to school, and Tracy had carefully called Marsh's home number, not his cell. Transparent, maybe, but all she'd been able to come up with to avoid him.

"Got it," he acknowledged. "What, two days ago?"

She joined him on the stoop, resting her hip against his and her head against his shoulder. "Where does the time go?"

"What's really going on, Trace? Are you still pissed about the camping trip? Locked in worry about all the work you need done here? Busy thinking about all the money you could make if you sell this place?"

"Busy, and still not feeling a hundred

100

percent like myself."

"Have you seen a doctor?"

Her heart sped up even more. "No need to," she said truthfully. "I know what's wrong, and it's not the kind of thing they can plop a bandage on. Besides, I just ate a good dinner at Alice's, and here I am, sitting on my steps talking to you instead of moaning over bad oysters."

"I was worried."

She turned a little so she could see his face. "That's sweet."

She was hoping for more, some undying pledge of love that would ease some of her anxieties, but he brushed a light kiss across her lips instead. "So what's been up, besides dinner with your neighbors?"

"Nothing on the property, if that's what you mean. Just the usual craziness at the rec center. Oh, and get this, there's a film crew coming to town, and Wanda's probably going to be baking pies for them. You've heard of Derek Forbes?"

He lifted a brow. "Aw, shucks, ma'am, I never did get myself to one of them talking pictures."

She poked him with her elbow. "I've actually met the guy. The last time I witnessed him in action, he was standing on a grand piano leading a group of awed partygoers in the chorus from the theme song of his latest blockbuster. He sang the verses, although not quite the sound-track version."

That was all Tracy remembered. Not where the party had been held or by whom. Why she'd been there, of course, was easier to put together. Undoubtedly CJ had promised to make the host or hostess richer than his or her wildest fantasies, and the poor sap had believed him.

"Ah, that fancy other life of yours," Marsh said. "The one I can't compete with."

She ignored the dig. "We were on the same guest lists at least half a dozen times. He has an impressive amount of energy and a wicked sense of humor. In an industry where people throw tantrums just because they can, he's one of a kind, even-tempered and friendly."

"Why is Wanda making pies for him?"

"Because it turns out he's a big fan of pie and everyone wants him to be happy. He's going to be filming here on our very own bridge. He's famous for doing his own stunts, so when the studios started screaming about insurance and liability, he started his own production company. The guy must be in his sixties by now, but nothing ever stops him. A friend of mine in the biz thinks he'll die in an explosion and be thrilled that he's gone out with a bang. Anyway, Wanda's beside herself trying to figure out what she can make that's good enough."

"Well, the guy may be larger than life, but so's Wanda Gray. If those two actually meet,

I'd like to be there to watch the room light up."

"Commutes are going to be a lot longer. Don't say I didn't warn you."

"I already heard about the film. You know the bridge that's going up beside the old one? One of the guys who won that contract is the brother of a law school buddy. Wild Florida was watching the whole business pretty closely, just to be sure the construction company that won the bid had the environment's best interests in mind."

"Did they?"

"Me, I'd rather see a passenger ferry, but yeah, Cardrake Brothers has a worldwide reputation for being environmentally aware. The plans they submitted are amazing. Even better, they did the repairs on the old bridge and brought them in under estimate. That convinced everybody they were the only ones to build the new one."

There'd been talk of a toll to pay for the new bridge, and the thought of having to fork over money each day to go back and forth to work had sent Tracy into a tailspin. With all her other financial worries, that had sounded like the credits rolling on a film of her life at Happiness Key. Luckily the city fathers had managed to find federal money to cover most of the costs, and the idea of a toll had been dropped.

"If I know Derek Forbes," she said, "expect

to see him dangling over the water or dodging cars. Wanda says they're calling the movie *Sunset Bridge*."

"You do know the best people."

"Do I?" She slipped her arm under his. "I always thought so."

"Officially the real bridge is named after some egomaniac who was mayor when it was built, but the locals really did call it Sunset Bridge, or at least they did when I was a kid." Marsh tugged her a little closer. "I haven't walked you out there when the sun's going down?"

"You probably thought you did. Maybe you had me mixed up with one of your other dates."

"We ought to do it before the movie crew arrives. Why don't you come over tomorrow night. I'll cook you dinner, then we'll take the pedestrian walkway out to the middle of the bay and watch the sun going down."

"You are such a romantic." She pulled her arm from his and slid away before she was tempted to say yes. She didn't want to eat with Marsh, not until her "all day" sickness was under control. And right now, in a moment of weakness, she was too apt to blurt out the truth about the baby.

"But I can't," she said, before he interpreted her silence as yes. "I have monthly reports, and I'm too busy to get them finished at the center next week. Plus, I'm trying to take things easy until I'm a hundred percent back on my feet. So I'd better take a rain check until I'm in better shape."

"I make a mean redfish Creole, and you could put your feet up and forget the bridge."

Alice's macaroni was beginning to writhe inside her. Tracy pictured hollow elbow-shaped serpents twisting and slithering up the walls of her stomach. Out of nowhere she felt icy cold, and her palms began to perspire.

"Another time," she said, getting to her feet.

"You're not in the mood for company, are you?"

She shook her head sadly. At least she hoped she looked sad and not eager to get rid of him. "Everyone says this virus lasts ten days to two weeks. I sure hope you don't catch it."

"You're sure it's a virus?"

For a moment she froze, then she forced a smile. "Oysters or virus, I just need more rest than usual. You understand?"

He didn't reply immediately. He rose and put his hands on her shoulders, and searched her face in the dim light. "Better get to it, then," he said at last. "We'll do the bridge another time."

"Give Bay a hug for me." She leaned over and kissed him on the cheek, then backed away. "I'll let you know when I'm over this."

"You do that." He nodded, then he lifted a hand in farewell, turned and started toward his truck.

She didn't watch him leave. She unlocked her front door and closed it with a bang behind her before she sprinted toward the bathroom.

CHAPTER SIX

Wanda wasn't satisfied with her Citrus Sunrise recipe. She wanted a pie that was both tall and airy, a pie that looked like the sun rising over a sandy graham cracker beach, growing lighter and brighter as it rose. She had based her idea on a tequila sunrise cocktail, then tried grenadine syrup, followed by cranberry juice, for the bottom layer, but so far hadn't produced a pie special enough to be on Phillip Callander's menu.

"All my pies have to be good," she told Janya, "but this has to be good enough that people come right over after eating a slice at the Shrimp and buy a whole pie to take home for the rest of the week. It's gotta be an intro-*duc*-tion."

Janya was helping but not tasting, since today's experiment included gelatin, something she, as a strict vegetarian, avoided. She pressed Wanda's graham cracker mixture into a pie pan as Wanda tried a little of this and a little of that to get the chiffon filling to reflect the blend of colors that she wanted.

"This is your Christian day of rest," Janya said. "You bake pie all week, and tomorrow, even if Wanda's is closed, you will be there preparing for Tuesday."

Wanda stared out the narrow rusty window with its view of scrub and one screeching blackbird. "Wanda's Wonderful Pies? That's work. But creating a new pie in my own kitchen, even this scrawny, good-for-nothing excuse for a real kitchen? Well, that's magic, pure and simple. You see the difference?"

"Like painting a mural," Janya said. "A wall is blank, then it is covered by colors and shapes and becomes a different thing entirely."

"It's the way Alice feels after she crochets an afghan or a scarf, or that tablecloth she gave Olivia." Wanda turned from the view to her eye-popping aqua walls and the friend in a gauzy white blouse framed against them. "I expect she'll be crocheting something for Tracy now. For the baby, I mean."

"She already showed me the yarn. She has been saving it for something special." Janya paused. "She said she has put enough aside for my baby, as well."

Wanda wasn't sure what to say to that. She knew she often said too much, and that this was not the time to experiment with anything except the pie in progress.

"It's odd the way these things work out,"

108

she said, treading as carefully as she was able. "Tracy getting pregnant when she didn't plan it. Those friends of yours with two little ones and an unhappy marriage. But I feel deep down in my heart that things will work out for you and Rishi. You'll need whatever Alice crochets for you."

"There are ways. Things we can still try to make a baby more possible." Janya looked up. "We are young, and there is time."

"Let me tell you. Whatever patience you learn now will help a whole lot once the babies start to come. You'll need it forever after. Trust me, you'll need gallons . . . acres. Even when they're grown."

"You need patience with Maggie?"

"Especially with Maggie. She keeps everything inside. And when'd you ever know me to do that?"

Janya smiled, and Wanda thought it was probably because they were talking about someone else now. "Is she happy to be here?" Janya asked. "Or is this something you don't know? Something she hasn't said?"

Wanda considered. "She's as happy to be here as anywhere, except home. And she locked *that* door behind her and threw away the key. Maybe she's happier to be here than, say, Hoboken or Boise, but not as happy as I want her to be. Your kids hurt, you hurt and there's not a lot to be done about it, either."

"What can we do to help?"

"Just let her know you'd like to be friends when she's ready. But it might be kind of hard to tell. She's not what you'd call transparent."

"Tracy said she and Maggie hit it off right away."

Wanda looked up. "Did she? That's news to me."

"They both have trouble with the men in their lives."

"I wouldn't say Felo's *in* Maggie's life anymore. Although he'll track her down soon enough, they'll have it out and maybe it'll finally be over."

"Sometimes that is best, isn't it? Putting a dream aside for good, then finding another to take its place?"

Wanda wondered if Janya was thinking about Maggie or about her own dream of becoming a mother. She was glad when somebody knocked on her front door. She waited a second or two for one of the neighbors to open it and call inside, but when a louder knock sounded, she wiped her hands on her apron and wound her way through the narrow kitchen.

"I'll see who it is, then we'll pour this new pie into that crust you worked so hard on." She called the last few words over her shoulder. The house was small, and it didn't take more than seconds to get from one end to the other.

She flung open the door and stared at a familiar face: Felo Estrada, who was clearly not happy to be standing on her doorstep.

When Maggie tried to remind herself of the good parts about living on the key and working in her mother's shop, having a normal work schedule was first on her conspicuously short list. In police work, regular hours were rare. Schedules shifted and emergencies took precedence. Now, with Sunday and Monday off, she could make plans without fear of disruption. Except, of course, what plans could she make now that had any appeal? She didn't quilt, knit or garden.

She did like the outdoors, notably swimming and kayaking, but her kayak was back in Miami, and the cost of renting one for even a day was prohibitive. She had spent the morning hiking a boardwalk trail through a swamp an hour's drive away, but now, freshly showered and rested, the remainder of Sunday and Monday stretched in front of her. Tracy had invited her to tour the rec center, and she supposed checking out the pool would be tomorrow's activity, but the promise of too many hollow, empty hours tugged at her.

Luckily she had come home to a message from her mother. Wanda and Janya were experimenting with pie, and if Maggie wanted to try a slice, she was welcome to come. She looked at her watch and did the math. She didn't want to stay for dinner, so if she went too late, she would have to argue the point. Going now would break up the afternoon; then maybe she would drive into town in the evening, buy a sandwich or burger and visit the beach. People watching was something of a hobby, although from a cop's/ex-cop's point of view, that often included guessing what crimes those who were passing by might commit or had already. Still, maybe eventually she would get over that. She could start today.

At a roadside fruit stand she had bought a trio of shiny Florida avocados fresh from the grove. Now she put two in a basket, along with several ripe tomatoes from the same stand, and started toward her parents' house. Outside, the harsh afternoon sun dried her damp hair. Even protected by sunscreen, her arms felt the sting.

On her mother's doorstep she opened the screen door, then, without knocking, opened the front door and stuck her head inside. "Mom?"

Her eyes took only seconds to adjust to the lower light level inside, but in that time, a figure stepped into view — and it wasn't her mother.

She stepped back, not to run, but from surprise. Then she stared at the man she had lived with for too many years.

"Felo."

Wanda came out of the kitchen, and her expression said it all. *I couldn't warn you. I couldn't get rid of him.*

"Felo just arrived," Wanda said. "I was offering him iced tea. Would you like some, too?"

Maggie gave a short shake of her head. "I'll pass."

She examined her ex-lover. He was tall and lean, and now, dressed as he was in khaki shorts and a silk shirt covered with palm trees and parrots, he seemed more of both. She remembered when the shirt had come home with him after a discount store shopping trip. She'd asked if he was serious, but even then she'd had to admit the shirt looked perfect against his olive skin. His black hair had been recently cut, short on the sides, as always, just long enough on top to show a hint of wave. His eyes were hazel and heavily, darkly lashed, and when he smiled — which, she could tell, was not in the immediate forecast — his teeth seemed impossibly white.

The word that had come to mind when she'd first met Rafael Estrada was *charming.* Now, years later, it was still the word best suited for him. Because Felo was more charming than handsome, a potent combination of hawkish features and genuine warmth that canceled out the ordinary things about him and added up to a charisma that rarely failed.

She, of course, was that rare exception.

"I didn't see your car," she said.

"If I'd parked it where you could, you probably would have disappeared again."

Felo's voice was one of the most seductive things about him, a musical rumble that suggested he could sing, although in reality he couldn't carry a tune. Even now, she felt his words amble along her skin in the same way they had from the beginning, as if each ordinary syllable was meant to seduce. He spoke Cuban Spanish like a native, but there was no hint of anything but generic Florida when English was called for.

"Wouldn't you know," she said lightly. "Tricky, like a cop."

Wanda stepped forward. "Janya and me were making pie. Why don't you stay a while and sample what we're putting together."

"I think I'll pass." Maggie held out the little straw basket. "I bought these today. I couldn't resist."

Wanda came forward to take the basket from her hand. "I think maybe you ought to stay here with *us.*"

Maggie smiled a little and gave a slight shake of her head. "Felo hasn't seen my house, and Rumba will be glad to see him. We'll leave you to your experiment. Save me some for later, okay?"

Wanda looked worried. She turned to Felo. "No funny business, you understand me?"

Maggie almost laughed. Two cops facing off, and Wanda, who was on her way toward sixty, was the one to be most afraid of.

"I would never lift a hand to your daughter," Felo said. "You *know* that."

"I don't know *what* I know. You two just remember you used to love each other, when you settle whatever it is you're settling today."

"Come on," Maggie told him. "Before she goes after you with her rolling pin."

"And a handy weapon it is," Wanda said menacingly.

"Good to see you again, Wanda," Felo said. "Tell Ken I said hello."

Maggie didn't wait. She turned and started toward her cottage, knowing Felo would catch up with her quickly. His legs were inches longer than hers, and he'd been a long-distance runner since high school. It wasn't unusual for him to do eight miles on a Saturday morning, then come home and make brunch for their friends. She'd given up running beside him early in their relationship and gone back to serious swimming, because Felo's most relaxed stride still quickly outdistanced her shorter, more determined one. She'd gotten tired of watching him jog in place while she struggled to keep up.

He did catch up, but he didn't speak. He just walked beside her, accommodating his stride to hers. She had known this day would

115

come. Felo was too good a cop not to track her down the moment she settled into Happiness Key. The fact that he had waited this long surprised her. She had also known it would be emotionally upsetting when he did, and that the longer she avoided him, the more upsetting it would be. Gauging from the extra breaths she seemed to be taking and the slight tremor of her hands, she had waited too long.

She led him up the path to her cottage and opened the door, preceding him. "I imagine Rumba already knows you're here."

A thump from the cat's favorite chair proved her right, followed by a streak of white heading toward the doorway. Felo scooped Rumba into the air and held her away from him, arms extended. A soft flood of Spanish followed, along with a feline purr Maggie could hear all the way across the room.

"She's missed you," Maggie said. "If you believe cats miss people."

"They can and do." Felo held the cat against his chest. "She's thin."

"She quit eating for a while after I left her with —" She broke off.

"You didn't keep her with you?"

Maggie saw no point in secrets. "I went camping for a while. Cats aren't the best companions in a tent. She was well taken care of, trust me. But she didn't like the change in routine."

"No, it wasn't routine she missed. She missed you. She missed *me.* She's not an inanimate object."

"If she were, I wouldn't have to change her litter box."

"You always denied how much you love this cat. Some things don't change."

"Some things do." She faced him. "You didn't get iced tea at Mom's. Want some?"

"How about something stronger?"

"Beer?"

He nodded. She strolled into the kitchen, deceptively calm, and rooted through the refrigerator. She rarely drank beer, yet she'd bought some to keep on hand. Now she wondered why. Had she bought it for Felo, knowing that one day he would show up on her doorstep? Was she still catering to a man she had walked out on? And what did that say about her?

"No Hatuey," she said, naming his favorite South Florida brand, "but I have Corona."

"Fine." He spoke from the doorway, Rumba still purring in his arms.

She took her time opening the bottle, finding a glass, pouring carefully so the beer didn't overflow. She didn't bother adding a slice of lime, since that seemed too much like something she would do for a lover. She handed the finished product to him. "Did you eat lunch?"

He stowed the cat under one arm and took

the glass. "I didn't come to be entertained, Mags."

She shrugged. "How did you find me? Or were you just hoping if you showed up on Mom's doorstep, she would cave and tell you where I was?"

"Your mother doesn't cave."

"Then you must have known I was here."

"Yeah, thanks to you."

She crossed her arms over her chest, then realized what he'd said and dropped them to her sides. "What are you talking about?"

"The GPS messenger I gave you? Well, I got an email message this morning with your location pinpointed on Google Maps."

For a moment she stared at him. "I didn't —" Then she remembered.

For her birthday two years before, Felo had given her a special GPS unit to carry along when she went hiking or kayaking on her own. He was a cop, always sure trouble was around the corner, and the unit was small and ingenious, able to pinpoint her location anywhere in the world by satellite. She had accepted the gift, but it had never pleased her. To Maggie, the GPS signaled a lack of faith in her ability to take care of herself. Like almost every male cop she'd known, there was a part of Felo that still thought she was weaker and more vulnerable than he was.

Weaker, and in need of a man's control and opinions.

In addition to summoning professional help in an emergency, the GPS unit allowed her to signal a contact — and of course, Felo had been that contact — to let him know that she needed assistance. The unit worked where cell phones would not, and it was waterproof, with a long-life battery, particularly long-lived for someone like Maggie, who rarely turned it on.

Unfortunately, yesterday she *had* turned it on when she found it deep in the pocket of the cargo pants she'd taken camping with her. She'd turned it on for a quick system test, and apparently she had pressed the wrong button while she was at it.

"Well, I hope they don't put me in charge of the witness protection program," she said.

"Not much chance of that, now, is there?"

She didn't wince. "No, I suppose not. Law enforcement isn't exactly knocking down my door for new jobs these days."

"You brought that on yourself."

She was glad to feel anger replacing what had been raw nerves at seeing him again. "Maybe I did, but you know what? Somebody had to point out what was going on, Felo. Not all of us are willing to just turn our backs on corruption."

He took a long drink before he answered. "You left without a word to me. You left, after all our years together, and you didn't even tell me where you were going. I had no way

119

to contact you and settle this."

"I got every message you left with my parents. The fact that I didn't call should have told you something."

"You know what it told me, Mags? That you were the same old Maggie Gray. Communication's never been your strong point. You're the only one who knows what's right, and you don't see any reason to share that with the rest of us. You quit your job in a blaze of self-righteous glory, and the rest of us, who stood firm so we could change the system from the inside out . . . ? We weren't worth a conversation."

"A conversation? You had plenty of conversations about what was going on, Felo — but not with me. With your best friend. You and Alvaro found plenty to talk about. And Alvaro had plenty of reasons to tell you to stay out of the whole mess and leave me twisting in the wind by myself."

"Alvaro?"

Felo never got loud when he got angry. He'd grown up in a family of shouters and learned early that the only way to be heard was to speak so softly that everyone else had to stop and listen. Now his voice was as soft as a cobra's hiss.

She tilted her head to examine him. "Most relationships have two people. Ours had three, maybe more. Alvaro was one of them. Remember your boyhood friend, the one who's slated to be one of the richest men in Miami if he continues along the track he's walking now?"

"Alvaro had nothing to do with anything."

"No? I heard you on the phone discussing this with him. More than once."

"He's my friend from way back, and an ex-cop. We were partners before he quit the force. I talk to him about a lot of things."

"He's also a friend of Paul Smythe and Jorge Famosa."

Famosa was the drug lord Maggie had so diligently collected evidence against. Jorge, Alvaro and Felo had grown up in the same neighborhood, and while Jorge chose a life of crime, Alvaro and Felo had gone to the police academy, served together and were bonded in a way only men in a job like the one they had chosen ever could be. Bonded forever, with little room for the women they worked with — or loved.

To her knowledge, Felo had never had any connection with Jorge as an adult, but Alvaro and Jorge often attended the same parties and had mutual friends. Alvaro had come up more than once in her investigation — so frequently, in fact, that she had considered taking herself off the case. But Felo had never listened to any of her suspicions.

Surprisingly, Felo didn't defend his former partner or himself. He put the half-empty bottle down on the nearest counter, then

121

faced her. "Maybe more?"

She shook her head to show she didn't understand.

"You said our relationship had three people in it, maybe more. What did you mean?"

She debated whether to answer. She wished that part hadn't slipped out. Yet wasn't that one of their problems? The very charm that had so attracted her had attracted other women, as well. And Felo loved women. Particularly women who needed him, the way Maggie never had.

"All those late nights, Felo. You think I didn't notice? You think I didn't see the . . . intimacy in the way you treated other women on the force and in the neighborhood? How many sinks or windows did you fix on our block? How many times did you sit in on interviews at the station house, just to be helpful? How many drinks did you have with how many women?"

A muscle worked in his jaw, and his expression hardened, but he didn't answer right away. He just considered the question, the way he might have considered a menacing reptile in the swamp.

"How long were you suspicious?" he asked at last. "How long did you silently accuse me of being unfaithful?"

"That would be hard to say."

"So what set off the big explosion? The one I never even heard until now?"

She realized there was nothing to hide. They were no longer a couple, and she had nothing else to lose. "The day I was told to drop the Famosa case, I came back to the station to find you. I thought I needed to talk to you, to get your opinion. Somebody told me you were in an interview room down the hall, so I went to find you, only the door was closed. I looked through the glass to see who you were with, because I didn't want to interrupt if it was important. I saw you sitting with Sal Freepoint, patting her hand, heads together like lovers."

He gave a short nod and waited.

"I'd been suspicious of her, of you, before that. She was always asking you for advice, getting you off to one side for who knows what. I told myself not to pass judgment on what I'd seen, that you'd tell me what was going on when we talked that evening. But you never mentioned her."

"What chance did I have? We fought about your decision to quit the force. We fought about what you should do about Famosa and Smythe. What chance was there to tell you that Sal just found out that her boyfriend was going to Iraq — the same boyfriend whose unit dismantles explosives, by the way, and who has a better-than-average chance of getting his head blown off while he's there?"

"Don't make me sound like some kind of

shrew, Felo. By the time we called it quits
—"

"*We* never called it quits. Don't pretend I was part of that."

"By the time *I* called it quits, then, you were hardly ever home anyway. How long did it take you to realize I was gone? We'd stopped spending time together. Are you really trying to tell me you were faithful?"

"I'm not trying to tell you anything."

She shrugged.

"But for the record?" he said. "I was. Have been. Still am, although God knows why. And if I'd stopped spending time with you . . . ? It's because you were never there, Mags. Oh, the physical Maggie Gray came home sometimes. But your head and your heart were on the Famosa case. You lived and breathed it. I wanted someone to look at me and see me. I wanted a wife, a woman who wanted a husband and children to help round out her life. And every time I looked at you, looked through you, that woman was moving further and further away."

"I was a cop. You know what that means. At least, you know what it means for a *man.*"

"No, I know what it means to *me.* What it meant to you? Apparently everything, but in the end, nothing. Because you threw it away. And you know why? Because you don't think anybody else's advice is worth anything. You don't trust anybody except Maggie Gray."

"I don't pander to other people, people who ought to be locked away forever, no!"

"Mags, you don't listen, and you don't ask questions. You're sure every male cop in the world, including me, is going to stomp on you again. But all you ever had to do was ask what was going on and listen to what I said. You could have asked if Sal and I were going to bed together, or who I was out with in the evenings when you were preoccupied. But that was beyond you. Just like telling me you were leaving was beyond you. Like telling me where you'd gone was beyond you!"

"*This* is not beyond me," she said carefully. "I'd like you to leave."

"You know what? I don't believe you. But I'll do it anyway. Because I don't want to be here anymore." He set the cat down carefully, and Rumba, who had picked up the tension between them, fled toward Maggie's bedroom.

"What do you want me to do with the rest of your stuff?" he asked.

"I'll come for it. Just tell me when you're not going to be there."

"I'll look at my schedule. Try opening my next email for a change. It's easier than a conversation. I'll let you know."

He turned and started through the house. She heard the door slam. The noise shuddered in her head long after she'd gone to bed, and kept her awake for most of the night.

CHAPTER SEVEN

Janya was pleased Rishi had made friends
with Harit Dutta. Her own friends were so
important to her that she had wished the
same for him. The only thing that didn't
please her was that Kanira was bundled into
the relationship. She didn't really dislike
Kanira, she only disliked the woman's com-
plaining.

"I know that you would rather not go this
evening," Rishi told her on Monday, as they
prepared to leave for a picnic at the Duttas'
house. Janya had been surprised at the invitation, since Kanira had made no secret of her
inability to cope. Janya hoped there would be
food on the table.

"Friends are important," Janya said carefully. "And perhaps these friends will benefit
from our company."

Rishi was tying his shoes and didn't look
up. "Their marriage is not happy."

Had she been there, Tracy would have said
"duh" to such a statement. Thinking of that

made Janya want to smile, although the subject was too serious. "It is hard to be so far from home when children are small and need so much."

Rishi finished and stood. "I suppose she's made her bed and must lie in it."

Janya thought Kanira had been in that particular bed at least two times too often. She had conceived her children with little thought of anyone's happiness, conceived them solely to make her husband give up his dream of writing. She found that kind of manipulation hard to accept, and she had not mentioned it to Rishi, who would find it harder.

"I should not judge," she said, "but the children exist, and so does the marriage."

"Harit has not said so, but I know he feels trapped. How can things go so wrong for two people who were once in love?"

Janya thought this conversation was extraordinary. She and Rishi talked of many things, but rarely love. "Perhaps arranging marriages is better," she said. "Perhaps if Kanira's family had convinced her to marry someone with prospects more to her liking, she would be happier now. She, too, is trapped. She can't abandon the children or Harit."

"Women do."

"Not women like Kanira. She would never be able to face her family or friends again.

127

She would certainly never be able to go home."

"Marriage is many things, but never simple, no matter how it comes about. Perhaps it's saddest, though, when love existed at first. Losing what we've found is harder than never finding it at all."

She was surprised he had thought so seriously about something that had not flashed by on a computer screen. She knew Rishi had hidden depths, but encountering them always unsettled her, as if, after more than two years of marriage, she was still living with a stranger.

She wondered what he would say next. "I worry less about whether Kanira and Harit are in love and more about those babies. Growing up is difficult enough, but doing it with discord in the home . . . ? It poisons the air."

"Children are affected by everything around them." Rishi nodded, as if in emphasis. "They sense when they are wanted and when they aren't."

Rishi knew better than most how it felt to be both, having been a beloved son, then an orphaned and unwanted nephew. He was speaking from his heart, and she heard the sadness in his voice.

She thought about what Kanira had told her. "Children who are brought into the world for the wrong reasons have a difficult time making their way through it. Perhaps we can find a way to help these two."

"What are the right reasons for having children?" he asked.

She looked at him, surprised. "Children brighten a home."

"Children are often ill. They cry and whine. They make much work and cost much money. There are already too many of them in this world. So why do people insist on having them?"

She touched her forehead. "To carry our love into the next generation." She touched her heart. "Because love is not simply a fatality waiting to happen. It is what helps us move forward."

"But it takes love to create love."

She thought of Kanira and Harit and knew they were back at the beginning. "We must do what we can to help. Let's find a way to lighten their load so they can give those children what they need."

On the trip to the Duttas' apartment they chatted of other things. Their first glance of the former motel showed peeling paint and rusting railings. A pool green with algae occupied the center of the complex, and the apartments hugged its narrow boundaries. Janya hoped Kanira kept a close eye on her little ones, since the gate leading to the murky water was wide open.

Vijay opened the door, but he didn't speak.

129

Behind him Janya saw Kanira in a short skirt and T-shirt sliding an overly fussy dress over a squirming Lily's shoulders. The living room was small and cluttered with children's toys. Harit greeted them, immediately volunteering to show Janya and Rishi the park where they would eat their picnic dinner, as if he hoped for a few minutes of fresh air and quiet.

"Janya will want to help me. Take Rishi and the children," Kanira said in a stern voice. "Don't leave me here to watch them *and* make the food. You, Jay," she said, pointing at little Vijay, "you must work. Work is not just for women, although one might think so around here. You will carry some things when you go."

The little boy didn't look surprised at his mother's tone, which indicated to Janya that he was used to it. Vijay resembled Harit, and Janya wondered if Kanira often addressed her husband's faults by disciplining the child. Her heart went out to him.

The men did as ordered, carrying Lily and what supplies they could. Vijay clutched paper plates and plastic cutlery against his narrow chest. He walked like an old man. Janya wondered if he ever ran or played, and if he did, where. She could not imagine Kanira simply taking the children to the park to let them behave like children.

"I would like to have entertained you at a restaurant," Kanira said once the men and children were gone. "That is what I suggested to Harit. But we have no money. So I am afraid the meal will be simple. I have no time to prepare food the way our servants did in Kolkata. I never realized how hard they worked, not until I came here."

"You were from the city, then? Not a village?"

"Me? No. That was Harit. A poor village, too. No, my family was rich and much different from his. A generation ago we would never even have met. But he was a gifted student, and given scholarships and chances well beyond his caste. We were introduced through friends. My family was appalled and told me I must cut all contact. Instead, I married him." She looked away, as if watching that sad scene unfold.

Janya knew the consequences of such a marriage and hoped she was wrong. "Did your parents learn to accept him?"

"We are dead to our families. Mine because Harit was not good enough to be my husband. His because my family refused to provide a dowry and insulted them many times over. His father expected Harit to offer the family support, and now Harit cannot, since he hardly supports us. Our parents have not acknowledged the children and never will."

"Perhaps in time."

"We send photos of Lily and Jay, and they

131

come back unopened. They will not take phone calls. There is no hope."

"You are very much alone." Despite a growing dislike of Kanira, Janya felt a stab of sympathy. She, too, had once disappointed her parents, but in the past year, her relationship with them had improved. Now her mother even talked about visiting Florida one day.

"I am strong, and I have resources." Kanira smiled a little. "Perhaps I will change my life one day soon, and for the better."

There was something about the smile, secretive, even a little arrogant, that put Janya on guard, but not enough to keep silent.

"I know this life must be hard, Kanira, but you have many things other women might envy. A handsome, talented husband who is trying to publish an important novel. Two beautiful children. A new life in Florida stretching out in front of you."

Kanira gave a derisive snort. "Indian women are taught to ask for so little."

Janya did not point out that Kanira had so much more than most women in the country of their birth. She remembered words her paternal grandmother had often repeated when the child Janya was unhappy.

If you think you are free, you are free. If you think you are bound, you are bound. Indeed, child, always, you are what you think, so you must think only the best.

132

Now Janya was afraid that if her grandmother's saying was true, Kanira would be unhappy the rest of her days.

Tracy had been blessed with boundless energy and a strong constitution. She had never been seriously ill, and she had never had a problem getting out of bed, unless she'd been plied with too much alcohol the night before. Those evenings were, for the most part, history, since she was well past the age for frat parties and well under the income level for socialite free-for-alls. She wasn't particularly sad about either.

Unfortunately, since the pregnancy, getting out of bed and getting to work on time had become as tough as hauling herself to the post office to mail her annual property taxes. In both instances she really wanted to pull a pillow over her head, block out reality and sleep right through the event.

On Tuesday she dragged herself to work with the same enthusiasm she had on Monday, because she was a big girl and pregnancy was not a life-threatening illness. She'd checked her calendar before going to bed and figured if she worked a ten-hour day today, she might be able to do everything she needed to. And if she didn't, the next day would be even worse.

While she hadn't yet seen her doctor, she had read an online dos and don'ts list and

133

learned that every morsel of food or drop of liquid she could conceivably put in her body was lethal to a growing fetus. Using common sense, she had whittled that down considerably, but she was avoiding coffee and tea, and drinking juice and water instead. She had a prescription for prenatal vitamins that the nurse had called in when Tracy explained why she wanted to move up her annual exam. Now she took one with a glass of water from the cooler beside the rec center's welcoming coffee urn, and wished she could follow it with something suitably high octane.

Gladys Woodley, the rec center's receptionist and wife of Woody, the director, rambled into the coffee end of the corridor and stopped at the sight of her. "Are you okay?"

Tracy glanced down to be sure she had pulled on the usual items of clothing. Pregnancy also seemed to be interfering with her short-term memory. She wouldn't be surprised if she'd forgotten to put on her jeans and was wearing pajama bottoms. But from what she could tell, all was well.

"Why?" she asked.

"You've been looking pale. You didn't lose too much weight, did you? After the contest ended?"

The center had held a weight-loss fundraiser over the summer, and Gladys and Woody had dropped an astonishing forty pounds. Tracy had lost the ten she'd needed

134

to shed. Unfortunately, the pregnancy diet plan was now in full gear, and she was dropping more.

"Tummy problems," she said, managing a bright smile. "Best diet plan out there."

Gladys tilted her head, a newly styled head at that, with a sleek chin-length bob that, along with the weight loss, made her look ten years younger. "Are you pregnant?"

Tracy could fudge the facts, but she knew better than to lie to Gladys. Gladys *was* the rec center, and a stickler for good behavior. A lie would come back to haunt Tracy when she slid from tight jeans to maternity clothes.

"I'm not telling anybody," she said softly. "And Marsh doesn't know, okay?"

"Tracy!"

"I just need to figure this out, that's all. But I'm not quitting my job. I'll need it more than ever."

"Are you and Marsh fighting again?"

Tracy wondered. "Nothing like that."

Gladys didn't say anything for a moment; then she nodded. "So how can I help?"

"Just cut me a little slack if I need it. Until I'm over the nausea. I'm not moving as fast as usual."

"You have time off. You've earned vacation days. You should take some and get a little extra rest."

"I'm going to save them to add to my

135

maternity leave. That's when I'll need them most."

"Marsh loves children. You've seen him with Bay."

A change of subject was in order, but before she could come up with one, Gladys took pity. "We're one class short for our Christmas-crafts segment," she said. "The woman who promised she'd do papier-mâché angels is moving to South Carolina. The program's about to go to print. Do you have any ideas for a replacement?"

Tracy felt she owed Gladys something for taking this news with only a minimum of angst and advice. An idea condensed from the hormonal fumes fogging her brain.

"Alice," she said. "Remember when my neighbor Alice taught the youth-camp kids to crochet? Before her son-in-law interfered? Well, good old Lee's not around these days, and I bet she'd teach snowflakes. She crochets all different shapes and sizes, and hangs them in her windows and on her tree."

She thought about her own suggestion and realized how perfect it was. "All that transportation for Olivia's wearing her down, so maybe we can time the class so she can pick her up after school and save two trips. Maybe early enough so she can enjoy the pool or even get involved with the shuffleboarders. She needs some fun."

"Perfect. You'll ask?"

"Right away."

Gladys turned as if to leave, then turned back. "You'll tell him, won't you? Eventually?"

Despite the change of subject, Tracy didn't have to ask who Gladys meant. "Just getting my head straight. Marsh will know when the time is right."

The time was not right late in the afternoon when she ran into Marsh and Bay in the hallway. Marsh was talking to a blond man Tracy didn't recognize. The guy was a little younger than Marsh, broad shouldered and a few inches taller, with three days of stubble ten shades darker than his shaggy hair. She approached warily, not in the mood for more subterfuge, but she managed a smile for Marsh before she gave his son a more genuine version.

"Hey, kiddo," she said, leaning down for Bay's inevitable hug. Now that he was ten, Bay was beginning to resemble Marsh more and more. He had his father's sandy-brown hair and both his parents' intelligence. Last year he had been one of her biggest challenges in the youth program, but now that they'd worked through the worst of their problems, they had a special bond.

She wondered if the child she was carrying would resemble this boy she had grown so fond of, and for a moment, she couldn't think of another thing to add to her greeting.

"Gotta get to practice." Bay waved his swim team bag. "Today we're going to dive. A lot."

"Don't forget to come back up," she told him, ruffling his hair, "or at least clean the pool floor while you're down there." He took off down the hall, and she watched him for a moment, composing herself before she turned to his father.

"So, what are you doing here?" She leaned over and kissed Marsh's cheek. He wasn't on his way to or from the courthouse; in fact, he was even more casually dressed than he was at the Wild Florida offices. Then she noticed the big clue: the racquet he held at his side. The other man had one, too.

"Racquetball," she said, answering her own question. "Did I know you played?"

"Don't very often. Tracy, meet Blake Armstrong. Blake's the brother of an old law school friend."

"The bridge builder?" She held out her hand. "Tracy Deloche. Welcome to the rec center."

"Tracy's a supervisor here," Marsh said. "She keeps Bay in line."

Tracy waited for him to explain further, to stake a claim of some sort, since Blake was looking at her appreciatively as he shook. But "supervisor" was as far as Marsh got.

"I try," Tracy said, "although it would take an army to whip that boy into shape."

"She's fond of him," Marsh said. He looked

at her, then at Blake, who hadn't dropped her hand. He finally seemed to get it. "And of *me*," he added.

Tracy felt the way she had the night CJ proposed. All glittery inside, with visions of a long happy life together.

"Although not so much lately," he added.

Blake dropped her hand. "Your loss," he told Marsh.

Tracy narrowed her eyes. "Your *fault*. Your . . . oysters."

"Tracy's been under the weather and she's blaming a virus on me," Marsh explained. "If she weren't, she'd beat your butt at racquetball. She's an athlete."

Tracy was just a whit mollified. "How long do you expect to be in town, Blake?"

"My colleagues and I are moving into a house out on the key, not far from Marsh's. We'll make it our office, and a couple of us will live upstairs, too, until the bridge is so far along we aren't needed on-site every day."

"I live out on the key, too. At the other end. You'll like it." She started to say something else, when she saw a familiar figure approaching.

"Hey, Maggie!" She waved the woman down. Maggie had a pie carrier in her hand, and Tracy wondered if Wanda had sent samples to the rec center staff, as she sometimes did when she wanted opinions. She was glad to see Maggie looking perfectly normal.

139

She'd heard that Maggie's ex had found her on Saturday, and she'd been debating whether to check on her or leave her alone to regroup.

Normally the sight of Wanda's pie carriers was a moment for internal rejoicing, but not so much today. In fact, the idea of pie was wrestling with the reality of the two slices of buttered toast and carton of yogurt she had managed to eat that morning. Quickly she averted her eyes.

She couldn't even enjoy Wanda's pies. She hoped, when the baby was born, she didn't hold this against the kid.

"Tracy," Maggie said with a nod. She stopped beside Blake and Marsh. "Mom wants opinions. I gather it's not the first time?"

"What do you have?"

"Chocolate Truffle."

Tracy's stomach flipped.

"And Tantalizing Tangerine," Maggie finished. "She's not too high on either, but she wants feedback."

"Marsh, this is Maggie Gray," Tracy said, and finished the introductions. "Wanda and Ken's daughter," she added.

"I'm a fan of your mom," Marsh said, shaking Maggie's hand after she transferred the carrier.

"So am I," Maggie said. "You gotta love my mom."

"Why?" Blake asked, offering his own hand. He seemed as interested in Maggie as he had been in Tracy, before Marsh had finally asserted himself.

Maggie was looking him over and seemed to like what she saw. "When I was a kid in Doral," she said, "there was a regular Wanda Gray fan club on our street. She fattened up every kid on the block. They're probably all cursing her now, but back then, anybody who needed consolation showed up on our front porch for pie."

"You grew up in Miami?" he asked.

"Did. You must know the city."

"Do." He grinned. "I grew up there, too."

Maggie and Blake began to compare memories. Tracy thought maybe Maggie had found someone to help take her mind off her ex. Marsh put his hand under her arm and propelled her away for privacy.

"You feeling any better?"

"Definitely. But not a hundred percent."

"Are you going to the doctor, or do I have to drag you?"

"I've got an appointment." Although not with the doctor he expected. "Time to be checked over anyway."

"Want me to stop by and check on you tonight? I've got some chicken soup in the freezer."

The soup sounded good; the visit did not. She was still too prone to emergency toilet trips, and Marsh wasn't stupid.

"Rain check," she said. "Ten-hour day ahead. I'll just want to go to bed."

"That could be arranged."

This was the moment to be seductive, to say something that left him wanting what he wasn't about to get. The prepregnant Tracy would have had a choice of quips. The one whose vision of chocolate truffle pie was still nibbling at a stomach that had been at least temporarily calm couldn't think of anything except . . .

"Not tonight, okay?"

"Gotcha."

She rested her fingertips on his arm. "Let's do something next week."

"It's only Tuesday, Trace."

She wondered why it felt so much later. "This weekend?"

"I'm feeling all fuzzy-gooey inside at how excited you are."

"Be a good guy and don't hassle me. I remember a few times when you were so busy you didn't even have time to call me for days at a stretch. Okay? Isn't that part of being in a relationship? A little patience?"

"Are we in a relationship?"

Tears threatened. She couldn't believe it. She seemed prone to cry over everything these days. She swallowed and hoped he hadn't seen the evidence.

"Not if you don't want to be," she said as

142

evenly as she could manage.

"What I *meant* was if I don't ever see you, it's hard to remember who you are."

"Is that really what you meant?"

"I'm listening so hard to the subtext here, I forgot what we were discussing."

She sighed. "How's Friday night?"

"I'll be at a conference."

"You could have said so!"

"I'll be back Saturday afternoon. I'll call you when I get in. We'll see how you're feeling." He reached for a lock of her hair, twined it around his finger for a moment and tugged. "Work for you?"

She nodded and hoped it did. That gave her four days to start feeling human again. Maybe she would set a record.

Maggie and Blake still had their heads together, but Maggie was shifting the carrier as if she was preparing to leave.

"I'll show you where the staff lounge is," Tracy told her, glad to have a reason to split.

Quick goodbyes, and the men started off toward the racquetball courts. Maggie stood a moment and watched them go.

"He seems nice," she said.

"Marsh or Blake?"

"Both."

"Blake looked like he wanted to eat you alive. There's probably going to be a lot of that going around."

Maggie smiled at her. "I could use the

diversion."

Tracy watched Marsh's retreating figure. "If diversion works to put another man out of your head, be sure and let me know."

CHAPTER EIGHT

On Friday morning Wanda gestured to three pies on the counter in front of her. "Well, I got three pies I can show Phillip," she told Maggie. "That rec center staff's as good as any focus group some fancy marketing person could have put together for me."

Maggie wasn't sure what part of that statement impressed her the most. That her mother had, after hours of testing, come up with three pies that satisfied her, or that Wanda knew about focus groups. She'd never doubted her mother was smart, but she'd had some doubts about her ability to learn new things. Clearly, everything about the move from Miami to Palmetto Grove Key had been a learning experience.

"I'm glad you axed Tantalizing Tangerine," Maggie said.

"That's the thing about ideas. Not all of them are good, and you have to know the difference, which is the hard part. At least Chocolate Truffle is good enough to sell in the store, just not good enough for the Shrimp's menu."

"Phillip might like it. It's so rich he could cut the slices smaller and get more for his money."

"We'll see if he likes these other ones first. I just wish I had a better name for this one." Wanda pointed to the last pie in the row, a towering creation filled with walnuts, chocolate chips and coconut. "Seven-Layer Pie doesn't much do it for me."

Maggie figured that her mother's three new creations probably totaled a week's worth of calories. She was afraid if she worked at the shop too long, she was going to start packing on the pounds. At least she had joined the rec center at Tracy's suggestion and could spend evenings working out now. In addition to the health value, the pool and weight room would give her a place to go.

The door opened and she glanced up, expecting to see Phillip Callander. Instead, Blake Armstrong walked through the door, looking considerably different than he had earlier in the week at the rec center. She wondered if he had come to Wanda's Wonderful Pies to make an order or a date. The question was more academic than personal, although at least the second would give her something to do some evening besides laps in the rec center pool.

"Hey," he said, homing in on her im-

146

mediately and bypassing Wanda. "This place smells like heaven. Did I die without realizing it? Hmm . . . pies in the sky, huh? My kind of heaven."

"Darn it, that's what we'll call it!" Wanda clapped her hands together, and Maggie jumped. "Pie in the Sky. Who is this guy?"

Maggie introduced them.

Blake shook Wanda's hand. "If I named one, I guess that's the one I'll have to buy."

"Can't. It's a sample, but we got plenty else to interest you." She glanced at Maggie. "Maggie will give you the tour. I've got things to do in the back. Nice meeting you."

They were quickly alone. Maggie shook her head, fully aware that her mother was trying to give them some privacy. "So, want to go over the list?" She nodded to the chalkboard behind her.

"Just tell me your personal favorite. We're moving in today, and a celebration seems in order."

"Key lime's always the most popular. Today's version has a shortbread crust."

"Sounds great. I'll take one."

She got a pie out of the refrigerator case and boxed it for him. Then she took Blake's credit card and rang up the order. "You're looking different. I really like the haircut."

"I clean up okay?"

She taped the box to ensure a safe delivery. "You do indeed." Blake was freshly shaved, too, and his hair was now tamed into masculine curls.

He had a nice smile, and she found herself responding to it. It wasn't alluring or seductive, like Felo's, but open and friendly, like the smile of someone who was used to being liked.

"I don't see a ring," he said, his gaze flicking to her left hand.

"No reason for one."

"Am I poaching if I ask you to a party tomorrow night?"

Maggie was not a party girl. She liked smallish dinners with friends, backyard picnics and barbecues. She thought she owned a little black dress, but if she did, it was hanging in a closet in Little Havana.

"Nothing formal," he said, reading her expression. "Just something simple to get us all off on the right foot in town."

She felt herself nodding before she knew she'd decided. "May I bring something?"

"We have it covered. I'll pick you up at six."

She handed him the box and told him where to find her. As he left the shop, Phillip Callander and another man, as thin as a pretzel stick and roughly the same color, squeezed around him and came inside. Maggie called for Wanda.

Her mother corralled her before she could head to the kitchen. "Stay," Wanda hissed quietly.

148

Maggie didn't smile, but she wanted to. Her brazen, in-your-face mother clearly needed support.

Phillip reached the counter and grasped Wanda's hand, sandwiching it between his. "Wanda, meet Larry Bly. Larry's the line producer for *Sunset Bridge.* He's in town firming up arrangements. I told him about you, and he just had to come meet you himself."

"Our success hinges on you," Larry said, grabbing Wanda's other hand for a moment. "Pie could make or break us."

For a moment Wanda looked like a gator trying to cross the busy Tamiami Trail: confused and ready to dodge anything that moved. Then she shook her head, as if untangling cobwebs. "You're having some fun with me, aren't you?"

Phillip dropped her hand and started to speak, but Larry interrupted. "Maybe I overstated it a tad, but it's my job to keep Deke happy, and nothing makes him happier than pie. Phillip tells me he'll love yours."

"Deke?"

"That's what Derek's friends call him."

"Well, there aren't any guarantees, are there? The man's a pie connoisseur, he probably has some strong ideas what he likes or doesn't."

Phillip waved that away. "Don't trouble yourself, Wanda. The man will move here for

149

good just to eat his way through your list."

Maggie was glad she hadn't left. Somebody had to tell this story at the next family gathering, and who would believe it if it came from Wanda herself?

Wanda didn't say anything, which was the only clue Maggie needed to the way her mother was feeling. Wanda pulled out the three new pies she'd set out for Phillip and took down plates, forks and her best pie server. Then she cut each man a small slice of the first, the Citrus Sunrise she'd worked so hard on all weekend.

"Try this and see what you think," she said, already cutting into the Dancing Dulce, a riff on *dulce de leche,* a Latin American treat Wanda had, ironically, been introduced to by Felo.

By the third pie, Wanda's newly named Pie in the Sky, the men looked as if Christmas had come early and Santa had been particularly generous.

"I really thought I might have to fly in pie from Deke's favorite restaurant in L.A.," Larry said. "But this is spectacular. He's going to love you. You'll come to the house where he'll be living and make pies if he's entertaining? Please say you can be bought."

"Almost any woman can be bought if the price is high enough," Wanda said, winking.

"He loves to meddle in the kitchen. Watching you make pie will keep him happy. We love it when that happens. I'm making room for this in my budget. Lots of room. You won't be sorry."

"I'll be thrilled to have these on my menu," Phillip said, sweeping his hand over the pies on the counter. "Between us, we're going to put the Dancing Shrimp on the map, Wanda. You wait and see."

Maggie watched as the men said goodbye and left; then Wanda turned to her. "You saw that?"

"I did."

"I'm not imagining this?"

Maggie stepped forward and gave her mother a hug.

By three o'clock Tracy knew she had to hang up her sneakers and crawl home. On Fridays she usually stayed until the last kid in the after-school program had been picked up and the swim-team coach assured her that practice was over. But there was plenty of staff to make sure those things went as planned, and she was too exhausted to look at more paperwork. She had finally seen the obstetrician that morning, and although nothing surprising had come from her first visit — Tracy was fine, the nausea was normal, the baby was due in early May — the whole experience had worn her to a nub.

She had heard the baby's heartbeat. That had been a surprise, even though she'd known she might. But the amplified *rat-a-tat* had been absolutely clear, and she'd been there alone listening to it, with only her doctor keeping her company. She knew any of her friends would have been glad to go along, but she also knew she had no right to ask. She'd gotten herself into this, and the man who had helped her didn't yet know he was a father again. If anyone should have been with her, it was Marsh. And that revelation was the most exhausting part of the day. Knowing she'd cheated Marsh of that moment and not yet being willing to change that.

Now she gathered her things and said goodbye to Gladys, who congratulated her for taking care of herself for a change. Then she dragged herself out to her soon-to-be-vintage Bimmer, which the feds hadn't bothered to impound when they took everything else she and CJ had owned in California, and turned up the radio so she wouldn't fall asleep at the wheel.

Once on the key, she slowed as she neared home. She passed the foundation of what had once been the office for Happiness Haven, the tourist camp that had originally occupied the property. The owners had harbored big plans for development, none of which had come to fruition. Most of the cottages had already been gone when CJ bought the land to construct a luxury condo complex and marina and optimistically renamed it Happiness Key. The sign CJ had commissioned still marked the beginning of Tracy's property, but now it lay on its back, staring up at the blue Florida sky.

The conservation easement with Wild Florida meant keeping Happiness Key was possible, but only just. The contractor interested in taking the whole property off her hands had called her at the center that morning to sweeten his offer by thousands. She hadn't told him yes or no. She'd just wondered how many big decisions one woman could make when she was both hungry and nauseated.

"Janya." Tracy found herself stopping in front of the Indian woman's house before she could figure out why. She certainly wasn't going to tell her friend about the doctor's visit and make her feel sad again. She sat for a moment and wondered why she was there, but the answer wasn't difficult. She was never with Janya when she didn't feel better afterward. Talking to her was like sitting next to a cool flowing stream. Though she was the youngest woman in the development, Janya wasn't young in insight.

She stepped out of the car and saw that Olivia was heading up the road in her direction. Immediately she felt better. Watching Alice's granddaughter grow up was a bonus Tracy had never expected when she moved to Florida.

"Hey, Olivia," Tracy said when Olivia was almost to her. "How's school these days?"

"I like it." Olivia was wearing a jean jacket over a ruffled pink skirt and matching high-top sneakers with no laces. Her hair was off her neck in two pigtails. Tracy had helped her shop before school began, and then they'd gone to see the latest Harry Potter movie, with Olivia catching her up on all the previous films. Afterward Tracy had gone to the library and read her way through the series because, clearly, she needed to know more. For the kids at the rec center, of course. Just for them.

"You're looking great," Tracy said, pointing down. "Love the shoes."

Olivia, at an age where looking good was half the battle, smiled her thanks. "I . . . well, I wondered if . . ."

Olivia was beginning to sound a little too much like her grandmother, but her agile brain wasn't the problem. Tracy smiled encouragement.

"There's a mother-daughter softball game at school in a couple of weeks. And, well, I wondered if you'd be my . . ." Olivia shrugged.

"Mother?"

"Well, everybody will know you aren't. But you could be my grown-up friend."

Tracy could see the dilemma. Alice couldn't do this. She was not Olivia's mother, she was

154

Olivia's grandmother, and not a young one at that. She had recovered as well as could be expected from the stroke, but running bases was not in the cards. Nor was pitching or playing third base. Tracy wasn't sure her aging friend was up to swinging a bat, either.

Yet here was Olivia, who needed a young mother and would again in the future. And this time she was asking Tracy to stand in for the one who had died, most likely at the hands of Olivia's own father.

Tracy felt her throat tighten. She imagined her nauseated self running bases, but despite that, she knew she couldn't say no.

"I am *so* hot on a softball field," she said. "We moms are going to cream you daughters."

Olivia's face lit up as if she'd swallowed the sun. "Great!"

"Does Alice know you're asking me?"

Olivia sobered. "I didn't really tell her about the game. Not yet."

"She'll want to be there."

"Maybe not. She . . . well, she feels bad she can't do everything, you know? She's doing a lot. Like too much. I . . . just don't want her feeling worse. I thought maybe . . ."

The girl wasn't going to tell Alice. Tracy could hear it in her voice. Olivia was perceptive and thoughtful, and Tracy realized she was feeling guilty about all her grandmother was required to do for her. Olivia was afraid this would make Alice feel inadequate. Or at least that's what Tracy was guessing.

"She adores you," Tracy said. "She won't feel one bit bad I'm the one on the field. She'll be glad you asked me. Do you want me to tell her?"

"I'll do it."

They talked about the date of the game, and Tracy promised to put it on her calendar. Then Olivia gave her a spontaneous hug and turned for home.

Janya, in a pink flowered sundress, met her on the front steps. "You decided not to work so long today?"

"I just pooped out. I'm on my way home for a nap, but I thought I'd see how you're doing."

"You need tea. Come have some with me."

"I'm not drinking tea these days. Or coffee. Or alcohol."

"Cold water, then. And sympathy."

Tracy followed her inside. The tiny house was filled with plants and murals. An impressionistic Taj Mahal dominated one wall, and the last time Tracy had seen Janya's bedroom, a jungle scene complete with tigers had nearly leaped off the wall. Unlike some landlords, she was happy her tenant liked to paint. Tracy would never be called on to freshen up Janya's house.

While Janya got ice, Tracy told her about Olivia.

"I am not surprised she asked you," Janya said. "Only that she has not yet told her grandmother."

Tracy leaned against the wall to stay out of Janya's way. "I think she's afraid she's draining Alice dry. Alice is a wonderful grandmother. Nobody could be better, but Alice is in a different phase of her life than Olivia's mother would have been. She'll never be up on a ladder decorating the gym for Olivia's prom, or throwing a boy-girl birthday party next year or chaperoning field trips. She dotes on that girl, but she's already been a mother, and her energy's flagging. Becoming one again's just too much."

"I'm glad Olivia could ask for help."

Tracy hoped the occasional softball game and shopping trip were going to be enough help. She took the glass of iced water and followed Janya into the living room. She was just about to choose a seat, when somebody knocked on the door.

Janya went to answer while Tracy made a nest on the sofa, arranging pillows against her back. According to Google, her prime source for pregnancy information, one of the more obnoxious effects of pregnancy was backache. She figured she might as well prepare.

Janya was speaking to someone on the steps, and the conversation continued for several minutes, so Tracy closed her eyes.

157

Then the door opened wider, and Janya ushered in an attractive Indian man carrying a little girl and holding the hand of a small boy. Janya looked worried, but she made a quick introduction.

"Tracy, this is our friend Harit Dutta, and his children, Vijay and Lily."

Tracy made a polite response and smiled a welcome at the children — impossibly small children, at that — who looked anything but happy. The little girl was sobbing, and the little boy was sniffing hard, as if trying not to.

"I have told Harit I will take care of his children for a little while," Janya said with a smile in their direction. But the smile was forced, and Janya definitely looked troubled.

Harit smoothed his daughter's hair; then, without another glance at her, he handed the baby to Janya. Lily wasn't happy to go. She leaned toward her father, arms pitifully outstretched, and began to cry harder. Vijay's sniffing became louder.

Harit squatted beside his son and spoke to him in a low voice. The little boy threw his arms around his father's neck, but Harit untangled them and set the child away. Then he stood.

"Thank you," he told Janya. "This will make my evening easier."

"I will take good care of them."

"I'll get their things. I promise I'll call to let you know when I'll be coming to get them

158

tomorrow." He paused. "Or the next day, at the latest."

Tracy had been surprised to see the father saying goodbye to his children, but this new information was more surprising. Janya was going to do overnight child care for this harried young man?

"It might be best if you leave their things on the porch," Janya told him. "We can get them later. Better, perhaps, to say one goodbye now?"

Harit Dutta nodded, ruffled his son's hair almost as if the gesture was only prompted by Janya's words, then made his escape.

Tracy stared her gathering questions at her friend. Janya shrugged. Lily was screaming now, as if her heart would break, and little Vijay was trying to open the door and get to his father.

Tracy leaped to her feet and got to Janya's side before Janya could stop the boy. She grabbed for Lily and slid her from Janya's arms. "You know him. Talk to him."

Her words were accompanied by a thump, as if something had landed on the front steps. Then, as Janya gently took Vijay's arm and led him away from the door, Tracy heard the start of an engine.

She was too busy to run to the window to watch Harit Dutta driving away while his children cried inconsolably. Lily was squirming in her arms with strength Tracy had, until

159

that moment, only equated with angry nine-year-olds piled on top of each other after an umpire's bad call.

"We can't have this," Tracy said firmly. "Let's go wash that sad little face." She took the flailing baby into the bathroom and soaked a washcloth in cool water, before she used it to wipe Lily's streaming eyes and nose. Lily was probably a pretty child, with delicate features and hair that would one day be as lovely and thick as Janya's, but right now her tiny face looked like a gnome's, angry and wrinkled.

"See the baby in the mirror?" Tracy asked. She leaned toward the bathroom mirror, then pulled away. "All gone. Where did she go?" She tried again. Lily continued to scream. "I can't find the baby," Tracy said calmly. "Where can the baby be?"

Lily took a deep breath to scream once more, but no sound came out.

Encouraged, Tracy tried a third time. "Baby's gone. Baby's gone. Where can the baby be?" She leaned over so Lily could catch a glimpse of her face before she pulled her away again.

"I saw her. I saw her!" Tracy jiggled Lily a little. "Did you see the baby, Lily? Let's look for her again."

Lily gave a pitiful screech, but the volume was lower than it had been. Tracy rinsed the washcloth, and used it to wipe Lily's forehead

160

and cheeks. She continued playing peekaboo with the mirror until Lily was only groaning a little.

"Such a pretty baby," Tracy crooned.

Lily leaned her head against Tracy's shoulder, and Tracy felt as if she'd been struck by lightning. For a moment she couldn't move, the sensation was so delicious, so unexpected, so . . . maternal. Finally, aware that the bathroom was not the best place to spend the afternoon, she reluctantly settled the little girl on one hip and went back into the living room.

"Lily tells me she's thirsty," Tracy said. "Vijay, what does Lily drink?"

The little boy was curled up on Janya's lap, sobbing quietly. "Milk," he said.

"How about you, Vijay? Do you drink milk, too?"

"No!"

"Well, neither do I," Tracy said. "I absolutely do not drink milk. I drink bug juice."

Vijay looked up, and his eyes widened.

"But since Janya doesn't have any, we'll settle for water, okay?"

He sniffed loudly, but his little head nodded.

He scrambled off Janya's lap and ran to the window, but he didn't make a sound when he saw his father was gone. He stood stiffly, like a soldier, and Tracy hoped he wouldn't stay that way for the rest of the afternoon.

Half an hour later both children were asleep on the sofa, worn out from crying. Janya had put pillows around Lily to keep her from falling off, and Vijay was wedged between the back of the sofa and one of the cushions.

Only then did Tracy raise a brow in question. "What is this about?" she asked softly.

"Kanira, his wife, disappeared without a word. Harit came to see if I knew where she has gone," Janya whispered.

"Do you?"

"No. I haven't seen or heard from her since we had dinner with them on Monday. And she said nothing of this."

"Did he come expecting you to take the children? Just like that?"

"He said they were going to look for Kanira, and that is why he had the children's things assembled. But I think, perhaps, he hoped I would offer."

The children's things had arrived in several pillowcases the women had retrieved from the steps. A few toys. Some clothing. Diapers for Lily. Very little, assembled quickly, but perhaps enough, since Janya had a washing machine and Harit had said he would be back for the children soon. While they were on the porch he'd given Janya some hurried explanations about schedules and diets, but it was precious little.

"Does he have any idea where to look for her?" Tracy asked. Vijay moaned in his sleep,

162

and for a moment both women went still until he was quiet again.

Janya bit her lip, then shook her head. "But he asked . . . he asked if Kanira had said anything." She looked uncomfortable.

"About what?" Tracy prompted.

"Another man," Janya said at last.

"Another man? Does he think she ran off with someone else?"

Janya's expression said it all.

"*Did* she say something to you?" Tracy asked, although the answer was written on Janya's features.

"She said . . ." Janya looked away. "She said she had resources, and that soon she might change her life for the better."

"You think she meant a man?"

"I cannot say what she meant for certain. But she has no family to turn to. She did not complete her education in India, and even if she had, here she would be expected to do more to qualify for a job. So what could she have meant? She was unhappy with Harit. She did not hurt the children, and she did not scream at them, but she was not happy to be their mother, either."

Tracy knew Janya was thinking out loud, but the possibilities did seem limited and, at best, uncertain. "Maybe she just took off to think a little."

"There is a shopping center not far from their house. She left the children with Harit

163

early this morning before he had to be at work and said she would return."

"Did he call the police?"

"He is afraid the police will not be helpful because he is from India. I think he is hoping Kanira will call soon, that this is her way of grabbing attention and letting him know how unhappy she is." Janya shook her head sharply. "As if everyone who has met her doesn't know this already. She is very clear about being unhappy."

Tracy could understand why Janya had agreed to watch the children. They were too young to be caught up in this drama, and if Harit *did* find his wife, the ensuing scene would be enough to give the little ones nightmares. Janya was trying to spare them.

"He *will* come back, won't he?" Tracy asked.

"Of course. He must. We are strangers to him, and they are his blood. Perhaps he did not want the children, the way Rishi wants ours, but I think he cares about them. In her way Kanira cares, as well. Only . . ."

"Only the gods screwed up big-time giving these two kids," Tracy said.

"This is the way it often seems to work."

Tracy realized that she was sitting there, pregnant through her own carelessness, and the conversation had inevitably led right to that all-consuming subject again. But before she could say anything, Janya smiled, as if she had read Tracy's thoughts.

164

"Not you, Tracy. The gods did not screw up. You were wonderful with Lily. You say you know nothing about babies? There you were, doing everything, as if you had always done it."

Tracy had been too busy to worry about what she was doing. Lily had been screaming like a gale-force wind, so to dampen the noise, Tracy had simply tried ways to make her feel better. Everything she'd done had come naturally. She'd simply watched, tried this and that, paid attention to what worked and then done it again. Could taking care of a baby be that easy?

"Just luck," she said, but she wondered. She had been surprised to learn she knew how to handle the kids at the rec center. She always described her prowess as benevolent disinterest. The kids at the center learned quickly that she didn't care why they misbehaved or have any particular stake in the outcome, so they toed the line because there was no point not to.

But maybe she had been wrong. Maybe getting along with children was a talent after all. She definitely needed a course or two on diapers and breast feeding, and maybe how to get through childbirth — which sounded physically impossible — but maybe she wasn't going to be as hopeless as she had expected.

"It will be strange to have children in the

165

house," Janya said. "I must call Rishi while I can and warn him. Will you stay here a moment and keep them safe?"

Tracy nodded. She suspected the best part of mothering might just be watching children sleep. She saw no reason to deny herself that innocent reward.

CHAPTER NINE

Tracy never knocked herself out when she cooked for Marsh. He knew her history. Before moving to Florida she'd left meals to household staff and restaurant chefs. After her life changed and all disposable income had been disposed of, she had survived happily on snacks and supermarket delis. Gradually she had taken a few basic classes at the rec center and begun to prepare more complete meals. Marsh loved to cook, so she saw little reason to become a gourmet herself, but at least now she could prepare salads, sauté vegetables and grill fish. She had even perfected several interesting entrées with multiple ingredients, just to prove she could.

None of those entrées were in evidence tonight.

Breathing through her mouth to avoid smelling her own cooking, Tracy stepped back from the kitchen stove to examine the meal she was preparing for Marsh and Bay, who were due any moment.

Mashed potatoes. Check. Broiled chicken breasts seasoned with salt and the barest dusting of pepper. Check. Salad of iceberg lettuce, celery and cucumber with the blandest ranch dressing she could find. Check. Sliced Italian bread and butter. Check. She hoped that with the addition of a sprig of bright green parsley, Marsh and Bay wouldn't notice that the meal completely disappeared against the shiny white ironstone plates that had seemed relatively sophisticated when she'd found them on sale at Target. Short of drawing a Magic Marker road map — turn right for potatoes — she didn't know what she could do. She had prepared a meal she might be able to eat. That alone was miracle enough.

That afternoon, when Marsh had called, she'd turned down an invitation for dinner at the funky old Cracker house that had been home to his family for generations. He was likely to make something fragrant and spicy, she'd thought, and there was no way she could sidestep eating at least some of it, with dire consequences. So she had invited the Egan guys here, claiming she wanted to host, since she needed to make this an early night. She told a skeptical Marsh she'd promised to go to an early church service with Alice tomorrow. Church was the only Sunday excuse she'd been able to think of on short notice, and she'd felt so guilty using God for her own purposes that later she'd stopped by Alice's to see if she could go with her after all. No question an hour in church was needed after so many half truths.

She turned off the stove and stepped into the bathroom to check her hair. She'd chosen a bright fuchsia blouse, hoping her pale cheeks might reflect some of the color, but so far it wasn't working. She'd planned to spend extra time on makeup, but she'd napped too long, so the face staring back at her wore minimal mascara and only a nominal coat of lip gloss. Anything brighter against her washed-out skin and she was afraid she would look like a vampire. She'd left her hair down and planned to lean forward a lot for maximum coverage.

Mentally she rehearsed her story, trying to stick with the truth as much as possible. She was definitely feeling better. The doctor had said everything was fine. No lie there. She was supposed to take things easy for a while and eat simply until her digestion was back to normal. Again, true. She was sorry she'd been so cranky, but she wasn't used to being sick, and work was sapping every bit of energy while she recovered.

For a moment she considered calling and telling Marsh she just wasn't up to this. But the longer she held him at arm's length, the more questions he would have. The bigger the final explosion would be, too.

She was filling water glasses with ice when she heard the familiar pickup. She had set out wineglasses and a freshly opened bottle of white wine, pouring some in the sink and filling her own wineglass with water and a squeeze of lemon to make it cloudier, as if she had already started on the bottle without him. She was afraid if she turned down a real glass of wine, his suspicions would be aroused.

The front door opened, and she peeked out to find she had one visitor, not two.

"Where's Bay?" she asked.

"At the last minute he got a better invitation. Adam invited him to a movie."

"Oh . . . great!" She pasted a smile on her wan face. "For him and us. Although I miss the kid. I've only seen him in passing lately."

"It happened as we were getting ready to come here, but I should have called. We were rushing around to get him ready, and it slipped my mind."

"No problem. It's a very simple dinner."

"There's a new Thai restaurant near Wanda's shop, and I could have taken you out if I'd known."

She imagined lemongrass and Thai basil, and had to immediately put the thought out of her mind. "Another time, when we can stay out later. Let's pour you some wine. I'm already sipping."

He followed her into the kitchen. "You look

cheerful in that color."

She glanced at him. He was wearing a shirt she particularly liked. First, it had no slogan. That was a start. Second, it had buttons. And third, it was a subtle leafy print that brought out the gold in his hair and eyes. He wore jeans without holes in the knees and polished loafers without socks. This was formal Marsh.

This was Marsh hoping to score.

Her heart sank. Along with nausea and the desire to pee every three minutes had come a dip in her libido that bothered her as much as the other symptoms tied together. She had never had to fake anything with this man. Not desire. Not enthusiasm. Not orgasm. Tonight she knew she was going to have to fake the whole nine yards.

And women wanted children why?

She remembered that rapid little heartbeat, and for no good reason at all, her eyes filled and spilled over.

"Are you okay?" Marsh asked.

"It's the chicken," she said, waving a hand in front of her face. "Something I used when I was spicing the breasts is making my eyes water. I must have an allergy." She split for the bathroom, shut the door, sniffed hard, carefully wiped her eyes, hit the toilet again and washed her hands.

When she returned, she grabbed her wine-glass, which she'd apparently set right beside the door, because there it was waiting for her.

She took a long drink, remembering halfway through that Marsh thought this really *was* wine. She pried the glass from her lips.

"On an empty stomach?" he asked. "A stomach that's recovering? Chugging wine? Is that a good idea?"

"White wine settles it. The doctor says it's fine." Two lies. She would probably need to go to church morning *and* evening tomorrow.

"So you saw the doc?"

"Did. Everything's okay. She did a few tests and said these things take care of themselves with time. I should just eat whatever tastes good until my appetite comes back."

"And tonight apparently white tastes good. We might need sunglasses. Dinner could be blinding."

"I know. It does look a little . . ." She tried to think of a good spin to put on things. "Monochromatic."

"Not a chromatic in sight. Even the wine's white. Very Zen."

"Exactly what I was going for."

He moved behind her and put his arms around her waist, pulling her close. "It's sweet of you to feng shui the dinner when you're not feeling well."

She leaned against him. "That's me. Sweet as sugar."

"Which is also white."

"You've been patient. I appreciate that."

He squeezed gently, but it set off a chain

reaction. For a moment she thought she was going to have to bolt for the door. She wriggled away, gasping for air and composure. "Let me heat up the chicken."

"Exactly what I was thinking. We can't eat lukewarm chicken breasts. What would that say about us?"

She was too nauseated for repartee. Instead, she switched on the broiler again and took more deep breaths through her mouth. "I'll just stick the potatoes in the microwave, too."

Marsh carried things to the table, and in a few minutes she joined him with their plates, his heaped with potatoes and chicken, hers barely dotted with the same. Even so, whatever appetite she'd gained had fled. Luckily she doubted that it mattered. Whatever she left on her plate was going to blend right in.

Marsh told her about Bay and work. She caught him up on the rec center. At one point he looked up from the chicken he'd been pushing around his plate. "Which seasoning do you think you're allergic to, Trace? Salt or pepper?"

"That's not very nice."

"The meal's a study in simplicity. Maybe *that's* what you're allergic to."

"I believe in tasting whatever I'm eating, unadorned, fully flavored. This chicken died for us."

"It's a brand-new concept. It might catch on."

She didn't tell him it had been in favor with the newly pregnant for thousands of years.

He helped her clear, and she was touched to see that somehow he had finished the contents of his plate. The meal, even by her skewed standards, had been horrible. Overcooked chicken. Lumpy potatoes. Limp iceberg lettuce with tasteless dressing. She doubted Marsh would ever eat anything she prepared again.

"So . . . tea? Coffee?" she asked brightly. "I have white tea, if you're interested. And milk to put in it."

He pulled her close. "You're a trouper. I pushed you into this. I'm sorry. I've just missed you. And I've been wondering if something else was going on." He waited, as if to see whether she had anything to add. "But I should have left you alone until you felt a hundred percent," he finished, when silence reigned.

She put her arms around him and rested her head against his shoulder. "I'm glad you're here."

"I should go."

She wondered if she ought to simply confess her charade while he was feeling repentant. She didn't plan to keep the truth from Marsh for long, just long enough to make sure she knew where they stood without a baby between them. But here they stood right now, arms around each other, and the baby *was* between them. Right between them, and she was the only one who knew it, the only one who had heard its pin-dot heart pounding.

"Not yet," she said, kissing him. Maybe she was trying to make up for the deception, she didn't know, but when he gathered her closer, she kissed him harder.

They left the dishes and the leftovers and undressed each other on the way to her bedroom. Marsh's shirt in the hallway, pants by the bed. Her outer clothing everywhere and her lacy underwear hanging from a doorknob. She'd changed the sheets and worn her prettiest thong, just in case. Thongs wouldn't be all that inviting in a couple of months, and she'd figured she ought to wear hers out while she could.

They fell to the sheets, and she told herself she was fine, she was good, better than good, and that this was exactly what she wanted to be doing. She didn't protest when he nuzzled her breasts, although they felt oddly tight and almost painfully sensitive. She couldn't complain, because that symptom would be a dead giveaway. She moaned, but not from pleasure. The bland dinner had helped with the nausea, but now everything else seemed out of whack. Breasts that didn't want to be touched, heartburn bubbling in her chest and worst of all, a strong desire to close her eyes and fall asleep.

She fought them all, responding the way

she knew he wanted her to. She was doing fine until he stopped, leaned over the bed and felt for his pants.

"What are you doing?" she demanded.

"I doubt you prepared, did you? This wasn't exactly a foregone conclusion."

For a moment she wondered what she was supposed to have prepared for. Then she realized he was talking about her diaphragm. He was searching his pants pockets for a condom. Marsh was worried about birth control at the precise moment when there was zero need to be.

For a moment she wanted to cry. Then she had the absurd desire to laugh. She couldn't control it. She giggled. He looked at her and smiled. "I like a woman with a sense of humor. But what's funny about taking precautions?"

"I'm just glad you're here and we have a reason to," she lied, the laughter dying. She wanted to cry again. Nobody had told her pregnancy was the gateway to insanity, but here she was, living proof.

"Me, too," he said, finishing what he'd started.

She welcomed him back fiercely and held him tight. She was lying to Marsh about too much, but at the last moment she was glad to discover that despite everything else, her response to this man was no lie at all.

■ ■ ■ ■

Blake drove an expensive copper-colored hybrid that was both environmentally sound and sleek. Maggie liked the way it purred softly, like a huge, tawny cat. This evening he wore a dark leather jacket over a lightweight cashmere sweater, and cowboy boots with vintage-washed jeans. She'd taken him at his word and dressed simply — dark slacks, green silk blouse with a darker scarf, a gold chain with the single diamond her mother and father had presented at her college graduation. She'd started to pull on a pair of suede pumps until she realized Felo had given them to her, and settled for dark flats instead.

The house that Cardrake Brothers had rented for their staff was beachy and sprawling, a two-story gray wood contemporary with a porch off Blake's suite that was high enough to catch glimpses of the Gulf in the distance and the remains of a tumbledown fish camp to the west. The area was sparsely populated, which made it perfect for parties, and Blake had told her that the company who managed it had been delighted to get professionals in for a long-term stay.

By the time she chatted with Blake in the car, then suffered through introductions to almost everybody, including a variety of city and county officials, she was ready to retreat.

Blake had been straight with her, this was a smallish party. But since she didn't know anyone but him, it was a smallish party filled with strangers, more taxing than the backyard bashes she and Felo had hosted, with him in the kitchen laughing and creating Cuban delicacies, and her filling glasses with beer and cheap wine.

When he had to leave to talk to the caterers, Blake turned her over to Ned, one of the partners who shared the beach house. Ned was older than Blake, lanky and socially awkward, but he gamely introduced Maggie to a few more guests before he found an excuse to leave her on her own.

Glad to be alone, she wandered the fringes of conversation, enjoying a beautifully prepared buffet of gourmet finger foods and champagne that probably cost more than a month of the house payments she had shared with Felo. The beach house was sparely but tastefully furnished, and she was particularly drawn to a series of professional photographs embellishing one wall, most with a bridge silhouetted against extraordinary scenery.

Even with the recession in full swing, this house still had to be worth a fortune. Maggie and Felo had bought their house together, fixed it up side-by-side, but with plummeting real estate prices, she was afraid the simple bungalow in Little Havana was worth, at most, what remained on their mortgage. When the time came to make a final financial break, she could just walk away and let him have it without a fuss. At least there was one positive coming out of the tense financial climate.

"Are you doing okay?" Blake asked after two hours, when he found her settled into a deck chair with a glass goblet filled with chocolate mousse. The deck was lit with tiki torches and soft lamps, and Maggie had been glad to find a seat in the shadows.

"Most likely not. Between working in a pie shop and your mousse, I'm going to have to work out every night for the rest of my life."

He lowered himself to a stool beside her and grinned engagingly. "I have a feeling you're not a party girl. More the quiet type."

She hadn't told him much about herself. She didn't publicize the fact that she'd been a cop. People got odd notions when they heard, as if they thought she was hoping to catch them doing something felonious. Instead, she'd mentioned a variety of jobs along the way, including education and PR. Both were true. She'd helped with the DARE program in the schools to educate children not to use drugs, and she had been the community liaison in her years in the sheriff's department. Important jobs, sure, but in that department, the only qualification an officer had needed to get them was breasts.

She told Blake a little more. "I guess I'm more or less the quiet type, but I'm not uncomfortable. I like to watch people, and I like to talk to them once I know them."

"What do you see here?"

She smiled. "Why?"

"Just curious. How does this group seem to you?"

She considered, because the question was interesting. "High octane," she said at last. "Upwardly mobile. Polite, but busy making contacts, so they move on fast. Your partners are working the crowd because they're newest to the community and still taking the local temperature. The city and county folks are trying to figure out how friendly is too friendly. They're investing a lot in Cardrake, so they're watching you carefully."

"We're not all work and no play. We have a couple of boats, and we fish. My group here just took a trip to Vegas together. Male bonding."

She had noticed there weren't any women on the team working on the bridge, an interesting omission. She wondered if the same good ol' boy network she'd fought so hard against in the sheriff's department also operated at Cardrake, and if it was as potentially lethal to women.

"Is it the gambling in Vegas that attracts you guys?" she asked.

"It's the supercharged atmosphere and

180

people watching, but I do enjoy losing my life savings now and then. Keeps me humble."

"Bet you were texting your contacts half the time, just to see what was going on."

"Your PR roots are showing. Are you going to pursue a job here?"

"Right now I'm committed to helping my mother make a go of the pie shop. She's had an array of incompetent assistants and needs a breather."

"So do you."

She cocked her head in question. "I do?"

"I'm guessing a breakup? Or maybe a job that got so bad you left, wounded and angry."

She was surprised he had hit those particular nails on the head and driven them home. "A little of both," she admitted.

"Dumb guy, whoever he is."

"Not dumb, no. I was the one who left, so maybe I'm the dumb one." The moment she said it, she wished she hadn't.

"Do you feel dumb?"

"No. Wounded and angry are more along the right lines."

"Too early to be going out with somebody else?"

She smiled. She liked Blake. He was easygoing, at least on the surface, and a better listener than most of the men she'd dated before Felo. He was the perfect guy to go out with after a breakup. Undemanding — at least so far — and successful enough that she wasn't going to have to hold his hand and encourage him while she was finding her own way.

"You'll have to tell *me*," she said. "I'm not in the market for anything except casual right now. If you're looking for more, you need to look elsewhere. If you're not, spending time together works for me."

"This is going to be an intensive, difficult time workwise. I don't want complications. Maybe we're ideally suited."

If they really were ideally suited, she knew she should feel something other than the vague interest stirring inside her, but she nodded. "Don't you need to get back to schmoozing?"

"People are starting to leave. My partners are going to head down to a club in Naples for a little more celebration. Want to come along?"

That was easy. She shook her head. "I promised I'd check out the adult swim team at the rec center in the morning. I told Tracy I used to swim competitively in college, and it was all downhill from there. I'd better make this an early night."

"You're a swimmer? Go on. I was on my high school swim team. Maybe we can train together sometime."

She tried to imagine Felo in a Speedo and goggles, and couldn't. "I'll let you know how it goes," she promised.

"Let me say goodbye to a couple more people, then I'll drive you home."

By the time she was in Blake's car heading back across the key, she was looking forward to slipping into casual clothes and flipping through the television channels. These days her attention span was, at most, three minutes long, which worked perfectly for most shows.

"Looks like you have a visitor," Blake said as they pulled up to Maggie's cottage.

She had already noted the same. This time Felo's car was parked directly in front of her house, and the man himself was sitting on her porch, Rumba curled in his lap. The front door had been locked, but Felo was masterful with a credit card.

"An old friend," she said as Blake pulled to a stop behind Felo's car.

"*The* old friend?"

" 'Fraid so."

"Want me to scare him away?"

She laughed. "He'd have you in handcuffs. He's a cop."

"A cop?" He sounded surprised.

"A good one, too, but impatient. I'd suggest dropping me off and turning toward Naples."

He didn't rev the engine. "I'm not leaving if there's going to be trouble here."

She was surprised, and a bit touched. After all, Blake really didn't know any of the important things about her.

She rested her fingertips on his arm to re-assure him. "I promise there won't be. He's not a psycho in uniform. Felo would never lift a hand to any woman unless she had a gun in hers."

"If you're sure . . ."

"Absolutely." She leaned over and kissed his cheek. "Thanks for inviting me tonight. I had fun."

"No, you didn't."

"Actually, I did. Great food, interesting people. Let's do it again."

He touched his fingers to his forehead in salute.

She got out and watched him drive away before she started toward her front porch.

"You broke into my house," she said in greeting.

"Don't you know any locks that take at least a minute to open?" He stood, Rumba in his arms. His black guayabera shirt was unbut-toned halfway down his chest, and despite a slight chill in the air, he wore shorts. "She heard me and started scratching at the door. I didn't want you to lose your damage de-posit."

"I didn't pay a damage deposit. Did you search the house just to see what I'm up to?"

"I opened the door six inches and hauled Rumba out to the steps. If I'd searched, what would I have found?"

"Remnants of a couple of pies in the fridge.

A brand-new *TV Guide*."

"And to think I just sat here."

They were face-to-face now. She couldn't summon outrage. Felo knew she hadn't left him for another man. There was nothing to search for, no evidence to collect. She doubted he was lying.

"Who's the guy?" he asked.

"Not your business."

He nodded. "Tell me anyway."

She debated, but what was there to hide? "His name is Blake Armstrong. He's an engineer, and his firm is building a new bridge to Palmetto Grove."

"Glad to hear it. The present one creaked when I drove across. And swayed."

"No, it didn't."

He shrugged. "Well, if they say they have to replace it now, they probably should have done it ten years ago. That's how things work."

"Are you stalking me?"

He stroked the cat thoughtfully. "Nothing that formal."

"Felo, what are you doing here?"

"I brought your things. Everything I could carry, anyway."

For a moment she forgot to breathe. He had moved her out. Just like that. She'd been steeling herself to do it, waiting for the right moment. But how long before that moment would have arrived?

"That's a lot of trouble," she said, not betraying her turmoil.

"Yeah, but I've got a few days off. I'm going to Alvaro's camp on the way home. So this wasn't that far out of the way."

His old friend owned a hunting camp off the Loop Road in the Big Cypress Swamp, about halfway between Miami and Palmetto Grove. Maggie had avoided it the way she avoided anything to do with Alvaro Hernandez, although it was the kind of place she would probably enjoy. Simple, almost primitive, surrounded by unadulterated nature and quiet. Felo often went there when he needed to be alone, or just to be outdoors without any motivation other than to enjoy sun and fresh air.

"There's some furniture I'd like to have," she said, gaze flicking to the car.

"Relax, I just got what was obvious. Things you might need here. There's still a bunch of stuff at the house. And anything you want is yours. Only . . ."

"Only what?"

"Don't be in such a hurry, Mags." He reached up and cupped her cheek. When she didn't pull away, he stroked it a moment. "I love you," he said softly. "That's not going away any time soon. But maybe this is good, huh? You being here, me being there. Maybe we need time to figure out what went wrong. Maybe you can figure out how to tell me what you need. And I'll figure out how to tell you the same."

"Telling me what *you* need's never been the problem. Telling me what to *do* was never your problem, either."

Something flickered in his eyes, but he waited a beat before he responded. "Then I'll learn to ask."

"Felo . . ." She shook her head.

"You want me to leave and never come back? You can say that right here and now? 'Felo, go home and stay out of my life'? Because if I'm going to listen to you, I guess I need to hear you say it right out loud."

She waited for the words to form, but she knew the sun would rise again before she found them. *If* she found them.

"You can't say it, can you?"

She remained still and quiet.

"Want to help me unpack the car?" he asked.

"Let me put Rumba in the second bedroom." She opened the door and took the cat inside. When she returned, Felo was lifting a box from the car. She moved aside as he carried it up the walk. Between them, the car was unloaded in five minutes.

"I'll head out now," he said, straightening up after the last box was sitting on her living room floor. "There's just one more thing. I almost forgot."

She'd expected another stab at intimacy,

something else to tie them together, but instead he left for the car and returned with a small cooler she'd noticed on the front seat. She had assumed it was food he was taking to Alvaro's camp, but Felo held it out to her and lifted the top. Fabulous smells emerged. "Some men give diamonds and some give BMWs. Me, I give *maduros, moros y cristianos, lechon asado.*"

Plantain, beans and rice, and spiced, marinated roast pork. "You brought this from Corrado's?"

"Maybe you left *me* for a while, but I figured you'd be mourning Corrado."

"Felo . . ." Again, she didn't know what to say. Corrado's was a hole in the wall near their house, but the food was a closely guarded neighborhood secret. Corrado, the owner, had more business than he could handle already, and Maggie adored everything about the peeling linoleum tables, and the dollar bills and business cards tacked on the wall behind the bar. She took the cooler and dipped her head lower to inhale. "Corrado can cook almost as well as you can."

"You take your time, but when you're ready, I'll cook for you again."

She finally looked up. "I can't tell you when or if I'll be ready, Felo. Maybe I've finally had enough of men telling me what to do. Maybe I just need a permanent vacation from relationships. Don't count on anything."

"You know what I count on? You love me, too, Mags. Somehow we lost our way. I'm still not sure how. But we'll find each other again." He leaned over and kissed her. Not as casually as she had kissed Blake in the car, but carefully, as if he knew he could push her a millimeter too far, too fast, and lose her forever.

"When you're ready." He left her standing there, Rumba yowling from the spare bedroom, the smells of garlic and cumin scenting the air, and Maggie wondering exactly how she and Felo had come to this.

CHAPTER TEN

Wanda was getting over her fluster. So she'd reacted a little to having her pies on a restaurant menu, then to having them declared good enough for the likes of Derek Forbes. Who wouldn't have? After all, she was human. Life was full of good things, only most of the time they flew right past a person's nose before she had the common sense to pluck the feathers out of her nostrils.

This good fortune had just landed, perched and flapped its wings, waiting for her to do something before it dropped a load she sure didn't want in her lap. And she *had* done something. She, Wanda Gray, could now be struck dead without a moment of regret. She had married a good man, raised two passable children and fulfilled her final purpose on earth. She had baked pies good enough for a movie star and a restaurant opening.

In the kitchen of Wanda's Wonderful Pies, she splayed one hand across her ample chest and realized, to her satisfaction, that her heart was still pounding away, and she might live to see even more fame and fortune. The thought was delicious.

"You all right?" Maggie asked, escaping to the back for a moment to replenish the pie case, which had just been the victim of a raid, thanks to a ladies luncheon at the local Pentecostal church and apparently no lady alive who had time to bake her own contribution.

Wanda dropped her hand to her side. "How many'd you sell?"

"Five. I wonder if there'll be anything on that buffet table besides pie?"

"Winn-Dixie's rotisserie chicken. And most likely Publix macaroni and potato salads right out of the plastic containers."

"I never realized how lucky I was to have a mother who made our meals from scratch."

"Maybe that's why you went for Felo. The man can cook."

"He brought me food from our favorite restaurant on Saturday."

Wanda looked up. This was Maggie *sharing,* unusual enough to make her wonder if she'd heard her daughter right. "Felo was here *again?*"

"He brought a carload of my belongings over. He's spending some time at Alvaro's camp."

"Moved you out?"

"More like *helped* me out." Maggie seemed

to shake off the sudden intimacy. "Anyway, want me to replace the pies I sold with the same ones?" She poked her head in the refrigerator, then back out. "We're already out of Key lime. Shall we make more?"

The hardest thing about running a pie shop was knowing each day what would sell and what wouldn't. A pie unsold was money down the disposal. Some pies held for more than one day, but many did not. And most of what she made couldn't be frozen without compromising the quality. The local homeless shelter got a lot of Wanda's miscalculations. The men had taken to making requests.

"Let's push Luscious Lemon instead."

"Fine with me, only there's just one back here and one out front."

Wanda thought about all the things she really ought to do, but nodded. "I'll make a couple more Key lime. If they don't sell, they're a favorite over at the rescue mission."

"They call you Queen Wanda, you know. When I told them I was your daughter, they started calling me Princess Margaret."

"They're all short on money, but a sense of humor's free."

The front doorbell tinkled, and Maggie, a pie in each hand, went to answer, while Wanda stooped to gather the ingredients she was going to need.

In a moment Maggie came back. "There's

192

a guy out front who says he has to speak to you."

"Who?"

"Tracy's guy."

Wanda snapped to attention. "Maybe Wild Florida needs a pie party. I'd better check this out." But even as she said it, she knew Marsh Egan was far too important to come tripping over to her shop to pick out pies. She was wary, and sorry the place was so small there was no way she could pretend she wasn't here.

"Want me to start juicing the limes?"

"You do that," Wanda said.

She marched out front, brushing off her apron as she went. There was a couple in one corner finishing slices of the apple pie she reluctantly included on her menu now and then. Her apple pie was good, no doubt about it, but the pie was so darned ordinary, even with her secret splash of whiskey. Another man was talking quietly on his cell phone by the door. He was waiting for people to join him, and he'd already picked out a slice of German walnut all his own and made her promise she wouldn't sell it to anybody else. Looked to her as if he was getting impatient.

Marsh was standing by the front counter in a suit and tie, which never looked quite right on him. Wanda liked Tracy's boyfriend. Marsh had been good for her landlady, straightened her out about a thing or two, and showed her she was a different person from the one she'd believed herself to be.

Of course, his politics were scandalous. Wanda liked the environment well enough in its place, but she wasn't sure Wild Florida ought to be halting development on every country road and patch of swamp. Still, she was glad he'd convinced Tracy not to let anybody turn Happiness Key into condos for millionaires. The houses she and the others lived in were no better than beach huts, but the land? The land was something special, and Wanda could see that, politics or no.

"Why don't I buy you a cup of coffee," Marsh said.

"We got coffee here."

"You've also got customers. I need to talk to you."

She debated. Of course, if she was the boss, she could take off whenever she wanted, right? Nobody was clocking her comings and goings.

"My coffee's better," she said. "We'll take cups and go over to the park."

"Black, thanks."

She told Maggie she was going out; then she poured coffee into disposable cups that said Wanda's Wonderful Pies above a pie slice logo Janya had designed, slipped a sleeve around and a lid over, then joined him.

The park was a block away. They chatted about nothing important as they strolled, then found a bench overlooking an empty ball field that would be in constant use after school let out for the day. The moment their behinds hit the bench, the chitchat ended.

"Tracy's pregnant, isn't she?" Marsh asked, the way he might ask if Wanda had sold more pecan or sweet-potato pies that month.

She'd been in the middle of a sip, and now coffee sprayed everywhere.

Marsh patted her on the back and waited patiently.

Wanda and all the rest of the women had been sworn to secrecy, but clearly, the secret was out. Faced with the truth, she couldn't imagine pretending otherwise, because this was one secret that was going to be pretty obvious in no time.

"It's none of my business," she said instead.

"True, but it's mine, isn't it? Don't I deserve to know?"

"Then why don't you ask her?"

Marsh was silent a moment. "Here's why," he said, as if he was explaining the law to a developer caught in the act of dredging up sea-grass beds. "She doesn't want me to know, or she would have told me by now. So before I confront her, it's up to me to find out *why*. And who better to explain?"

"If you're worried it's not yours, don't be. No question about that. She and that rat CJ never slept together after their divorce. Never even got close."

"Thank you, but that wasn't on my list."

"Good for you. I like a man who trusts a woman."

"So she *is* pregnant."

Wanda realized she'd as much as told him so. "I don't feel comfortable talking about this."

"Some things are out of our comfort zone, Wanda, but that doesn't make them wrong. I could shake the truth out of her. We could have a huge fight. I could say all the wrong things because I don't know what's going on, and in the long run, would that be good for Tracy or the baby?"

"I see why you're good at what you do."

Marsh sipped his coffee and gave her time to consider.

"How'd you figure it out?" she asked.

"I had my suspicions, then Saturday night she had me to dinner. Never has anyone cooked a meal more perfectly suited for a woman in her first trimester. But the clincher . . . ?"

He'd been staring straight ahead, but now he glanced at her. "She pretended she was drinking white wine, then she made an emergency trip to the bathroom. So I took a sip, just to find out. Water, with lemon juice in it. It was clear what that was all about, what this mysterious stomach virus was about, what the whole damn thing is about. I waited all night for her to break the news, even went through with birth control, but no go."

"She's planning to tell you, you know."

"When? When the kid needs college tuition?"

Wanda pointed a finger at him. "It's your own fault."

"Yeah, I know when it must have happened, and it *was* my fault. Hers, too, but neither of us was thinking straight that night."

Wanda covered her ears. She didn't mind talking about sex, that was for sure, but not sex between good friends. "Too much information. Lordy."

He smiled just a little. "Wanda, you must know how this goes. You have kids, too."

"Why'd you come to me?"

"You can't keep a secret."

She just shook her head sadly, because it was true.

"Why isn't she telling me?" he asked. "Is she trying to figure out what to do?"

She debated, but she decided not knowing could be the source of some harmful guesses. Like that one. It was better to put them to rest. "She's having the baby, if that's what you mean. Never in doubt." She paused.

"Here's the thing." She started slow, but that didn't last. "Tracy and you, you've got some kind of weird history, don't you? Don't deny it. Enemies, then friends, then you hardly spoke while your exes were both in

197

town this summer making trouble. Then suddenly, bingo, you fall into bed together and this happens. You were just starting to get to know each other, be a couple, and now, whammo, she's got a little peach pie in the oven. And how's she supposed to know how that's going to affect your relationship? I mean, one minute you're jumping down each other's throats, the next you're jumping into bed together and now you're jumping into diapers and training wheels."

"Tracy knows how I feel about my son. Why would she doubt I'd love another child?"

Wanda wondered how dumb a smart man could be. "You think I'm saying *that's* what she's worried about? Whether you could love another child? How about whether you love *her?* Knock me naked! Have you ever told her? Have you even thought about your own feelings?"

"That's the problem?" He sounded as if it was way too minor to be real.

"This is no small thing, Marshall Egan! Any woman with a brain wants to be connected to a man and sure where she stands before she has his baby. And you know what? Nobody ever loved Tracy Deloche enough, you ask me. Not her parents, and surely not that no-good ex of hers. She's just started realizing she's lovable, really lovable, on account of all her neighbors, and now this. She's got a baby on the way and a man who's never said the words she needs to hear."

"I don't know what else I could have done to prove I care about her."

"Oh, really? You think demanding she go off and do the stuff that appeals to you over and over again and not do anything *she* loves is a good way of showing how much you care?"

"Wow, I've been missing out on some fascinating conversations, haven't I?"

She refused to let him off the hook. "She doesn't complain, if that's what you're getting at. But from what I can read between the lines, it's all about you and none about her. Like you're trying to make her prove she could be the right woman for the head honcho of Wild Florida. Like camping in the Everglades is some sort of initiation ritual."

"That's not true."

"When's the last time you took her somewhere *she* wanted to go? A nice restaurant? A play? Maybe some fancy hotel for a weekend?"

Marsh was silent.

"You think about it," Wanda said.

"And that's why she hasn't told me? Because we didn't cuddle up in a suite at the Ritz last month?"

"This isn't a courtroom, and I'm not your enemy."

Marsh sighed. "Help me understand, okay?"

"It's real simple. She wants to be sure you're together, *if* you're together, because you want to be with *her.* Then this baby will be a bonus. But if you're together because the baby forced you into it? Nothing like a bonus. A wedge. You have a son. You know those early years aren't the best for romance. You let a baby come between you, and it sure as shootin' will. You got to be strong, and you got to be together and you got to be *sure.*"

"And she's not sure."

"Are you?"

He didn't answer, but of course Wanda knew she wasn't the one he needed to tell.

"So what do I do?" he asked when she glanced at her watch.

"You figure it out. I told you what she needs, what she's trying to find out. Now you figure out a way to give it to her. Or not. I can't make you. It's all up to you. But just a word of advice?"

She waited until he nodded. "Take a good look at Tracy sometime, okay? You ever walk down the street with her? You ever watch heads turn? Male heads? She's hanging out with you for a reason, and it's not because she can't find somebody else. You understand what I'm saying here?"

"Yeah. If she were a fish, I'd be stupid not to make sure the hook's in good and tight."

"Your metaphors need work, son. Too Wild

200

Florida for me." Wanda got to her feet. "I'll walk myself back. You stay here and think. But you tell anybody we had this conversation and I'm going to create me a new pie in your honor — the Ground-Glass Special. You get my meaning?"

"You talk tough."

"Try me."

"I can't believe I'm asking you for advice about my love life."

"Believe it," she said. "And take it seriously. This is a woman you don't want to lose."

Alice had agreed to teach the class on crocheted snowflakes, and on Tuesday at four she came to the center with Olivia to fill out paperwork and see the classroom Tracy had assigned her. Cozy, comfortably furnished with armchairs and a large coffee table, all the needlework classes met there, and the rec center quilters had their weekly bee in the room. Unless dozens of people signed up to crochet, Tracy thought it was perfect.

"Sign right here," she told Alice after the room had been approved and they were back at the reception desk. Gladys was temporarily absent, and Olivia was down at the pool watching swim team practice.

Alice signed one last time, and Tracy gave her copies of the contract. "No questions?" Tracy asked.

"I might come early some days."

"I hope so. Why don't we take you down to meet the shuffleboard gang while you're here. We can go out by the pool, then you can pick up Olivia on the way back in."

Tracy accommodated her steps to Alice's slower ones, and they started down the stairs. Tracy's office was a cavernous space nicknamed the rec room, but today she and Alice only used it as a pass-through to the state-of-the-art shuffleboard courts, which were just outside. She slid open the glass door and they stepped out. Florida could be quite warm in October, and today was no exception. The sun was moving toward the horizon, but the heat would stay with them well into the evening.

"Our shuffleboard team likes to practice late afternoon, early evening, to avoid the worst temperatures," Tracy explained. "They practice a lot. They're champions."

"I played. A long time ago."

"They love any and all newcomers, but they'll make sure you're at the peak of your game before they let you compete." She lowered her voice. "Remember, I've, um, had a few little problems —" she held thumb and forefinger half an inch apart to demonstrate "— with the shuffle board, who run the program. They're the ones who keep things going. We're doing okay right now, but you could put in a good word for me. I just keep stepping on toes, even when I'm careful."

"Not you, dear."

"Believe it." Now the sun was beating down on Tracy's head, and although she'd felt halfway decent all morning, suddenly she was sure her oxygen supply had been cut in half. She took a deep breath and hoped she wasn't wheezing. Her stomach was doing the wave.

"Well, it's certainly . . . bright out here," she said, trying to sound cheerful.

"When I was pregnant —" Alice paused and put her fingers on Tracy's arm to slow her down "— with . . . my Karen, I couldn't go out in the sun. Not for a long time. Made me . . . sick." The older woman nodded.

Tracy knew that must have been more than forty years ago, but it was still fresh in Alice's mind. She supposed pregnancy was like that. A life-altering event that stayed tucked in your memory no matter how long you lived. She'd assumed she could ignore it, at the very least push aside her awareness, but the baby had a way of asserting itself and making sure that never happened. She imagined this was just the start, too. Once born, the kid was going to control her life. She was being trained.

They stopped at the edge of the concrete shuffleboard court and watched four men at practice. Tracy waited until they had finished their turns before she stepped up and Alice followed.

"Roger, do you have a moment?" she asked.

Roger Goldsworthy turned as if to say

"You!" She still thought of him as Mr. Moustache, since the first day she'd met him at a local park, she had noticed his hairline moustache and not the intelligence in his sharp eyes. That was before she realized Roger would figure prominently in her job at the center and forever keep his gaze fixed on her to be sure she behaved. He was thin and wiry, and needed a good ten pounds to keep his pants from sagging without a belt cinched tight. His gaze flicked to Alice, and he nodded.

She introduced them, and Alice extended her hand. They shook, and Roger almost smiled. Tracy wasn't too surprised. He came from a generation when good manners had been taught at home. Here at the center she was constantly having to make up for that lack in the new generation, although Roger would probably laugh at the idea of Tracy Deloche as a role model.

"Alice is my neighbor," Tracy said, "and she's going to be teaching a class. I'm trying to talk her into hanging around the rec center a bit and taking advantage of some of our activities. I thought she might be interested in shuffleboard."

"We can always use more players," Roger said.

"Will you introduce her to the others for me?" She turned to Alice. "I can come back and get you in a little while."

204

"I'll be fine, dear. Will you tell Olivia where I am?"

Relieved she wouldn't have to go back out in the sun, Tracy went to find Olivia.

She quickly found more than she had bargained for. Olivia was waiting in the rec room, but so were Janya and the two Dutta children.

Tracy was stunned to see Vijay and Lily. She had stopped by on Saturday to see how everyone was faring, and found the house quiet and the exhausted children napping. Rishi had just run out for milk, but Janya had expected to hear from the children's father any moment to return them.

Sunday had been a day of thunderstorms, and Tracy had used the weather as an excuse to rest and clean house. She had even made vegetable soup for those nights she came home from the center too tired to fix a healthy meal, although the effort had exhausted her, and she had slept the rest of the afternoon and evening.

Yesterday Janya's car had been gone when Tracy drove past their house, and she'd figured her neighbor was making up for lost time, now that the children were back home with their parents.

Clearly she had been wrong.

"Janya?" Tracy looked down at Vijay, who was rolling a ball back and forth to Olivia, who was sitting cross-legged. Lily was snuggled sleepily into Janya's arms, eyelids drooping.

Janya moved away from the little boy and kept her voice low. "Rishi left us here for a little while so the children could play on the playground, but it is too hot outside. He did not want to bring us to the barbershop when he inquired about Harit."

"I thought the children were back at home. What does Harit say?"

"He says nothing we can hear. The last time I spoke to him, he was on my doorstep and you were in my living room."

"Yikes."

"We just went to the Duttas' apartment. The manager let us in so we could get more clothing. She recognized the children and believed our story."

"Story?"

"More or less the truth. I said that we were watching them and just needed a few extra things to make our job easier until the Duttas came home. I did not tell her the parents are missing, and we wanted to see if there was anything in the apartment that might help us find them."

"Missing?"

"I have no other word that fits. Harit left these little ones in our care, then he disappeared in search of his missing wife."

"What are you going to do?"

Janya absentmindedly stroked Lily's hair.

The little girl was now sound asleep. "Perhaps Harit did not bring our phone number."

"Your number's in information, Janya. He could find you that way."

"Or perhaps he has gone somewhere with no telephone service."

"In Florida?"

"I think it is more likely he and Kanira are battling, and he has no idea what to tell us, so he tells us nothing. Or perhaps he's afraid if he calls, we will insist he return, and he has yet to find her."

"Would you insist?"

Janya shrugged. "They are good children, sweet children, and having them is no hardship. Worrying? *That* is the hardship."

"You don't really believe what you've said, do you?"

"I believe these are possible explanations. But I am afraid the real answer is worse."

"What are you going to do?"

"I don't know." Janya lowered her voice even more. "We are afraid if we notify the police, somebody in authority will take the children away, and Harit and Kanira will have problems regaining custody."

Tracy could imagine that might happen. Once the courts got involved, the process of getting the children back could take months. But did the parents deserve custody after this?

"What about Ken? Won't he run interference and make sure things go as well as they

207

can? Does Wanda know?"

"I have yet to tell her we haven't heard from Harit. Only that we are taking care of the children for a while." She clutched the baby closer. "They cried at first, but now they are calmer. They have settled in. But what will happen if they are left with strangers again?"

"I don't know, but, Janya, you can't just sit back and wait forever."

"We've set a deadline of three more days. If we haven't heard from either Harit or Kanira by then, we will have no choice but to report them missing. We will go to Ken if we must."

"How is Rishi handling this?"

"He is good to the children and good to me, but he is worried. Still . . ." She glanced down at the sleeping baby and smoothed her hair again. "Having children in the house is a good thing, but a good thing for bad reasons. And that is what worries us."

"So Rishi's at the barbershop?"

"He said he will pretend he thinks Harit is cutting hair today. He is hoping to pick up information. But the apartment had nothing of use we could find under the eye of the manager. And I am afraid the barbershop will turn up nothing, as well."

"Would you like me to come over tonight and help?"

Janya looked sad. "The only help we need is finding Harit and Kanira. If you have an idea how to do this, please let me know."

CHAPTER ELEVEN

Tracy so rarely dressed up that when Marsh told her on Friday they were going to try a new restaurant getting rave reviews from his staff, she'd figured that like most of the places they went, at most this one deserved clean jeans and maybe the new smocked Henley she'd bought at a discount superstore because the fit was loose and long, and hid the fact her jeans no longer buttoned. She was glad that last week, when she and Marsh made love, the lights had been off in her bedroom. He'd seen her gain and lose weight.

But pregnancy? A different story.

Not until she mentioned her dinner plans to Gladys on her way out of the center did she discover that the Baithouse Bistro was not just another of Marsh's endless seafood dives.

"Baithouse Bistro?" Gladys fanned her face with a hand. "Did our Marsh come into a fortune?"

Tracy had been examining her nail polish

and wondering if repairing it was worth the time, since inevitably she would be cracking crabs or shelling barbecued shrimp she had no stomach to eat.

She looked up. "What?"

"That's the kind of place where you have to save for months just to walk through the front door."

"Baithouse? Come on."

"It's a redo of a historic building that used to be a tackle shop, baithouse and charter fishing service until some time in the eighties. They renovated it last summer and turned it into the best restaurant within fifty miles of the city. It's a good twenty-minute drive from town, right on the water. I'm trying to convince Woody to take me there on our wedding anniversary."

On her way out to the car, Tracy punched in Marsh's number. "Did you actually say the Baithouse Bistro?" she asked without preamble.

"That's the place."

"You do realize you probably have to wear a tie."

"I think I have one somewhere, me being a lawyer and all."

"I'm thinking this place doesn't have a kids' menu."

"I have a babysitter."

For a moment that word struck terror in Tracy's heart. Babysitter, the expensive and infrequently budgeted alternative to twenty-four-hour parenting. She hadn't thought about babysitters. There was so much she hadn't thought about.

Like not getting pregnant in the first place!

For a moment she couldn't remember why she'd called Marsh. For a moment she was afraid all this mommy stuff was beyond her, outside her emotional repertoire, too difficult to figure out.

"Trace, are you there?"

She looked down to be sure. She thought her knees were knocking.

"Are you going to propose?" she asked. "I mean, this is the kind of place where men propose. You probably proposed to Sylvia in a restaurant like this one."

"I proposed to Sylvia on the subway between Columbus Circle and Rockefeller Center. The tax benefits swayed us."

"So I'm safe? No subways in Florida, unless you count the Walt Disney World monorail."

"I just thought you deserved a night out someplace a little fancier. Sometimes I forget where you come from, or at least I try to. It's hard to compete."

Panic ebbed, replaced with a warm glow. "You don't have to compete," she said. "Nobody in my past was ever in your league, Marsh."

She snapped her phone closed and jogged

211

to her Bimmer, covering the miles home in record time.

By the time Marsh arrived, she was wearing a filmy flowered Tory Burch dress that she'd brought with her from California. Never formfitting enough to excite her, now it flowed gently over her expanding breasts and not-so-flat tummy. Somehow she'd found the energy to wash and dry her hair, even throw a few hot rollers on the wisps she didn't pin up with the rest of it. She'd managed real makeup and Miu Miu pumps that put her eye to eye with Marsh. For insurance against an evening chill, she carried Alice's lovely crocheted shawl.

"You look fabulous," he said. Marsh himself was wearing a sport coat she couldn't remember and a designer tie. So, okay, it was a swamp scene, clearly not from London or Milan, but a tasteful swamp scene. Just one alligator, and impeccably tied.

"So do you. Love the tie. So Florida." She leaned forward and kissed him. He put his arms around her and pulled her close, and for a moment they just stood like that in the open doorway, their unannounced baby between them.

Marsh usually fetched her in his pickup, since they rarely went very far, but tonight he was driving his hybrid. In the car they chatted about the past week, bringing each other up to date. She told him she was still mulling over the developer's offer, although not with enthusiasm. He told her about the latest Wild Florida fundraising appeal.

Just before the bridge she was surprised when he pulled off the road and into a parking lot at the boat launch. He turned off the engine, and before she could ask why, he came around and opened her door. "Now I've got you, I want to take full advantage."

"I thought you took full advantage last time we were together."

"Not sex, romance." He helped her out, an old-fashioned gesture that was romantic in itself. "The sun's going to set in a few minutes."

She thought she was probably a little overdressed, considering that most of the men in the lot — fishermen and shrimpers coming back for the night — were in shorts. If they wore shirts at all, the fronts sported beer advertisements or raunchy slogans. Still, she didn't want to object. This was thoughtful. Thoughtful was good. Not perfect, but good.

They held hands as they strolled toward the pedestrian walkway on the east side of the span. "My father used to bring me here when I was a kid," Marsh said. "He said Sunset Bridge was the best place in the world to see the sun go down. That's an exaggeration, but not for him. He was in Vietnam during the war, and after he came home, he never left this part of Florida again. He'd had his fill of travel."

Tracy knew that Marsh's parents had both died in the years just after he completed law school. Like his father, Marsh had tried living elsewhere — Manhattan, in fact — but now he, too, saw no reason to leave the state he loved so well.

"I like the way it smells up here," he said as they walked up the stairway to the bridge. "Gulf air, sulphur from the mangroves, sunshine beating down on salt-crusted lumber."

"Fish. Dead fish."

"Yeah, that, too. Even that."

A breeze ruffled her dress and wrapped the skirt around her legs. She untangled it and leaned over the railing when they stopped. They weren't alone. Others had come out to watch the sun go down, too, and the moment was nearly at hand.

"I like living in a place where dawn and sunset are a ritual," Tracy said. "Most of the time in California I didn't even realize they were happening. I'd be inside the house, or hurrying to get home and annoyed I might not get there before dark."

"The sun rises and sets everywhere."

"It's all about seeing what's right in front of you."

They both fell silent. The sun was a fiery ball hanging over the water and turning it a hundred different shades of pink and orange. Clouds feathered above it, and the sky slowly turned a milky gray. Then, as they watched, the sun slipped lower until, between one blink and next, it was gone.

Tracy was sorry to see it go. "That's always kind of sad."

"I've heard a rumor there'll be another tomorrow. That's the thing about sunsets."

"Will they have a walkway on the new bridge? Because if Blake and his gang aren't planning one, a lot of people are going to be unhappy."

"They know better. I've seen the drawings. Simple, sleek, safe and pedestrian friendly."

Tracy hoped she and Marsh didn't wait until the new bridge was built to enjoy another sunset.

Back in Marsh's car, she closed her eyes. Almost immediately the purring engine lulled her to sleep. She woke up with a start when they came to a stop, and was immediately embarrassed.

"Long, exhausting week," he said, as if reading her mind. "Besides, I like watching you sleep."

"I was probably drooling."

"I'm partial to drooling women."

She wondered if he was partial to pregnant ones. How would Marsh behave when she needed a back rub or a late-night pickle run, or as a partner for childbirth classes where she would learn to pant and blow and look altogether ridiculous?

And what about labor? Florida country boy, for sure, but how would he do when the offspring emerging wasn't feathered or scaled but uniquely human? She was acquainted with Marsh's ex, and without inquiring, she was absolutely sure that Marsh had not been invited to attend his son's birth. Hotshot attorney Sylvia had probably had an epidural so she could continue working on her current brief.

"I think we ought to go in." Marsh touched her cheek, as if to bring her back from wherever she'd wandered off. "I had to use more lines than a deep-sea fishing guide to get us this reservation."

Tracy had been to Baithouse Bistro hundreds of times, only the name of the restaurant had been different, along with the city, and the man at her side had been different, too. Menus with entrées priced at a week's worth of groceries. Tablecloths so heavily starched that if she held one up to the wind, she would sail away. Serving staff in pearl-gray vests and pleated tuxedo shirts, crystal and china as fine as any she'd possessed in her former life.

She let Marsh seat her, an unusual event in itself, and dreaded the moment the menu arrived. Her appetite had picked up a little, and most of this week she'd managed to eat

216

and retain three small meals a day. But she wasn't yet out of the woods, and she didn't want to get lost when the ladies' room was all the way on the other side of the restaurant.

"It's lovely," she told Marsh after their server had presented the wine list with commentary, then offered to send the sommelier to the table for more advice. Marsh had tactfully sent him away, and the list was lying unopened beside him.

"Somebody told me they pay attention to the local Seafood Watch List. You can order anything off this menu without guilt."

She smiled a little. "And I was so worried."

"Don't give me that. I've seen you pass over Chilean sea bass and monkfish. You're a better environmentalist than you claim." He took her hand and squeezed it. "If we order a bottle of wine and depend on me to finish it, I'll drink too much, and I'm driving. What do you think?"

Tracy was relieved, because she hadn't yet come up with a satisfactory excuse for turning down alcohol. "Like you said, it's been a long week. I'll just go with a glass of that New Zealand chardonnay he mentioned."

Marsh signaled and ordered two glasses and, after a brief consultation, a plate of steamed seafood in a simple lemon butter sauce to share. The wine arrived as they decided on their entrées, and they toasted each other. Tracy took one tiny sip, then put

217

down the wine and picked up her water glass in its place.

"Somebody at work said the broiled mahi is amazing," he said. "Very simply prepared."

She looked up, surprised. This was a man who couldn't broil anything without using half the condiments and herbs in his amply stocked kitchen. "Sounds great."

"What else looks good to you?"

They debated the menu, but in the end she was hopeful that most of what they'd ordered would pass the baby's personal taste test. He hadn't asked if her "virus" had finally abated, but the selections had been, by his standards, plain, bland, ordinary. She felt a return of the warm glow she had experienced on the telephone. First a romantic sunset and now concern for her comfort. What more could any woman ask from a man?

Well, okay, a lot of things, but paying attention to her was high on the list.

"We have to do more of this," he said.

"This really isn't your kind of place, is it?" She played with the wineglass, as if she were heavily engaged with the contents.

"I like being with you almost anywhere."

"What made you think of this for tonight?"

"Because you're a good sport, Trace. And I've taken advantage of you."

She was fascinated. "Have you?"

"We don't have to do everything my way. It was a tough summer for both of us, but you hung in there, and I wasn't much help. I just appreciate you, that's all, and I wanted you to know it."

Being appreciated? Good. Great, maybe. Just not as great, say, as being loved. She kept the smile on her face and nodded, as if she was with him every step of the way, but she imagined herself in, oh, eighteen years at her baby's high school graduation. Would she hear the same speech from this man? *Sorry I wasn't much help during the kid's childhood, but I'm glad you hung in there. Oh, and by the way, I appreciate you.*

"Well, you must appreciate me a lot to bring me here," she said when it was clear he had finished.

The steamed seafood arrived, and Tracy busied herself pushing around bits of it on her plate so it looked as if she was eating more than she was. She dipped and nibbled, and was happy to discover that the baby was something of a seafood fan. Of course "baby" was a technical misnomer. The creature inside her was actually a fetus recently upgraded from an embryo, according to the pregnancy guide her college roommate, Sherrie, had sent her the moment she heard about Tracy's condition. Sherrie, who lived in Arizona, had been safe to share her news with, since she'd never even met Marsh and was unlikely to blab.

She wished she could tell Marsh how

ridiculous all the scientific nomenclature sounded to her, but like almost everything that really mattered to her — the baby, her own future and whether the two of them were going to spend it with the oh-so-grateful Marsh — this was definitely off-limits.

"What's happening with Janya and Rishi?" he asked, after the waiter removed the shells and sauce.

She debated, then decided she could tell him about the Duttas, since tomorrow was their deadline for talking to Ken. Janya and Rishi had made every inquiry they could think of, but there had been no sign of the missing Indian couple. Now the authorities had to be notified and the fate of the children decided. Tracy had warned her friends that sometimes bystanders got swept into a legal tangle just for helping out. In her opinion, for their own protection, it was past time for that phone call.

She described the situation to Marsh, pausing only for the delivery of their salads. Hers was ridiculously plain, a wedge of iceberg lettuce with a creamy herbal dressing. She took a bite, then another. The dressing tasted like all the good things in the world whirled together. She dived in as if she hadn't eaten in weeks, which was more or less correct.

"Like that, do you?" Marsh asked.

She had managed with great aplomb not to pick up the plate and lick every drop of dressing off it once she'd finished.

"Very nice," she said.

"Must have been. You never finished your fascinating story. Why didn't you tell me about this before?"

"They've been hoping the parents would show up again on their own, and they didn't want to involve the authorities." She sadly watched the waiter carry off her plate, but managed not to grab his arm.

"I'm the authorities?"

She turned back to him. "You're a lawyer."

"Since when does going to bat for diamond-back terrapins and sandhill cranes make me such a scary guy?"

"Consider yourself one of the anointed few, Marsh. This has been kept under wraps. I'm only telling you now because they set a deadline, and it's up tomorrow. They're going to tell Ken in the morning and let him figure out what to do. But I think it's going to be difficult. They're already attached to the children, and they don't want to give them to strangers."

"It's a messy situation. Those maternal hormones get flowing, and all kinds of things can happen. Secrets, lies, bad decisions . . ." He raised a brow in punctuation.

"Which is why it's disturbing that the Duttas just abandoned the children the way they did and never got back in touch. Janya says Kanira was beleaguered and angry, but the children were all she had. She wasn't a model mom, but the children were cared for, clean, fed. They had toys and clothes and everything they needed."

"Is that the hallmark of a good mother?"

"I didn't say she was a *good* mother. An adequate mother, though, and Janya says unlikely to just leave them without a word."

"So there's a difference between good and adequate?"

"Duh . . . you can't tell?" She didn't add that Marsh, of all people, should be able to, since he'd married a woman who was at best adequate, with little real interest in their son, even now. Bay had come home from his recent weekend in California evincing no interest in going back. At the center, he had told Tracy that California was okay and he liked the San Diego Zoo. Whatever else he liked or didn't, including his mother, he kept to himself. But at the end of the conversation he'd given her the biggest hug she'd ever gotten from anybody.

"I *can* tell, most of the time," Marsh said. "It seems to revolve around how much a woman wanted the child in the first place, and what her reasons were for having it."

"The same could be said for a man," Tracy said. "Although too many don't take responsibility."

Their entrées arrived, which pleased Tracy, because with them came a change of subject.

She was full now, satiated by iceberg lettuce, but she gamely pushed her fish around the plate, taking bites now and then until half of it and all the rice pilaf were gone. Marsh had already finished and suggested she take her leftovers for tomorrow's dinner. She agreed happily. Tomorrow could be a whole new story, and she might be hungry again.

"Didn't like the wine?" the waiter asked as their table was being cleared and her full glass was removed.

"A little too dry for me," she said. "A little too oaky."

He looked surprised but didn't argue. "May I get you something else instead? Our compliments?"

She pretended to glance at her watch. "Thanks, but I'll fall asleep if I drink at this hour. I'm just fine."

They were offered dessert menus, and both declined.

The time had slipped by. She hadn't really expected a proposal — nor would she have known what to say if he'd made one — but as nice as the evening had been, there had also been a curious lack of intimacy.

She thought about all the things she knew. Marsh appreciated her. That was clear now. He liked sex with her. That had been clear before. Despite all the old-fashioned warnings she'd been given as a girl — *who'll buy the cow when he can get the milk for free?* —

this man hadn't abandoned her when they finally slipped between the sheets at summer's end. So apparently he also enjoyed being with her — or else he was secretly scouting for his next conquest, and she was just a convenience in the interim.

Of course, she knew better. She knew *him* better. Marsh *was* better. She definitely meant something to him. She just wasn't sure exactly what.

It was time to go, but he reached across the table and took her hands just as she expected him to stand.

"This has been nice," he said. "We need to do more of it."

"It's not exactly your thing, though, is it?"

"When I'm with you, Trace, I don't care where we are. Here, the middle of a swamp, filling water balloons for a dozen screaming ten-year-olds . . . I hope you know that."

She thought of all the lines she had heard from other men, all the lavish compliments CJ had paid her when he wanted something in return. She weighed Marsh's words against those of men with names she couldn't remember.

She would never forget this man's name. She would never forget this *man.* Now if she could only figure out what she should do about him. Luckily Marsh didn't know she was pregnant, and she had weeks yet to test the waters of their relationship without that life-altering complication.

She squeezed his hands in hers. "Speak for yourself, Nature Boy. This has been better than a swamp any day. Now let's go to my place and do a test."

"What's that?"

"Let's go measure how much you like being with me in my nice soft double bed."

They were almost to Tracy's house — somehow she had managed to stay awake and carry on a conversation — when she realized the police car in the distance was not Ken's normal ride, parked for the night in front of the Grays' cottage. This was another car, lights slowly flashing, parked in front of Janya's.

She didn't have to tell Marsh to pull over. By the time she realized what was going on, he had parked and turned off the engine.

"Let's check this out," he said. It wasn't a question.

Tracy got out and started up the path to the Kapurs' front door. Jasmine scented the air from one of Janya's clay pots, and the police radio blared with unfamiliar codes and chatter. The car doors were closed, and no one was inside. She was relieved that nobody she knew was sitting in the backseat in handcuffs. Stranger things had happened at Happiness Key.

The front door was ajar, and Tracy could

see lights inside. A uniformed officer was standing in the doorway, writing on a pad.

"Excuse me," Tracy said. "I'm the owner of the property. Is there a problem?"

"Nothing that concerns you, ma'am," he said.

"These are my friends, and —"

Ken came into view, a Ken in a polo shirt and jeans. Even in informal clothes he still looked like a cop, with close-cropped salt-and-pepper hair, and eyes that saw everything set deep in a serious face. Ken was definitely attractive when he smiled, but he wasn't smiling now. Just beyond him, Tracy thought she could see Janya's shadow drawn out along the floor.

"Ken!" Tracy beckoned, hoping he would come to the door.

He nodded at the other officer, who moved out of the doorway so Ken could fill it.

"Did you know about this?" Ken asked her.

Tracy was genuinely confused, but she wouldn't have answered anyway. She'd had her own encounters with police in California after her ex-husband was arrested for his shady financial dealings. Even though this was Ken, Wanda's husband, her neighbor and friend, she knew better than to blab.

"Did I know about what?" She could feel Marsh's arm come round her waist, and, at her answer, his fingers digging into her side.

"That the parents of the children the

226

Kapurs have been caring for were missing?"

"Does it matter?" The fingers were digging deeper now.

"Tracy . . ." Ken's tone made it clear he was in no mood to coax.

She gave in to both men. "Janya told me. She and Rishi have been trying to find them. They were almost sure they were going to return. Did they?"

Ken looked as if he was trying to decide how much to say. Then he shook his head. "They aren't going to return. Not in this lifetime, anyway. The Miami police found them dead in a hotel room late this afternoon. From the look of the crime scene, they think it was probably murder-suicide."

CHAPTER TWELVE

This morning Wanda wasn't just preparing pies in the kitchen of her shop. After a fitful night's sleep — and who could have slept after the story Ken had told her? — she had decided what to send to Janya and Rishi's house for the Dutta children. Even though it was only seven o'clock, she had already finished a batch of oatmeal chocolate-chip cookies, along with two quarts of citrus ambrosia liberally sprinkled with coconut. She knew Janya liked her ambrosia, and she figured it was something little ol' meat eater her could make for the vegetarian Kapurs, who must surely be at their wits' end about now.

"It's just about the worst story I ever heard," she told Maggie, who had just come in and was learning what had happened from Wanda's own lips. "Your dad says they were in some seedy motel room and the gun was in the husband's hand. Awful scene, and they'd been there for so long, some of the evidence was destroyed, if you know what I mean."

"I wish I didn't." Maggie made a face. "But I don't understand why Janya and Rishi never reported that the parents had dropped off those babies and never returned for them."

Wanda understood only too well. Both the Kapurs were as tenderhearted as anyone she'd ever met, and even without having the chance to talk to Janya herself, she guessed her friend had wanted to shield the absent parents from the long arm of the law. She and Rishi had probably hoped that the Duttas would settle whatever problems were between them and return, ready to take their children back home.

"Your daddy told me Janya and Rishi went looking for the Duttas themselves, with no success. They'd set today as their deadline to tell him the whole story and see what to do next."

Instead, sometime this morning the Kapurs were facing an interview with Child Protection Services, and Ken hadn't been able to predict the outcome. Quite possibly the agency would remove the little ones and place them with a trained foster family, if one was available. He had promised to vouch for his neighbors if they wanted to keep the children while a search for relatives began, and Janya and Rishi had been grateful.

"They'll want to keep the children with

them as long as they can," Wanda said. "They're settled in now. Of course, that house is no bigger than a minute, even though it's got an extra bedroom. I don't know what an agency will say about that."

"Good foster parents don't grow on trees. Besides, there's the cultural issue. The Kapurs will better understand any customs the kids might have been raised with, plus the father did ask them to care for the children. That will add weight to their request."

"So you think they have a chance?"

"It seems possible. Are they citizens?"

"Rishi is, and Janya will be once she jumps through all the right hoops."

Wanda certainly hoped the Kapurs could keep the children. Of course, she knew Janya — and probably Rishi, too — was growing attached to little Vijay and Lily. And who wouldn't? They were sweet and bright, and the boy, especially, was mature beyond his age. Wanda just hoped that if they were allowed to keep the children while relatives were contacted, they didn't get so attached that the final separation knocked them off their feet.

"I don't understand how the children were traced to Rishi and Janya," Maggie said. "Who told the cops where they were?"

"Nobody." Wanda hated everything about the situation, but she did enjoy being the one to part with the facts for a change. "They found Rishi's phone number on Harit Dutta's cell phone. They were calling everybody who was listed, and Rishi immediately told them that the children were with him and his wife, and how that had happened. The Palmetto Grove police were asked to go and interview them, and that's how your dad found out what was going on."

"Murder-suicide, huh?"

"They think maybe she left him for another man, and somehow he found out where she'd gone and went there to talk some sense into her. With a gun."

"But there was no man with her?"

"Not so's I've heard."

"Where did all this happen, do you know?"

"Some ratty old hotel on Biscayne Boulevard. Just over from Little Haiti." She glanced up and saw Maggie frowning. "What?"

"Nothing."

"You always did that. Right from the time you could manage two syllables. Something bothered you? Didn't matter. 'Nothing' was always the right answer."

Maggie chewed her bottom lip, a sure sign she was either thinking or trying not to snap at her mother. Then she gave a short nod. "That's my department's territory," she said. "I should say, my former department."

Wanda understood immediately, and she knew Maggie wasn't saying she was glad she hadn't caught this case herself. She was

231

mourning her life as a cop. The instinct to get in and find out what had happened was still strong.

"I don't mean to do that," Maggie said.

"What?" Wanda was mystified.

"Shut you out."

Wanda just stared at her. She was at a complete loss for words. They were talking about their relationship. Feelings. History.

"Maybe sometimes you have to," she said cautiously, after she'd recovered for a moment. "I can be overwhelming. It's just who I am."

"And I can be underwhelming. Do you think you picked up the right baby in the hospital?"

Wanda wanted to wrap her arms around her daughter and squeeze, but she knew better. She just nodded. "Doesn't really matter whether I did or didn't. I got the baby I wanted, and don't you forget it."

Janya wasn't sure she slept at all after the police finally left. She tried, knowing that she had the children to think about. Now, more than ever, they needed patience and support. But instead of sleeping, she'd lain in bed asking herself over and over how she and Rishi would explain Harit and Kanira's deaths to Vijay. No matter what they said, baby Lily would not understand, but Vijay, young as he was, seemed to understand more than he should. The first day he'd come to stay at Happiness Key, he had barely spoken. But in the days since, he had frequently asked about his parents, and once he had said that his mother was often angry at him, and now she might be gone because he had teased Lily on the day she left.

When did children learn about death? Had Vijay lost a pet? Killed a fly or an ant, and watched it go still and lifeless? Did he understand that when someone died, they never returned? She and Rishi had very little time to discuss this and figure out together what to do. Children's Protective Services would be visiting this morning, perhaps taking the children with them to a foster home. Would the news be better understood and accepted if learned from a stranger? That answer, at least, was easy. Of course not. Vijay was still wary and far too self-contained for a four-year-old, but slowly he had warmed to both Rishi and her. Bad news was best heard from someone who cared about you.

So how was she also going to explain that he might not be able to stay in this tiny house with people who were at least familiar?

She got up at six, because she was more exhausted from trying to sleep than from not sleeping. She wasn't alone long. In the midst of beating eggs for one of the omelets both Rishi and the children enjoyed, she felt a presence behind her and turned to find Vijay, hair standing on end and eyes crusted with sleep. He looked somber, as he always did, and he didn't smile when she greeted him.

"Is my daddy coming today?" he asked.

Janya considered how to answer, as she had considered all night. "No," she said as she had decided. She would let the boy take the lead in this conversation and answer only what he asked. At least at first.

"When is he coming home?"

She squatted in front of him so they were eye to eye. "I am so sorry, but your daddy and mommy will not be coming home."

He bit his lip, as if trying to decide what this meant. "Not at all?"

She shook her head. "They can't come. Never again."

"Why?"

She was sorry Rishi was not yet up, but in the end, the answer must be the same, no matter who gave it.

"We found out last night. I know they wanted to come back for you and Lily, and planned to. They loved you very much, but there was an accident, and they died."

"No, they didn't."

She waited, hoping he would say more, but instead he went back to the tiny bedroom he shared with Lily and closed the door.

Janya felt tears running down her cheeks and wiped them with the palm of her hand. When she stood she saw that Rishi was in the

234

doorway.

"I heard," he said.

"He does not believe me."

"I think perhaps he does, at least a little. It will take time. He is too young to understand this."

"Do you understand it? I do not. Not even a little."

Rishi put his arms around her and held her close.

Breakfast an hour later was a silent affair. Vijay said no more about his parents, and when asked a question, merely nodded or shook his head. Afterward, the telephone rang, and Rishi answered it in their bedroom. When he returned he took Janya to one side and told her that Protective Services was on the way. Together they decided not to explain the visit in advance, since nothing would be gained. They also decided not to pack what few possessions the children had.

"I will not make this easy for the authorities," Janya said. "And I will not look as if I can hardly wait for them to take these children away. It's wrong, Rishi. They have been through enough."

"We will have little to say about it today, but I will speak to a lawyer if the children are removed."

Janya was surprised. "You would do that?"

"Harit was my friend, and that is more connection than anyone else in this country can claim. He left them with us. He wanted us to care for them. This is a wish we can honor, until someone from the family makes arrangements."

"Kanira told me the families wanted nothing to do with them, including the children. They would not answer letters or phone calls."

"Yes, and Harit's family is poor, and his village is remote and susceptible to floods. Sometimes it is what they call here a ghost town. The family could be difficult to track down."

"If we are allowed to keep them until the family is contacted, they could be with us a very long time."

"Will you mind?"

She shook her head. "And you?"

He smiled just a little. "No." The smile disappeared. "But this is not the way I wanted to put children in our home. I . . ." He paused; then he pulled her farther from the bedroom door, as if to be sure their voices didn't carry into the living room, where a long-faced Vijay was guiding metal cars between blocks of scrap wood Rishi had brought home from work yesterday. Lily knocked down the blocks the moment the cars passed between them.

"I have thought and thought about this, Janya. I thought of little else all night. I don't believe Harit killed Kanira. In fact, I am sure

236

he didn't."

"How can you be sure? You certainly weren't there."

"He is — *was* — not a violent man. He was a follower of Gandhi. And his novel? I read the first chapters. It was brilliant. He was so . . ." Rishi swallowed, as if swallowing tears. "He was remarkably talented, and the novel was destined to be an important one. It is about a young skeptic alive during the time when Gandhi was leading India to freedom and the young man's journey toward non-violence. Once he told me it was not so hard for him to write because he, too, took that journey in this modern day. Before coming here, Harit was a community organizer devoted to peaceful solutions, and he despised the way people in this country so often settle problems at gunpoint. He would never buy a gun. I can hardly believe he would even pick one up."

"They found it in his hand. People change when they get angry."

"I don't think he changed enough to give up all his ideals, abandon the children he loved, seek out someone to sell him a gun, hunt down his wife and shoot her in a strange bed before turning the gun on himself."

Janya had her own doubts. Yes, Kanira had made comments that *could* be construed as admitting to an affair. But what had she really said? That perhaps soon she would change her life for the better. And couldn't that mean almost anything? A job she had secretly applied for so that the struggling family had more income? A chance to go back to school to learn a profession? Even, perhaps, some new hope that a distant relative or friend might welcome her and smooth the way with her own family if she left Harit and returned to India with the children.

"It is hard for me to believe Kanira, with all her faults, would have deserted her children for a man," Janya said. "If anything, she would be unlikely to trust any man to give her a better life, not after Harit failed to give her the one she wanted."

"The police seem certain they know what happened."

"The police can be wrong, here as well as in India."

Janya heard a car engine, then silence as the car stopped. Her limbs felt heavy as she went to answer the door, and her stomach was in turmoil. Only as she reached for the knob did she realize exactly how badly she wanted to keep the Dutta children with her in this house. The revelation frightened her as much as the thought of losing them to the state of Florida.

Maggie wasn't sure why she had agreed to another date with Blake Armstrong. He'd arrived at Wanda's Wonderful Pies almost the moment they'd opened that morning and invited her to dinner. He'd promised someplace casual, saying that after a long day at the shop, he guessed dressing up and late hours wouldn't appeal to her.

Maybe, she thought, that was why she had agreed. Blake seemed like a considerate guy, thinking ahead about how she might feel and working around it. He'd already scouted a mom-and-pop spaghetti joint and promised the best calamari in town. Partial to calamari, she'd heard herself agreeing.

Of course, the best reason for spending the night in Blake's company was to avoid her own. Evenings were the worst time for her. She disliked television, was out of the habit of reading and was usually too tired from working at the shop to whip herself up to try something new. A quiet evening with a pleasant, attractive man would be a respite. She had warned Blake she didn't want a relationship. She certainly wasn't ready for a new lover, either, and even if she had been, she wasn't sure he would make the cut. Nice as he was, good looking as he was, she didn't yet feel that electric charge that was so important.

The man who still made all her nerve endings sizzle was back in Miami, surrounded by women who would be only too happy to soothe his battered ego.

"You want to go home a little early so you

239

can get ready?" Wanda asked when Maggie glanced up at the clock over the counter. The clock, shaped like a fruit pie with crinkled crust edges, was a new addition. The distance between the hour and minute hands — a knife and a fork — was always in shadow, as if that portion of the pie was a slice — or more — that had already been eaten.

"No reason to," Maggie said. "I'll just shower and throw on my good jeans."

"In my day, unless you were some kind of hippie type, a girl got a little dressed up when a man asked her out."

"I'll add a belt, how's that?"

Wanda shook her head, but she couldn't quite control her smile. "This is why children move out. Saves everybody these conversations."

"But clearly you miss them." Maggie went back to the kitchen to finish six sweet-potato pecan pies that were heading for a ladies tea late in the afternoon. She planned to deliver them, go home and change, then meet Blake at the restaurant for an early dinner.

She was just setting the oven timer when her mother called her back to the front.

"Janya here wants to talk to you."

Maggie hadn't realized their neighbor had come in. She greeted her and expressed her sympathy.

Janya nodded her thanks. "From such a terrible situation has come one good thing. We

240

will be allowed to keep the children with us until their family in India makes arrangements to take them. Ken spoke to the agency and convinced them this is what the Duttas would have wished, and after their visit this morning, they agreed. We will take a parenting class that starts soon, but until then, the case worker will come to check on them from time to time and be certain all is well."

"I'm so glad," Wanda said. "They'll be better off with you than with strangers. But, Janya, you got to be careful. You got to be sure you don't get too attached. They'll be going to India by and by, and you have to remember that."

Janya didn't look annoyed at Wanda's advice, as Maggie would have been. She obviously took it seriously. Maggie realized how much the young woman respected her mother, and she felt a ridiculous jolt of pride.

"Some things are easy and some are not," Janya said. "But I think it is better for the children if I do not put myself at a distance. They need to know that someone cares about them now that their parents are gone."

Wanda didn't argue. Clearly the respect cut both ways. "Does Vijay know?"

Janya gave a graceful shrug. "I have told him, but what he knows and what he understands are different. The social worker, Miss Crede, has promised to make an appointment with a psychologist who works with children.

Perhaps that will help."

Maggie was glad Janya had wanted to fill her, as well as her mother, in on the situation, but she was a little surprised that Janya had made such a point of including her. She could see the relationship that counted here was between Janya and Wanda. The surprise disappeared when Janya turned and addressed her directly.

"I have not only come to tell you the news but also to ask for your help, Maggie. Both Rishi and I believe the police in Miami have made a grave error. We did not know the Duttas well, but we are both certain that Harit could not have murdered Kanira."

Maggie listened as Janya explained her reasons for that conclusion. She knew, from her years on the force, that murder was difficult to accept. Unlikely people sometimes picked up a gun and used it in the heat of anger. Often there was nothing in their background to indicate such a decision was even possible. She had investigated a heartbreaking case in which a devoted mother had shot her disabled son as he lay sleeping, then turned the gun on herself. The boy had been a real-life poster child for his disease, and the mother had raised half a million dollars for research. No one could believe she had killed him, yet in the end, it was the only possible explanation. She'd snapped after learning the boy was declining and there was little hope of stopping it. In her troubled mind, ending his life before his suffering increased had been her final act of devotion.

"I called your father," Janya said. "He told me the police in Miami are looking into these deaths, but he thinks they have made up their minds. There has to be another explanation, but I am afraid they will stop looking before they find it."

Maggie thought Janya might be asking for reassurance, so she gave it. "It's a good police force there, and they won't take the easy way out. If they decide it's a murder-suicide, then they'll have all the evidence they need to support that conclusion. They will treat the deaths seriously and with respect."

"This was your department, not your father's?"

Maggie nodded.

"You still have contacts there? I know I must be asking a great deal, but could you find out what they learned? Could you tell them we would like to talk to them? That we knew the Duttas and are sure Harit would never fire a gun?"

Maggie debated. She liked Janya, and she knew the woman and her husband had a difficult road ahead of them. Caring for the newly orphaned children under the eyes of a social worker, taking classes to become certified foster parents, waiting to see who gained final custody, then having to send the children away, even if the situation with the families in India was less than ideal. Asking old friends for information seemed easy in comparison. But, of course, some of Maggie's old friends on the force now held her at arm's length, worried a continued relationship could jeopardize their own positions.

But not Felo.

"Let me think about it," she said. "I'm not sure what I can do, but there might be something."

"This is all I ask," Janya said gravely. "It will ease my husband's mind if he knows someone takes our view seriously."

Wanda presented Janya with the ambrosia and cookies to take home, and Maggie left to check on pies. When she returned, Janya was gone.

"You gonna follow through for real?" Wanda asked.

"I guess I am."

"You're going to ask Felo to look into it, aren't you?"

"I guess I am."

"That'll be interesting."

Maggie waited for more — inevitable, she was sure. But Wanda just nodded, proving that Maggie didn't know her quite as well as she had always assumed.

After that cryptic exchange, they worked in silence. Maggie cleaned the kitchen as the pies finished baking, then took them out to cool while she called a supplier and gave their order for tomorrow. It was nearly four by the time she left the shop, a pie carrier in each hand. She delivered the pies, then headed over the bridge for a shower and change of clothes. In the end, she didn't wear jeans. Since the weather was warm, she wore bronze roll-up capris and a cocoa-brown crop top that bared just enough midriff to be worthy of the name. She pulled her hair up in a ponytail and wore gold hoop earrings. And that was as dressed up as she planned to get.

Blake, in a casual sports jacket and jeans, was waiting for her when she got to the restaurant. As promised, the place was a hole in the wall, but all the tables were overflowing with diners by the time she arrived. Dean Martin — a favorite of her mother's — was singing "That's Amore," courtesy of loudspeakers in the corners, and garlic wafted through the air like a ghostly presence.

"It's everything you promised and more," she said after he'd kissed her cheek and seated her.

"We even have a stain shaped like Texas on the tablecloth. A very old stain, I'll add."

"But it's been washed in between."

"More than a million times, I'd say. I ordered a carafe of Chianti, but don't feel compelled to drink it. The other option is chardonnay. They're nothing here if not prepared for all tastes."

"Simple decisions are good. No time wasted."

"So you're up for the calamari? I can order it while you check out the menu. Or I can recite the whole thing between one heartbeat and the next. Spaghetti with marinara, clam or alfredo sauce. Meatballs or Italian sausage are extra, as are mushrooms. Remember all that and apply it to rigatoni. Lasagna comes with or without ground beef. So does manicotti. The salads are green, and you can choose creamy or regular Italian dressing."

"My head's spinning. What are you having?"

Their waitress, a lithe young brunette wearing impossibly high heels, arrived with the Chianti and two glasses. Blake ordered calamari and garlic bread, and since Maggie didn't really care, they both ordered the manicotti without meat and regular Italian dressing on their salads.

"But bring those after the calamari, okay?" Blake told the young woman.

She flashed a blinding smile at him, something that Maggie guessed happened a lot with Blake and strange women. Just like Felo. Blake poured the wine, and they toasted.

Small talk lasted through the introduction of the calamari, which covered a dinner plate and was served with both marinara and aioli sauce. At first bite, Maggie was in love. After the second, she found herself thinking how

246

much Felo would like the unpretentious restaurant.

"So I gather things went okay with the old
boyfriend after I dropped you off? You're in
one piece. You don't look wounded."

"Should I?"

"That would be up to you. But cops have a
reputation. They can disturb the peace just as
easily as they enforce it."

"Cops are like anybody else, only they have
a lot more temptations."

"You don't think the profession appeals to
budding psychopaths who use their uniforms
to live out their own violent fantasies?"

"I don't, although there are always excep-
tions."

"I gather you know a lot of them. Cops, I
mean."

"Why do you gather that?"

He passed the marinara sauce so she
wouldn't have to reach across the plate.
"Well, if you and the cop on your porch were
ever serious, you probably knew his friends."

She debated, but the time had arrived to be
fully honest. Otherwise it would look as if she
was hiding something she was ashamed of.
"He wasn't the only cop in our house. I was
a detective."

"Wow."

"My father's a cop, too. A regular blue
epidemic."

"What happened? Did you get tired of the

grind? The danger? The paperwork?"

"Always tired of the last. But no, I was sick of working hard, doing everything right and having a crooked prosecutor dismiss my evidence in an important case for no good reason. I quit in the middle of a press conference. Turned in my gun and shield and any hope of ever working for that department, or probably any other, again."

"So that's why you're here?"

"That and trying to keep my mom from working herself to death before she's sixty. By the time I leave, maybe she'll have some reliable staff and a strong customer base. Then she can settle down to making pies, which is what she loves best."

"Still, going from a life on the edge to making piecrust . . . It has to be hard."

"A lot of what I did was boring. Same in this job or any, I guess."

"I love every part of mine."

She studied him. The first time she'd seen Blake, she'd thought he looked like a California surfer. Tonight he looked like the Ivy Leaguer he probably was. He had almost classic features, although the nose was a bit snubbed. His eyes were a pale blue, rimmed by dark lashes and just a hair too close together. Added up, the effect was endearing, as if somebody upstairs had tried to soften an overload of perfection.

"What do you like best?" she asked.

"Seeing a project through to conclusion. That final moment when it all comes together successfully."

"And you've done that a lot? You don't seem old enough."

"My group's made up of the hotshots of Cardrake, which used to be a pretty stodgy company. Cardrake does roadways, all sorts of bridges, site development. As civil contractors go, it's one of the larger companies on the East Coast. When they got some criticism for not being green enough, they went looking for younger talent with those credentials, and nothing's been the same for them since."

"And you're one of those?"

"I have degrees in civil and environmental engineering, plus as much experience as someone my age can acquire. But the bridge to Palmetto Grove Key is the first time I've been in charge of a project. Of course, I'm consulting constantly and reporting to more warm bodies than sailed in the ark, but this baby's mine."

Maggie imagined that as bridges went, this was one of the smallest Cardrake had constructed. But still, she supposed, if all went well, this entire project would be a star on his résumé, and he would have nowhere to go but up.

"They must think a lot of your work to give you this kind of responsibility," she said.

"I — we proved ourselves when we brought

the bridge repairs in under the estimate. We used new technology and good old-fashioned horse sense. In the long run, though, the financials made the decision. Everyone likes saving money. The city was so happy, they chose Cardrake to build the bridge, and Cardrake was so happy with *us,* they asked us to design and construct it."

"It's nice to see someone so enthused about his work."

"Cops aren't?"

"In their own way."

They waited until their waitress had taken away the calamari platter, which was now mysteriously empty, and their salads were sitting in front of them before they resumed.

"What did you like about being a cop?" Blake asked. "What kept you there until you finally gave up?"

"No sound bite intended, but I like helping people. Sometimes we could and did. Sometimes we only put the bad guys away for a while, but that still helped everybody who never came in contact with them."

"Do you still think like a cop?"

She started to ask what that meant, but she didn't really need to. She thought about the Indian couple who had died in Miami, and her own curiosity at the scenario Janya and her mother had described.

"I guess I do." She found herself telling him about the case. "I've been asked to look into a murder-suicide that happened this past week in Miami. Some things don't add up, and a neighbor asked me to see what I can find out."

"Why is she or he interested? Miami's not Palmetto Grove."

"They were living here. The neighbor was keeping their children."

He listened while she told him the Duttas' backgrounds and the little she knew about the case. He shook his head sadly as she talked, his blue eyes flashing compassion and concern. She wondered if this was a man who could be dragged to a chick flick and shed a tear when a scene warranted it. Felo, for all his machismo, had been one of those.

"That's an awful story," he said when she finished. "What's going to happen to the children?"

She explained, and he looked relieved. "At least somebody has them who cares. So what will you do next?"

"I still have friends on the force. I'll check around a bit, just to relieve my neighbors' minds."

"So you think there's something to your neighbors' suspicions?"

"It's doubtful. Mistakes can be made, but generally the investigations are thorough, and this looks cut-and-dried. So often we think we know somebody, but in the end they turn out to be somebody completely different."

"Amen." He nodded solemnly.

Their dinners arrived, heaped to the edges of their plates. She looked up. "No more talk of murder. Let's discuss your amazing ability to choose great restaurants."

He smiled, too, then he reached over, took her hand and squeezed it. "Nobody can say you're a boring date. And you can talk about anything you want. That was a lot more interesting than where you buy your clothes or the last movie you saw. Promise me updates?"

"Yikes, I'd forgotten how boring dating can be. It's usually that bad?"

"Worse. But not this time."

They unclasped hands, but Maggie realized she was glad to be here with Blake, surrounded by strangers laughing and talking over platters of aromatic marinara and bottles of cheap wine. Her past was best forgotten; her future was a monstrous question mark. But for this moment, the present seemed just about right.

Chapter Thirteen

Wanda had promised herself she would stay out of Maggie's life. Of course, that promise had been made the day Maggie turned twenty-one and Wanda was still working at it, like one of those fancy tablecloths Alice crocheted that took practically forever.

Still, it was Tuesday, the start of their work week, and here was Wanda's own daughter making a phone call to her ex-lover. Maggie's cell phone was giving her problems, wouldn't hold a charge or some such technical gobble-dygook, and she hadn't bothered installing a landline. So now she was calling Felo right in Wanda's very own kitchen to find out if he would ask around and see what he could turn up about the Dutta murder case.

Of course, she hadn't exactly *told* Wanda this. Wanda had surmised as much by careful listening. Very, very careful.

Five minutes passed, and Maggie finally walked into the front, where Wanda was finishing preparations so she could open the door and welcome the public.

"I couldn't help but overhear," Wanda said.

"Of course you couldn't. You were standing in the doorway."

"I wasn't! Not quite that close, anyway, and this is a small shop. Don't forget it."

"Just so you won't fill in the blanks with erroneous information —"

"And just so *you* remember, I stood on my feet and served hush puppies and shrimp for decades to send you to college so you could learn words like 'erroneous.' "

Maggie ignored the customary inducing of guilt. "I've done everything I can from here to learn more about the Dutta murders, but I haven't picked up anything helpful. I couldn't think of another way to get hard information, so I had to ask Felo to help. He knows about the case. It's been in the news, and he *is* in Homicide."

"It's not his?"

"Someone working closer to the motel caught it, which I knew. But Felo said he'd nose around." She paused. "For a fee."

Wanda bristled. "What's wrong with that man? It's a simple favor. Is he too angry to help?"

"He wants to cook me breakfast. This weekend."

Wanda pondered that. A man who could cook and liked it, to boot. That was a man a woman couldn't let go of easily.

254

"Some fee," she said. "Your dad fries an egg so hard it could stand in for a hockey puck. Felo wants to cook for you, how hard is it to say yes?"

"Apparently not very. He's coming on Sunday morning."

Wanda heard the ambivalence in her daughter's voice. "You sorry?"

Maggie looked as if she didn't know what to say, or perhaps she didn't want to say it to her mother. But finally she shrugged. "The whole time we talked, I wondered if I was calling to help Janya and Rishi, or just using that as an excuse to talk to him. It's hard. All of this. We were together a long time. He meant everything to me."

Wanda wasn't sure she'd heard her daughter right. This was Maggie, who, when her beloved grandmother died, hadn't shed a tear except in the privacy of her bedroom. The girl had only been ten, but she'd already made up her mind that emotions were, if acknowledged at all, a private matter.

"I know it's hard," Wanda said. "Your dad and I went through a bad patch after he killed that drug dealer back at his old job. He stopped talking, stopped paying attention to anything, especially me. Somehow we got through it, but I'm not sure what we did to make things right."

"I don't know if Felo and I can. Make things right, I mean."

"Well, while you're waiting to figure it out, you'll get some of that tasty cooking of his on Sunday. Don't set yourself up to ruin breakfast by fretting and doubting yourself between now and then."

Maggie smiled a little. "That's actually good advice."

"Didn't think that was possible, did you?"

"You think I'd answer that?"

Maggie disappeared back into the kitchen, and Wanda, smiling, finished arranging pies in the display case and listing the day's selections on the blackboard.

The shop had only been open for fifteen minutes when her first customers walked in. For a moment she was rooted to the spot. Then she was afraid she might swoon, like the sweet young thing in one of her beloved pirate novels.

She might not be a sweet young thing, but this man had definitely been a pirate. Captain Pierce Arrowhart in *Under an Azure Sky,* a movie so bad it had gone straight to DVD, but what did she care? She'd bought three copies, afraid if she bought one she might wear out the disc and never be able to replace it.

"Derek Forbes," she said, surprised that sound could still issue from her throat.

"You must be Wanda." Derek Forbes extended his hand, moving past Larry Bly. Larry had his razor-thin nose tilted toward the ceiling, as if better to capture the fragrance of the pies baking in the back.

Wanda held out a trembling hand. "Derek Forbes," she said again, when nothing else occurred to her.

"I get that a lot," he said with his noteworthy grin. And, of course, the grin had been noted a million times. He was a little older than she was, his hair just beginning to thin and thread with silver, neither of which he tried to hide. His skin was leathery, as if he spent his life in the sun, but the tan was the perfect setting for his deep green eyes, eyes compared so often to emeralds that seeing them in real life should have been disappointing but wasn't. He had a man's face and body, nothing pretty or soft but angles and planes and toned muscle. And even if he was a little shorter than he seemed on film, he was still half a head taller than she was.

Wanda recovered just a little. "I bet you do. I needed preparation. A facial. Manicure." She fanned herself with her hand.

Derek laughed. "You look exactly right to me. A woman who can bake a good pie is a woman any man finds beautiful."

"Then I'm on a par with Liz or Demi or Meryl."

He gave a bawdy wink. "The stories I could tell about those three . . ."

Wanda wanted to pinch herself, but she wasn't sure she had regained enough coordination. "We just set out all the pies for the day. I bet you'd like a sample or two."

"The way some men want a cold beer and a willing woman."

"I could rustle up the first, and the second's no problem at all."

His eyes crinkled when he smiled. Both seemed completely genuine, too, as if he was enjoying himself. "I bet you're married to a good man. You deserve to be."

"Right on both counts."

He moved forward to study the blackboard over the counter. "Are these today's selections?"

"What's baked already. We'll be adding pina colada as soon as my supplier gets me more coconut, and Elvis Surprise if we need more pies 'cause we get a morning rush."

"Elvis Surprise?"

"Crushed peanut brittle, bananas and chocolate chips. After the King's favorite sandwich. One of my special pies."

"Would you make me one someday?"

"Was Dorothy wearing ruby slippers?" By this time Wanda had managed to get her legs working again and circled the counter, taking out the pies destined to be served piece by piece and cutting small wedges. She chose three, a mocha pecan, a new lemon-blueberry chiffon she was debuting today and a raspberry crumble. They were all newish recipes, part of her eternal quest to find the perfect pie, and while not the Holy Grail of pastry, they were, by her own high standards, passable.

"Want coffee with them?" She looked at both men, although Larry had yet to say a word. "Milk, soda — although I don't really recommend anything that competes with my pies."

"Just pie," Derek said, taking a seat on the first red stool at the counter. "And maybe some water?" Larry nodded in agreement.

Wanda served both men pie, then went into the kitchen and grabbed her daughter's shoulder. The mixer was on, and Maggie was whipping cream. "Do you know who's out there?" she mouthed.

"I figured it out."

"Come out with me this minute. I need you to catch me when I faint."

"Can't leave this right now."

"Girl, you are some piece of work." Wanda grabbed two of the glasses she reserved for private pie parties and filled them with ice, then bottled water. She went back to the front and set them in front of the men.

"I think I've died and gone to heaven," Derek said. "This lemon pie? I've never had anything like it in my life."

"It's my newest recipe. Glad you like it. I wasn't sure about the blueberries."

"Did you try it with raspberries?"

Nothing was easier to talk about than pie.

Wanda figured if countries at war could just sit over pie at the negotiation table and talk about recipes before they delved into who invaded what strip of land, then everything would work out just fine for everybody.

She felt herself warming to the subject. "I did, but I liked the sweetness of the blueberries as a contrast to the lemony lemon. You know, you have to get blueberries when they're just ripe enough, soft but not mushy. So I'll have to gauge when I offer it according to what's available. But that's nothing new. I don't use any fruit that's not right at its prime."

He was interested, no mistaking it. About this time most men's eyes were glazed, their brows furrowed. They wanted to eat, no explanations necessary. But Derek Forbes? He loved pie the way she did.

Ten minutes later they hadn't even scratched the surface. She'd dished up new plates with small wedges of everything else being served that day. Larry Bly looked a little green at the gills, but Derek Forbes was in his element, eating slowly, luxuriating in every little crumb.

"Will you come and make pie with me soon?" he asked, when most men would have been groaning with the calorie overload. "I want to see you in action."

That was the kind of sentiment most women would kill to hear. But Wanda knew he was talking about pies, and that was good enough for her. "Any time you want me. I hear they moved you into the Statler mansion. I've been in that kitchen of yours, and I'd pretty much give a toe or my appendix to get back in there and cook."

"Then it's a deal." He pushed himself up. "I don't remember a morning this good. I'm going to be thinking about these pies all day. We'll buy four to take with us." He named his choices.

Wanda packaged them and turned them over to Larry Bly. Derek Forbes moved around the counter to hug Wanda, while Larry fished in his pocket for his wallet.

"Now, don't forget, we have a date." He kissed her cheek; then the two men left together.

"Did I hear him right?" Maggie asked from the doorway. "What are you going to tell Dad?"

Wanda fell into the nearest chair. "Call and tell him all those CPR classes he had to attend are going to come in handy. And better call him quick."

When Tracy had agreed to be Olivia's mother at the middle school's traditional mother-daughter softball game, she'd worried about the way she might feel. But now that it was time, she wasn't worried, she was resigned. Although the worst of the nausea was beginning to abate, lethargy was settling in. Prepregnancy, she had usually stayed at the rec center until the last match had been won and the last swim team parents had taken their shriveled, shivering children out for pizza or hamburgers. Now she was dead on her feet by four.

"I could take your place. I am good at cricket," Janya told her. "I have watched your baseball games on television, and Rishi has explained what is happening. I understand touchdowns."

"Apparently not well enough." Tracy laced up her sturdiest sneakers. She had cleats, but wearing them didn't seem sporting. The other mothers probably couldn't catch a ball if their gloves had built-in radar. She supposed being pregnant was a fair handicap.

She straightened and clasped her hands over her head to stretch. "Besides, you have your hands full, and I'd rather be out on the field kicking butt than in the bleachers wiping it."

"You are getting very good at changing Lily's diapers."

"How are the kids today?" The question was a daily one. As often as possible, Tracy made sure to stop by Janya's house, bouncing Lily on her hip, bearing small gifts for both children and for the worried new mother. Most important, she knew Janya could use a listening ear.

She hadn't thought of it before, but today she and her Indian neighbor had even more in common than usual. Tracy was mothering Olivia, and Janya had Vijay and Lily. They were both pitching in to help raise other people's children. *Pitching* in at the softball game. At least she was still thinking like a recreation professional.

"You think you will not harm yourself or the baby?" Janya asked. "By running and throwing?"

"I asked my obstetrician, and she said I'll be fine doing anything, as long as I don't overdo." Tracy got to her feet and tried to summon energy. Rishi had the children outside on the toddlers' playground. With all the turmoil and sadness in their household, the Kapurs still hadn't wanted to miss this chance to cheer on Olivia. They were hoping, too, the game might cheer up Vijay, who rarely spoke now, and whose first visit with a play therapist had ended with a full-blown tantrum.

"The flowers on your desk are lovely," Janya said as they passed the vase of roses and tiny purple iris on their way outside to gather Janya's family for the trip to the middle school.

"Marsh," Tracy said.

"The same Marsh who is not romantic or in love with you?"

"I never said that."

"Not in those words, I suppose."

"He's been . . ." Tracy searched for the right words. "Attentive. Sweet."

"Does this help you?"

Tracy thought it might. Marsh hadn't suggested one "Marshy" thing to do since taking her to the Baithouse Bistro two weekends ago. No bird watching. No hiking, camping or canoeing. No chaining their bodies to trees in protest of something or other. Of course, only a little more than a week had passed, but she was encouraged, even though she was also just the least bit sorry there was nothing adventurous planned for their immediate future. She hoped some muscular woman with spiky hair, twenty-two earrings in each lobe and washboard abs wasn't enticing him into the swamps with promises of albino alligators or double-billed wood storks.

"He seems to care," she said. "He's bringing Bay to watch me play this afternoon, then he's cooking for us at his house. I just wish he'd come right out and declare his undying love, buy me a huge diamond and beg me to marry him."

"Would you?"

"It's possible."

"Without the diamond?"

"You know him pretty well, don't you? We'd probably stand barefoot on a beach somewhere and weave wedding rings out of palmetto fronds while some shaman chanted

264

environmental slogans in Swahili or Sanskrit."

"I studied Sanskrit. Should I prepare?"

"No, I'm counting on you to draw intricate designs all over our bodies with henna, as another symbol of our togetherness."

"What will it take before you tell him about the baby?"

"The moment I can't button my newest pair of pants, I'm going to storm into Wild Florida's headquarters and tell everybody their boss left me barefoot, pregnant and a size eight."

They were outside by now, and after they gathered up Rishi and the children, they piled into the van Rishi had borrowed from his company, and drove the mile to the middle school.

As they walked to the softball field where a group of mothers was warming up, Olivia came to meet them. A bunch of girls were off to one side huddled and giggling. One of them yelled for Olivia, who ignored her.

"I'm so glad you came!" She hugged Tracy, then Janya, even though her friends were watching. "This is so cool."

"Is your grandmother here yet? Janya and the gang can keep her company in the bleachers."

Olivia paused just a second too long. "No."

Tracy realized immediately what this meant. "Janya, you go ahead and get settled with the kids. Wave down Marsh when he gets here.

265

We'll see you after the game."

She waited until goodbyes were said and the children were carted away before she turned back to Olivia. "You didn't tell your grandmother about the game, did you?"

Olivia looked guilty, but she nodded. "I just didn't want her to feel bad. And she would have. She was invited to a Scrabble tournament with some friends, so I told her I'd go home with Jessie after school and work on my homework. She thinks Jessie's mother is going to drive me home after dinner."

"Olivia, there are at least a couple of lies in there."

"Not really. I *am* going home with Jessie after the game, and her mother said she'd drive me home. So the only lie was, like, not telling Nana about the game and you being my stand-in mom today."

"Well, if I'm your mom for the afternoon, I get to remind you that it's not cool to make up stories, even if your reason's good."

"It *is* a good reason."

"I get that. But not being completely truthful puts us both in an awkward position. What if I mention the game by mistake?"

"You're too smart to do that." Olivia's friend yelled for her again, probably the aforementioned Jessie. Olivia waved back. "Gotta go. We're going to beat you moms."

Worried, Tracy watched her run toward the other girls. On the surface Olivia appeared

266

unselfish and thoughtful, even if she was also being a trifle dishonest. But how much of her decision had been related to Alice's schedule and how much to just wanting a "young" mom today, just like everybody else's.

With nothing to be done about it, Tracy walked across the field to the group of moms pitching balls back and forth. She wasn't far away when a ball whizzed by her head before she could duck to avoid it. She heard the whap of the ball slapping against a glove, then it flew back the other direction, missing her by several feet.

"Am I invisible?" she shouted.

The last mother to throw, a tall woman with broad shoulders, red-blond hair and legs like tree trunks, glanced at her. "We have it under control." She held up her glove, and the ball slammed into it again. "You ever play softball?"

Tracy had wondered how much she should tell these women. Would they be intimidated by her credentials? After all, she was a supervisor at the rec center, with a related degree and a growing body of experience. She was a natural athlete, good at every single sport she'd attempted. She, unlike them, didn't spend her days helping with car pools, bake sales and field trips. She was fit, strong and, well, pregnant, but that was just temporary.

"I've played a little," she said modestly.

"We're pretty good," the mom said. "We've been playing together for years. This game's a tradition. Who's your kid? She new?"

"Olivia Symington."

"I guess you can play center field. Glenda Spitz is left field. Whatever you miss, she'll catch."

Tracy was beginning to steam. "I thought you might need a pitcher."

The woman laughed. "That would be me."

"You planning to pitch the whole game alone?"

The woman's eyes narrowed. "Yeah, unless I have somebody to relieve me who knows what she's doing."

Tracy held out her hand, slipping her glove on the other one. "Try me."

"I don't want to sound unfriendly, but we don't have time to train you."

"Throw the ball. Now." Tracy realized she sounded as if she was addressing the sixth-grade boys at youth camp, but she figured this really wasn't that different. Macho posturing came in all genders, ages and sizes.

The woman shrugged, looked at her friend and grinned, then backed up to throw the ball to Tracy. Tracy no longer felt even vaguely nauseated. She didn't feel tired. She just felt annoyed. When the ball whizzed in her direction, she didn't even raise her glove until the last minute. Then she leaped for it, caught it easily, wound up and pitched it back to the woman, who almost let it fly by when the ball curved neatly at the last minute.

"I noticed you're taking both feet off the ground at the last moment when you pitch," Tracy said conversationally. "Just so you know, that's against the rules. If you don't drag the toe of your pivot foot, then you could be called for leaping. *I* have time to train you, if you like."

"What did you say your name was?" the woman asked.

"Tracy Deloche. I'm the supervisor over at the rec center."

The woman stared at her, then a grin lightened her face. "Let's just not beat the girls by too much, okay?"

"They're pretty good. I've coached some of them myself."

"Yeah, but can you bake a chocolate-chip cookie?"

"Not unless someone's holding a gun to my head."

The woman nodded right before she threw the ball again. "We'll get along."

Tracy thought she might actually like this mom thing. That was a huge revelation, and she was still getting used to it. First she'd discovered she was okay with babies. Now, whenever Tracy visited, Lily clapped her hands and screeched Tey-Tey-Tey, which could have meant anything, but delighted

Tracy anyway. She had maternal instincts she hadn't known she possessed. She could soothe little Lily, entertain her, even change her diaper with efficiency. And now there was this mom-bonding thing that might just work out for her. Turned out there were jock moms as well as cookie bakers and Sunday-school teachers. She would find friends on the playground, maybe even start a softball league with day care.

Finally there was Olivia, who had been thrilled to have Tracy stand in for her own mother. "Thanks, Mom," she'd said afterward, with a huge hug, even though the girls had lost. She had apparently forgiven Tracy for striking her out when it was Olivia's turn at bat. Since the girl had later gone on to hit a triple, she was content.

"You look happy," Marsh said, stepping out of the kitchen with a platter of bruschetta that held a variety of toppings. Her stomach didn't even spiral in place. In fact, the bruschetta looked delicious.

"I was just thinking about Olivia." She looked around to be sure Bay wasn't in earshot.

"He's on the phone upstairs," Marsh said, reading her mind.

"She called me Mom. I think she was only joking, but it sent shivers up my spine."

"Why, because you don't ever want to be one?"

She almost laughed. "I was thinking more along the lines of her needing a mom and me being her stand-in. She adores Janya, too, but I think Janya's more like a big sister. I'm just older enough that she can pretend with me. I would have been, what, twenty-three when she was born? That's not out of the ordinary. I fit right in with the other mothers on the field."

"Do you think she'll be asking you for more of this kind of thing?"

Tracy was sure of it. Olivia had glowed. There was no other word for it. "She was pretty happy to see you there, too. She might need a stand-in dad now and then. Would you be willing?"

Without answering, Marsh set the food in front of her. "I'm betting after all that running around on the field, ice water's your drink of choice."

"Perfect."

He left and returned with a pitcher, and two glasses filled with ice and lemon slices. "I like Olivia," he said. "I always wanted a daughter. Maybe she'll stand in for me?"

She almost blurted out the truth, that she might well be carrying that daughter he'd yearned for. But she wasn't quite ready.

These pants still buttoned.

"I'm hearing great things about that play down at the civic auditorium," he said as he filled her glass and handed it to her. He told

271

her about it, and she tried hard not to wince. There were few things in life she disliked more than dysfunctional families dissected onstage. She'd grown up in her own and didn't need a dramatic replay.

"Interesting," she said when he finished.

"I thought you might like to go. I could get tickets."

He was being so nice, working so hard to please her. She wasn't sure what to say. She asked a question instead. "I didn't know you were that fond of the theater. Are you?"

He took a long swallow before he answered. She was afraid he might drown. "Not usually," he said, just before she grabbed the glass for his safety.

"But the play appeals to you? People tearing each other apart onstage? That's your thing?"

"Not usually."

"You were doing this for me, weren't you?" She almost cooed the words. "You thought I might like to go."

"It occurred to me."

"Waste no time worrying. I love film — after all, look where I grew up. But I'm not a huge fan of the theater unless it's something light. Does that solidify my reputation as an airhead?"

"No, it solidifies my desire to hang out with you."

She thought about his words. "Hang out

with you." She supposed that was as good a description of their relationship as any. Had he added "and get it on with you," it would have been perfect.

"What would you like to do?" he asked when she didn't reply. "Would you like to plan something for Friday night?"

She realized something was nagging at her, something she couldn't quite get hold of. She sat in silence, worrying the instinct like a cat with a cornered mouse. At the same moment, Bay came roaring down the stairs, demonstrating the reckless energy with which he did everything. He was too often in trouble, because social skills weren't one of the places he excelled, but he was learning.

"Can I go to the movies with Adam Friday night?" he shouted. "Will you take us? Can he sleep over?"

"So much for you choosing our night out," Marsh told Tracy.

She was still trying to figure out what was bothering her. She nodded. "I'll come hang out, too, unless Bay doesn't want me here."

"Will you play Guitar Hero with us?" Bay asked.

"I'll cream you, kid."

They munched bruschetta while Bay told them all about his class field trip to a wildlife rehabilitation center; then they moved into the kitchen for one of Marsh's fabulous meals. He had breaded and broiled catfish

273

with herbs, lemon and garlic, and served it with pasta with a light cream sauce and a medley of roasted vegetables.

She was dishing up reasonable portions of each when he leaned over to refill her water glass.

"Where's the wine?" she asked. She didn't want any, of course, and had decided to plead dehydration, but there was no opportunity. Marsh always had a glass of wine or beer with his meal, but he seemed to be drinking water tonight, too.

He hesitated. Not long, but just as she'd correctly read Olivia's hesitation earlier in the afternoon as guilt, she read this one as subterfuge. Marsh was working on an excuse.

"I just forgot to open a bottle," he said. "What would you like? I probably won't have any myself. It's been a long week."

And then she knew.

She put down her fork. "Marsh, can I see you in the living room for a moment?"

He looked surprised. "Your fish is going to get cold."

"You're right about that." She stood and walked out of the kitchen, leaving him no choice but to follow.

When he joined her, she leaned in close so Bay wouldn't hear them. But her tone said it all. "You know!"

He feigned ignorance. "Know what?"

"You know! Who told you?"

When he didn't answer, she grabbed his shirt. "Wanda, right? Wanda told you?"

He stopped pretending. "I wrung it out of her. I lived with a pregnant woman, remember? I'm not stupid, even if it did take me a little while to put all the facts together. Oddly enough, it never occurred to me that if you were carrying my baby, you wouldn't tell me yourself."

She shoved him. "That's why you've been so nice to me, isn't it? That's what the Baithouse Bistro was all about. The flowers. Coming to the softball game. Telling me I could choose our date this weekend. You've been buttering me up so I'd tell you."

"That's simplifying things a whole lot. But let's back up a little. Let's not only talk about horrible old me doing all those nice things to make you happy. Let's talk about why you never told me in the first place."

They were only one decibel level above a whisper, but Tracy didn't want Bay to hear any of this. She lowered her voice another notch.

"Because I didn't want to." She glared at him. "Because we didn't plan this, we aren't married and as far as I know, I'm just a passing phase in your life. This baby isn't a passing phase. It's *real,* and I want to be sure it gets off to the best possible start."

"Without its father?" He glared. "When were you going to tell me? How long did you think you could hide something like this?"

"Until I was ready, that's when!"

"Don't think you can cut me out of my own child's life anymore. This is my baby, too."

"Yeah, well, you got that right, but I'll sell Happiness Key and fight you every step of the way in court if you get grabby, Marsh. I'm warning you."

He looked shocked. "What are you talking about?"

"I want this baby. I didn't plan it, but I want it. I'm going to be a good mother, unlike a certain other woman you were married to. You can be involved, but don't think you'll have any control about what I do and how I do it."

"You still haven't given me a good reason why you didn't tell me. You're keeping the baby. You weren't wrestling with that. Wanda said you needed reassurance. Is that all this is about?"

All. To Marsh, making sure the father of her child loved and wanted her was simply "all this is about." It was inconsequential, irrelevant. She was just a silly pregnant woman with insecurities and a need to have her dainty little hand held. He would do his duty, be a good father to their child, and heck, he had proved in a pinch that he could even consider her needs and pamper her a little.

Was that enough?

"I'm going home," she said, looking for her

276

purse, which she'd left in some corner. She spied the handle peeking over an ottoman and headed to reclaim it.

"Trace, don't do this. Finish dinner. I'll get Bay in bed, then we can talk things over. Hormones are flowing like mad right now. But we have to use good sense."

Hormones? For a moment she wanted to slap him. And maybe that part *was* hormones. But the rest of it?

"You should have told me you knew," she said, "instead of pretending you were so interested in pleasing me."

"And you should have told me, period."

She shook her head, grabbed her purse and headed for the door, fishing inside for her keys as she walked. He followed her outside.

"We have to talk," he said as she opened the car door. "Surely you see that?"

"I need time alone."

"Trace." He grabbed her arm. "This should be a happy time. I want this baby, too. If you doubt that, you shouldn't. You know how much I love Bay. I'll love this child every bit as much."

She tried to breathe deeply, to consider his feelings, to move beyond her anger and insecurity. But all she could do was repeat what she'd said.

"I need time alone."

He dropped her arm and moved away. "Call me when you're ready. But please, call me?"

277

She slid into her seat and jammed her key in the ignition. Then, before she shut the door, she added, "If you call me first and start nagging, all bets are off, Marsh. I won't be rushed, and I won't be lectured again about my hormones and my lack of good sense. Got it?"

She didn't wait to see if he did. She slammed the door, backed up and sped away.

CHAPTER FOURTEEN

On Sunday, Maggie rose early to clean the cottage, which was so tiny that cleaning was never much of a time sink. She did what chores there were to a Latin rhythm, a favorite Miami radio station that often, but not always, was clear enough to listen to here, if she didn't mind occasional bouts of static.

Afterward she showered and washed her hair, leaving it loose to dry. The moment she caught herself wondering what she should wear for Felo's visit, she decided to stick her hand in the closet and pull out whatever she touched. She didn't want to primp, but she didn't want to send him screaming back to Miami, either, not before he told her what he'd been able to dig up about the Duttas. Luckily she wasn't forced to pair her fuchsia capris and tomato-red blouse. Khakis and a turquoise cotton pullover won the closet lottery.

She was zipping her pants when the local Miami news came on. The story at the top of the hour was the acquisition of several large cattle ranches by Peerless Sugar.

She snapped off the radio, sorry she'd indulged just before Felo arrived. This wasn't the best start for their morning together.

Felo, Maggie and Peerless had a history. Peerless Sugar was one of the largest sugar companies in Florida, founded by a man named Fernando Echemendia after the Cuban revolution propelled him to the United States. Peerless had been handed down from father to son until the present CEO, Miguel Echemendia, had expanded it into the success it was. In addition to vast acres of sugarcane, the corporation owned miles of citrus groves and other properties, making Peerless a substantial employer and a carefully cultivated player in state politics.

Felo's ex-partner and boyhood friend Alvaro Hernandez was the Peerless vice president.

Like Felo, Alvaro's start in life hadn't been easy, but while Felo had chosen to escape his dysfunctional childhood by earning good grades and college scholarships, Alvaro, who was two years older, had taken a different route, heading straight to the police academy after high school graduation and moonlighting after hours working security at local clubs. He was already established and able to pull the appropriate strings to partner with his boyhood friend once Felo graduated and joined the force.

But Alvaro's lucky star had really shone on the night when Miguel Echemendia was attacked by a business rival inside the Miami Beach nightclub where Alvaro was working the floor. Alvaro had intercepted and disarmed the attacker before Echemendia's bodyguards looked up from their dinner plates. A grateful Echemendia had hired him to head security at Peerless, and Alvaro had risen steadily through the company and now was close to the top.

Maggie didn't have a problem with powerful people, but this particular one *was* a problem. Alvaro had a hold on Felo she couldn't understand or countenance.

There were reminders everywhere, it seemed, of the problems between her and Felo. And still she had invited him back into her life when she had asked for his help.

When he called at nine-thirty to tell her he was crossing the bridge to the key, she started the coffeemaker. He preferred Cuban coffee, a thick, sweet espresso he made with a traditional stovetop pot. By now, though, he would have already enjoyed two, his morning ration, before setting out. Since she'd never quite developed a taste for it, he wouldn't feel obliged to include cafe cubano on his breakfast menu.

As she had done incessantly since their conversation, she wondered about the point of this visit. Surely nothing he'd learned was such a secret he couldn't tell her over the telephone. He'd mentioned interviewing Janya and Rishi, and she'd agreed that was a good idea, but since a phone call would have sufficed, she knew there was more. Whatever the reason, sadly, she was looking forward to seeing Felo every bit as much as she was dreading it.

By the time he knocked, she was setting out plates and mugs. She called for him to come in but didn't rush to greet him. He found her in the kitchen, not a treasure hunt of any magnitude, since the cottage was less than six hundred square feet.

"Hey, Mags," he said casually from the doorway, as if they had never been apart. "Didn't I give you that sweater?"

Too late now, she realized he had. A traitor to her gender, she found little pleasure in shopping. Felo, on the other hand, loved buying clothes for her, and while Victoria's Secret was his favorite stomping ground, no matter where he was, he could spot something that would look good on her.

"You did," she said, still not turning around, as if his arrival was of no consequence. "You always paid attention to whatever women were wearing at the moment." Left unsaid? That maybe his fashion sense was a by-product of his interest in women, period.

"My mother and I went shopping a lot

when I was a boy. We walked to the mall to get out of the house whenever my dad started drinking. We never bought anything — we never had money. But I used to tell myself as soon as I could, I would buy her those things she'd loved so much. By the time I could, she was gone."

The rest of his sentence lay in the air between them: and so he had bought things for Maggie instead.

She finally turned. He was holding a loudly purring Rumba blissfully draped against him. "You never told me that."

"It's not a happy memory."

He looked just the way he always did. Vibrant. Seductive. Very, very male. But this morning there was a hint of sadness in his eyes, as well.

"Did you have a good drive?" she asked, not sure what to say about his revelation and trying to forestall more of the same.

"It was better than driving through rush hour."

"Coffee's ready. I made it strong. That was the best I could do."

"Are you hungry?"

She was starving, but she hadn't wanted to ruin her appetite. Felo's breakfasts were amazing.

"I can wait," she said. "I know it'll be worth it."

"I brought pastries. JoJo's. Pour the coffee

while I set things out."

They had been together so long, this was the way their relationship had developed over time. He told her what to do; she told him the same. No please or thank-you needed. It was a form of intimacy, accomplishing the little things together with no fuss or bother. An unusual request, of course, was different, an excuse for old-fashioned good manners, but now old habits were showing.

She did as requested, spooning sugar into his cup. With Rumba rubbing against his ankles, he rifled through cupboards and found a plate, which he filled with pastries from their favorite bakery. JoJo, the old man who'd owned the place for almost forty years, never turned out a failure. Her mouth watered.

"Want me to get started?" he asked. "I'll snack while I cook. I brought fruit to cut up, if you're interested."

The kitchen was small, really only large enough for one cook. But they had worked together in smaller. The first apartment they'd shared, nothing more than an efficiency, had come with a creaky old Murphy bed that took up most of the floor when it was lowered. By the time they lowered it at night — or any time of day — neither of them had cared about floor space. Their world had shrunk to a double-size mattress, their hands and lips, and skin gliding over skin.

She couldn't refuse to help, not even when it meant brushing against him, finding he was just inches away when she turned, feeling the warmth of his breath against her cheek when he spoke.

"Sounds good," she said. "I'll get started. What are you making?"

"Pisto Manchego, if that sounds good."

"You know it does."

"I wanted to make the pisto last night, and I got everything chopped. But I got a call just as I was turning on the burner."

"Work?"

"What else?"

Such a simple answer, but these days so fraught with meaning. Was Felo seeing another woman now? Or still? Was his lover calling at night, wishing he was there with her instead of in the house he and Maggie still owned together, chopping vegetables for the woman who used to live there?

Had Maggie simply taken Felo's natural warmth and charm and turned it into infidelity in her head, his sympathetic ear into an affair with a colleague? His anger at her failure to marry him and have his children as a growing disinterest in her?

"I'm surprised you were able to come this morning," she said, struggling to accept his answer at face value. When Felo was assigned to a homicide, he worked it steadily for the first forty-eight hours, and a trip out of town would have been unthinkable.

"It didn't take long to figure out the death was an accident. Plenty of witnesses and no questions by the time we finished up around midnight. Gary says hello."

Gary was Felo's present partner, a man on the cusp of retirement, and Maggie had always been fond of him. Some months before she left, Gary had taken her aside, at a sports bar where so many cops went after work, and warned her that guys like Felo didn't come around very often. "Stop hanging around the edges of his heart and plunge right in," he'd said, the grisly image a product of one beer too many and a harrowing day of investigations.

Onion was sautéeing in olive oil now, pleasantly redolent, and in a moment Felo added garlic, making it more so. She found mangoes and papayas in a bag and began to peel and slice. Felo had always been in charge of shopping for fruit, instinctively knowing when it was at its peak. Her luck in this endeavor had never been half as good.

He put down his spatula, reached over and broke off a piece of a pastelito, a flaky, buttery pastry. He stretched out his hand and poised it in front of her. "Open up."

There was no point in trying to protest the intimacy. She knew Felo would feed it to her, anyway, the minute she did. She chewed, appreciated and swallowed. "Pineapple."

"I think there's guava, too. JoJo said only the best for you."

"Did you tell everybody in Miami you were coming to see me?"

"Not Alvaro."

The moment he said the name, he realized what he'd done. His annoyance at himself was obvious.

"Why not?" she asked as his eyes shuttered and his lips thinned into a grimace. "Did you think he'd disapprove?"

"No, I didn't. He likes you, even if the feeling's not mutual. I didn't tell him because I don't want Alvaro involved in us."

"Us?" She refrained from saying there was no longer an "us."

"That's right, Mags. *Us.* You and me. Didn't we spend enough years together for the word to have some meaning?"

She knew better than to touch that. "Alvaro was *always* involved in 'us,' Felo. He was always right there, hanging out on the sidelines."

"Alvaro is my friend. I made it through the streets of my childhood because he was there to protect and guide me. He's not an easy person to know, and these days he's got a reputation he deserves. But he only deserves it because he's cultivated it carefully, so no one messes with him. If he was half as ruthless and dangerous as you think, he'd have every law enforcement agency in the country

287

investigating every move he makes. But he's walking the streets and nobody's following him."

She couldn't believe they were talking about this. His relationship with his ex-partner was a good part of the reason she had left Felo. She knew better than to continue, but she couldn't seem to leave it alone.

"Since when does walking the streets mean a man isn't guilty? These days Alvaro has friends everywhere, and most of them owe him favors. Don't tell me the bad guys are all in jail. We both know most of the ones with connections are fat, flourishing and free."

"He's vice president of Peerless Sugar, not a two-bit gang leader."

Maggie took up Felo's challenge. "Your buddy started out doing all the dirty work for Miguel Echemendia, Felo. You think Eche-mendia's bodyguard could keep his nose clean? You think he stayed on the right side of the law all those years he was working his way up to second in command? And now that he's the de facto CEO, because Echemen-dia's too befuddled to butter his own bread, he's got even more reason not to play fair."

"You think there's a businessman in this country of ours at Alvaro's level who got there by playing fair every second of every day?"

She wasn't a fool. She knew Felo was right about that, if not about the extent of Alvaro's criminal activity. But one fact was indisputable, the important one, the one that had severed their relationship.

"Alvaro was behind your decision not to support me when I challenged Paul Smythe, Felo. You've never denied that."

"No, you just never listened to what I was saying."

"Alvaro wanted me to keep my mouth shut, to let the crookedest state's attorney in Miami's history continue his dirty tricks unchallenged. And he had lots of reasons. Famosa was his childhood friend. Yours, too, for that matter. And Smythe is a good friend to Peerless. Your old boyhood pal used you to make sure things happened the way he wanted them to, never mind that he used to be a cop. And you let him! You took his side against *me*."

Felo's anger was clear from the way he softly punched his next words. "Nobody uses me. Not my friends. Not you. The situation was never as simple as you wanted it to be, Mags. It was complicated. It *is* complicated. And you're not good with complicated, or with listening. Or trusting."

She was stung by the criticism, even if it wasn't new. "I'll agree, trust was an issue for us." And there was that "us" word again.

Felo put down his chopping knife and, in one fluid motion, put his hands on her shoulders and turned her to face him.

289

"Let's not talk about Alvaro, because he's not important. Let's talk about *us.* I loved you then, I love you now. But at the end, I wasn't getting anything back. You were obsessed with the Famosa case, then later with getting even with Smythe. The whole thing became personal to you. You were trying to prove something. When I talked about our future, your mind was always somewhere else. So I found other people to talk to, and I stayed out late because what was the point of going home? Yeah, it was childish and stupid, but how long did it take you to notice things were changing between us?"

"This isn't getting us anywhere."

He dropped his hands, as if he was tired of trying. "It never does."

Part of her wanted to ask him to leave, to be done with the anger and recriminations for good. But a larger part, a part that would not be easily silenced, knew that Felo leaving was not the answer, just as her leaving him had accomplished little except create an emptiness that continued to grow with each passing day.

He had given her something. He had tried, at least a little, to explain what he had been feeling. She knew that for them to settle this, to part as friends or even to reunite, she had to give something in return, no matter how hard, how alien, it felt to talk about her feelings.

"I'm sorry." She bit her bottom lip, as if tasting the aftermath of the unfamiliar words. "I . . . I *was* obsessed. The case felt important. It made up for all those years I had to fight for every single inch I climbed the career ladder. You don't know what that was like, Felo, how rare it is for a woman to be put on an investigation like that one. Maybe Smythe even asked for me because he figured I wouldn't do a good enough job."

"That's not true. You earned it, that's all."

He had never understood the day-to-day politics of discrimination.

"Either way, getting Famosa was important, and working on that kept me from —" She stopped.

"Making a commitment?" he asked when she didn't finish.

"Maybe," she conceded. "I wasn't ready to stay home, have babies, keep house. I wanted what we already had. I thought we were good the way we were, but you were pushing me into a corner."

"And you never wanted more?"

"I just thought we would work it out together when the right moment came, only every time we tried to talk about it, we ended up not talking at all."

She expected him to be angry, but instead he shook his head, then put his arms around her and pulled her close.

She knew better than to stay that way. The

feel of his body was so familiar, so easy to relax into, so seductive. The warmth and scent of his skin filled her, seeped into her pores, slid along her nerve endings. She tried to pull free, but only in her mind. Her body would not give an inch except to strain closer.

"I don't know how we got along as well as we did," he murmured against her hair. "I speak, you hear things I don't say. You don't speak, and all my fears speak for you."

She looked up, knowing what would happen, and it did. He kissed her, a slow familiar kiss that felt like all the good things that had once filled her life then fled. She knew better than this. She knew how dangerous it was to succumb to temptation, dangerous for both of them. She didn't want to lead him on. She was no surer of how she felt about him, whether or not she trusted his word and his affiliations. Yet she couldn't seem to pull away. Felo was like a drug in her system, and not one that tempered reality but one that gave life, brought energy and feeling coursing through her.

"I didn't come to seduce you," he said.

She wasn't sure she trusted that, either. But in the scheme of things, whether he had or hadn't was a ripple in a pond of misgivings.

"I didn't expect to say yes if you did," she murmured against his lips, although it was probably a lie.

He took her answer for the assent it was.

He folded her closer, his fingers reaching under her sweater, stroking her back, unhooking her bra with long practiced skill. She wondered, as he lifted the sweater and inched it up over her shoulders, if "yes" was yet another way to avoid talking about their differences. Because if they talked at last, would Felo leave once and for all, never to return?

"What?" he asked, pulling away for a moment.

"Nothing."

"No, there was something. You gasped. Do you want me to stop?"

She finished pulling her sweater over head and dropped it on the floor. "If I did, you would know," she said.

"I'm not sure."

She smiled sadly; then she traced the fine curve of his lips. "No more talking."

"Let me turn off the stove."

She rose on tiptoe to kiss where she'd touched, and her bra drifted down her arms and joined the sweater on the floor. "You do that."

By the time Maggie got out of the shower, the smells drifting from the kitchen were remarkable. She doubted the little beach cottage had ever experienced anything as fabulous as Felo's Pisto Manchego. The chorizo alone would linger in the air for days, reminding her of this morning.

As would the pleasant ache in sensitive places and the tingle of every nerve ending in her body. She smiled as she dried her shoulders and breasts, but by the time she'd finished and was dressed again, the smile had disappeared.

Acting on impulse was Felo's trademark, not hers. Yet she had more than complied. She had encouraged. She had cut off conversation, afraid it would cool the fever in their blood, blocked out every warning her brain had tried to send her. They had come together as if something outside themselves had kept them apart these months, but she had ignored the truth. She had left him, and nothing had really changed since she walked out their door. She had only his word that he had not been unfaithful. And she still didn't believe he hadn't heeded Alvaro's counsel, but had refused to support Maggie's plan to unmask Paul Smythe for his own reasons.

The table was set when she joined him. He smiled, but his expression was wary, as if he, too, knew that all was not yet well.

"That was a bad idea," Maggie said, sliding into her seat.

"It wasn't a mistake, and it wasn't a commitment. We know sex isn't the problem in this relationship. Until we can talk about the things that really are, what's the point of talking at all?"

"I'm not coming home."

"I didn't ask you to."

"Why do we do this to each other?"

"Because it's better than saying goodbye."

That was true, the answer she didn't want to hear, but the real one. She couldn't say yes and she couldn't say no, and that kind of indecision was foreign to her. She had left Felo, believing that their relationship was finished. Yet in those weeks alone in the Blue Ridge, the true depth of her feelings for him had become clear. And though she rarely changed her mind once it was made up, this time she'd felt none of the certainty and relief that came with a decision. Instead, she'd just felt more confused and unsure.

"We are who we are," she said. "And neither of us is likely to change."

"What we are is hungry. Starving, actually. And it's time to do something about it."

He piled food on the little table. The Pisto Manchego with eggs nestled on top of the savory vegetables laced with shrimp and cho-rizo. More of the pastries he'd brought. A salad of avocado and diced red onion, along with the fruit Maggie had sliced.

As if they'd silently agreed that they'd plumbed the depths of their troubled relation-ship enough for one morning, they talked about friends and changes to their neighbor-hood. When she had eaten enough to sustain her for a week, she pushed her chair back and got more coffee to refill his cup.

"Are you going to tell me what you discovered about the Duttas?" she said.

"I thought I'd wait and tell your friends at the same time, unless you'd rather hear it first."

She shook her head. "No hurry, I guess. They've been given custody of the children for the time being."

"How are the kids doing?"

She knew that wasn't an idle question. Felo loved children, and they loved him in return. He partnered with a church group that made teddy bears for children in crisis, and he'd convinced some of their fellow officers to carry them to help soothe distraught children when a parent was taken away or, worse, when the children themselves were taken from their parents. At Christmastime, nobody worked harder soliciting toys and clothes for children in need than Felo. His own difficult childhood had made him even more aware.

"The little boy is hardly talking. The little girl — she's hardly more than a baby — has settled in pretty well, although she's afraid of men."

"Was the father violent at home?"

"Rishi says he was a confirmed pacifist. More likely Lily, the baby, rarely saw him, so she's not used to men. Between his job and his novel, he was gone a lot."

"I was surprised you called me. You had other contacts."

She started to say she'd tried them all, but that wasn't strictly true. There were others who could have helped her find the information she needed. If she was really honest with herself, she knew that calling Felo had been a way to test the waters between them.

"You're the best," she said, and it wasn't a lie.

"Shall we head over now and see what we can find out from your friends? I'll tell all of you what little I've learned." He got up and started to clear the table. When he stopped to one side of her, he leaned over and kissed her head.

"Don't spend the next weeks regretting what happened, okay? Let it go. We'll take this one step at a time."

"In what direction?"

He ruffled her hair. "Let's get these dishes in the sink."

Maggie phoned Janya before they left the house, and once they arrived, the other woman opened the front door before they could knock, baby Lily perched on her hip. The little girl wore a bright pink T-shirt and a diaper. Settled that way, one hand rhythmically tugging a lock of Janya's hair like a miniature bell ringer, the child could have been hers. No one would have disputed it.

Janya held out her hand to Felo as Maggie introduced them. From her mother, Maggie knew that in India women rarely shook hands with strange men, but now the gesture seemed effortless to Maggie's neighbor.

"We thank you for coming," Janya told Felo. "It is a long trip, and your time is valuable."

"I'm glad I could be a little help."

They followed Janya inside, and she introduced Rishi, who was trying to coax Vijay to eat a plate of sliced melon. The little boy didn't look at them, and his expression was glum. The melon appeared untouched.

"Lily needs a nap," Janya said. "I will be with you as soon as she's in bed."

"Vijay, would you like to watch television in our bed?" Rishi asked the little boy, who gave a sullen nod. Both Kapurs left to settle the children, and Maggie and Felo made themselves comfortable in the tiny living room.

"This place is small for four," Felo said softly.

"If the children were older, it would be really difficult."

"Will they look for a larger place?"

"They don't know from one day to the next whether the kids will stay here or be sent off to India. It doesn't make sense to move if they don't need to."

"And the kids have had no contact with family there?"

"None. Can you imagine what it'll be like for them?"

"Like me being sent to Cuba to live out the rest of my days."

Janya returned, closing the door to the children's bedroom — not much larger than a walk-in closet — behind her. In a moment Rishi came out of the other room and pulled the door, too, without closing it all the way. In the background Maggie could hear the high-pitched voices of children from a television show.

"Vijay has difficulty sleeping at night," Janya said. "So he is tired during the day, but he fights a nap."

"Bad dreams," Felo said. It wasn't a question.

"If so, he will not tell anyone about them."

"That's too bad. It would help."

Janya and Rishi settled themselves in chairs, and Rishi took the lead. "We appreciate that you've taken the time to help us."

Felo waved this away. "I was happy to. Since we don't know how long we'll have before the children need you again, let me just tell you quickly what I've learned."

Maggie admired the way Felo had already put Janya and Rishi at ease. She sat back and listened.

"The day Mr. Dutta left the children with you, Mrs. Dutta was seen with an unidentified man going into the motel room where she died. The man had made the reservation earlier in the day, but the information he gave, name and address, doesn't check out. We know it wasn't Mr. Dutta. Several people, including the reception clerk, saw the man when he checked in and are sure it wasn't your friend, although the description has some similarities. Dark hair, olive complexion, not too tall. Neither of them were seen after that, but late that evening, someone did see Mr. Dutta knocking on the door of the room. They gave a positive ID."

"So she went into the room, but no one saw her leave again?" Rishi asked.

Felo nodded. "At some point after that, the Do Not Disturb sign went up. The room was paid up for a week, cash, and it was at the end of a walkway with nothing to one side but an overgrown vacant lot and Biscayne Boulevard running right in front of it. The room next door was trashed and slated for what passes for renovation there, so it wasn't in use. Vagrants regularly troop through and stay a couple of weeks at a time. It's the kind of motel where nobody's going to do any extra work if they don't have to. So the maid ignored the room, figuring she could plead 'do not disturb' if anybody got around to asking why she hadn't gone in."

"Lord . . ." Maggie shook her head, imagining the scene the cops had found.

"The money ran out, the manager asked the maid if the guests had checked out yet, and when he found out what had been going on, he went down to see for himself. He unlocked the door and called the cops."

"They did not deserve this," Janya said.

Maggie wished she was sitting closer so she could pat Janya's hand, but Rishi did it instead.

"Crime scene and Homicide arrived quickly, and the scene was gone over thoroughly," Felo said. "They canvassed the area around the motel, as well as all the rooms and staff. Nothing major was found to refute the theory that Mr. Dutta found his wife hiding from him and killed her, then himself."

"Nothing *major?*" Maggie asked, aware that this word was the most important one he'd uttered.

"What does that mean?" Rishi asked. "There were little things that didn't add up?"

"More than one," Felo said. "First? The other man. Where was he when the deaths occurred? If he was out getting dinner, or doing almost anything, why didn't he report the bodies once he came back?"

"He and Kanira could have fought before all this happened, and he could have left for good," Maggie said. "Or maybe he did come back, saw what had happened and was afraid he might be implicated."

"Possible. That's what the detective in charge assumes. But here's the next thing. Mr. Dutta's gun? Or I should say the revolver he was holding when they found him. A

Smith & Wesson .38. It was stolen two months ago from a registered gun owner in Hialeah and reported at the time. Maybe it made its way here to Palmetto Grove and somehow Dutta got hold of it, but it seems more likely that the gun never left Miami-Dade and somehow Dutta bought it not far from where it was stolen."

"Impossible," Rishi said.

"Unlikely," Felo agreed. "One, nothing's been turned up to link Dutta to anybody in Miami. As far as we know, he's never been there and has no friends there. So how would a man like him know where to go to buy a gun on the street without getting himself killed for his trouble?"

"But he did get himself killed," Maggie said. "Somehow."

"But not during a gun buy. And let's not forget he was seen knocking on the motel door that evening, and seen here in the afternoon when he left the children with you, Mrs. Kapur. That means there was very little time for him to buy a gun anywhere, here or there, before he went to that motel."

"It's still possible," Maggie said, playing devil's advocate. "Maybe somebody at the barbershop sold him one. Maybe he was worried about protection for his family."

"Never," Rishi said. "Harit was a pacifist. He hated guns. He would never own one, and certainly never use one. He hated violence. I tell you, he hated it!"

This time Janya covered her husband's hand. "Let Felo go on, Rishi."

"There are two more inconsistencies," Felo said. "Small, but real. First, Mrs. Dutta had bruising on her wrists and a scratch on her cheek. Of course, as you know, the bodies weren't discovered for almost a week . . ."

Maggie shook her head, hoping Felo wouldn't go into detail. And of course he was too nice a guy for that. He just let the words hang in the air for a moment before he went on.

"It's hard to tell, but the assumption is that she got them during a struggle. However, there was no corresponding evidence Harit had participated. Of course, both the scratch and the bruises could have happened before her death, maybe by a day or so. It's not possible to tell now. And she was the mother of young children, active, busy, so it's not a stretch."

"What else?" Janya asked.

"Two microscopic fibers were found in Mr. Dutta's mouth."

"Gagged?" Maggie asked.

"Certainly not when they found him. And when I say microscopic, please remember the length of time they were there, the state of the room, the placement of his head on the floor."

"Is that all?" Rishi asked, glancing at Janya,

303

who looked pale beneath the warm brown of her complexion.

"I am bothered by the fact that Mrs. Dutta was found lying in a comfortable position on the bed, as if there was never any attempt to escape."

"She would have tried to get away from him if she saw he had a gun," Maggie said. "So could someone have repositioned her after the murder?"

"Forensics didn't come up with anything conclusive, but it's possible."

"She could have been trapped there," Maggie said. "Told not to move, convinced it was the only way to save herself."

"This is very hard," Janya said, her voice husky with tears.

Felo leaned forward and took her hand for a moment, as naturally as if they had always been friends. "I'm done. But it's your turn, yours and Rishi's. What can you tell me that helps us put this together?"

"They were not happy," Janya said. "Kanira was angry with Harit because he would not get a better job. She told me she had something planned to better her life, but she didn't tell me what."

"Harit was my friend," Rishi said. "And he knew his wife was unhappy."

"He could not have missed it," Janya said.

Rishi nodded gravely. "His book was important to him, but he told me he might have to put it aside for a while. He knew Kanira's patience was at an end, and, worse, he knew her impatience was bad for their children. So he began cutting hair in the afternoons, during his writing time. It was something of a secret, because he was visiting clients at their homes — charging more, of course. He knew his boss at the barbershop wouldn't look kindly on this, but he was desperate."

"So there was more money recently," Felo said.

"He told me the tips were good, and that it made a difference. He hoped to buy a better car, or at least get theirs fixed."

"So things had improved?"

"He was trying to make them better."

"Kanira was impatient and critical," Janya said. "This is true. But when I was with her, she watched over the children, perhaps not with as much love as we would wish, but carefully. She would not leave them and go away. I feel this strongly. Had she decided to leave Harit, she would have taken them with her."

"Perhaps she was going to send for them when she was settled with this other man?" Maggie asked.

"I think not. She would have been afraid Harit would not let her have them." She hesitated, then shook her head. "And I believe, as sad as this may sound, that she knew if Harit did make a success of his writ-

305

ing, if his book sold well, the marriage might be worth something to her." Tears filled her eyes and she blinked them away, looking down at the floor. "She never said this, but she might have thought it. I just know she would not, for many reasons, have abandoned the children." She looked up at last. "One more thing. Where would Kanira have met a man to run away with? She usually had her children with her. And like me, she would never talk to strange men in parks or stores, especially not with her children at her side. It is just impossible to believe."

"What can be done?" Rishi asked. "There must be justice."

Maggie looked at Felo and found he was looking back at her.

"I don't know what to tell you," Felo said, getting to his feet. "But I *will* tell you *this.* I won't drop it. Not yet. I'll see what more I can learn, okay?"

Everyone else stood, and the Kapurs walked them to the door. And then Maggie and Felo were alone outside.

"You're really going to keep at this?" she asked. "Even if it pisses off the guy in charge of the case?"

"I know how to make things happen without pissing him off."

"And I never did."

"Not your strong point," Felo agreed. "What about you? Are you going to see what

306

you can do from here?"

"I'll try hard not to antagonize anybody," she said.

"Good. We can work on the case together."

They reached his car, and she leaned against it, her arms folded. She supposed the message was clear. Their morning was finished, and it was time for him to go back, even though he still had to get a few things from inside.

"I'm surprised you're so helpful," she said. "You really have nothing invested in whether the Duttas were caught up in a lethal love triangle or something more insidious."

"I'm always helpful," he said.

"That so?"

"It's not something you'd notice, Mags. You never want help."

He headed back to the house to get whatever he wasn't planning to leave behind. She wanted badly to think of a good comeback, but what could she say when she'd just been told the truth?

CHAPTER FIFTEEN

Tracy was now fourteen weeks pregnant. She found it hard to believe the baby inside her weighed only an ounce when she already felt like an elephant. So, okay, for most of her life her entire self-image had revolved around fat cells, how many, where they landed and how to obliterate them. Early last summer she'd been disgusted to learn she had gained a dress size, so she'd participated in the rec center weight-loss program to regain the slender, toned body she had once been so proud of.

Now? Worries about her weight had flown out the window. Her appetite was back, she was eating everything in sight, and she really didn't care how much weight she gained. She felt good again, energetic and strong, and nothing would change the fact that before long the whole world would clearly see the truth. She was now cycling through her wardrobe looking for all the pants with drawstring waists and every top that fell loosely past her hips. She'd bought larger bras and marveled at the way she filled them out. She was pregnant! Whether she was a size three or a blissful plus size waddling through the maternity section, who cared? There was a baby growing inside her, and she, Tracy Deloche, was nurturing it with every bite.

"So you can tell me all that with a straight face?" Wanda asked as she packed up the fifth raspberry chiffon pie from her display case for Tracy to take back to the center. "That you need these pies for that baby of yours? The way some women need, oh, spinach or calf's liver?"

"Not exactly *need.* But you have no idea how nice it is to think about food again without my stomach jumping on the old Knott's Berry Farm Silver Bullet and taking all those curves upside down and sideways."

"And you promise you're not going to eat all these pies alone?"

Tracy didn't quite tell Wanda the truth, that though four of the five pies were indeed going to a rec center staff luncheon to celebrate the retirement of one of their maintenance men, one was going home to be savored and enjoyed alone during the upcoming weekend.

"I am not going to eat all these pies by myself," she said, throwing Wanda's words back at her, since, technically, they were true.

"And if I come over to your place . . . say, tomorrow night, I won't find any pie remains in your fridge?"

"You know, in case you don't recognize my visit here this morning for what it is, it's a goodwill gesture, an all-is-forgiven notification to the woman who told Marsh Egan I'm pregnant with his baby."

Wanda waved that away. "You forgave me for that a couple of weeks ago. And it was your own fault for trying to keep it away from Mr. Marshall Egan in the first place. You're lucky he didn't figure it out before you even bought the pregnancy kit."

"Whatever."

"You talk to him lately?"

Tracy didn't answer. Marsh had told her to call when she was ready, but two and a half weeks had passed, and she hadn't yet picked up the telephone. She'd waved to him once at the rec center after he picked up Bay from swim team practice, but before he could close the distance, she'd headed for the ladies' room. Even Marsh wasn't going to tackle her there. By the time she finally decided the coast must be clear, it had been.

Which had been something of a disappointment.

"I guess that means no, you haven't talked," Wanda said. "When are you going to call the man? When the kid needs braces?"

"Nope, I'll call my father for that. Orthodontist to the stars, remember? He might even give me a discount. His only grandchild,

310

after all, even if the most I've gotten from Dr. Dad since my divorce is a Christmas card with an engraved signature and a funny picture of Santa wearing orthodontic head-gear."

"I gather you're not flying back to the bosom of your family to have this baby."

Tracy almost shuddered. Denise Deloche, her mother, had been aghast to learn she was going to be a grandmother, and Tracy's father hadn't returned the obligatory phone call she'd made to inform him. She had never doubted she and the baby were on their own, but now she had final confirmation.

Of course, there was Marsh . . .

"You can't duck and cover for the rest of this pregnancy," Wanda said. "You ask me, you're not being fair."

"Then I won't ask. Now, tell me all about *you*. Maybe I can find something to criticize with the same enthusiasm."

"Sorry to disappoint, but nothing to tell."

"No movie star sightings?"

"Haven't heard a word." Wanda finished a knot in the string surrounding the final boxed-up pie. "I tell myself it's not those pies I sent off with Derek Forbes, but I wonder."

"He loved them, Wanda. He told you he did when he was sampling. You've got to understand, at this stage of a film, every-body's jetting all over taking care of this and that. He's probably not even in town."

"No? Ken tells me there's a party at the Statler house tonight, where he's living. They've got special police patrols just to keep out the riffraff, never mind it's a gated community."

"Did you ask Phillip Callander what's going on?"

"He's off somewhere scouting seafood suppliers for the new Dancing Shrimp. Somebody else must be catering."

"Well, Forbes is missing a good bet. Whatever they're serving, it won't be as good as what you'd bake."

The doorbell tinkled, and Tracy turned to find Marsh coming toward her. She didn't blink, and she didn't run, although of the two, the latter was her favorite option. Her stomach started to roll, however. Confrontation ahead, and nowhere to go but right toward it.

"Have a sudden craving for pie?" she asked as nonchalantly as she could manage.

"Sympathy pains. Now that I'm all over my morning sickness."

"Well, have at it." She lifted the stack of boxes and angled her body away from Marsh so she could circle him.

"You'll put these on the rec center account?" she asked Wanda, who was on her way to answer the telephone.

"I'll give 'em to you for free if you two will just stay right here and have your fight so I can watch, once I'm off the phone."

"Sorry . . ." Tracy nodded goodbye to Marsh and started toward the door.

He followed close behind. "What kind of gentleman would I be if I didn't help with those?"

"The kind who reads minds."

"You'd rather stumble and fall, and end up with pie all over the sidewalk?"

"Sounds pretty good to me, considering the alternative." But she stopped, resigned and let him take three of the boxes.

He opened the door so she could precede him. "My car's just down the block," she said.

"I'm parked behind you."

So he had come in looking for a fight? She supposed she couldn't blame him. If he'd left this up to her, the cricket ringtone on his iPhone, the one reserved just for her, would never have chirped again.

They walked in silence. Only when the pies were safely wedged into her backseat did Marsh begin.

"I thought you were going to call."

"Actually it went more like this," she said. "You told me you would wait until I called. I never said I planned to follow through."

"Didn't you?"

"No, I guess you just assumed since that's what you wanted, that's what I'd do."

"More like I assumed that since we're both grown-ups, you'd call once you calmed down

313

and we would work things out."

She opened her mouth to reply, but he held out his hand like a traffic cop. "I'm sorry, Trace. I'm sorry I didn't trust you to tell me you were pregnant once you were ready and went digging for the truth myself. And I'm sorry I didn't tell you I knew, but really? Wanda was right. I hadn't done much to show you your needs were important, too. I just wanted a chance to make that up to you, to do something other than drag you through the swamps for a change."

"At least when you were dragging me through the swamps it was genuine. What part of the new stuff was, and how am I supposed to know?"

"I didn't do one thing I didn't want to. I'm happy being with you anywhere. I just never realized everything we did was all about me."

"I like all the outdoors stuff. I just like a little variety and glamour along with it."

"I know that now."

She could feel her spine unkinking, one vertebra at a time. She had dreaded this discussion. She'd imagined it in her mind, over and over again, and somehow it always ended with Marsh telling her he was sorry they were in this boat together, but he planned to row it his way, thanks, and she'd better jump on board fast or she'd be swimming alone.

"It's not about that, anyway," she said, try-

314

ing to retrieve some of her righteous indignation. "You weren't honest with me."

"And *you* weren't honest with *me,* okay? Or you wouldn't have pretended you had a virus for weeks and weeks, instead of just telling me the test was positive."

He was right, of course. There was nothing to say to that.

He reached out and tucked a strand of hair behind her ear. "Trace, what's the real problem? We both want this baby. We have enough in common to keep us happily occupied. We're great in bed together. You love my son, even though he's not always the most lovable kid on the block. I'm a fine cook, and you love to eat. I don't make a bundle, but I do make enough to keep us happily solvent. I'm a passably good dad, and you'll be a terrific mom. What's the big deal here?"

She dissected his words, looking for something other than all their shared virtues and interests. There wasn't a wisp of emotion interlaced among them.

"So what are you saying?" she asked, probing for more and hoping she'd been wrong. "Where is this leading?"

"Let me rub your back when the baby's feeling ornery and paint your toenails when you can't reach them anymore."

"I can pay people to do that. They have professionals who do it better." She waited.

"Move in with me — with us. Let me take

care of you and be part of all this."

She didn't feel deflated, because her expectations had been low. But she did feel a jab of disappointment. Expectations low, hope just a tad too high. Move in with Marsh and let him watch the fun from a safe emotional distance.

"I can take care of myself," she said. "I think I've proved that. I've got some financial problems, sure, but I'll find a way out of them or sell Happiness Key if I'm forced to. Physically I'm fit, and my job's guaranteed after my maternity leave's over. Gladys is talking about instituting a real day care now that the nursery renovations are all done. The baby can be right at the center with me. And I've got great neighbors, as you know."

"And what about me?"

"Once he's weaned —"

"He? You know this is a boy?"

"No, it's too early. That happens at the next ultrasound, if I decide I want to know. I just think it's a boy, that's all."

"Weaned?"

"I'm going to breast-feed. It's better. But once he's on a bottle or solid food, you can have him for longer periods. I won't keep him away from you. We can work out joint custody if you want."

"You've obviously thought a lot about this."

"And why wouldn't I? This was a huge surprise for me, and for you, too. But all those *hormones* don't keep my brain from processing information, Marsh. Neither of us asked for this, but that doesn't mean we can't turn it into a good thing. Things are different now, and we just have to go with that, right?"

He looked perplexed; then even that disappeared and there was no emotion on his face at all. "So I gather my offer's been turned down."

"What offer was that? The toenails? The back rub?"

"Moving into my house."

For just a moment she hesitated and tried to imagine it. Living with Marsh, seeing him morning and night. Helping raise his son, then their son — or daughter. Looking like a family. Acting like a family.

Never really becoming one.

They had drifted together after one bad marriage apiece. She knew she didn't want more of the same, and now Marsh wasn't even offering that much. Move in with him. Pretend they were together. Look happy for the sake of the kids.

"I'll pass," she said. "I'll be fine where I am, but I won't shut you out of the pregnancy again. This *is* your baby, you're right. You deserve to be informed and involved."

"Informed and involved." He nodded, as if the words were foreign to him.

"Look, why don't you come to the ultrasound, if you want to be part of things? My

317

next appointment's in three weeks. I'll text you the date and time."

He was silent for so long that she thought she'd offended him by asking, but at last he nodded. "I'd like that."

"Great. And now I've got to get back before the pies melt. So we're good? All settled?"

"Just as comfortable as an old sneaker."

She wanted to shake him, but she smiled brightly. "I'll let you know if anything exciting happens in the meantime."

"You do that."

He was still standing there when she drove away. No longer smiling or even hungry, she wondered if Marsh was silently celebrating his good luck at dodging the moving-in-together bullet, or simply thinking about the next thing on his long list for the day now that he had crossed off "Talk to Tracy about our kid." Whichever it was, she hoped he developed a good case of heartburn to go with it.

Wanda wouldn't have abandoned Maggie and left her to finish pies and handle customers by herself that afternoon if just anybody had asked for her help. But the man asking was the new household manager, calling on behalf of Derek Forbes, and he'd frantically informed Wanda that when Forbes discovered that the menu for tonight's party didn't include Wanda's pies, he had nearly lost his job.

Wanda had graciously offered to send over what she had on hand, but Zippy — and Wanda was sure no sane mother had named this man Zippy — begged her to come to the lavish Statler mansion herself and make the pies right there. Mr. Forbes had mentioned how much he'd like that to happen. Mr. Forbes had said he might come down and help.

Wanda had been hooked immediately. By Derek's enthusiasm for her pies. By the promise of cooking in the perfect kitchen where in May she had deposited pies for a party and sworn that, in heaven, she would have that exact setup. By the possible assistance of Fabulous Forbes himself. Heck, she would bake pies in a third-floor walk-up smack on the border of two warring drug lords if Derek Forbes was going to be there to help.

The Statler house was in the most exclusive gated community in Palmetto Grove. At the gatehouse, Wanda gave her name to the guard, who waved her through immediately without even checking his clipboard. The waterfront Mediterranean-style home didn't look as if it had fallen on hard times, although the former owner, Edward Statler, certainly had. One of the very banks he had tried to defraud had foreclosed on the house with both haste and relish. From what Wanda knew, the bank was now making whatever money it could by leasing it to high-ticket clients while loan officials scoured Florida to find somebody who could afford to own it. This made sense to her, since the two-story house spread out over the gargantuan lot and looked to be as large as most motels and a bunch fancier, to boot.

She sat behind the wheel of her six-year-old Japanese sedan and imagined what it would be like to actually belong here, maybe to be coming home from an exhausting afternoon of manicures, massages and martinis. She would have a Lilly Pulitzer shopping bag on the seat beside her . . . no, the store would have anything she bought delivered, of course. What was she thinking? Maybe a little blue box from Tiffany & Company. Something she could carry in her Gucci purse, a big one, like the one she'd seen in a photo of Halle Berry. Even bigger, maybe.

Or she could just be little ol' her, trotting inside to bake pies for her favorite movie star.

Wanda could feel herself grinning so wide, her back teeth felt a zing from the air conditioner.

She got out and crossed the marble courtyard, two well-washed canvas bags from some forensics seminar Ken had attended slung over her arms. While Zippy had promised she would have everything she could possibly need right here, she didn't trust the man. She had her favorite pastry mat, crust shields and double-sided pastry cutter, and her new fancy-schmancy silicone rolling pin. She still used her well-seasoned, tried-and-true maple one more often, but the silicone wasn't half bad, either. She was superstitious about the maple one, though, because her mother had given it to her, and she never took it any-where, just in case.

The door opened before she got to it, and a little bald man with huge red glasses and a tie hanging loosely over a white T-shirt leaped forward to hug her.

"You came! I told myself you would. Told myself and told myself, but —"

"Zippy," she said, trying to wriggle free, "I presume?"

"Zippy, here," he agreed, releasing her. "Let me get your bags. Let me get you a drink. Let me get down on my knees and kiss your pretty toenails."

"Not necessary," she said, leaving out the part where she would kick him in the nose if he dared try. "You get all the ingredients I told you to?"

"Double. Triple. I bought everything in the store that looked like it could be baked in a pie."

"Well, that ought to be interesting. Got me those blackbirds I asked for, too?"

Zippy chortled. "I like you already. I'll show

you to the kitchen."

"Been here before, so I know the way. Made pie for a party here back in the spring."

"Weren't they the lucky folks!" Zippy was practically chirping.

"Your boss at home?"

Zippy started toward the kitchen. Apparently the Statlers had moved out but their heavy dark furniture and elegant Oriental carpets had refused to go with them. The house was much as Wanda remembered it.

"Not yet, but he will be," Zippy said. "And he'll be in a much better mood if he finds you here. He was unhappy with me. But how was I to know the man's completely addicted to pie in general and yours in particular? I mean, I had a pastry chef making cupcakes, all kinds of cupcakes. That's all people are eating these —" He seemed to realize his mistake. "With the exception of your wonderful pies," he went on smoothly after the hiccup. "And, of course, we only want the very best for this party. Everyone who's anyone in this part of Florida will be here. But it won't be o-*ver*-whelming. Just the cream of the crop, the best of the —"

"Got it," Wanda said. "And ten pies will do?"

"It was too late to cancel the cupcakes, so yes, that will be perfect. We'll put them in the front. Plate the slices beautifully. Guest list is seventy-five or so, and you know women.

They'll drool themselves silly, but they won't eat dessert in public."

Wanda's head was beginning to throb. Any woman who was afraid to be caught eating pie was a woman in need of a brain transplant.

The kitchen really was a stunner. She hadn't blown the memory out of proportion. Stainless-steel appliances and dark cabinets lined the walls. A sun-dappled granite island the length of a canoe divided the kitchen, and over it, a skylight provided natural light, filtered gently through glass shelves that had held pots of herbs when the house was constantly occupied. Now the shelves were sparkling clean but empty.

"Nice, huh?" Zippy said, watching her face. "The best of everything, but I don't think it's been used very much. Does that seem fair to you?"

"Life's just full of stuff like this," Wanda said. "Bet they never used their swimming pool, either."

"Derek certainly uses it. Bring your suit to the party. He's determined to get people in the water. He'll throw them in if he has to."

She turned. "Me?"

"Didn't I mention that?" Zippy looked stunned. He slapped his own cheek. "Tell me I told you Derek insists you come tonight. Insists! Please, please, tell me I told you that!"

She just stared at him. "Me?"

"I was so upset about the pies. I was so worried you'd say no." Zippy looked as if he was about to burst into tears. "I can't believe this. Tell me you'll be there. Bring a friend, a lover, a husband, but come!"

"Me?"

"Who else?" The question was not Zippy's. The voice was lower, warmer, less affected. Derek Forbes came into the room. "So Zippo managed to get you here. He can be persuasive when he remembers." He glanced at Zippy, but not with rancor. "He's excitable, aren't you, Zip?"

"She's here and she's coming tonight, right?" Zippy's expression was pleading as he stared at her.

"Sure. Of course," Wanda said. "Wouldn't miss it."

Derek walked over and kissed her cheek. Then he rested his hands on her shoulders. "You really are priceless, you know? And now, let's make pies."

"Let's, as in let us, as in you and me?"

"Why'd you think I wanted you to come *here* instead of making them at the shop? I need lessons. I need instruction. I need Wanda Gray."

"You planning to get that shirt all covered with flour?"

"Want me to take it off?"

For a moment she couldn't move or speak.

Then he laughed. "Zippo, find me an apron."

"Good idea," she said, having discovered her lungs still worked. "And wash your hands good. You and me are about to turn pie into an art form right here in God's favorite kitchen, Mr. Forbes."

"Deke," he said. "Everyone I love calls me Deke."

She smiled and felt that zing on her back teeth again. "You got it . . . Deke."

CHAPTER SIXTEEN

Janya hung up the telephone just as someone knocked at her door. Behind her, from the children's bedroom, she heard the rhythmic thump of a tennis ball hitting the wall. The thumping had been nonstop for half an hour, and she hoped the arrival of company would convince Vijay to do something else. Nothing she had suggested had worked, and she sensed another tantrum in the offing if she took away the ball. Tantrums were frequent now, and increasingly hard to manage, and today she preferred the coward's way out. Lily was happily working on a plastic bowl of diced fruit at the little play table Rishi had bought and installed for her in the corner, seemingly oblivious to the noise.

Wanda and Tracy were waiting on the doorstep and came right in as soon as the door swung open. Tracy was still in shorts and a loose top, but Wanda was wearing black capris and a matching linen shirt.

"She's a basket case," Tracy announced.

"We're here for a consultation."

Since Wanda herself had called just minutes before, Janya knew the story. Wanda had been invited to Derek's impromptu pool party, and since Ken was working late that night, Tracy had been tapped to go with her.

"I am to be the fashion consultant?" Janya asked.

"More like the critic," Wanda said. "More like the one to tell Ms. Deloche that she can't mess with my image and make me over."

"No makeover in the works," Tracy said. "We're just going to fix your hair and makeup. The outfit works great, and I have some jewelry we can use to brighten it even more. Janya does, too. And maybe one of her gorgeous scarves? I remember something turquoise and silver."

"When I invited you to be my date at the party, I didn't know you were going to take the night so seriously!" Wanda said.

Janya knew Wanda well enough to realize this was all part of her act. In reality, Wanda was delighted Tracy and Janya were going to help her prepare.

"We'll sit you down at the table and work on the hair a little," Tracy said.

"My hairdresser's on vacation. How could she do this to me?" Wanda frowned. "What is that god-awful noise? You got a woodpecker in a birdcage?"

"Vijay."

"Where is he?" Wanda demanded.

Janya nodded to the bedroom.

Wanda pursed her lips, then she rummaged through a polka-dot handbag the size of Nebraska and pulled out a spiral notepad and three different pens. Without another word she marched into the bedroom. Janya watched from the doorway.

"Hello, Vijay. You stop that noise this minute, you hear?"

Vijay looked up, his eyes suspicious.

"I got a job for you," Wanda said matter-of-factly. "I need a book to read tonight, and I don't have time to go to the store and buy me one. So I want you to write one for me. Write about anything you want, you hear? Just make it interesting. You don't know how to write, just draw me some pictures. Got it?" She picked up the tennis ball and walked out.

"Now, let's get down to business," she told the other women.

Janya waited in the doorway for a moment to see what Vijay would do. He threw himself facedown on the floor, and she waited for the tantrum to begin. Instead, he just lay there, inert, and after a moment she left him in hopes of his getting a little rest before the next assault.

"Things not going any better?" Tracy asked softly. She had Lily balanced on one hip and was feeding her a melon cube.

Janya shook her head. "His therapist says it will take much time. But it is so difficult just to get him into her office, I am not sure we do anyone a service by trying."

Tracy handed her charge a grape. "Any news?"

Janya lowered her voice so Vijay couldn't hear it. "The social worker just called. She says they have found one set of grandparents."

"And?"

"She would say nothing else except that they are still searching for the second."

"Have you spoken to an attorney?"

"Rishi has engaged one. She believes we have a case for keeping them. Rishi is an American citizen, and I soon will be. The children were born here, and the grandparents refused all contact."

"But it's not a slam dunk," Tracy said, aptly reading between the lines.

"It will not be simple."

"And that's all this social worker said?" Wanda asked.

"I inquired if I could get into the Duttas' apartment to collect the rest of the children's toys and clothes. She said she believed that could be arranged, since the police have been and gone. The rent has been paid for another month. I think they will be most comfortable with as many familiar things around them as we can provide."

"You take Maggie with you if you get in," Wanda said. "She'll want to see that apartment."

Tracy handed Lily to Janya and motioned to the dining table. "Okay, let's see what we can do to make you Hollywood gorgeous," she told Wanda.

Wanda complained; Tracy ignored her; Janya ran interference. They did this so well and had so many months of practice behind them that the roles felt natural. Forty minutes later — and just sixty before the party was to begin — Tracy stepped back.

"I don't wear my hair down," Wanda said flatly. "Makes me look dumpy and old as a Studebaker."

"What's a Studebaker?" Tracy asked.

"I rest my case."

"I spent the first decades of my life learning how to be gorgeous and snag a man. Look in the bathroom mirror first, before you show Vijay how to have a real tantrum."

Janya and Tracy looked at each other as they waited for the shriek of indignation from the bathroom. Tracy had loosely pinned up part of Wanda's hair, but she'd left the back down and curled a few wisps around her friend's face. Gone was the trademark layered eye shadow, in its place two shades of a soft gray, with Wanda's eyes outlined in a warm brown. The lipstick Tracy had chosen was peachy and clear, and her friend's cheeks

330

glowed peach, as well.

"One, two, three . . ." Tracy counted slowly.

Janya smiled.

Wanda returned. "Well, it's different."

"Definitely," Janya said. "And different is good for a party."

"You like it," Tracy said, nodding. "I can tell. You aren't cursing."

"I am a lady."

"And you are a lovely lady at that," Tracy said. "You deserve diamond earrings. We'll go back to my house, and you can take your pick of all my jewelry. The feds left me a few nice things when they put CJ in prison. I'll wear what you don't."

"I will get a scarf." Janya returned with the one Tracy had remembered, and another that was black with a gold-filigree design laced through it and a long fringe with gold beads.

"You really think I could pull this off?" Wanda asked, running the filmy scarf along her wrist. "You're the exotic type, not me."

"In India, *you* would be exotic. Pretend you are in India tonight."

Wanda gave her a quick hug. "Off to make a fool of myself. Come on, Ms. Deloche. We might as well try those diamonds."

Janya was still smiling ten minutes later when Vijay came out of his bedroom. Lily was lying on her back on the floor, playing with a rag doll, and Vijay had to walk around her. He was clutching the notebook Wanda had given him and forgotten to take back with her.

Janya squatted so they were eye to eye, something the therapist had said might help bring him out of his shell. She had become accustomed to one-sided conversations with the little boy, who was silent most of the time, except when he was screaming.

"Miss Wanda went home. Did you write a book for her? We can take it to her house."

Vijay held it out, which surprised her. She took it and nodded seriously. Then she paged through and found six pages filled with childish scribbles, but there were recognizable letters, as well.

"Why, Vijay, you write very well." She nodded again. "Miss Wanda will be happy."

"I want to write a real book."

For a moment she was so surprised by an entire sentence that she didn't know what to say. "Do you?" she asked after she recovered. "Do you need more paper?"

He shook his head angrily. She considered. "Do you need a little help?"

He nodded so hard she thought he might fall over.

"I can help if you wish," she said. "It does not surprise me you are a writer, because your father was a wonderful writer himself."

"Now," he said fiercely.

"Of course." She sat on the floor beside Lily and crossed her legs. "What shall I do?"

332

"You write. I will talk."

"Good. We can get started." She turned to a fresh sheet of paper and waited.

The little boy was silent for a long time. Janya began to wonder if he had changed his mind.

"Once there were very bad parents," he said at last. "They ran away and left their children."

Through a mist of tears, Janya carefully printed Vijay's words.

Tracy remembered when parties like the one at the Statler mansion had been a normal part of her life. She knew how to dress, who to talk to, how much to drink and how little to eat. The last two rules were irrelevant tonight. She was drinking sparkling water and eating everything in sight. The food was fabulous — not the least of it Wanda's pies — and the water kept her cool, since she was not about to get into the pond-size infinity pool where some of the other guests were splashing and playing.

Derek Forbes had greeted her warmly and laughed when she reminded him of the party back in California. Then he'd dragged Wanda off to meet his friends, and for almost two hours Tracy had wandered and chatted and nibbled until she was finally full.

Now she stood in the shadows of the house admiring the twinkling lights that adorned the shrubbery and palms, and the jazz quartet that was playing just loudly enough at the edge of the patio. She was growing tired, and she imagined Wanda was even more so. Adulation could be wearing.

"I thought I recognized you," said a male voice.

She turned to find Blake Armstrong beside her. "You're Marsh's friend," he said.

Since Maggie had mentioned their dates, she knew more about Blake than he probably knew about her. She doubted Marsh had mentioned her at all. She put on a smile, gratified that he remembered their brief encounter.

"Yes, Marsh's friend," she said, and wondered if that could be said now. "And wow, do you look different."

He seemed surprised. "Do I?"

She touched her hair in emphasis. "You were pretty shaggy last time I saw you. Long hair. On your way to a full beard." Blake had curly hair, which a lot of men cropped nearly to their scalps for easy management. But now his was beautifully cut and styled, and she told him so.

"The shaggy look wasn't the one I needed for this job, that's for sure. Just takes a good barber and a little bit of gel." He rippled his hands over his head in demonstration.

"Maybe we could convince Marsh to give your guy a try."

"I'm guessing Marsh might cut his hair for a big donation to Wild Florida, but not for any other reason."

She was more or less partial to Marsh's ponytail; in fact, at the moment, she was more partial to the ponytail than the man. She laughed at the suggestion, and they chatted about the party and the food.

"So how's the bridge going?" she asked. "When do you break ground? Or is that even what they call it when you're building in the water?"

"Works for me. There's a lot to do in advance, so we won't start construction until well after hurricane season ends. I'll be more or less part of the scenery for some time to come."

She wondered how Maggie felt about that. Her newest tenant walked a fine line between sharing her life and keeping the truly intimate parts to herself. Tracy liked Maggie and enjoyed their conversations, but she was always aware that Maggie kept secrets.

"Might be here even longer," Blake said when she didn't pick up the conversational gambit. "If one of those tropical depressions brewing off the coast of Africa strengthens and turns this way."

"Tropical storms?"

"Nothing to worry about now, but you don't keep track?"

Tracy felt a little foolish. But she wasn't going to list the topics that were uppermost in her mind these days, not to a friend of Marsh's. "I confess I don't," she said. "I figure when the cops come knocking on my door to tell me to evacuate, I can pack anything of value and cross the bridge in fifteen minutes. The advantage of being poor."

"I'm surprised Marsh doesn't keep an eye out. Hurricanes wreak havoc on the things he holds most dear."

The things Marsh held most dear. Alligators. Swamps. Barrier islands. "Pretty much anything that doesn't shave its legs," she said.

"Ouch."

"Forgive me. Marsh and I have our ups and downs."

"The path of romance. Never easy."

"Sounds like you know what you're talking about."

"Had a long-term relationship that went kaput right before I moved here. That's what the scruffy look was all about. I did the human-vegetable thing for a while, just to recoup."

"Did you? Recoup?"

"I now consider myself lucky to be rid of her."

She wondered if she would ever feel that way about Marsh. Of course, she would have a lifelong walking, talking reminder of her failed love affair. Better make that "affair" and leave out the love.

"So how bad are these tropical depressions?" she asked, to change the subject.

"Not bad enough to be on everybody's lips at the moment. I'm just a tad sensitive, since if any of them hit southwest Florida very hard, we'll have to make changes in our plans to accommodate any and all alterations in the landscape. Roads could get washed out and so forth. Lots to delay us."

"I can see why you worry."

"And I can see why Marsh is so crazy about you." He rested his hand on her shoulder for a moment. "Figure out what the problem is and fix it. The two of you are a nice fit."

She smiled, despite every inclination to tell him to talk to his friend, not her, and watched him melt into the crowd to shake more hands.

Tracy was glad when Wanda found her a few minutes later, because her feet were beginning to hurt, and she was tired of talking to strangers. She'd been having an internal conversation in which the old Tracy tried to explain to the current Tracy why parties filled with chatting strangers were actually fun. Not having come up with a good reason, she was afraid she looked disgruntled, but Wanda was too elated to notice. She glowed, and not from anything Tracy had done with foundation and blush.

"That man introduced me to everybody. I never heard so many compliments. Of course, it doesn't hurt that he helped make the pies. That's what it's all about. Everybody loves Deke. That's what I'm supposed to call him. Everybody wants to go along with anything the man says or does."

"How much help was he?" Tracy asked.

"He does know his way around a kitchen. He cooks to relax. But he's not much of a baker. He chops fruit pretty good, and he whips cream like he knows what he's doing."

"You made Derek Forbes do the dirty work?"

Wanda lifted a brow. "Was there someone else in that kitchen who should have done it?"

"Next you'll get out the dominatrix outfit and brandish the whip."

Wanda put her hand on her chest. "Be still my heart!"

"What does Ken think about all this?"

"I stuck it out with Ken when times were tough. He says he can stick it out with me when times are plush. Besides, the man knows he's king. I just wish he could be here to see this. Closest I ever thought I'd get to a party like this one was delivering pies through the back door."

Tracy felt better. She was happy to witness Wanda basking in her own success.

The man in charge of who basked and who didn't approached. Tonight Derek Forbes was wearing a flowered silk shirt that Tracy could tell had been hand tailored for a perfect fit. She was always suspicious of actors, since assuming the personalities of others was what they did best, but she thought it was possible Derek Forbes was exactly the man he seemed. Larger than life, audacious, kind.

"Good, you found your friend," he told Wanda. "I wanted her to hear this, too. Wanda, I'm getting deluged with raves about our pies from all my film friends. Everybody's asking if you've got shops in other towns."

"Me?" She gave a delighted laugh. "I've got enough problems paying what little staff I have and my suppliers. What would I open another shop with? Flour and graham crackers?"

"You're not thinking big. You've got a great product. Pie could be the next cupcake. One minute nobody even thinks cupcake, the next every main street of every small town in America has a shop. And we know how much better pie is, right? Pie like you make, anyway, not that sacrilege from the grocery store. Did anybody's grandmother make cupcakes? No, that's something a harried mother makes with a mix and takes to her kid's school on his birthday, so little John and Jill Classmate don't fight over the size of their pieces. But pie? That's America, that's our heritage, that's our grandmother in the kitchen with a checkered apron and a rolling pin!" As if he realized he'd said enough for the moment, he stopped. "I know this is a little overwhelming."

Wanda was staring blankly at him. "You think I ought to open more shops? *Me?*"

He glanced at Tracy. "She doesn't really think like this, does she? That she's just ordinary, that she can't be a star."

"I think I'm just going to get her home," Tracy said, watching her friend growing paler. "She's had a big night and a long day."

"More Wanda's Wonderful Pies?" Wanda asked again.

"You could start small. Open a shop in Naples or Miami. I have contacts. You could talk to my business manager."

When Wanda didn't speak, Tracy repeated herself. "I think I'm going to get her home."

Derek gave Wanda a spontaneous hug, then stepped back. "I had a great time with you this afternoon. We'll do it again." He smiled at Tracy and left.

"Do it again?" Wanda said. "And he thinks I'll live to tell about it?"

"Let's get you home. You're ready, right?"

"I was never here. I'm going to wake up any second."

Tracy put her arm around her friend's shoulders and led her toward the house. "Well, let's make sure you do it in your own bed, okay?"

"I figured all this was too good to be true. I'm going to wake up with Chase slobbering all over my pillow and Ken snoring beside me."

"I was ready to go anyway. I don't think I'm a party girl anymore."

"It was a good one, though, wasn't it?"

"It was."

"You remember all the details so you can tell me in case I wake up."

CHAPTER SEVENTEEN

Tracy missed Marsh's cooking. Okay, she missed more than his cooking, but she was trying to keep everything else in perspective, or better yet, deeply buried, where it was less disturbing. But the cooking? Every meal was a reminder of what she could be eating if she just moved in with him. So, regularly, three times a day, she was reminded of the relationship she'd ended, as well as Marsh's fried catfish, his sautéed greens, his peach cobbler. From the man, and from Wanda, she had learned to love food. Having them cook for her when she dieted had been no real gift. But now that she was pregnant? Now that she should catch back up on the calories morning sickness had heartlessly stolen? Now that her obstetrician had told her to eat everything healthy that appealed to her?

How fair was that?

"Clearly you're on the road to a healthy pregnancy," Maggie said as Tracy helped herself to another serving of Janya's basmati rice.

"Making up for lost time," Wanda said, pushing a dish of potatoes and spinach fragrant with ginger and turmeric in Tracy's direction. "You sure all this spicy food's a good idea?"

"Nothing here's on the list of things I need to watch out for."

"I remember when I was pregnant," Alice said dreamily. She paused to form the next sentence. "I ate potato salad with every meal . . . for a month."

Tracy had noted a change in Alice. She was pausing less, talking more. The color had returned to her cheeks since she'd begun teaching at the rec center. Her snowflake class was popular, and she'd agreed to teach shawl making after the holidays. Meantime, she was at the core of a regular group of women at the center who were working on an afghan for a fundraising raffle. Alice had turned Olivia's difficult schedule into a plus by spending the hours she had to wait in town for her granddaughter into activities at the center and a new set of friends. She had even joined the shuffleboard team, and, from all reports, they were glad to have her.

Tracy had to say, she was proud, as well as worried. Now when Olivia was at the center waiting for her grandmother to finish an activity, she camped in Tracy's office to do homework. Tracy loved having her there, but Olivia's revelations about school, sports and friends worried her just a little. What was Alice missing, and was that Tracy's own fault for enjoying Olivia so much?

"I wanted chocolate," Wanda said. "Didn't matter how I got it. IV hookup would have been fine by me."

"I'm just craving food in general." Tracy took just a bit more of the potatoes. Once the baby came, she would probably want to regain her figure, although at the moment, the reason why evaded her. What man would be looking for a single mother with a time-consuming job and a massive amount of debt? Who besides Marsh? And even *his* interest was questionable. She reached for another spoonful of potatoes, a larger one this time.

"I am eating more, too," Janya said. "I run after the children all day, and in the evening, when Rishi comes home, I work on the mural at the yacht club. It is small, and they are patient, but it must be finished. The work makes me hungry."

"You should have let me host dinner at my house," Maggie said. "You have so much on your plate right now, and it's past time I did it."

Janya looked puzzled, and she glanced down at her place setting. "I have very little on my plate. I seem to have eaten it all."

"It's an expression," Tracy said. "Means you're busy. Your schedule is too full."

Janya smiled. "Oh, no, this was a pleasure. And Vijay helped me make the aloo palak. He helped me measure and stir. He is a wonder in the kitchen, and understands numbers and even, I think, fractions." She smiled in the direction of the little boy, who was entertaining his sister by rolling a ball for her to catch and roll back.

Tracy had noticed that Vijay seemed marginally more at home now than he had the week before. He was interacting with his sister, and so far there had been no sign of a tantrum, even after Lily knocked down a block city he had built to entertain her. The little boy didn't smile, and his conversation had been limited to a "hello" without eye contact, but she thought Janya and Rishi were making progress.

"Well, I got news to share," Wanda said, "and it's not about my weight, which suits me just fine even if I am closing in on a size sixteen. Ms. Deloche and I went to a party at Derek's house, as you all know, but what you don't know is that he thinks I ought to open more pie shops. He thinks I'm that good. I like to have dropped my teeth, even if they are still attached to my jaw, the way teeth are meant to be."

Everybody made all the appropriate noises. Maggie was the first to move beyond them.

"But you're not going to," she said, clearly in the know. "Because even one shop's a lot to handle."

"She's right," Wanda told the others. "But it's a kick, somebody like Deke thinking I'm that good. You know how many years I had to live to hear something like that?"

"Don't let her fool you," Maggie said. "The family heaps praise on her at every turn. Where do you think this ego comes from?"

The front door opened, and Rishi walked in. Lily clapped her tiny hands when she caught sight of him, and Vijay stopped rolling the ball. He didn't get up to go to Rishi, but he looked interested — another good sign, Tracy thought.

"I apologize for being late," Rishi said after greeting them.

"I have explained that your secretary is sick," Janya said. "Have you eaten?"

"Yes, at my desk, and now it is time for ice cream with my favorite children." He approached them slowly, as if he knew that Vijay needed time to make this transition. Janya had told Tracy the little boy had problems moving from one thing to the other now, as if every change was a reminder of all the other changes in his life.

Rishi squatted on the floor beside Vijay. "I am thinking that an ice-cream cone would taste good now, and I wonder if you think so, too?"

Vijay seemed to consider. No one at the table spoke, aware that leaving the house with Rishi, like so many things in the little boy's life now, was something new and untried.

He finally gave a brief nod. Rishi smiled and got to his feet. "Is Lily ready?"

Tracy got up before Janya could. "Let me check her diaper while you put Vijay in the car. I need the practice. Janya, stay here and entertain your guests."

Janya looked grateful, and Tracy scooped up the baby and took her into the children's tiny room, where a foam pad on a low dresser served as a changing table. Tracy was becoming adept at this and accomplished the diaper change quickly, with the help of a musical mobile above the dresser. Then she straightened the little girl's embroidered skirt and pulled on her socks and shoes, since the nights were finally cooler. She zipped up a hoodie and stood Lily on the table to look her over. Satisfied, she whisked her back into the living area.

"This okay?" She held the child out for inspection.

Everybody cooed. Tracy grabbed the diaper bag, a rag doll and a book for the ride, and met Rishi on the front doorstep as he came back for the little girl.

"She's all yours."

He smiled, and Tracy thought how nice he looked. Rishi wasn't a handsome man, but he had made changes in his appearance, and he was definitely more attractive. He looked particularly nice tonight, in his dark jacket and white dress shirt.

She said as much when she joined the women at the table again. "And he's awfully good with those kids, too. He was singing to Lily when he drove away."

Janya smiled. "He is growing very attached to both of them. Vijay misses his father most of all, and Rishi is finding little ways to help."

"What's Rishi doing to his hair that's so different?" Wanda asked. "It looks good."

"A good cut and a little gel." Janya moved her hands over her head in explanation. "Harit convinced him to try it that way. He had many talents."

Everyone was silent as they worked on their dinners, until Wanda put her fork down. "Well, that's as good a lead-in as any, I guess. Now that the children are gone for a while . . . Maggie, you got anything to tell Janya and the rest of us about the investigation?"

Tracy thought Maggie looked the way she must have throughout her adolescence whenever Wanda asked a question she didn't want to answer. But she put down her fork, too. "I've been talking to everybody I can think of. I even went to the barbershop to see if they would trim my hair —"

"No way!" Tracy put a hand over her heart.

"Don't worry, every strand's safe. It's a real

male bastion. They didn't even like me walking through the door. The only woman in there was watching her little boy get a Mohawk."

"Did you find out anything anyway?" Wanda asked.

"I told them who I was, and that I was concerned Harit might be cast as a murderer before all the evidence was in. The owner said it was pretty clear what Harit did, and that nobody there wanted to talk about it anymore."

"Did he say anything about the other customers?" Janya asked. "The ones Harit was seeing in their houses?"

Maggie explained that piece of information to the others. "Rishi thinks Harit was going to some of his customers' homes to cut their hair. They paid extra and tipped well, and his family needed the money."

"I can tell you no boss would like that," Wanda said. "Be like one of my employees going off to bake pies using my contacts and recipes."

"Maybe not quite as bad, but you're right, the owner didn't like it," Maggie said. "I asked about Harit's regulars, and he just shrugged. Then I asked about the others, because I had to. I could tell it wasn't a surprise to him. I would guess that's why he doesn't care if we clear Harit's name. He's angry Harit went out on his own. But he told *me* whatever I'd heard about private clients was wrong. And that was that."

"*That* is never *that* with you," Wanda said.

Maggie didn't dispute it. "I parked across the street and talked to everybody who came and went for the rest of the afternoon. The guy who gave that kid the Mohawk came out about an hour before they closed, and I talked to him. He said after Harit disappeared, the owner discovered what he'd been doing because some guy called and said Harit had missed a private appointment. I told him I wanted to talk to Harit's personal customers, but he said he didn't know who they were, only that Harit attracted the pickiest ones. He said Harit got the guys who thought they were too good for the old-fashioned stuff."

"I can get them for you," Wanda said. "Those names. Could have days ago, if you'd just told me."

Maggie looked skeptical. "I don't think anybody knows who they were, Mom."

"I can get them." Wanda stood up. "Mind if I use the phone in your kitchen?" she asked Janya, who nodded. "I'll need something to write on, since ol' Vijay still has my notepad."

The two women went into the other room, but Janya returned in a minute. Wanda's voice was low and unintelligible in the background. "Vijay is writing a book in Wanda's notepad," Janya explained. "About bad parents who leave their children and never come back. We work on it together."

Everybody was silent.

"I think it might be helping," Janya said. "His therapist is encouraged. He is talking more, and his story grows more complicated. Yesterday the little boy went in search of his father and encountered a bear. But the bear was kind. I think the bear is Rishi."

"I'm glad a therapist is working with him, but what's going on with their social worker?" Tracy asked.

"She keeps the facts to herself, and right now she is on vacation," Janya said, and Tracy detected frustration in her friend's voice. "But she has made arrangements for us to get into the Duttas' apartment next week to collect the children's things. For that I am grateful."

"I'd like to go with you," Maggie said.

"I thought you might. I asked if I could bring a neighbor to help sort and carry, and she said yes, but she will need to be with us while we are there, which is why we can't go sooner."

"Bummer," Tracy said.

"Maybe I can still look around a little," Maggie said.

Wanda returned at that moment. "Got it."

"Got what?" Maggie asked.

"That list of customers Harit was visiting on the sly. Now, ask me how I did it."

"How did you do it?" they chorused.

"One of my best customers manages the shop, you know, answers the phone, keeps the appointment book, gets equipment fixed, assigns the walk-ins to operators. The owner's hardly ever there, so he was probably being honest when he said he doesn't know anything that would help. Seymour pretty much runs the place."

"Wow," Maggie said. "Seymour. Now I'm embarrassed. As the barber I talked to was leaving, he called something over his shoulder like 'see more next week.' I couldn't figure out what he thought I ought to see, so I was planning to go back and talk to him again."

"Well, Seymour just got back from a cruise. Could have saved you some trouble."

"Stop gloating. Seymour gave you a list?"

"I promised him a whole Charleston pie if he did. That's his favorite, and you'll be making it tomorrow." Wanda handed the paper to Maggie. "And here's how he knows who Harit was seeing on the sly. Turns out Harit figured what the shop should be paid for each customer he saw and turned money over to Seymour to add to the till. Honest to a fault, it sounds like. That way he figured he wasn't hurting anybody by working on his own time and keeping the bigger tips for himself. He and Seymour kinda kept the arrangement to themselves, just in case the owner didn't like it. Harit had begun to see eight men in private, at least those were the ones Seymour knew about or remembers. Harit settled with him at the end of the month."

Tracy thought Harit's honesty was another sign he was an unlikely murderer. "Eight haircuts a month doesn't sound like a lot of extra money."

"Rishi did say that Harit was encouraged by the money he was saving," Janya said.

"Let's say he charged seventy-five dollars to go to somebody's house and cut their hair on *their* time," Wanda guessed. "Sound right?"

"So much?" Janya asked.

"When I was rich and bored, I used to drop a hundred just for a trim at my favorite salon in Bel-Air," Tracy said. "Men's cuts were cheaper, but they started at, like, forty-five, and that was right there at the shop."

"And Harit was more a stylist than a barber," Maggie said. "So let's say seventy-five because he traveled to their homes, and he gave maybe, what, twenty to the shop as their share? That's fifty-five, plus a tip of, say, twenty more?"

"I think you're way out there," Wanda said, "but if you're right, that's six hundred dollars a month extra."

"Three hundred would have made a difference to his family," Janya said.

Maggie scanned the list. "No names I've seen before, but I haven't seen much of anything so far. It's not like the case files are

353

in my possession."

"Are you going to check them out?" Tracy asked.

"Definitely. Maybe Harit talked while he cut hair and somebody remembers something I can follow up on."

"You don't sound all that hopeful."

"Ninety-nine percent of the leads a cop chases down in an investigation come to nothing. But it's a place to start."

Something had been nagging at Tracy, something the conversation about haircuts and stylists, as opposed to barbers, had triggered. Now it came to her, and she pushed back from the table to get more comfortable.

"You know what? Let me see that list." She studied it after Maggie handed it to her; then she frowned. "Okay, this is wrong. He's not here."

"What?" Maggie asked. "Who's not there?"

"Blake Armstrong. Of course, if he had been, you would have recognized his name, so I guess I should have figured that out."

"Why did you think he should be here?" Maggie retrieved the paper.

Tracy put her hands over her head and wiggled them. " 'A good haircut and a little gel.' What Janya said Rishi learned from Harit. I saw Blake at Derek's party, and I commented on his hair, which is curly, like Rishi's. He told me virtually the same thing, made the same wiggly motion. I thought maybe Harit was his barber, too."

"He's not on the list," Maggie said. "And I told him about the murder-suicide. I probably said Harit's name, and he didn't react. He just seemed sad two strangers had died that way."

"It's possible he never knew the name of the man who cut his hair," Alice said. "Didn't connect them. Men . . . don't pay attention."

"Yes, and if he wasn't a private client," Tracy said, "maybe he just called and said something like, 'Is that Indian barber available at two?' "

"Reduced to our nationality," Janya said as she cleared plates off the table to make room for dessert. "Nameless."

Wanda stood to help. "Because people have trouble remembering names they didn't grow up with. They take the easy way out. I bet in India I'd just be 'that American woman.' "

"Nobody uses 'just' in a sentence with your name in it," Tracy said. "You can bet on that."

"If Alice is right, and Blake didn't make the connection," Maggie said, "then the next time he tries to make an appointment with 'that Indian barber' he'll find out."

"Surely he'll mention it to you if that happens," Tracy said. "Or you can just ask him."

"At least I have something to follow up on," Maggie said.

Tracy doubted her new tenant would admit outright how much she missed her former

355

job, but it seemed clear Maggie wasn't investigating the Duttas' deaths solely to help the Kapurs.

She changed the subject as Wanda left to get her latest creation, the Orange Blossom Special, and bring it to the table. "I've invited Marsh to come to my next doctor's appointment. They'll be doing an ultrasound, and we'll probably be able to tell the baby's sex. Do I want to know? Will that spoil the fun?"

Wanda returned with the pie, which was topped with mounds of whipped cream and mandarin oranges, and Janya set plates and forks beside it. "You asked Marsh to go with you?" Wanda said. "The two of you are back together? This is an announcement?"

"No, I'm just being civilized. Thoughtful."

"You're being stubborn, that's all." Wanda carefully moved slices of pie to plates, and shook her head when they listed to one side. "I'm going to have to work on this one. Doesn't hold its shape."

"If you were managing a bunch of shops, you wouldn't have time to work on recipes," Maggie said, "and why is Tracy being stubborn? Why is everything always the woman's fault?"

"Because she's letting pride get the better of her. You have a problem with a man, you tell him so. You demand some answers. You don't just cut off your nose to spite your face."

Despite herself, Tracy's hand went to her nose, which luckily, was still there. "That's not what I'm doing," Tracy insisted. "You don't *ask* a man if he loves you. If you have to ask —"

"You have to ask," Wanda said. "Anything you really need to know, a man won't bother to tell you. That's how that works. He figures you already know. It started in the Garden of Eden. You think Eve ate that apple 'cause she really wanted to know what was going on in the world? No! She ate it 'cause she forgot to ask Adam what the good Lord had told him. That idiot woman figured if he wanted her to know, he'd have mentioned it. And that serpent? That serpent was just chattering away, all friendly like, and that was a nice change after all those nights with Adam watching the hyenas and the jackals playing football on the Animal Planet. She was desperate for conversation. The apple was just a bonus."

"I think I like Wanda's church . . . better than mine," Alice said.

Everybody laughed, except Maggie. "You're still making everything the woman's fault."

"You know what, Maggie? You and Tracy, you're two of a kind. No wonder the two of you hit if off the way you did. Maybe both of you are afraid to find out what's what with your men, so you figure if you don't ask, you don't have to hear the terrible truth. Only,

357

having tried that myself, it seems to me that what we get is worse than a simple answer would ever be." Wanda held up her hand. "I'm done."

Tracy paused with the first bite of pie halfway to her mouth. "All I asked was whether I should find out my baby's sex at the ultrasound."

"What does Marsh think?" Alice asked.

Tracy shrugged. "I haven't asked him."

No one said a word in response. Together they finished their pie in silence.

CHAPTER EIGHTEEN

Maggie heard her telephone ringing when she was still twenty yards from the front door. She had finally broken down and installed a landline because her cell phone, despite a new battery, was still unreliable, and coverage at her house was spotty. Since she had eighteen months left on the contract with her carrier, she had given up and gone the traditional route so she could avoid dropped calls when she made inquiries about the Duttas.

By the time she picked up the receiver, she was out of breath and certain she would hear a click as her caller gave up. Instead, she heard a familiar voice.

"Mags? I was about to hang up and try your cell again. Did I pull you away from something important?"

Maggie collapsed into the chair beside the phone. "I was having dinner down the road at the Kapurs'. What's up?"

Felo paused. "A lot, as a matter of fact. But

I don't want to go into it on the telephone."

"What's your choice? I'm here, and I assume you're in Miami?"

"No, I'm just down the road, but I'm not bucking for an invitation. I've got to be at work early in the morning, so I need to head back tonight. Any chance you can drive south a little and meet me at a place called Joe's just off 75 outside Pelican Point? It'll take you about forty minutes to get here, but I'm finishing up something anyway."

Maggie was tired. The village of Pelican Point might be in the same county, but forty minutes each way to the middle of nowhere didn't sound appealing. Still, she was interested in the reasons why Felo wasn't coming here if he was that close. Did he regret their last encounter? Was he trying to avoid another? Or was it just that he was trying to save himself a longer drive home?

"What are you doing in this neck of the woods?" she asked, buying a little time.

"Tracking a witness in a case we caught. We're finishing up, and we'll be done by the time you get here, if you come."

"You've got Gary with you?"

"I'll drop him off at the local steak house so we can talk in private."

"I'll be there." She'd said the words before she knew she'd decided.

Fifty minutes later she slid into a booth at Joe's, clearly a popular hangout, since she'd had to leap to get the booth when its previous occupants departed. She thanked a young man with a multitude of tattoos and piercings for clearing away a drained-dry pitcher of beer and half a dozen glasses. He even wiped off the table and brought a fresh basket of pretzels. She figured she'd either been honored or hit on.

Felo arrived ten minutes later, when she was halfway through an anemic mystery brew. One draft tasted just like the others at a place like Joe's.

"Next time, send Gary here and *we'll* do the steak house," she said in greeting as he ignored the seat across from her and slid in beside her.

"Somebody told me Joe's wings are the best in Florida."

"I ate, you go ahead."

Her tattooed conquest shuffled back and took Felo's order; then they were as alone as they could be with Carrie Underwood belting out "American Girl" in the background and standing room only at the bar ten feet away.

"Get what you need from your witness?" she asked.

"He was happy to cooperate after we pointed out we were saving him a trip back to Miami, where his name's on a warrant for three outstanding parking violations."

"So you'll head home after this?"

"Have to. How are things with you?"

She couldn't imagine telling the truth, that whenever she wasn't totally immersed in something else she missed him and their life together so much that more than once she'd had her car keys in her hand, ready to drive to Miami. Instead, now she was immersing herself in the Dutta inquiry to dull that impulse, even though she doubted she had a prayer of turning up anything useful.

"No problems," she said. "I'm working hard."

"How's Rumba?"

"Sleeps all day and prowls all night. Nothing new."

"I miss picking cat hair off my pants when I'm sitting in meetings."

"Next time I'll bring you my vacuum bag."

She had turned just enough that he could lean over and kiss her quickly. "I'll take whatever I can get, Mags."

She didn't turn away, but she didn't smile, either. She just tried to read his expression and figure out what, exactly, that kiss really meant.

Their server approached with Felo's beer and another for her, although she hadn't asked and wouldn't drink it. She was careful not to look too grateful when he set it down in front of her.

"Wings on the way," the man told Felo, and vanished back into the crowd.

"So?" she asked. "I'm pretty sure you didn't ask me down here to talk about cat hair."

"I wanted to let you know what I've turned up in the investigation. I figured you'd want to hear it in person."

"I'm glad you've got something. I turned up a big fat zero. From what I can tell, the only friends the Duttas had in Palmetto Grove were the Kapurs. Vijay wasn't enrolled in nursery school. Nobody at the library, the supermarket, the Laundromat or the drugstore either knew the family or had any anecdotes, although a guy at the video store said some Indian woman had come in and asked for a job ordering and writing up descriptions for a new Bollywood section. She wanted to be paid under the table."

"Kanira?"

"She fit the description. If it was her, that may have been all she was talking about when she told Janya she was going to change her life."

"Anything else?" Felo asked.

"The landlord's counting the days until their rent comes due so he can clear the apartment and rent it out again. He claims he doesn't know a thing except that their money was good. Every avenue led nowhere."

"And the husband's job?"

"I'm still working on that. But initially, nothing."

Felo slowly sipped his beer, as if he was

363

thinking over what she'd said. For a guy some labeled impetuous, he was slow to form opinions, one of the things that made him such a good investigator.

"The answer's there," he said when the beer was half gone. "If he didn't shoot his wife and turn the gun on himself, the answer to who murdered them is in Palmetto Grove. One thing's pretty clear. Dutta had no ties to Miami. There's not a shred of evidence he'd ever been in the city before he died there. He and his wife entered the country in New York. He was enrolled in some kind of writing course at NYU, where he had a fellowship. Apparently she got pregnant right away and couldn't work because she didn't have a green card, so with another mouth to feed, he quit before graduation and they moved to Palmetto Grove."

"Why?"

"She hated the cold and claimed it would harm the baby. He thought he had a job teaching at the community college in town, but it fell through. By then, whatever resources they'd come with were gone. So they stayed on, and he wrote and cut hair, a skill he'd learned in India."

"They were never in Miami?"

"I can't say they never visited, but there's no connection anyone can find, plus no gap in the family history. India, New York, Palmetto Grove. No missing months. Not even weeks."

"So was that what you couldn't tell me on the phone?"

The wings arrived, and Felo waited until the server was gone before he answered. "No, but that's part of what I found out. Here's the other thing, and it's potentially more interesting. I got a look at the evidence and what the victims had with them."

Maggie watched him dig into his food. "You haven't eaten in how long?"

"Breakfast. Long day, sorry."

She had always loved watching Felo eat. He loved food, relished it, couldn't get enough. His delight was almost sexual, it was that intense.

Almost.

She looked straight ahead, curiously aroused as he sucked on a wing. "So what was so interesting about what they had with them?"

"Most of it was what you'd expect. Nothing in the mother's purse of interest. Wallet, house keys, photos of her children in a little sequined carrying case, tissues. The father had a wallet, too, a pad with notes in Bengali, which turned out to be nothing more than grocery lists and what are probably random reworked sentences from the novel he was writing. His car keys were on the floor beside him, which was interesting to me. Put

365

keys deep in a pocket and they stay there, right? So I think they were in his hand when he walked in."

"And he dropped them when he died?"

"Or on his way to pull out the gun. But why would he wait until he was inside for that?"

Maggie wondered the same thing. That scenario was highly unlikely.

"He had a paycheck he hadn't cashed, about thirty dollars in bills and change, and one thing that made no sense."

Maggie perked up. "What?"

"Dice."

"Dice? Harit Dutta was a gambler? Maybe that's why the family had so many financial woes." Her mind was racing now.

"Not just any dice. Blue dice with green marbling and the name of an Atlantic City casino embossed in gold. The Atlantis."

"I don't think I get it."

"Neither did I, so I took a photo and sent it over to Alvaro."

"There's that name again."

"Cut it out, okay?" Felo's tone was sharp. "I'm trying to help you here. How about a little respect?"

Maggie knew he was right. She was a broken record. Alvaro was his friend. He and all the other male cops that Felo had ever been friends with were always going to be part of the package as far as Felo was concerned, and there was no point in pretending it wasn't so.

"Yeah. Okay."

She felt him relax a little. "I'm not an expert on gambling. Alvaro spends a lot of time at casinos these days, entertaining. He says he likes to see how people treat money. Along the way, if the people he's with are losing, he loses, too. If they're winning?" He shrugged. "He knows his way around."

It was one thing to be polite, another to cheer from the sidelines. She nudged him forward. "So what did he say?"

"He thinks the dice are a special giveaway to high rollers, the kind of thing a casino will put in a gift basket in a player's suite. Collectible, but not necessarily valuable. The kind of limited-edition memento people stick in collections, but without much value, at least at first."

"So Harit Dutta, who never went anywhere and had, at best, a minimal income, was carrying dice only the high rollers at Atlantis ever get. Odd, to say the least, unless he had a secret life we haven't uncovered, and you've pretty well discounted that."

"The next step is to find out how many dice were in that batch and who they went to. Alvaro's going to do it."

She felt a surge of anger. "You know, it's one thing to ask Alvaro about the dice, but it's another to involve him in the investigation. He's not a cop anymore. He's not even the next best thing."

"Why not? He has connections there, and I don't. It's a stretch, even for you, to think he was involved in this case, too. You think Alvaro's got his fingers in every murder, every fragment of corruption, in the city?"

"He knows everybody. Who's to say he doesn't know the people who did this?"

Felo slammed his glass on the table so hard Maggie was surprised it didn't break. "You know what, it's time you understood something. Past time, which is why I'm really here tonight. I didn't come to tell you about the dice. You think I couldn't tell you that over the phone?"

"Then why *did* you get me here?"

"Because I finally got the all clear." He waited a moment, to collect himself, but she knew he was still angry, because his voice dropped. "I've told you all along that Alvaro had nothing to do with my decision about Paul Smythe. Let me tell you who *did.* There's been an ongoing federal investigation of Smythe for two years now. His decision not to prosecute Jorge Famosa? That's peanuts. The corruption's so deep even *you* wouldn't believe it. When the word got to the feds that you were trying to blow the whistle, they talked to the chief. And he . . ." Felo blew out a long breath, as if he hoped that would steady him. "He asked me to calm you down and keep you from grandstanding at the press conference. And I tried. God knows I tried to get you to back off."

Her mind was spinning. His words didn't make sense, and she didn't trust what little she did understand. "What are you talking about?"

"I'm talking about *me* trying to get *you* to listen, and you blaming my ex-partner, who'd been feeding the feds useful information about Smythe for a full year before that point. Alvaro's no friend of either Jorge or Smythe, even if he looked like one to you. He's been working with the feds. Not because he's a saint, but because he believes in that badge he used to wear, and he knew Smythe was bad for the city. And bad for Miami is bad for Peerless."

"Oh, please! If the chief wanted me to keep quiet, he would have talked to me. He would have brought *me* into the investigation. He wouldn't have talked to you."

He was quiet for a moment, as if trying to find a way to reach her. "That's where you're wrong," he said at last. "And you know why? You know what you don't see? You don't see *yourself.* You look in the mirror and don't see the woman who got hurt so badly during her first two years in police work that she's still sure every man on the force is patronizing her. It's your line of first defense, your immediate reaction. It's what makes your world go round."

"That's not true!"

"The chief knew you wouldn't listen, just like you're not listening now. You were absolutely convinced exposing Famosa and Smythe at that press conference was the right thing to do. He was sure even if you had all the facts, you'd go ahead, and while you were at it, you might blurt out something that would ruin the feds' case. You know what he said to me? He said when Joan of Arc rode through town on her big white horse, anybody who got in her way was trampled, only the history books forget to tell that part of the story. So he enlisted me as a last resort, to do what I could."

Maggie didn't want to believe this. She searched for something to say, some way to prove it wasn't true. But nothing came to her.

"Why are you telling me *now?*" she asked at last.

"Because Smythe's about to go down. You'll be reading about it before long, so why not? And you know what's funny? You'll probably look good once he does. Most people won't figure out that you almost compromised years of careful investigation and undercover work. You'll look good, like you were the first to figure things out and challenge him. You could probably even come back to Miami City, because if they didn't take you back, they would look bad to the press and the public. But nobody there will ever look at you as a team player, even if they did before. You would do better to go somewhere else, without all the baggage attached."

Maggie didn't know what to say, but worse, she didn't know what to feel. She had been right about Smythe, but, of course, that had never been in doubt. A man who deserved to lose everything was finally about to. Maybe Jorge Famosa would go down at last, too. Maybe all that work she had done would be resurrected and used at last. She felt no remorse, no sympathy for either man, because they were lower than pond scum.

But there were larger issues. One, that she hadn't been trusted with this information because her own chief had believed she wouldn't keep it under wraps. And worse, much worse, by not listening, not trusting, she had, as Felo pointed out, nearly brought down an investigation and undone years of work by fellow law enforcement officers. She'd been so convinced she was right, so sure everyone else was corrupt or lazy, that she had ridden her big white horse through the streets of Miami and never looked down to see who had fallen beneath its hooves.

"I can't believe this," she said, hanging her head as the truth began to hit her.

He didn't reach for her hand. He simply watched her. "You don't know how many times I came close to telling you."

"Why didn't you?"

"Because I thought they might be right, and I couldn't take that chance."

"How can you say that?"

"Can you honestly tell me you wouldn't have gone ahead with that very public resignation? That you're sure you would have done the right thing and backed off? Because you wanted somebody to pay. You were so furious at everybody, Mags, me included, that I don't think you would have known the right thing to do. Whatever your reasons are, you're a loner. You don't ask for help, and you don't accept advice. Not ever."

The awful part, the part she would live with for the rest of her life, was that she really didn't know if he was right. She just looked up and shook her head slowly. "I'm going home."

"I'll take care of the bill. Just drive carefully."

"It's a little late to worry about me, Felo," she said with a burst of anger. "Don't you think you're a bit after the fact?"

"Since this thing came up, I've worried about you every minute. And if you don't think that's true, then whatever we had together really is over."

She didn't know how to answer that. She just grabbed her purse and waited until he'd slid out of the booth before she headed for the door.

■ ■ ■ ■

Tracy wasn't sure why she phoned Marsh when the pain in her abdomen woke her up. The pain was a slicing, stabbing fury that made her head swim when she bolted upright just before midnight. Disoriented, she reached for the telephone and dialed his number with moonlight illuminating the keypad. Voice mail picked up after half a dozen rings, and she heard Marsh drawl a new recorded message. He gave a number in Washington where he could be reached while he was visiting legislators on Capitol Hill all week.

Tracy hung up, infuriated that Marsh, the father of her baby, had left town without telling her. Never mind that he'd left behind a carefully detailed message, something he normally didn't do, and that he had a perfectly reliable iPhone. He was in D.C., hanging out with senators, and she was here in her tiny cottage doubled over with cramps.

Was she losing the baby? She was far enough along in the pregnancy that she'd felt safe. Most problems occurred earlier, although certainly not all. Yet here she was, pain in her abdomen, chest constricted, pulse racing. Exactly what was she supposed to do?

She turned on the bedside light, and the second call went out to her obstetrician. She listened to the entire automated menu of possibilities before figuring out which corresponding number to press next. Three numbers later she listened to the final message, scribbled down the emergency on-call number and hung up. Then she dialed again. This time the call went immediately to voice mail. She left a message, explaining who she was and what was happening; then she hung up once more.

"Great." She wondered how many patients died or had triplets between option one and two on the voice-mail menu. She could dress and head to the emergency room, but she wasn't really sure she should be driving. Shouldn't she just lie quietly and hope for the best? If she was losing the baby . . .

Tears sprang to her eyes. Where was Marsh when she needed him? Who else would understand how she felt right now? If she'd had any lingering doubts about whether this baby was a good idea or not, the pain in her abdomen sent them fleeing. She wanted this baby. Wanted it! And right now she wanted the baby's father, too. Her friends would be sad if she miscarried, but Marsh, like her, would be losing a child. Their son or daughter, conceived together, if not in love, then in affection and, okay, sexual heat. But he would understand.

She decided she couldn't just lie there and wonder. Some doctor in the obstetrics practice would call eventually. In the meantime, she probably ought to get up and dress, in case she was told to proceed to the hospital. It probably made sense to pack an overnight bag, too, just in case.

Tears dribbled down her cheeks, and she wiped them away with the back of her hand. "Marsh, why aren't you here?"

She let herself cry for a moment, or rather, she gave up trying to stop the flow. After a minute she sniffed, wiped her face with a tissue from the bedside table, then got gingerly to her feet. The pain wasn't any worse. It was intermittent, releasing, then beginning again, but it wasn't getting stronger. Which was good, she thought, since stronger would have sent her into total panic. She flipped on the overhead light; then, blinded for a moment, she flipped it off again. Waited, flipped it on and squinted until she could see.

She had showered when she came back from Janya's house, had a snack, brushed her teeth and climbed into bed. Now she turned on all the lights in the house and dressed as quickly as she could, gritting her teeth as the pain stabbed at her. She got essential toiletries and a nightgown, and put them in the Louis Vuitton canvas overnight bag that had been an afterthought in her previous life. Now she would have to save for weeks just to buy one used.

That thought didn't give her a pang, as it

might have before. Right now she was pretty sure she knew what was important and what wasn't.

The telephone still hadn't rung. She debated what to do next, then debated calling Marsh at his hotel. She was so tempted. He couldn't do anything from Washington, but at least he would know. If she was going to be miserable, he should be, too.

A knock sounded on her front door. Surprised, she stopped pacing and listened to be sure, then crept toward the door and flipped on the outside light. Maggie was standing on her doorstep. Tracy unlocked the door and let her in.

"It's like a strobe light at a sixties rock concert over here. Lights on, lights off. I was getting dizzy. What's going on?"

"Why are you out and about?"

Maggie looked pale, and her eyes were red. "You don't want to know. You didn't answer me. Are you okay? You're holding your middle."

"I'm having a lot of pain. I have a call in to my doctor. I'll probably have to go to the hospital."

Maggie made a comforting noise. "Why don't you sit down. Need some help?"

"I can make it." Tracy more or less stumbled to the sofa and gingerly lowered herself to a cushion. She bent forward, which seemed to relieve the pain.

"When did it start?"

Tracy told her, then recited the facts of what she'd done since. "I called the doctor. Somebody ought to be getting back to me before too long."

"I don't know anything, but Mom does. Why don't I call her."

"Wanda?" Tracy wrinkled her nose, but the thought of sensible, opinionated Wanda at her side was actually comforting.

Maggie gauged her response correctly. "I'll call."

"But she'll be asleep. And she has to get up so early."

"She'll want to be here."

Tracy let her dial, and when Maggie hung up, Tracy cocked her head in question.

"On her way. She hadn't undressed for bed. She was reworking the recipe for the Orange Blossom Special."

"Where were you?" Tracy asked. "Did you go somewhere after dinner?"

"Felo and I met for drinks down in Pelican Point. He was there doing something on a case."

"Any info on the Duttas?"

"You don't feel like talking about that now, and neither do I. Right?"

They were saved from further discussion by Wanda barging through the front door. "Why didn't you call me?"

Tracy was still bent forward, resting her

forearms on her thighs. "I honestly didn't think about it. I called the doctor." She didn't admit she had also tried to call Marsh.

"Where's it hurt?"

"My abdomen."

"Mind if I poke a little?"

Tracy considered. "Will that help?"

"Could be helpful. Then, when your doctor calls, you can tell her exactly what's what."

Tracy leaned back, and Wanda sat beside her, then pressed on her abdomen. "Right side painful?"

"It's all painful."

"Try to concentrate here. Degrees, okay?"

Tracy closed her eyes. Wanda pushing against her abdomen didn't increase the pain. "Try the other side."

Wanda did.

Tracy tried to imagine which was worse. "The left side's worse. Not there." She waited until Wanda moved her palm up. "Right there. Could it be my appendix?"

"Do you have one?"

"It can't be my appendix. I'm pregnant!"

"I had a friend had hers out in her eighth month. Had a healthy baby boy four weeks later. Besides, I don't think that's it." She started massaging Tracy's belly gently, right where Tracy had said it hurt. "Feel any better?"

Tracy started to say no, but she realized the pain really was dissipating a little. "Maybe.

Yes, I think that helps."

Wanda shook her head, as if she knew something she didn't want to share. "Maggie, you do this for a minute, okay? I want to check something."

Tracy grabbed her hand. "What is it? What do you think's going on?"

"Don't go getting yourself in a lather. Just let me look around a little."

"Some home remedy? I'm not taking anything until the doctor says I should."

"Maggie, give this a try, okay?"

Maggie and Tracy looked at each other, but Tracy shrugged. Wanda showed Maggie where she'd been gently pressing, then she stood. "I'll be back in a minute."

"What's she doing?" Tracy asked when Wanda disappeared.

"She's Wandaing. That's what Dad calls it when she wanders off to snoop."

"What does she think she's going to find?"

The answer arrived almost immediately. Wanda returned with a can and a paper bag. "You had you a little snack when you got home from dinner, I see."

"I'm making up for lost pounds. I was hungry."

"For spicy canned chili and corn chips?"

"Corn and beans are healthy. They're good nutrition."

"Honey, I don't know how to tell you this, but what you got is plain old indigestion and

379

gas. First Indian food at Janya's, now this."
She held the can higher. "You were just asking for it."

"I have a cast-iron stomach. I never get
indigestion. I never have —"

"Gas. Which is why you didn't know what
it was. And don't tell me cast iron, either. A
little while ago you couldn't keep down
water, remember? Pregnancy throws everything for a loop. So honestly, can you put two
and two together on your way to the bathroom to do what Mother Nature intended?
Because something tells me you'll be heading
that way in about one minute, and Maggie
and me, we're heading out the front door to
avoid air pollution."

Tracy didn't know why she was arguing. If
Wanda was right, she was okay. The baby was
okay. She was flooded with relief at the same
moment she realized Wanda had hit the nail
right on the head.

She sat up, then she got to her feet. "This
would be a good time for you to leave."

"You call if you need us, but something tells
me you're going to be just fine."

Maggie still looked worried. "You're sure?"

"You stay if you want," Wanda said. "Me, I
know when to abandon ship."

They glanced at each other; then they both
headed for the door as Tracy headed for her
date with Mother Nature.

Later in bed, the pain mostly gone, her fears

allayed by both Wanda and the doctor on call and sleep slowly descending, she realized she had one additional thing to be grateful for.

Marsh would never know how close he had come to sharing these moments with her.

CHAPTER NINETEEN

Wanda knew she had spent too many hours trying to perfect her Orange Blossom Special recipe. She had added another egg to the custard base, cooked it longer, tried freezing it, let it set in the refrigerator for eight hours before slicing, added gelatin once and cornstarch the next time. The men at the homeless shelter liked it any which way, runny or as stiff as sheet metal, and at least she was fattening them up with all the rejects.

Now she was so busy thinking about what Maggie had told her that morning that she nearly missed the right moment to take a new batch of orange custard off the stove.

Ken would know what to make of her daughter's news about Paul Smythe and the way Maggie's own chief hadn't trusted her enough to tell her about the federal investigation. Maggie hadn't elaborated, and at least Wanda had been wise enough not to push her for details. She was just glad Ken wasn't off doing one of his training sessions and could help her put everything Maggie had said together. He'd always understood their daughter better than she did, and Wanda had always understood their son, who said anything he pleased and let the chips fall wherever they wanted. Seemed like a cockeyed way to distribute talent in a family, but the kids had turned out okay anyway.

She was still trying to make sense of it all when she realized someone was in the kitchen with her. She hadn't heard the front door jingle. Startled, she nearly dropped her spoon.

Derek Forbes bent over the pot on the stove and inhaled. "Orange juice, and possibly zest, as well? And are those little chopped bits of orange in there?"

Wanda wished she hadn't been standing over the stove for the past half hour. Her hair had frizzled, and her face was splotchy and red. She patted the former self-consciously. "You like to have scared me to death."

"You were deep in thought."

"Yeah? Well, I hope nobody took that rare moment to make off with the till."

He laughed. "Your daughter's out there guarding your well-deserved profits. What do you call this pie?"

"Nothing, if I can't figure out how to get the filling to hold its shape. I get that right and I'm calling it the Orange Blossom Special."

"Perfect, and it smells heavenly."

She told him a little, since she knew he would be interested. "This time I'm using yolks instead of whole eggs, and more corn-starch. Gelatin, too. We'll see if it does the trick. Means I'll have a lot of whites left over, but I can never make too much meringue, not even if all the biddies in the universe line up outside my door to donate an egg. Might even use it on this pie."

She moved the pan off the stove into a bowl of cold water so it would cool faster. "You here for a pie for yourself? Things are slow this week, so you have lots of choices. Next week they'll be buying pies in droves on account of Thanksgiving."

"I'm here to talk about your future."

For a moment Wanda didn't know what to think. A future with Derek Forbes? She nearly panicked; then the humor hit her. Even in her most outrageous pirate novels, nothing that unlikely ever happened.

"My future," she said carefully, "is all about getting this recipe right, and that's all. If you're here to nudge me into opening more shops, I don't have the time or money. This one is like to kill me as it is. Besides, I'll drop dead in this kitchen trying to get this recipe right before I get the chance to do another thing."

"Hear me out," he said. "I have an idea, and I've got my business manager looking into it. I'm looking for another tax shelter.

384

Some of my colleagues open restaurants, Clint, Kevin, Jennifer." He waved his hand as if to say everyone was doing it. "But I've been thinking pies. What I really want is to franchise your shop."

"What?" She stopped worrying about her hair and complexion. "What did you say?"

"Pies. Your pies. Like I told you, I'm convinced pies are the next cupcakes. If we get in there now and take advantage, we'll do well. We'll use your recipes. I like the look of your shop, and even if we spiff it up a little, I want to keep the same feel. We'll bring in some top-flight talent to handle the business end, but you'll have most of the say on how things are run. We can work out what you want from our collaboration. A percentage, a salary, we'll make it work."

She wondered if she had heard him right. "You want to franchise Wanda's Wonderful Pies yourself?"

His grin had been seen around the world, and he used it to great advantage. "It's not a spur-of-the-moment thing. I've been looking around for just the right avenue. A while back I hired a team to design a shop and secure recipes, but they never got it right. Then I stumbled upon you. You know what a good product you create. You have all the expertise, and you're still young enough to pull this off. It'll mean a lot of traveling at first, making sure the shops we open are up to your standards. A lot of administration, publicity, but nothing you can't handle with the right kind of assistance. And we'll hire anybody you want. Your husband and kids can work for you, if you like. Your daughter might even want to take on some of the management duties. You'll have freedom and control."

"Me? I can't even get this recipe right. You know how many of these pies I've made?"

He laughed, a wonderful thing to hear. "That's what makes you so perfect. You won't accept second best or cut corners. You'll ride herd on everybody, even me, just to make sure the product's always first rate, along with the service, the locations, the look of the shops we open. I think you've got everything you need to make this work for both of us, and I've got the money."

Wanda didn't know what to say. One minute she was worrying about Maggie and how to make a pie filling set up just the way she wanted it to. The next she was immersed in high finance, jetting from Kalamazoo to Sacramento to make sure window curtains were starched and piecrust was flaky.

"I think I'm going to have to sit down," she said.

"What can I do? Need more facts? Figures? Encouragement?"

"Just need a chair." She fanned herself.

"I'll have my business manager bring by some of the paperwork we've put together.

You can look it over, see what you think. See what your family thinks. It's big, I know. But I think the sky's the limit on this."

He must have seen the shock written on her face, because he laughed, and then he kissed her cheek. "Ah, Wanda, you and I will make beautiful pies together."

He was long gone by the time she recovered. Maggie poked her head in the doorway and didn't seem to think it was odd her mother had just finished a tête-à-tête with one of Hollywood's A-list actors. "Okay if I run out for a sandwich?"

Wanda waved her on.

"Sure you don't need anything?"

"Just a good head on my shoulders, that's all."

"Then I guess you don't need a thing. You're all set."

Tracy wasn't sure what to do about Olivia. The girl was a delight, despite good reason not to be. She'd been through so much, losing her mom under suspicious circumstances, then having her father convicted of attempted second-degree murder on a different case and imprisoned. Alice was Olivia's stabilizing influence, the one unbroken link to Karen, Olivia's mother. Alice could talk about Karen's childhood, tell Olivia the ways she resembled her, and emphasize how much Karen had loved her daughter. Alice adored

Olivia, and the two were exceptionally close. But these days Olivia seemed to need more.

"I feel like I'm letting Alice down or something," Tracy told Wanda. The two were sitting outside on what passed for Tracy's patio, draining a pitcher of margaritas made without tequila, since Tracy couldn't have it and Wanda said she was too tired to chance it.

"Seems to me you're just helping out."

Wanda poured another glass for herself and held out the pitcher to Tracy, who shook her head. "I don't want to gouge a path to my bathroom. I'll be making a couple of trips, as it is."

"Just because Olivia likes confiding in you doesn't mean you're being disloyal to Alice," Wanda said. "We agreed a long time ago, everybody in Happiness Key has to pitch in to raise that girl after everything she's been through."

"It's just that she needs a mom. She's got a wonderful grandmother, but Alice can't be both. I mean, people do it all the time if they have to, but there are things *I* know that Alice just doesn't anymore. Like music and clothes and what it feels like to kiss a boy for the first time. And I'm closer to my own adolescence, close enough to help Olivia through hers. I remember all that like it was yesterday."

Wanda was staring into the distance. " 'Course, you were an adolescent a lot longer than most people."

388

Tracy could hardly quibble, since it was pretty much the truth. She had been a spoiled brat until she moved to Happiness Key.

"I just wonder if I ought to say something to Alice," Tracy said. "Just explain that I'm not trying to cut Olivia out of her life, but that I'm supplementing what Alice does for her."

"Alice seem upset to you?"

Tracy pondered for a moment. "No. I'm not even sure she notices."

"Doesn't seem upset to me, either. In fact, she's looking good. Happy, maybe. For a while there, she was exhausted all the time. But now that you've got her hanging around at that center of yours, not doing all the back-and-forthing, she seems rested. And she's having a good time with the other seniors, right?"

"She's the crochet queen. You ought to see the snowflakes her class made. They donated some to the center for our holiday tree."

"I suspect you'll drag me there for some event or other and I'll see them."

Tracy thought Wanda was particularly subdued tonight, which meant she was only twice as outrageous as most people, a subtle difference. She had already told Tracy about Maggie and the Paul Smythe case. Wanda was frustrated that she hadn't learned more details from her daughter, but Tracy thought there might be something else bothering her.

Wanda kept looking away, as if her thoughts were somewhere else.

She put down her glass and rested her fingertips on Wanda's knee. "Are you okay?"

"The strangest thing happened today. You know Derek Forbes?"

"Duh. You mean the actor Derek Forbes who loves your pies?"

"That would be the one. He wants to go into business with me."

Tracy wasn't sure she'd heard Wanda right. "Doing what?"

"He wants to help me franchise Wanda's Wonderful Pies. Says he's been looking into starting his own pie franchise, but why should he, when he and I can do it together?"

"Are you kidding me?" This time Tracy slapped Wanda's knee. "That's fantastic. And you didn't say anything until now?"

"Because I don't know how I feel about it." Wanda looked right at Tracy. "Do you think he means it?"

Tracy thought that for Wanda, this was like having an angel come down from heaven and offer her a mansion on a street paved with gold. It just didn't compute. There had to be a catch, or maybe she was hallucinating.

"Nothing bad with any basis in fact has ever been said about the man," Tracy said. "He has an army of loyal friends. He's been married a couple of times, but —"

"Twice. He's still friends with both of them.

He told me he's just not one to settle down."

"He told you that?"

"We spent a whole afternoon together making pies for his party. What else were we going to talk about? He says he's sorry he never had kids, though."

Tracy tried to get to the point. "I think he means this. Why aren't you jumping up and down? Wanda, this is a dream come true, only you never dreamed this big, did you?"

"My head's not screwed on straight or something. I can't wrap my brain around it."

"What does Ken say?"

"Kenny doesn't know yet. You're the only one I've told."

"Wow."

"It'll take a day or two just to believe it. His manager's going to get me some paperwork. Maybe then it'll seem real."

"Something's bothering you." As hard as it was to believe, Tracy could see that Wanda was more than just skeptical. She was worried.

"I'll get back to you on that." Wanda drained the rest of her fake margarita and got to her feet. "I guess I'd better get home and break the news to Kenny. He'll want to take me out to dinner. That's his best way to celebrate, and I'm not going to think about the money it costs tonight. I'm way too tired."

Tracy knew better than to push. Her neighbor was working this out in her own way and time. Nothing would budge her.

She got to her feet, too. "Well, whatever happens, the offer itself must feel good, right?"

Wanda shrugged, but she also smiled.

"I'll walk you partway," Tracy said. "Olivia's off camping with her class for the weekend, and she asked me to stop and check on Alice this evening. You and I think Alice looks better, but Olivia says she's been forgetful and preoccupied. I think she's just not comfortable leaving her alone."

"The girl shouldn't feel guilty. She's not supposed to be taking care of her grandmother. We're here if Alice needs something. Olivia's got to live her life."

Tracy agreed, only she wasn't sure how to make that a reality. She had done what little she could by getting Alice involved at the center. She hoped that once Olivia realized her grandmother was enjoying herself more, she would begin to feel freer just to be a kid.

Wanda peeled off toward her house, and Tracy went to Alice's and knocked. When nothing happened, she knocked louder and began to worry. Finally she peeked around the side of the house and realized Alice's car wasn't even there. Olivia's concern was making her paranoid, and Alice was probably off having a good time. Tracy started home, the rest of the evening stretching in front of her.

Once there, she wandered the tiny house

and, with nothing better to do, considered how she would arrange everything once the baby came. Her cottage had only one bedroom, and once she squeezed a crib in beside the bed, there would be no place for the baby's things, no room for a changing table or another dresser.

After an hour of trying to work out logistics, she'd settled on the easiest. Even though she liked the sofa she had, she would look for a comfortable sofa bed to replace it and move out to the living room. That way the baby could have her bedroom, and once Maggie moved out of the fifth cottage, with its tiny second bedroom, then Tracy and the baby could move there.

Or she could simply sell Happiness Key before she had to begin making astronomically expensive repairs, and settle into a child-friendly neighborhood in a child-friendly house. She could sock away enough for college expenses and work part time.

And what would her renters do? Where would they go?

By that point it was late enough that she decided to check on Alice again. She knew it probably wasn't necessary, since Alice had obviously felt well enough to drive somewhere. But she hated to break her promise to Olivia.

This time Alice's car was parked beside her house, so Tracy knocked, fully expecting the older woman to answer. No lights came on, and no footsteps were heard. Maybe Alice was in the back of the house, or maybe she had already gone to sleep and didn't hear the door. Tracy knocked harder; then, when her knuckles rebelled, she gave up.

Alice had to be fine. She'd driven somewhere and driven back. She was probably taking a shower, or maybe she had the television too loud — although Tracy probably would have heard that through the door. She debated what to do next. She had no reason to worry, except that Olivia herself had been worried. Worried enough to ask Tracy to check on Alice, and Tracy had agreed, which meant she didn't feel comfortable just walking away.

"Alice?" she called loudly, banging on the door one more time with her fist.

No answer. Great.

She backed away. She could just go home and assume Alice's reason for not answering the door was a perfectly acceptable one. But she was reminded of another night when Alice *had* needed help, a night many months ago, when Olivia's father was still living there. Had she not intervened . . .

"Well, that bites." She couldn't just go home. Now she really was worried. Maybe, without knowing it, Olivia had seen signs of impending health problems. Maybe all the activity at the rec center hadn't been as good for Alice as Tracy had thought.

"Right. Like I'm going in there alone." From too much experience, she knew emergencies at Happiness Key were best shared with friends. She started down the road to Wanda's house.

Wanda answered the door wearing satin pajamas, Day-Glo orange with purple piping.

"I guess you didn't go out to dinner after all," Tracy said.

"Kenny brought home chicken and all the fixins. Why, you hungry? I think there's a drumstick left."

"I just knocked at Alice's. Her car's there, but she's not answering."

"Thought you did that a while ago."

Tracy explained as Wanda nodded.

"Think we need to check it out?" Wanda asked.

"I know we do. But I hate to do it alone. This could really suck."

"Well, I'd loan you Kenny, only he went off for a walk on the beach. We can wait, or you can take me."

"Door number two. Are you going to get dressed?"

"I am dressed."

"And you don't care if anybody sees you like that?"

"Not a thing showing that shouldn't be."

"If Ken can sleep with you, I can manage

to walk down the street. Let's get it over with."

Wanda turned on the porch light and slid into flip-flops. The two women started down the road.

"Maybe you'll knock and she'll answer right away. Could have been in the bathroom, or asleep."

Tracy hoped it was true, but when they got there and she knocked again, there was no response. The lights were off, and she tried to remember if they'd been off before. She wished she'd paid more attention.

"You think she might be over at Janya's? Only place she'd walk besides our houses. She doesn't know Maggie that well."

Tracy pulled out her cell phone and hit speed dial. She spoke to Janya, then hung up. "Not there."

"What do you want to do?"

"Go get my keys and let myself in. You with me?"

"Stay here. She leaves a spare under one of those garden gnomes in the flowerbed. In case somebody drops off Olivia, and she's not home."

The day was beginning to catch up with Tracy. She wanted this over. She and baby X were ready for a good night's sleep.

"Let's do it."

Wanda lifted gnomes and retrieved the key from under the third, her pajamas pulsing with radioactive energy in a shaft of moon-light. She returned and handed it to Tracy. "You're the landlady. I'm the witness. You have no evil intent and enough evidence to check out the place."

"Thank you, Miss Law and Order. Let's get this over with."

Tracy inserted the key in the doorknob. The door had a dead bolt, too, which wasn't locked. The door swung open.

The women tiptoed inside. "Alice?" Tracy called. "Are you home? Are you all right?"

Wanda switched on the lamp beside the door. The living room smelled like lilac air freshener, and it was neat as well as empty of living beings, with the exception of Alice's flourishing aquarium, which glowed with a soft amber light in one corner.

"Alice?" Tracy walked through the living room and into the hallway. She pushed open the door that led to Olivia's bedroom, but she wasn't surprised to see that Alice wasn't there. Then she got to Alice's bedroom and stopped. The door was closed. Although she hadn't noticed it before, now she thought she heard the air conditioner humming, which could explain why Alice hadn't heard her call. She debated returning the way she had come, locking the door and going home. The house looked fine. Perfectly normal. Alice wasn't ly-ing unconscious, or worse, on the living room, kitchen or hallway floor. Olivia's room was empty, too.

But if they left, she would spend the whole night worrying.

"Let's get this over with," Wanda said. She knocked on Alice's bedroom door; then, without waiting more than a few seconds, she pushed it open.

Tracy's eyes took a few moments to adjust. In those moments she was sorry she'd invited Wanda along, since without her, she might have retreated.

Then she saw movement. Someone sat up in Alice's bed. Then someone else did, too.

"What are you doing here?" a familiar masculine voice cut through the darkness. "What in blazes are you doing here?"

Tracy turned to Wanda, who already had her by the shoulder. "Leaving," Tracy screeched as Wanda pulled her back into the hallway. "We were just checking on Ali—" She screeched again as Wanda jerked harder.

In a moment they were in the living room, and in another they were outside, slamming the door behind them.

"Lordy," Wanda said, flip-flops clacking madly against the oyster-shell road. "Lordy, Lordy, who'd a thought? She will . . . *never* forgive us."

They were in front of Wanda's before they stopped. Tracy was wheezing from the pace Wanda had set. "I've lost everything." She drew another wheezy breath. "Gone. All gone."

"What are you talking about?"

"Do you know who that man was?"

"You didn't get a good look at him, did you? Tell me you didn't look that hard. Because he didn't have a stitch of cloth—"

Tracy held up her hand. "Too much information!"

"Then how do you know?" Wanda demanded.

"Because I'd recognize that voice anywhere. That was Roger Goldsworthy. Mr. Moustache. The shuffle in our shuffleboard *and* the rec center board. Remember him, the guy I insulted in that park way back in the days when you thought I was lower than a snake's belly? The guy who made my life miserable my first summer at the rec center? Roger knows everybody in town. And I have now screwed with him one too many times to recover."

Wanda's eyes were large. The two women stood together huffing and puffing. Finally Wanda spoke. "If they fire you, you'll get unemployment. That's a good thing."

Tracy didn't know whether to laugh or cry. But she was sure whichever she did, she no longer had the problem of where to put the baby in her little cottage. Without an income, the expenses here would quickly become impossible. She doubted she would still own this land and the cottages sitting on it by the time her baby made its debut in May.

CHAPTER TWENTY

Tracy spent the hours from dawn until she left for work inventing reasons not to make an appearance at the rec center that morning. Earthquakes might have served in California, but they were a no go in Florida. The tropical depressions that Blake had found interesting two weeks before had died away, and even though there was another on the horizon, now that it was nearing the end of November, nobody was taking it seriously. She had grudgingly ruled out an invasion of killer bees. She couldn't use the pregnancy, of course, and she didn't want to claim illness, because if all her New Age friends in California were right, that was bad karma and liable to backfire.

In the end she went into work early, determined to plead her case to Gladys, who might understand why Tracy, out of concern for a neighbor, had sabotaged the privacy of a board member. Between bees and earthquakes, she'd come up with a hint of good news. Marsh was now on the board, too, and it was possible Gladys would at least be torn between loyalty to Roger and the father of Tracy's baby. Gladys might appear to outsiders to be nothing more than the receptionist and wife of the rec center's director, but everyone on the inside knew she was the power behind the throne.

Unfortunately, she was also absent.

Tracy arrived to find a stranger behind the desk, a pretty brunette who looked bewildered to be sitting there. "Gladys has a cold and doesn't want to give it to anybody," the woman said after Tracy introduced herself. "I'm a temp."

Tracy figured she'd better try Woody, who was actually her boss, but when she asked, the woman shook her head. "Mr. Woodley's going to be late. Maybe around lunchtime? And short of that, I don't know a thing about this job except that you're probably in charge for a while."

Downstairs, Tracy stared blankly at the day's schedule. Without either of the Woodleys at the center, she would probably be particularly busy this morning. Maybe she could prove how indispensible she was, so that when Woody finally came in, the temp would sing her praises so loudly that Roger Goldworthy's voice would be drowned out.

"Tracy?"

She looked up to find Alice, of all people,

standing in her doorway in a pretty rose-colored dress. Tracy jumped to her feet, slamming a knee against the desk drawer. Holding it with both hands, she said words even her negligent parents would have reprimanded her for.

Alice took the long path across the room, obviously concerned. "I . . . I didn't mean . . ."

"No, no, it's not your fault. I didn't close the drawer, that's all. I was looking at my schedule, and I wasn't paying attention. I . . . I —" Tracy stopped babbling. "Omigosh, I am so sorry! About last night."

Alice smiled. Her eyes twinkled, and her cheeks were pink. "Not me."

Tracy came around the desk. "We shouldn't have been there, but we thought something had happened to you."

Alice waved that away. "You were being good neighbors. We just . . . didn't hear you."

"I really, really didn't know you had, um, company, Alice. Olivia . . . I just wanted to be sure everything was fine, and when you didn't answer . . ."

"You . . . don't have to explain." Alice put her hand over Tracy's on the desk. "I understand. I remember the last time you checked . . . on me."

Tracy hugged her friend. "I'm so embarrassed."

"I'm not."

Tracy hugged her harder. "Oh, wow."

"We've been spending a lot of . . . time together." Alice's smile was warm when Tracy stepped away. "I never expected to find another man. Not after my Fred died. Roger feels . . ." She shrugged. This time it wasn't a pause to pull together words. This time it was clearly a search for the perfect one, which never arrived.

"Life is very short," she went on after a moment. "You won't learn that, not for a while. We . . . we want to be together while we can."

"Of course you do." Tracy grabbed her hand. "You don't have to explain. I'm so glad for you and Roger, Alice. He and I haven't always had an easy time of it — you know that from the stories I've told — but I like him a lot. I respect him."

"He won't . . . retaliate." Alice's smile broadened.

Relieved, Tracy led her to the couch, and they sat. "You know, if you'd told us about this, I never would have gone into your house. I would have figured you probably had company."

Alice settled herself against the cushions. "I . . ." She shook her head. "It's complicated."

"You mean love's still complicated at your age? I thought, well, that just doesn't seem fair. When does it get better? You're supposed to be my role model."

Alice laughed a little. "It's not complicated for us. When you're our age?" She paused and looked straight into Tracy's eyes. "You know better. No time to wait and . . . wonder."

Tracy thought that was a little pointed, as if Alice was making a comment about her own relationship with Marsh.

"But sometimes —" Alice stopped.

"So how is it complicated?"

"Olivia."

"Why? Doesn't she like Roger?"

"She's only met him . . ." Alice appeared to be counting. "Three times. Two at the center. One shopping. No, you see . . . Roger and I? We want to move in together. Maybe even marry, but my cottage is too small for all of us. And Roger lives . . . at Shell Horizon."

Tracy considered that. Shell Horizon was a senior retirement community with differing levels of care, one of the nicest in the area. She knew a number of the seniors who used the center were residents. Shell Horizon had a bus that brought them and picked them back up at regular intervals. She hadn't realized Roger was a resident because he still drove his car to the center, but he was a retired geologist and probably had a sizable pension. Shell Horizon offered a host of activities, along with pools and restaurants. They even had a shuffleboard team, although not a very good one, which was probably why

Roger preferred the rec center's.

She realized now what the problem was. "Olivia wouldn't fit in, would she?"

"Not until she's fifty-five."

"Oh, it's a fifty-five-and-older community. Of course. So she can't be there."

"Grandchildren . . . are welcome. Weekends and summer vacations mostly. There's even a clubhouse for when they visit. But they can't live there."

"I guess I never thought about that."

"We could buy a house, but we don't want that . . . responsibility."

Tracy could certainly see why. Both Roger and Alice were at a point in their lives when they should be enjoying sunsets together, strolling on the beach, beating the pants off other seniors at any number of games. They shouldn't be tied up fixing faucets, or hiring lawn services and exterminators.

"A condo?" she asked. "A nice complex somewhere that doesn't have age restrictions?"

"So many . . . are for singles or young families. Parties. Loud music. Not right for an . . . impressionable young girl."

Tracy could see that, too. And it sounded as if Alice and probably Roger had looked around to see what was out there.

"I would miss my friends," Alice said. "At Happiness Key."

"We'd be nearby. We'd see you all the time.

One phone call away." But Tracy tried to imagine Olivia living a distance from the rest of them with her grandmother and Roger. Alice struggled to make life as normal for her granddaughter as she could. She accommodated Olivia's schedule, her music and television preferences. She worked hard to make sure Olivia was able to take part in any activity she wanted and to have friends over whenever she could. But no matter how nice Roger was to Olivia, or how accepting of having a preteen in his home, the girl would still be living with two people in their sunset years, with different needs and preferences from her own. Alice was not a young grandmother, and Roger might be even older.

Alice gave the tiniest sigh. "We have to keep things as they are. But we can . . . find time together."

Tracy heard the wistful note in her friend's voice. Alice's life hadn't been easy since her husband's death. And now she bore the full burden of a tween rapidly turning into a teenager. The other women at Happiness Key tried hard to make things easier, but at the end of the day, Olivia was Alice's responsibility.

She deserved a more leisurely life, one without so many household chores. At Shell Horizon she would probably have at least some meals provided, and maintenance on the apartment, too. Everything she really needed would be a short distance away, and as she got older, she would have people right there to care for her medical needs.

Best of all, she would have Roger, who was obviously a man with superior taste.

"Before you know it, Olivia will be off to college," Tracy said, but even as she did, she was adding up the years, and the sum was sobering. Alice and Roger really shouldn't wait that long. Not if they wanted to have any meaningful time together. Six or seven years was not a small thing at their end of the timeline.

"I don't want . . . Olivia to grow up too fast. She's my heart," Alice said.

"And you're the best grandmother in the whole world. If I'd had a grandmother like you, I might have been this fabulous a lot earlier."

Both women laughed, but Tracy knew that under it, there was a discordant note of sadness.

Maggie and Janya's plan was simple. Once they were inside the Duttas' apartment, Janya would pack up the children's toys and clothing to take back home, and Maggie would look for anything that might add some insight into the couple's deaths. Janya also intended to pack up photographs and mementos that the children might like when they were older. If their family in India didn't want any reminders of their parents, Janya would keep those boxes herself and contact the children later, if she could find them. There was no guarantee the agency would tell her where they had gone.

Unfortunately, even simple plans could easily become complicated. After a quiet morning canoe trip through a nearby mangrove wilderness with only her GPS as guide, Maggie arrived at the apartment to find Janya and a stranger getting out of an unfamiliar car in the parking lot. Janya's expression was inscrutable, and Maggie was sorry she hadn't stayed on the water.

"Maggie, this is Miss Crede. She's the children's social worker."

Miss Crede had a rectangular head and body, a blond Dutch-boy bob and sensible shoes. She looked to be in her late forties and ready to take on the aging process with enthusiasm. She also looked to be in a hurry.

Maggie shook her hand and made all the polite responses.

"As you know, it's against our rules to let you have the run of the place alone," Miss Crede said, glancing at a leather-banded watch above a sturdy wrist. "We have to protect the deceaseds' possessions."

"What will happen to everything?" Maggie asked. "Was there a will?"

"No, and no family in this country. The court's in the process of appointing a personal representative, and he or she will probably sell what they can, and the money will go to the children's estate."

"I think there will not be much money," Janya said. "They had so little. But I hope you will keep Kanira's jewelry for her daughter and not allow it to be sold. It will have meaning to her. And Harit's books for Vijay."

"I will certainly make a note of that."

Miss Crede led the way, giving Janya and Maggie a chance to exchange glances. Maggie hoped her friend would be able to keep the social worker occupied while Maggie dug a little deeper.

Miss Crede — who, if she had a first name, was not willing to share — unlocked the door and ushered them inside. Just as she crossed the threshold, her cell phone rang and she stepped outside again. Maggie wished the call had happened later, when she'd had time to figure out what she most wanted to see without the social worker watching her.

Luck was with her anyway. Miss Crede came back in, snapping her phone closed just a few feet from the door. "I'm going to need to leave, I'm afraid. It's an emergency I've been dealing with all week, and it's just come to a head. Would you like to reschedule?"

Maggie stepped forward so she and Miss Crede were eye to eye. "There's nothing here for you to worry about if you leave us alone, is there? Like Janya said, this family had very little. We'll put everything for the children in boxes, and you can go through them and have them sent to her house if you like. For the record, I used to be a cop until I moved here. You can call my department in Miami right now and ask for a reference."

Miss Crede was a woman required to make snap decisions. "I guess staying without me will be okay. Can you wait until I get back? Then I'll do a once-over of the boxes and you can take them with you. It's a matter of policy."

Maggie figured that social workers, like cops, had seen the worst of the worst and weren't the most trusting of professionals. "Boy, do I understand policy," she said, pasting on the same friendly smile she had used when she tried to coax information from witnesses.

"I'll be gone —" Miss Crede glanced at her watch "— an hour. Maybe an hour and a half. Do you have a cell-phone number, in case I'm going to be later?"

Janya jotted hers on a slip of paper and handed it to the social worker.

"Got to go." Miss Crede dropped the number into her sensible purse. "I'll see you then." She paused, then put her hand on Janya's arm. "If it were me, I'd choose a little jewelry and a few books for the children now. I don't think anybody could possibly care."

She nodded; then she disappeared out the door.

"An hour," Maggie said, when she was sure Miss Crede was gone. "Let's get to it."

"What will you look for?" Janya asked.

"Everything, expecting nothing. Keep your eye out for anything unusual while you pack. Papers, items that seem out of place, anything that gives new insight into the parents or the family relationships. And if you notice anything that's missing . . . ? Something you would expect to find? Make a note of that, too."

"The police have been through the apartment."

"They were looking for reasons to pin the deaths on Harit. We're looking for reasons not to."

Janya nodded gravely, but Maggie could tell she doubted anything useful would still be left in the apartment. Since Maggie felt the same way, she could hardly tell her to buck up.

Janya went into the bedroom the children had shared and began making piles. Maggie started in the kitchen, opening cupboards and drawers, examining contents, pulling out the drawers and looking beneath them. She didn't expect to find anything hidden, although that wasn't out of the question. She was more interested in items in plain sight that might have meaning. Calendars. Notes by the telephone. Phone numbers. Although she was doubtful the police would have left anything important, the murders had not taken place here. This had never been a crime scene, so according to her father, it hadn't been treated to the same thorough going-over that the murder scene itself had received.

The kitchen yielded nothing except a phone number penned on the inside of a matchbook. She pocketed that, and went to the living room phone and dialed. Pizza delivery. She tossed the matchbook into the trash. Desk drawers held pens and little else. There was an address book, with characters in an alphabet she couldn't read. She called Janya, who took it and shook her head. "I do not read Bengali script."

"Do you know anyone who might?"

"That would not be difficult to find."

"See if you can put this in one of the children's boxes, perhaps among the books you're taking with you."

The living room was tiny. Maggie thought it was probably smaller than the one in her own cottage. She searched behind and under furniture, under sofa cushions, in the television cabinet and a small bookcase, shaking each book to be sure nothing was hidden between the pages. She lifted the edges of the sisal rug that covered a scarred vinyl floor. The Duttas had not been collectors. There was little to search.

Their bedroom was the next stop. In her experience, bedrooms were often hiding places. Once, she had found a pound of heroin hidden in the false bottom of a drawer filled with lacy underwear. This room, like the rest of the apartment, was sparsely furnished and remarkably clean. Kanira Dutta had apparently spent her days chasing dust. Maggie wondered if the woman had known she was soon to die, would she have chosen other pursuits? Taking her children to the park so that would be the place where they remembered her best? Watching sunsets at the beach and collecting shells? Trying one more time to mend fences with her family in India, or with her husband?

Thirty seconds into the bedroom search, Maggie struck gold. A laptop sat under the rolltop of a battered desk. She examined it and decided the computer was probably at least five or six years old, heavy by current standards and almost surely slow to load. She flipped the top and turned it on, but the battery was dead. Five minutes later, after a thorough search of the room had turned up nothing else of interest, she found a cord in a backpack in the closet. She plugged in the laptop and turned it on again, only to find it was password protected.

"Great." At least the keyboard used the alphabet she was familiar with. She typed in Harit's name, then Kanira's, with no luck.

She tried Vijay, then Lily, with no success either, but when she typed in Vijay&Lily, she was in.

"It's a miracle."

"What did you say?" Janya asked from the other bedroom, which was right next door. The walls were thin.

"I have Harit's laptop. I wonder if the police went over it." Maggie filed that question away to ask her father, who so far had been happy to let her know anything he could about the case.

Janya came to see what was up. "Is his book on it?"

Maggie was looking through files and directories for addresses, phone numbers, anything relevant. She was elated to find a calendar, but unfortunately it hadn't been updated since the previous year. Obviously Harit had kept his private appointments elsewhere, perhaps because the laptop was old or unreliable.

"I don't see the book, but . . ." She went directly to Harit's word-processing program and found a large folder named Passage.

"This could be it," she said.

"The children should have those chapters. Their father was a talented writer. They should have proof of it. If they are sent to India, no one there will ever tell them. They will grow up thinking their parents were bad people. Perhaps they will grow up thinking *they* are, too."

Maggie was sorry Janya had to wrestle with the children's future. She couldn't imagine how hard it would be for her friend to lose Lily and Vijay to people who probably didn't want them.

"Was Harit's novel in English?" Maggie asked.

"I think perhaps it was. His grant was from a literary foundation here or perhaps in Canada. I am not certain."

"This is it, then." Maggie had figured out the way the folder was organized and had pulled up what looked like a first chapter. She scanned it quickly.

"I'm going to email this whole file to myself," she said. "It should only take a minute. Then we'll make copies for the children. I'll put the chapters on a CD. We can print it out, too, and keep it for them."

"It will be important someday," Janya said.

Maggie returned to the folder, attached it to an email to herself and tried to send, with no success. The laptop was just too old and the file too large. She went back and began sending individual files. A clock ticked inside her head. Miss Crede was due back before long, and Maggie didn't want to be caught with the computer whirring.

At last the folder was all accounted for. She went over the rest of the files, looking for anything of interest. Clearly, though, this was

Harit's work computer. There were no letters or personal notes, or even games he had played. Harit Dutta had been serious about his writing and possibly afraid that anything else might slow the computer more. His mail folder was empty, and while Maggie knew there were ways to access deleted email from a hard drive, she was not a computer expert, and she was running out of time.

She turned off the laptop, put the cord back where she'd found it and searched the dresser. When she had finished that, she checked the little bathroom, and finally she went into the children's bedroom to help Janya sort.

"Nothing?" Janya asked.

"Nothing's jumping out at me. I doubt the address book will be useful. It looks like something the wife brought with her from India. Unless the murderer tracked them here, it's unlikely it will help, and I can't go there to interview everybody in it."

"I am nearly done. I will leave clothes the children have outgrown. There is nothing special, nothing sentimental. Kanira was fond of ruffles, but Lily is not."

"Do you need help with the toys?"

"I have sorted Lily's." Janya pointed to a toy box. "She will be happy to have some of these things to play with. Vijay's toys are in the closet. Will you look through them?"

"You'll know better what he likes, but I can

417

start." Maggie went into the closet and began to take things off a shelf system along the back wall. Books. No surprise there. A plastic case of small metal cars. A can of logs that fit together to build a house. She remembered those from Junior's childhood. She had rarely sat still long enough to build anything herself.

She reached for the next item, trying to figure out what it might be. She stepped to the doorway, where the light was better. She was holding a small metal slot machine with Atlantis Casino emblazoned in gold across the front. The little slot machine had an arm with a red knob on the right side, and Maggie pulled it down. The reels spun, but none of the images matched. Cherries, bananas, a red balloon. She turned it in her hands and saw a slot in the back. The slot machine was a toy, but it was also a bank.

And it had Atlantis Casino painted on the front.

She'd told Janya about the dice in Harit's effects. Now she held out the slot machine. "Look at this." Maggie pulled the arm again to show her. "Does this seem like something his parents would have bought for Vijay?"

"No, this is a toy for an older child, and one with no imagination. Vijay would be bored very quickly, I think, and he had no money to save."

Maggie jingled the slot machine, but there was no sound of coins clinking together inside. "*I* would be bored. But it makes its point, doesn't it? A slot machine. Atlantis Casino, the same Atlantis Casino the dice came from."

"I know you think perhaps Harit gambled there, but they had no money, Maggie. And Kanira told me all the things that were wrong with her husband, but nothing about gambling."

"I believe you. I think this came from the same person who gave Harit the dice. Perhaps somebody he knew. One of his customers?"

"Could that be important?"

Maggie doubted it. Harit had been carrying the dice in his pocket when he died, but that only indicated they'd been given to him near the end of his life, perhaps by one of the last customers whose hair he had cut. Did that mean it had something to do with his murder? Probably not.

"Why don't you put this in a box to take home," Maggie said. "Just in case."

"I wish we had found something more important," Janya said.

Maggie wished the same. "It's usually this way. Leads are hard to come by. This case is baffling, unless it's exactly what it looks like. An angry husband, a cheating wife, a moment when self-control disappears."

"This will be very hard to explain to the children when they are old enough to understand."

As hard as that conversation would be, Maggie knew Janya fervently hoped that she would be the one to have it with them. Because if she had to sit them down someday to explain that their mother and father had quarreled and both had died as a result, that would mean the children were permanent and beloved members of the Kapur household.

CHAPTER TWENTY-ONE

Some people believed that a baby in utero benefited from slow circular massage to the mother-to-be's abdomen. On the day after Thanksgiving, the closest Tracy got to giving her little one a massage was sliding the waistband of her warm-up pants up and down over what was now a noticeable bump, in hopes of finding a comfortable place to tie the cord so she could get to her ultrasound appointment.

"I guess Marsh is going to be there," she told Janya, who had a snoozing Lily on one hip and a blouse, which she'd brought for Tracy, draped over the other arm. Janya had asked about Marsh with studied nonchalance, but she wasn't fooling her friend.

Tracy settled the pants high and hoped they would stay there. She reached for her water bottle and took a long sip. She was under instructions to drink a quart of water before the appointment, and this was the last of it.

"I texted him the date and time. Maybe he

went out of town for Thanksgiving, I don't know, but he didn't say anything to me. You're sure about the blouse? You won't miss it?"

"It has much room this way." Janya spread her hands sideways. "It will grow with you."

Although the blouse, a gauzy peacock blue with flowers embroidered at the neckline, was nothing like Tracy's usual style, now it looked light and comfortable, which was quickly becoming her design of choice. "I'll enjoy wearing it, thanks. Something tells me I'm going to be as big as a mini mansion before too long."

"So Marsh will meet you there?" Janya asked, hanging the blouse over a chair in Tracy's dining area.

"If he comes." Tracy was trying to sound nonchalant, too, but it wasn't easy. She hadn't seen Marsh for weeks — not to speak to, anyway. Yesterday she had eaten Thanksgiving dinner with Alice, Olivia and Roger Goldsworthy, who had not poisoned her serving of white meat and oyster stuffing. In fact, he had been almost solicitous. She wasn't sure if his demeanor was a reaction to her pregnancy or an expression of his desire to impress his lady love. Whichever it was, she thought her job was probably safe.

"You could phone him and suggest you drive together," Janya said.

"It's too late for that. I need to leave in a

few minutes if I'm going to get there on time. And I can guarantee I'm going to. I have a quart of water hanging out in my bladder with no place to go until this thing is finished."

"Why don't you let me drop you off."

Tracy realized what Janya was up to. "You are *sooo* transparent. If you drop me off, Marsh will have to bring me home, right?"

Janya wasn't a good liar. She looked away. "I just thought perhaps you might not be comfortable driving after drinking all that water."

"Nice try, but I don't even know if he's coming. And I don't want to get stuck there."

"This seems like a —" Janya stopped short, struggling for the correct word, which was unusual for her. "An intimate moment," she said at last. "The sound of the baby's heart. Pictures of the baby itself. I am told they sometimes suck their thumbs. The baby will seem real to you both."

"Right. And?"

"Would this not be the proper moment to talk to Marsh? To tell him, perhaps, what you are feeling?"

"What I'm feeling is annoyed. He hasn't called or spoken to me in weeks, and I did make a point of inviting him to the ultrasound. I made the first move."

"What move was that? The baby is his. You told him he could come with you to see what is, after all, his by rights. You did not tell him that you love him or need him, which is important in this country. You did not say you want him in your life. You only said he could, at last, be a tiny part of this miracle you carry inside you."

"Whew." Tracy fanned herself. "The air is heavy with recriminations."

"No, that isn't true. But you are my friend, and I think you might be afraid. What would be different in your life if you told Marsh you miss him? If he said, 'Too bad, but I am a busy man,' then you would know what you now only suspect. If he said, 'Tracy, I miss you, too,' then you would know something new, and it would help you make your next choice."

"What would be different?" Tracy gave a humorless laugh. "I would look pathetic, that's what. Like I was whining for attention. And it's clear, isn't it, that the man has no real feeling for me? If he did, I would have heard from him."

Janya was silent for a long moment; then she shook her head. "I think it's better the way we do things in India. We marry. We have babies. Then, if we are lucky, we fall in love. But our lives and our futures are set first. We do not hold happiness or sadness over the heads of the people we must live with. We cannot test them and hope they get a passing grade. By the time that is a question, our lives are too entwined."

"So if Marsh and I marry and have this baby before we're sure we're in love, we'll be better off? Love will just grow? I don't see that working."

"Is love all there is? There is a baby here, and two people who want it. Until the baby was a fact, the people were happy together. Is there not something wrong with that, Tracy? Is not something a little off, as you say?"

Tracy refused to show that her friend's words were softening her resistance. "Your timing's no accident, is it? You're trying to get me riled, throw me off my game, so when and if Marsh shows up, I'll be off balance and more apt to blurt out something stupid."

"Will it work?" Janya asked, not denying Tracy's assessment.

Tracy pulled her long-sleeved shirt down over the pants. It was loosely tailored, hiding the evidence. But soon she would need the blouse Janya had loaned her, and real maternity clothes, to boot.

"Gotta go. In more ways than one." Tracy grabbed her purse and smoothed Lily's dark hair as she passed on her way out the door. "Lock up, will you?"

"Are you going to find out the baby's gender?"

"I'm going to see how I feel when I get there."

"Perhaps Marsh will help you make that

decision."

Tracy kept right on walking.

By the time Tracy got to the five-story doctor's office in suburban Palmetto Grove, the sun-flooded, palm-dotted distance to the front door looked to be ten miles long. A new tropical storm, recently named Phyllis, was said to be heading in their direction, but there were no signs of its imminent arrival in this parking lot.

Tracy shifted uncomfortably behind the steering wheel and asked herself if she could make it up to the office. From previous visits she knew there was a ladies' room near the lobby elevator. Was she really capable of breezing right past it to the third floor? She thought maybe she'd been a little careless on the water front. She had figured four glasses of water would do it, and since that sounded like a lot, she had begun too early. She also hadn't exactly measured the glasses. She might well have drunk a quart and a half.

And wow, did she feel every single ounce sloshing around inside her.

She had no choice, really. If she visited the ladies' room, the whole thing was off. If Marsh had managed to clear his schedule for this, he would have to clear it again for a second try. And even though that thought gave her a little zing of pleasure, she knew it was unworthy. Besides, she had scheduled

426

the ultrasound for today because the day after Thanksgiving was a holiday for everyone at the rec center. She wanted to save every minute of paid leave for the weeks after the baby's appearance, and luckily her doctor's office was open today.

She waited until the worst of the urge to pee passed; then she got out and locked the car behind her. The stroll across the blacktop was more like a wobble, but she made it to the door and into the air-conditioning.

She rested for a moment, feeling a little better, but not for long. The sound of running water brought her up short. She'd forgotten about the lobby fountain. The building where so many of Palmetto Grove's doctors had their offices was serviceable, but some interior designer, hoping to soothe the transition from parking lot to blood tests and X-rays, had designed a fountain against the wall opposite the elevator. It came complete with a "pond" the size of a throw rug, into which a steady stream of water fell and was recycled to fall again. And again. And . . .

Tracy sprinted across the hall, only to find one of the two elevators was marked Out of Service. She punched the button labeled Up. A glance at the space above the door confirmed her worst fears. The one working elevator was on the fifth floor, and it wasn't moving.

"Great. Just great!" She punched the button again, as if that would suddenly send the car hurtling through space.

She felt someone move up beside her, and she glanced around to find Marsh not three feet away.

"In a hurry, are we?" he asked.

She told herself to stay focused. "I don't know about we. And don't use that word."

"What word?"

"The W word!"

He looked perplexed. "Are you feeling okay?"

She faced him, hands on hips. He looked tanned and fit, his ponytail neat and shorter than the last time she'd seen him. He looked deliciously masculine, too, in worn jeans and a lightweight dress shirt. He also looked perplexed.

"I am not feeling okay," she said. "I am a dam about to burst, if you really have to know. And why didn't you call to tell me you were coming?"

"I didn't see any sign you wanted to know."

"Fine. Great. Be like that."

"Like what?"

"Like somebody with no feelings."

"I don't have feelings? Wouldn't somebody have noticed that by now and told me?"

Tracy looked up and saw the elevator still wasn't moving. She punched the button again.

"That won't help," Marsh pointed out.

"They're probably loading something. Take a deep breath."

"*You* can say that because *you* don't have a quart and a half of water inside you yearning to do what that fountain is doing!"

"Oh, got you." He leaned over and punched the up button. "I'll help. That should do it."

Of course it was only a sad coincidence, but as Tracy watched, the fourth-floor light went on. The elevator was moving down.

"Damn fountain," she said. "Whose idea was that, anyway?"

Marsh glanced up at the elevator lights. Four was still illuminated. He sighed, backed up to the fountain behind them, looked it over, then flipped a switch just to one side of the rock face. "Better?"

The hall was suddenly quiet, except for the low hum of music in one of the nearby office suites. The fountain had stopped flowing.

"That's amazing," she said, shifting her weight in hopes of relieving the pressure on her bladder. "You can do everything. That's hard to live with."

"You aren't living with it. You refused, remember?" He rejoined her.

"I'm nobody's charity case, Marsh. I'm doing just fine on my own."

"Charity case?"

She looked up and saw that the elevator had progressed to three. "How many people are coming and going in this stupid building?

There must be herds of them getting on that thing. We'll be trampled when they exit."

"I asked you to live with me because I wanted you there," Marsh said. "How pig-headed can you be? You think I don't know you can manage without me? You could manage on the surface of the moon. You'd find a way to manufacture your own oxygen. You're a survivor, I know that."

"Why did you want me there, then? Because you're afraid I won't take care of our baby?" The elevator was on two now. Her gaze was locked on the lights.

"I have no doubts you'll be a good mother." The elevator doors opened, and one old man with a walker began to slowly shuffle off. Marsh kept the door from closing, and Tracy shifted her weight from one foot to the other. Once the doorway was finally clear she bolted inside, and Marsh joined her.

She punched three and watched as the doors closed.

"This is no time to talk about past arguments." She faced Marsh, who was leaning against the side of the car. "No point. Let's not ruin today."

He looked pained, as if he wanted to speak and was weighing the consequences. The elevator jerked and began to move.

"I haven't decided if I want to know the sex," she said.

"I like the idea, myself."

"And that's it? You do, so we find out?"

"Trace, why are you trying to start a fight?"

She looked at the lights over the door. They had progressed as far as the second floor. They had only moments together alone in here. She could handle that, couldn't she? She could take the high road — particularly if it was the quickest way to a toilet.

"I just want to make it clear I have some say in this," she said.

"Seems to me you have all the say. I'm just the invited guest. But let me point out that I can find out the sex from the technician without you needing to know. That way we both get what we want."

"And that's what this is all about, isn't it?" She shifted and began to lightly stretch, hoping she was moving the ocean of water inside her to a better shore.

"What?"

"Both of us getting what we want? Individually. You. Me. Baby makes three."

There was a jolt, and the elevator stopped. The light still said two, but the elevator was no longer moving.

"We aren't moving," she said, hoping for once he would disagree.

"Afraid not."

"What's the problem?"

He leaned over and read the metal plaque to the left of the console. "The problem is we should have taken the stairs. I'm guessing there weren't herds of people getting on. I'm guessing this car's on its way to that rickety-elevator graveyard in the sky."

"No!"

He seemed to realize the full import. "Not a good time to get stuck in an elevator with me, is it?"

"Not with you, not with anybody." Tracy pondered her options; then she simply slid down the wall behind her to the floor, where she folded her legs campfire style and sat forward, elbows on her thighs.

"I've hit the alarm," he said.

She could hear a bell ringing faintly somewhere in the building. "Pry open the door. They do that in movies. Pretend you're Derek Forbes and escape through the top. Do something!"

He did. He sat down beside her, knee against hers. "I hit the alarm. Someone will come. Are you claustrophobic?"

"You don't even know! I'm having your baby, and you don't know the simplest things about me!"

"That works both ways. Am *I*?"

She took a guess. "No, or you wouldn't sleep in that stupid backpacking tent."

"Good call, and using that measure, I guess you aren't, either. So there are only two problems left. Me, and all that water."

"*You* are the least of it."

"I like the sound of that. I like not being

432

the cause of all the bad things in your world. It's encouraging."

She glared at him. "How can you make jokes?"

"I'm not."

Tracy could still hear the alarm in the distance. "Doesn't this thing have a speaker? Shouldn't somebody have talked to us by now?"

"Old elevator."

"This really sucks." Tracy wondered how long she could hold out. Minutes, at best, possibly only moments.

Marsh scooted closer; then, before she could protest, he lifted her to his lap and tilted her forward, propping her back with one arm and holding her at the waist with the other. "Is that any better?"

Miraculously, it was. The pressure eased almost immediately.

They hadn't been this close in weeks. Months. She had trouble catching her breath. She leaned forward, away from his chest.

"Trace, try not to squirm, okay? It's not helping."

"I'm just trying to get comfortable. How do you know it's not helping?"

"It's not helping *me*."

It took her a moment to get that. Despite herself, she felt a little jolt of pleasure that she was turning the guy on. "This was your idea, remember? I didn't target your erogenous zones."

"Well, we hit a bull's-eye anyway, didn't we? By the way, pregnancy agrees with you. You've never been sexier."

She knew better than to let that go further. She reminded herself that she didn't want to be sexy, she wanted to be loved. Well, okay, both. Both would be good.

That was getting her nowhere. She changed the subject. "So why do you want to know whether the baby's a boy or girl?"

"Baby. Oh, right. Now I remember. That's why we're here." He tightened his arm around her a little, and his hand stole down to the mound where their baby lay, and rested lightly, fingers splayed. "I guess I like imagining what he or she will be like. There are so many possibilities, it just seems like a good idea to limit them a little."

"Do you care?"

"Care?"

"Boy or girl. Do you care?"

"Nah. Although if I had to choose, I think I'd ask for a girl. One who looks like her mother."

Tracy didn't know what to say. It was one of the most intimate things Marsh had ever said to her.

"Rather than me," he added. "That would be a lot for her to contend with. I wouldn't make a pretty girl."

She deflated. "Well, I don't care. The

chances I'll have another baby are nil, so I'll take potluck."

"Do you want more?"

"Weird, weird question. You think I have a postpartum date at the sperm bank?"

"You're young enough to try again. I've been raising an only child. It has its problems."

"Well, you won't be raising one anymore. And mine will have Bay to fight with whenever they're together. Why isn't somebody doing something about that alarm!"

"Somebody is, you can count on it. And I've told Bay about the baby, in case you were wondering. He's confused, but that seems to run in the family."

Before she could answer, there was a grinding sound and a jerk. The whole floor of the elevator shook, then it began to move again. Tracy scrambled to her feet. "We're going down!"

"Up and down. Sounds familiar to me."

The door slid open on the second floor, and Tracy made a flying leap into the hallway. The exit sign pointed left, and she hobbled in that direction. Marsh kept pace. In the stairwell, she gripped the banister and told herself she could do this. Marsh had the good sense not to speak.

They arrived on the third floor after she'd pulled herself up by the railing, hand over hand, and she threw open the door to her

435

doctor's office with just a minute to spare until her appointment.

"Now." She leaned into the reception window, practically falling over the desk that ran in front of it. "Now, now, now! I have to have the ultrasound right this minute."

The woman grinned. "They all say that."

Tracy leaned closer. There must have been something in her eyes that made it clear she wasn't kidding.

Marsh spoke from behind her.

"I think she means it," he said. "You don't want to mess with this lady right now."

The receptionist stood. "You can come back, Miss Deloche. Right this way."

The first part of the ultrasound was excruciating and happily uneventful, but after Tracy was allowed to visit the ladies' room, the second part was much more fun.

"It looks like one of those aliens with the big eyes," she said, staring at the fuzzy pictures of the baby on the monitor as the technician moved the transponder over her gel-slick belly.

Marsh stood on the side away from the monitor, gazing over her reclining body. "I think it looks like a king-size peanut."

Tracy was trying to put the experience in perspective. Marsh was here to see his child. He had jollied her along in the elevator to keep her from freaking out. She should not exploit this connection. Sperm meets egg = baby created. Conception was just that clinical, even if they had enjoyed it.

Okay, "enjoyed" wasn't quite the right word. They had created this tiny alien creature the very first time, or at least during the very first night, they had ever made love. And they had waited a long time for that moment, held off until they were sure the situation was right, so the moment had been, well, ecstatic.

Sperm ecstatically meets egg = creation.

Marsh touched her shoulder, and his hand stayed there. "Trace, Gwen here asked you a question."

"I'm sorry." Tracy looked at the monitor to see if something was obviously wrong. Then she looked at Gwen, young and blonde and still clearly enjoying her job. "I didn't hear you."

"I said I can tell you the gender of the baby if you want to know."

Tracy considered. Marsh squeezed her shoulder. "You don't have to find out now," he said. "I can wait, too. Let's leave this decision up to you."

She looked away from the monitor and up at him. For a moment, despite her better judgment, she felt the thrill of a real connection. Marsh was smiling down at her with something she might even call tenderness.

"Let's find out," she said. "You want to, and I'm ambivalent."

"You'd do that for me?"

"I'm actually a nice person. Believe it or not, most people like me."

He smiled. "Then let's not."

"Not what? Like me?"

"Not find out."

"What? Why the switch?"

"Because not knowing will give us something fun to talk about. Wonder about. Life's filled with surprises. Maybe not knowing will stir up a few more."

"Then we'll leave the sex a mystery," Gwen said before Tracy could respond.

"I'll just paint the baby's room green, I guess," Tracy said. "I like sage green, and it's good for a boy or a girl."

"What room?" Marsh asked.

"The one I use now. I'll be sleeping on a sofa bed in the living room. It's the only good solution."

"The only one, huh?"

"Better than making a nursery out of the dining area."

"Definitely better than that." He removed his hand and stepped back a little.

She looked at the monitor again. "I've thought of all the alternatives, and that's what it comes down to. I'm going to need a crib, a changing table. I'll have to get Janya watching out at garage sales for me. It's so hard to believe, but there's the baby. It's real, isn't it? This whole thing is real."

Marsh didn't answer. Tracy watched the baby, who was floating happily inside her, and wondered how, at the same moment that she was watching her very own son or daughter, she could still feel lonely, just because Marsh was no longer touching her.

CHAPTER TWENTY-TWO

Blake definitely wasn't a typical date. On their first evening together they had attended a posh party at his beach house. The next time they'd eaten at the shabby little Italian restaurant with the limited menu and fabulous food.

Now, miniature golf.

"I used to play with Marsh and Bay," Tracy told Maggie after Maggie explained what Blake had planned for the evening. "Bay was better than both of us put together. Played real golf, sure, although mostly just to dress up the scenery, even if I was a lot better than most of the guys I went out with."

Maggie was sure there were a lot of things Tracy had never done on a date, at least in the old days, on the road to becoming a trophy wife. She didn't think her friend and landlady regretted changing, but today she seemed glum, even though she had reported that the morning's ultrasound had shown that her baby was already totally adorable and growing appropriately.

Maggie rummaged in her closet for a thin black cardigan to wear over her T-shirt. Blake was going to pick her up in ten minutes, but she was almost ready.

"He's fun to be with," Maggie said. "Undemanding, too. No groping."

"There's something wrong, then."

Maggie laughed. "He knows about Felo, and he just got out of a relationship himself. I think that's all it is. We're taking it slow."

"How slow?"

"Undetectably." Maggie found the cardigan and backed out of the closet. Tracy was sitting cross-legged on her bed, staring out the window.

"Your mind's a million miles away," Maggie said.

Tracy glanced at her. "You won't like what I was thinking."

"Thanks for the warning." Maggie waited.

"I was thinking I hope my life doesn't come to that. Going on dates with guys I don't really want to be with, even hot guys like Blake, just so I won't have to think about the one I threw away."

"Well . . . wow."

"Yeah, I know. I warned you to duck."

"Not loudly enough."

"Have you talked to Felo since he told you about that state's attorney you went after at the press conference?"

"He's left a couple of phone messages, just to tell me he's still looking into the murders, and I faxed him a photo of that slot machine we found at the Duttas'. He's probably emailed, but my internet server's almost as bad as my cell-phone carrier. They're supposed to repair it this afternoon."

She didn't add that she had also asked another friend in her old department to send her any information she could gather about Blake Armstrong, including his credit report — and not because they were dating.

"So you're going to drop it? Him, I mean?" Tracy asked.

Maggie was beginning to feel annoyed. "Do we know each other this well?"

"Uh-huh. I think I know you well enough to realize talking about this isn't easy or normal. It's a lot easier for me, and I'm not enjoying it, either. But I'm beginning to wonder if both of us are just crazy. Janya says in India they work out the problems after their relationships are in place."

"Yeah, and they set brides on fire because their dowries aren't big enough or they happen to get pregnant with a daughter."

"Well, there's plenty of abuse in this country, too, and some of it's gold plated. But maybe Americans are so careful, so sure we have to dot every *i* and cross every *t*, we don't take chances."

"I'd say the divorce rate in this country

doesn't back you up."

"Yeah . . . Maybe not." Tracy's brief spurt of enthusiasm drained away.

Maggie hated to see that. "You're talking about Marsh and you, right?"

"I kind of thought you'd get what I'm talking about, since you're jogging along in a parallel groove."

Maggie could feel her defenses tumbling. "I do get it." She dropped to the bed beside Tracy to lace up her sneakers. "I'm still sorting this out."

"You're a careful sorter."

"When I was a kid, I made piles of clothes, and matched them by size, type and color, just so I could find everything when I needed it. Mom would go into my dresser when I was at school and mix the panties with the shorts, the socks with the T-shirts. She said it wasn't healthy to care that much about having everything in the right place."

"Wanda's not the most predictable person out there, I guess. You probably drive each other crazy."

That was too clearly true to acknowledge. "Why don't you just sit Marsh down and tell him how confused you are? Ask him how he feels about you."

"Good idea. You first."

Maggie finished tying the second shoe before she spoke. "It's not the same for me. I know how Felo says he feels. I just . . . I just don't know if I'm ready to trust him." She glanced at Tracy, who still looked pensive. "But tonight I'm just going out on a date with a friend." She paused; then she decided to tell the whole truth. "A friend who might have had his hair cut by Harit Dutta, but didn't admit to me that he even knew the man."

"Is that why you're going? So you can find out what's up with that?"

"Yeah. Part of it. I mean, it's probably nothing. Maybe Harit wasn't Blake's barber, and that gel thing —" she shook her hands over her head in imitation "— was just a co-incidence. When I followed up last week, Mom's contact at the shop didn't remember Blake's name, but he said a lot of their business is walk-in, and if a walk-in pays cash, there's nothing on file unless the guy asks for a receipt."

"For all you know he's been getting his hair cut when he goes out of town."

"I'm just keeping my ear to the ground tonight to see if anything comes up. It's the longest shot around, but what else do I have to do right now?"

"You're asking the wrong person. Me, I'm going home to watch the weather reports and find somebody to nail plywood over my windows if need be."

As a native of the Sunshine State, Maggie wasn't worried about the tropical storm picking up steam in the Caribbean after a lazy start. From experience, she knew storms this late in the season, when the waters had cooled, were disorganized and short-lived. In her opinion there was too little real news at the moment, so the local media were harping on this last-gasp attempt by Mother Nature.

"Well, I'm going to beat Blake at miniature golf while the sun shines," she said. "Wish me luck."

"You got it." Tracy slid off the bed. "Glad we had this little talk."

"Why?"

"So I won't feel like a total loser tonight while I contemplate my rapidly changing belly button."

"Because you have company in the failed-relationship department?"

"Because somebody else on Happiness Key is just as confused about her life as I am."

There was no good way to just ask Blake if Harit had been his barber. The name for that was "interrogation," and Maggie was on a date with the guy. Blake knew she was looking into the Duttas' deaths, and if she asked him if he had a personal connection to the case, her motive would be clear.

Instead, she decided to find out more about him. This was their third date, and delving a little deeper made sense on a number of levels.

445

"Are you half this good on a real golf course?" she asked after he hit a ball through a tunnel, around a hillside curve and into the correct lobe of a four-leaf clover.

"One of the smartest things an engineering professor ever told me was to find a good golf pro. You'd be surprised how many deals are sealed on a golf course."

"That was true in my profession, too. Any suspect I played with would have confessed by the third hole, just to keep from having to finish the course with me."

"You're not that bad." Blake grinned his Beach Boy best. He was definitely an appealing guy. Open, friendly and courteous, but not to a fault. Maggie always hated guys who treated her like a piece of fragile china, and Blake was much too smart for that. He was a good judge of people, and she wondered if the same professor who had recommended the golf pro had also recommended a few helpful psych classes.

"I'm coordinated." Maggie followed Blake's fabulous shot with one that took her to the wrong lobe, but not the worst of the four. "But not infallible," she added. She watched him sink the ball into the hole.

"You strike me as somebody who's probably good at everything you try. A good cop, I'm sure."

"And I can bake a cherry pie, Billy Boy."

"But are you a young girl who cannot leave

446

her mother?" he asked, impressing her by quoting the same song.

"Nope. Just a regular Renaissance woman, that's me."

"You must have plans to do something else with your life."

"You don't think working for my mother at Wanda's Wonderful Pies is my life goal?"

His cell phone rang, and he apologized after he read the caller ID. It was the second call he'd gotten since they began. "I have to take this. I'm sorry."

She sat on a bench as he wandered off, and removed sand from her shoe, glad for the chance. Blake rejoined her once her shoe was back on, followed her to her ball and watched her put it through a second tunnel.

On the way back, he draped his arm over her shoulder. "I think you're trying to re-assess your life. Keeping one finger in the law enforcement pie, baking pies with the rest of them."

"We've about used up the pie sayings, wouldn't you say?" She stepped onto the green and moved around the ball, which was at an awkward angle uphill from the hole. From experience, she knew this was the kind of shot at which she did not excel. She debated whether she should simply chip the ball to the flat area on the other side of the hole and put it in on the next stroke. Or should she try to sink it, against all odds?

There was really nothing to debate. She tried to sink it and almost did, missing the hole by half an inch. The ball rolled back to her feet.

"This could go on all evening," she warned.

"And I bet if I said you could just add the six maximum to your score and go on to the next hole, you'd laugh at me, right?"

"Darn right." She positioned herself and tried again. This time the ball went in.

"Wow." He laughed. "Dogged determination coupled with a lot of luck and a little skill. Does that describe you?"

"A lot of skill and a little luck. What about you?"

He waited until they were at the next hole, the tenth of eighteen. Lucky Putt was all about good fortune. The four-leaf clover they'd just finished, a horseshoe, a wishbone. This one was the pot of gold at the end of the rainbow. The goal was to hit the ball between strategically placed concrete leprechauns and down a steep incline into a pot of gold sunk into a hill. A painted rainbow pointed the way.

"I'm one of the lucky ones." Blake made the first putt because he'd done better on the previous hole. He watched as his ball clipped the second leprechaun and tumbled down a level. Now he would have to hit the ball across a small wooden bridge over a running stream.

"Not if that's any example." Maggie positioned herself carefully and managed to get her ball through the leprechaun gauntlet and into position to hit it into the hole on her next stroke. Which she did.

"*Usually* I'm lucky," Blake amended as they walked down to his ball. "Good parents, plenty of money, good schools, driving ambition."

"Where did you go to school?"

"Carnegie Mellon. Georgia Tech. How about you?"

"I stayed close to home. University of Miami."

"Did you always want to be a cop?"

He was asking more questions than she was. Good manners or evasiveness? she wondered. "Apparently not," she said, "because these days I'm baking pies."

"But doing a little investigating on the side. How's that going?"

Maggie was careful not to show any particular interest in the question. She stepped aside to let Blake aim for the bridge. He missed, and his ball went into the water.

"Man, I thought I had that," he said. "Just hooked to the right."

She wondered why he'd flubbed a fairly easy shot, although she told herself that was silly. Was she so hard up for something to do that she was seeing nerves where there weren't any?

She waited until he brought the ball out of the water and got it easily across the bridge; then she walked around and watched him sink it.

"I looked into some things, but nothing panned out," she said when Blake joined her off the green and they started toward the next hole, which had a slowly revolving roulette wheel in the middle and two narrow passages to each side. The wheel was low enough that it would send a ball spinning in a collision, but any golfer who lifted his ball into a black slot went right to the final hole.

"You got me interested, so I read about the case online," he said.

She waited, a perfect study in nonchalance. This was where Blake announced that the dead man had, in fact, cut his hair once or twice, something he hadn't realized until he saw the photograph. He would talk about coincidence, and how shocked he had been. Murder so close to his own life, and he hadn't even known.

But Blake went a different route. "I can't get those children out of my head," he said. "I keep thinking how difficult this is going to be for them. Bad enough the parents were killed, but the article said there's no family in the country."

"True, but the kids are being well taken care of."

"I lost an uncle to violence. Somebody

grabbed his wallet, and he went after him. The guy shot him through the heart. I was ten. I still remember how awful I felt when I found out what happened."

She supposed that *could* explain Blake's curiosity, that and the fact that she'd been a cop and generally people found her former job interesting, due mostly to the plethora of inaccurate cop shows on the networks.

Or maybe Blake's interest was something more.

"Well, it's a dead end," she said. "No pun intended. I think we just have to assume the deaths were what the Miami police believe they were. A murder-suicide. Love gone awry."

"And doesn't it far too often?" he asked, as if he understood that all too well.

His cell phone rang again. He lifted it from his pocket and looked at the number, then answered, moving away to carry on his conversation. Maggie played through, managing this one in three strokes.

Blake rejoined her.

"Sorry."

"Something come up?"

"There's always something. I'm getting regular reports on the storm. People are starting to worry. It looks like we're going to get hit."

"Take my word for it, it won't amount to anything. Too late in the year."

"Did you know they've revised the hurricane season a couple of times over the decades? It gets longer and longer, stretching into November now, and who knows how long it'll be in a couple of years. The water's staying warm later. Phyllis might surprise you. I think she's surprising the meteorologists."

"I guess it's your job to worry."

He smiled, but with a noticeable lack of enthusiasm. "I'm afraid so. In fact, I'm not going to be very good company tonight. Would you mind too much if I take a rain check on dinner? I've got to pick up some papers for a colleague and get them over to his hotel, then we're going to make some phone calls."

"Not a problem. Where are the papers? I can drive with you to get them, if that saves you time."

"No, they're at my house. I'll just take you back."

She had driven to Blake's and parked so he wouldn't have to make the trip out to her end of the key. She held out her hand for the scorecard and checked it. "You're ahead. But not by much. Give me one more hole to catch up, then let's call it a night."

He leaned over and kissed her. Not casually, but not with inordinate enthusiasm, either. "You're easy to be around. I was looking forward to getting to know you much better tonight."

She smiled, glad, then, that the date was ending. She wasn't ready for "much better," and now she wouldn't have to remind him.

She didn't catch up to his score, but by the end of their last hole, she wasn't so far behind that she had to hang her head. They turned in their clubs and balls at the little stand, and headed for Blake's car.

On the trip home they chatted, but only intermittently. Clearly his mind was elsewhere. After he parked, they both got out, and she went around to his side to say goodbye. She knew something was bothering him.

"Can a tropical storm do that much damage?" she asked. "Enough to delay your project or make you rework your plans?"

"Anything's possible, and that's what worries us. You can bet the odds all you want, but sometimes, no matter what they are, they'll go against you." He rested his hands on her shoulders. "I had fun, even with the phone calls. I owe you dinner."

"Not to worry. When things settle down."

She kissed him lightly on the lips, then raised a hand in farewell. He didn't linger and headed right for the house. As she walked toward her car, which was parked on the side of the road so as not to block his driveway, she watched Blake out of the corner of her eye. He didn't go to the front door and use a key to get into the beach house. He went to the garage door and raised his hand to the door frame. She realized he was punching a code into a keypad at the side, because after a moment, the door slid open.

She wondered if the keypad had been programmed before he moved in, or if he had programmed it himself with a code he could easily remember. A birth date, the last four digits of his social security number. Numbers a cop could get hold of with very little effort. Numbers that would probably show up on the report her friend was supposed to fax her tonight.

She slid behind her steering wheel and thrust her key in the ignition. One thing was perfectly clear about her date with Blake. She had set out to learn more about him, but for every question she had asked, he had asked two. Perhaps he was just a polite guy with a real interest in people.

Or perhaps he wasn't.

The rest of the evening dragged. Maggie filled the time by vacuuming up cat hair and cleaning out the refrigerator, but by the time the clock struck eleven, she was glad it was time to go to bed. She was pulling on her nightgown when the telephone rang. She didn't even check caller ID. She was so bored she was willing to talk to a telemarketer.

Of course, the man on the other end of the line was the person she was both most and least happy to have a conversation with right before going to bed.

"Felo," she said. She couldn't think of another thing to say.

"I figured you'd be up," he said. "Wasn't sure you'd be home."

She pondered that for a moment, then told the truth. "There's nobody here I'd want to stay out late with."

He didn't pick up the cue. "Well, I'm glad you're there. I have some information you'll want."

She felt a stab of disappointment. So the call wasn't personal, but what had she expected? She had yet to respond to the bombshell Felo had delivered in the bar at Pelican Point. She seemed incapable of dealing with it. These days she was like a tree that had been cut down, only to send out new shoots in every direction. She couldn't let go of what she'd believed. She couldn't simply trust Felo again. She had been wrong about Alvaro, as well as Felo's own reasons for asking her not to confront Paul Smythe, but there was so much more. Anger that he was pressuring her to become a wife and mother. Confusion about who she was when she was with him, and who she was when they were apart.

"You got my messages?" she asked.

"Right. I'm glad I have voice mail, since you're good at calling when you know I won't be able to pick up."

She didn't protest, because it was true. "I don't know what to say to you," she said, which was also true.

"Let's just concentrate on this case right now. Alvaro's been able to get some interesting information about the dice and that slot machine bank you faxed the photo of. Good thing you found it. The dice were a limited edition of two thousand. The bank was a limited edition of three hundred. And guess whose name was on both lists? One of the highest of the high rollers?"

She had a feeling she knew. The very man who tonight had talked about playing the odds. The one who had claimed to be lucky and wealthy. The one who had so casually asked her what she'd discovered recently about the murders. The one who had told her, on their first date, that he and his partners had just returned from Las Vegas. He'd made some joke about it, but even then she had wondered idly if he was one of those guys who really *didn't* go to Vegas for the shows and the camaraderie.

"Blake Armstrong?" she asked.

"Dead on. How did you know?"

She was silent for a long moment. Felo let the silence build.

Maggie finally broke it. She told him about her suspicion that Harit had been Blake's barber, though unacknowledged, then told him what else she knew.

"Nice of you to keep me up to date," he said once she had finished.

"I'm sorry, but all we really know now is that Blake is a gambler, and he probably gave Harit Dutta the dice and the bank, most likely for his children. Little gifts he happened to have on hand."

"Seems likely."

"I can't figure out how or why they're connected, though. Harit had no money for gambling. And I checked with the manager at the barber shop. He didn't recognize Blake's name."

"You asked him directly?"

"Did. Of course, it's possible Blake was one of Harit's private clients, but unless he was just a walk-in who paid cash, the manager should have recognized his name. Harit paid the shop what they were owed for those clients, even though he didn't have to."

"Is it possible Armstrong was referred to Harit by somebody else, another customer maybe, so Harit saw no need to pay the shop for someone who never would have gone there in the first place?"

Maggie had been standing, but now she found a chair and lowered herself into it. Rumba jumped up on her lap, and she stroked the cat as she wondered how she could have missed that possibility herself. Now it seemed so obvious.

"I didn't think of that," she admitted,

although she didn't want to. "It's definitely possible."

"That's why the Lone Ranger had Tonto, Mags." He moved on quickly, as if he knew she wouldn't appreciate the reminder. "Even if it's true, that's a long leap — from cutting hair to murder victim."

"Right. Maybe they met when Harit cut Blake's hair, but what would that have to do with his death?"

"Probably nothing."

"No, Felo, I think this is something. Blake knows I'm looking into the case. He asked me about it tonight."

"You were with him?"

"Twelve holes of miniature golf, then something came up. He kept getting phone calls. He dropped me back at his house so I could get my car and come home. Something to do with the tropical storm, he said. Work stuff."

Felo was all business. "You said he knows you're looking into the case."

"I told him a while ago. And he asked me about it tonight, but he's never admitted Harit was his barber, or that he even knew him. But he *did* know him. Harit's children have the toys to prove it."

"Not a slam dunk, Mags. We could be missing something else — probably are."

"I don't know where to go from here. I need some kind of connection between the men. Right now I don't know any reason why Blake would have been involved in the Duttas' murders. They were from completely different worlds."

"Maybe Armstrong gave *Mrs.* Dutta the toys for her children. Maybe they were having an affair."

She wondered, but it didn't feel right. "I guess it's possible, but Janya says Kanira Dutta had no family, no friends, no resources. When would she have gotten away from those kids to have an affair? How would she and Blake even have met?"

"We need more information about Armstrong. What he's been doing in his free time. Who his friends are, if he has any locally. Anything suspicious in his past. Anything shady going on with his personal and work life."

"I tried to ask questions tonight, but for every one I asked, he asked two."

"That's not a good thing. Maybe he's aware you're on to something. Maybe he's checking *you* out."

"I told him I hadn't found anything, and that it was likely the deaths were exactly what the police said they were."

"You need to be careful."

Maggie still couldn't believe that Blake Armstrong — fun, transparent Blake — had anything to do with the murders. Were she and Felo grasping at straws? Were there perfectly good explanations for everything that bothered them? But one thing she had learned from her years on the force — sociopaths were perfectly capable of lying without detection.

"I noticed tonight he has a keypad on his garage door," she said. "It might not be too hard to get in."

"Stay out of his house. You're not a cop anymore, remember? And if you were, no judge would give you a search warrant based on the little you have. You don't even carry a gun, Mags. You gave it back, along with your badge. Don't take chances."

"You're right," she said, because he was. Although that didn't mean she was going to listen.

"We'll figure out the connection," Felo said. "If there is one. But back off for now, okay? Look like you've given up. We need to sit down together and see what we can come up with, before you go any further."

Despite herself, a part of her was warmed by that possibility, even though another part was annoyed that he felt she required his assistance. "Sit down together?"

"I don't like this storm. Phyllis has been erratic from the beginning. And now she's heading your way. The water's warmer than usual this time of year, and that could lead to anything. Why don't you get out of town. Your mother will close the shop, and she won't

460

need you."

"You want me to come all the way to Miami because of a wimpy tropical storm?"

"Why take a chance? And not Miami. Meet me at Alvaro's camp. That's where I'll be."

Alvaro's camp was halfway between, in the middle of nowhere, but inland. If Phyllis really did make it to hurricane status, the camp wouldn't be a bad place to wait it out. Because he was in the middle of a swamp, Alvaro had a generator, his own water supply, enough food for weeks. Not a bad place at all.

Particularly if Felo was there.

"Is Alvaro there?" she asked.

"No."

"Will he *be* there?"

"Maybe. Does that matter?"

She considered. If she said no, that was a gift to Felo, a sign she was sorry about her doubts, that she trusted his word. It said that despite all her previous misgivings, she was willing to accept the truth that his old friend and partner was more good guy than bad.

If she said yes, then she wondered if Felo would simply write her off for good.

"You know what they say about three being a crowd," she said instead.

"I know what they say about a lot of things."

She couldn't go deeper, couldn't concede. "I'll think it over, Felo. I need to check with Mom, see if Tracy needs my help getting things done around here in preparation. I'll let you know."

He didn't argue; instead he changed the subject. "I'm sending you an email with an attachment. The two lists from the casino and something even more damning. You'll see when you get it."

She didn't want to hang up. But she didn't know what to say to keep the conversation going.

"Let me know one way or other whether you're coming," Felo said.

"I will. And thank you for doing all this legwork." She paused. "Will you thank Alvaro for me?"

"Maybe you can do that yourself." He hung up.

Maggie held the phone against her cheek for a long moment. Then she replaced it in the cradle and went to her computer. She turned it on and waited until it had booted up, then she tried going on the internet, to see if the cable company really had repaired her connection.

Surprisingly, they had. She downloaded her mail, then found Felo's email and downloaded the attachment so she could print it out.

It consisted of three parts. The two lists, and a copy of both the back and front of a player's card from the Atlantis Casino with Blake's name and photo. There was a note at the bottom from Felo:

This is the highest category of card, with the largest number of perks attached, meaning your friend Armstrong is well known and loved there for the money he loses. Basically the card keeps track of everything he spends, and tallies up what he's worth to them and how badly they want to keep him. I wonder if his employers know?

Maggie fingered the paper; then, on a whim, she folded it and put it in her purse to examine more closely when she had a free moment. Was it possible Harit had discovered Blake's gambling addiction from the toys Blake had given him? Had he tried to blackmail him? It seemed so unlikely, yet it also seemed possible.

Harit.

Maggie realized she had never downloaded Harit's book to her own computer. Now she found the emails she had sent herself with the chapters of his novel attached and downloaded them all, taking time to put the files on a CD so she could give it to Janya tomorrow for the children.

She debated turning off the computer. It was late, and she was finally tired enough to go to sleep. Instead, she opened the first file of Harit's novel. She began to read and immediately was caught up in the prose and the story. A young man, searching for truth in a place and time she knew nothing about.

The chapter's ending was most surprising. There were several spaces, then notes, segmented into paragraphs. She read a few and realized Harit had used the chapter end as something of a diary. Notes to himself about what he needed to do in the next chapter and research he needed to conduct. But not everything was about the book. With surprise she saw a list of groceries he'd apparently needed to buy. Another had to do with a doctor's appointment for Lily the next day. A third was a long rambling account of a philosophical debate with Rishi. Everything around him had been fodder for Harit's fiction, and he hadn't wanted to lose or waste any of it.

She paged forward to the end of the next chapter. Again, more notes. Chapters three and four were the same. She imagined the others were, too.

Maggie stared at the end of chapter four. There were dates, although no year. She had no idea how long it had taken him to write these chapters, but she suspected that tomorrow, after some sleep, when she read them all and especially when she read the notes at the end, she would know a lot more about Harit Dutta. And if she was really lucky, she would know something about the person who had killed him, as well.

CHAPTER TWENTY-THREE

Maybe Maggie slept well because she knew that when she awoke, she had something interesting to investigate. Or maybe she was simply tired from a long day at the shop and an evening that had only really gotten interesting at bedtime. Whatever it was, she woke up earlier than usual, feeling rested. She rose and stretched just as raucous banging started outside her house. Rumba yowled loudly in protest as she slipped into shorts and a T-shirt. She opened the front door and found two tattooed men in cutoffs and three-to-a-pack white undershirts nailing plywood over her living room window.

"What's going on?" she asked, although the answer was perfectly clear.

"Miss Deloche told us to start with yours and work our way down."

"Why? Did that stupid storm turn into a hurricane?"

"Depends on what station you listen to," said the first guy, who had a red, white and blue bull stampeding down his forearm.

The second added his piece. "Miss Deloche said she doesn't want to take any chances."

"Bang away," Maggie said.

Inside, she noted the time. It was only six, and while she normally got to the shop by seven, she suspected today wasn't going to be just any day. Did people buy more pies before a tropical storm? She imagined her mother was asking the same question. She dialed her parents' number, and Wanda answered after one ring.

"Are you going to open today?" Maggie asked on the edge of a yawn. "Earlier? Later? On time?"

"What do you think?"

Maggie could probably count on the fingers of one hand the times her mother had asked her that question. "You don't have a generator, so you might start early, but I wouldn't make too many. Use up what you have and see if the supplier will cancel today's order. If the electricity goes off, you don't want pies in the oven and stuff spoiling in the coolers."

"Did that part already, but we're thinking alike on this."

Maggie wasn't sure thinking like her mother was a good thing, but she felt a warm glow at what amounted to praise from Wanda. She wondered if this was something a woman never outgrew, the need for her mother to be proud of her.

"When do you want me in?" Maggie asked.

"Take an extra hour, and pack up whatever you might need for a few days and anything too precious to lose. Your dad says they'll be going door to door on the key telling people to leave and find shelter inland."

"Ordering?"

"Suggesting, at least for now."

Maggie knew the difference. Nobody was terribly worried. Yet.

"I'll throw a few things together, then I'll be in," she said. "I'll probably leave my stuff here with Rumba, then I can come back for everything if I have to evacuate. What are they saying about the storm? Somebody's outside nailing plywood over my windows."

"Winds low seventies, turning this way and picking up speed. Technically still Tropical Storm Phyllis, but only just."

Maggie didn't need a storm in her life. Not when things were just starting to get interesting on the Dutta murders. On the other hand, maybe a storm was *exactly* what she needed. Especially if Blake left the island and she didn't.

While Wanda detailed her plans for the day, Maggie turned on her computer, determined to read a few chapters of Harit's notes before she made the trip to town. She wondered if Blake's name would show up; then she wondered what kind of woman was most excited by a man when she thought he might

468

be involved in a murder.

"See you in a little while," she said as Wanda wound down.

"This will be a good day to be a baker and not a cop."

Maggie didn't tell her mother that she planned to be a little of both.

If Wanda had been paid a nickel for every hurricane and tropical storm that fizzled out before it did any real damage, she figured she would be rich in her own right, and able to hang up her apron and pot holders. Not that she would, but maybe she would hire a little more help and just concentrate on recipes.

Recipes were the center of the fun at Wanda's Wonderful Pies, and now she knew that for the truth it was. Oh, sure, she liked the other parts all right, talking to customers, making ten crusts at a time in her industrial-size food processor, then rolling them out by hand the way God had intended. But the part that made having the shop worthwhile was developing her very own, one-of-a-kind, completely extraordinary pies.

Now that she finally had the Orange Blossom Special just right, she felt like a million bucks. Nothing better — well, maybe sex was better, and that first time a grinning nurse brought you a new baby with ten fingers and toes — but next to that, nothing was better than knowing you'd created something other

469

people would enjoy for years to come.

Windy old Phyllis wasn't sparking any real fear in Wanda's breast. She was more worried the power would go off before the pies in the shop oven were finished. People hunkering down to ride out the storm would probably be out shopping for the long haul. One of those pies would taste mighty good to a houseful of people with nothing to do but eat and wait for their roof to blow off.

The door tinkled and Maggie blew in, a suitcase in one hand, an umbrella in the other. Rain was falling steadily now, and every minute or so a particularly strong gust of wind rattled the front windows. Ken had promised to come over on his lunch break and install the hurricane shutters, and Wanda wouldn't be sad to see him. This could be the last time for a while, if Phyllis caused any real problems for the Palmetto Grove police force.

"Pies already in the oven, apple and pear," Wanda said. "You have a problem getting over the bay?"

"The light at the intersection on the key turned red three times before I could get on the bridge." Maggie shook her umbrella dry behind her with more energy than Wanda had felt in years. "Lots of people evacuating already. Do you know what the neighbors are doing?"

"I haven't talked to everybody yet, but Tracy's planning to leave, and she advised me to do the same. I can't imagine anybody will want to stay now that our windows are boarded up."

"She called me, too. What are you doing?"

"Oh, my stuff's more or less together. I'll go home and get the rest of it once we close, get Chase and the stuff I didn't throw in the car this morning." She was about to ask Maggie if her plans had changed when the door flew open and Derek Forbes filled the doorway behind her daughter, with dour Larry close behind him.

Maggie greeted them before she turned her attention back to her mother. "Want me to start moving stuff from the bottom shelves up higher?"

Wanda didn't expect flooding, but she knew almost anything could happen. Maybe most of the storms that whipped through came to nothing, but she had also lived through Hurricane Andrew, and Maggie, who had only been a bit older than Olivia was now, obviously remembered the aftermath.

"You do that."

Once Maggie was on her way back to the kitchen, Wanda smiled brightly at Derek, then at Larry, who flopped down at a table and slipped off his wet sneakers.

"You're a tad early for pie right out of the oven. But I made half a dozen cold pies last night so I could serve them up today. Unless

471

you came to say you're heading back to California. If the airport's still open."

"Open long enough to send back everybody who's not essential. We're close to finishing what we need here anyway. Just a couple more scenes before we head back to California." Derek was practically dancing with excitement. "A big one on the bridge. You have no idea how perfect this storm will be! We tried the scene in a regular thunderstorm, but I want the real thing, not special effects. It wasn't big enough, grand enough." He swept his arms out and around to make his point.

"You want *that* big, you'll be here a long time. Phyllis won't amount to much. You mark my words. And how can you film in a storm, anyway? It'll ruin all your equipment."

"We're professionals, so we know all the tricks. We have everything we need. We're going to wait as long as we can, then pop over to the pedestrian walkway, jump the police barriers and film the scene one more time. The local cops have told us we can't, of course. So we'll have one chance and one chance only before they catch up with us."

Wanda put her hands over her ears. "Don't tell me that!"

Derek wrapped his arms around her for a huge hug. "You're not going to report me, Wanda. And we'll pay our fines and make a nice contribution to the police benevolent league in penance."

Wanda's knees were weak, but, of course, they were weak whenever Ken hugged her, too. Still, this hug would be good for a whole lot of conversation in her future.

"Just don't tell me another thing," she said as she came back to earth.

"Well, since we're practically business partners, you've got to be on my side. Right?"

She felt herself nodding, but she wasn't sure to what. "But no more revelations. I don't want my loyalties tested. I don't need trouble at home."

"Not another word about it, then."

"You'll be careful? Even if Phyllis isn't something to stick in your memoirs, these storms can stir up some gusts. Don't want you sailing off to Key West on one of them."

"I hope somebody remembers to film it if I do."

"You can bet we will," Larry said with a trace of venom, as if that might be a wish come true. Clearly the daredevil moments ahead were not ones he looked forward to.

She had to smile, because Derek Forbes, for all his macho good looks and considerable charisma, reminded her not of Ken, the man she loved and counted on for everything important in her life, but of Junior in his early adolescence. She supposed it was no wonder none of Deke's marriages had lasted more than a few years. His enthusiasm, vigor and charm were delightful, but along with them came a restlessness and penchant for risky behavior no woman would tolerate for long.

How long would he be interested in pie shops, and at what point would he turn his attention to something totally alien?

"You've been thinking about my offer?" he asked, as if he were reading her mind.

"A woman doesn't get an offer like that more than once in her life. It's taking up a lot of real estate in my head."

"Well, it should."

She smiled, because he was so clearly in love with the idea — and life right along with it.

"We'll have that conversation when this storm's over," she promised.

He looked confident things would go his way. "So will you give me all the pies you've got ready? We're hanging out in our trailers on the key, and I've got to keep everybody happy while we do."

She was glad he hadn't pressed harder about the franchise. She was in no mood to make a decision.

Maggie came out, and they packaged all the pies while Derek chatted on about the movie, and plans to fly back to California, then return to Palmetto Grove in a few weeks to wrap up final camera work and other details.

He left, trailing good spirits and enthusiasm

behind him, along with the unsmiling Larry, who had pies stacked under both his flabby arms.

Maggie spent the morning organizing and moving everything perishable. The shop was some distance inland, and she didn't really expect it to flood, so she figured she could leave the one suitcase she'd hauled in up on a table, since there was nothing in it she needed for the next few days.

Most likely any water damage would come from above, holes in the roof or shingles blown off to funnel water below, but preparation was mindless work. While she squeezed things in on the higher shelves, she considered what little she knew about the Duttas' deaths.

She was nearly finished when Wanda came into the kitchen. The pies were cooling on racks, but the oven was off now. With the wind picking up, she had told Maggie they were finished cooking for the day.

"Your dad's here."

"Putting up the shutters?"

"Nah, now he's got somebody coming later to do that. He doesn't have time."

Maggie followed her mother out to the shop, where her father was sitting at the counter with a slice of pear pie and a mug of coffee. Since Maggie's adolescence, Ken Gray had been her role model. He was the quintessential good cop, convinced his job was important and that it was important to do it right. He was fair, thoughtful and always on the alert for the best way to defuse any dangerous situation. There was a genuine rapport between her father and mother, too. Her mother talked and her father listened. It worked for them.

"Any news?" Maggie asked after she walked around the counter to kiss his cheek. "Sounds like you're going to be busy."

He pointed at the pie. "Lunch, dinner and tomorrow's breakfast. And I should be out on the roads already. Came to talk some sense into you and your mother while I eat."

Wanda sniffed. "I have good sense to spare."

"Then you'll close up right now and get back across the bridge, pick up whatever you can, along with that greyhound of yours, and go stay with the Greens. They're far enough inland you won't have problems there. By this afternoon at some point, the bridge will be closed to traffic in both directions."

"I'm way ahead of you. I told them I'd be there by five. Even saved them a couple of pies."

Stu Green had been a cop with Maggie's dad in the old days and had retired with his wife to a lake about thirty miles northeast of Palmetto Grove.

"What's wrong with *now?*" Ken held up his mug for more coffee.

"I got pies to sell, and Maggie's getting

things put up, in case we get a little water."

"What are the chances the storm will amount to anything?" Maggie asked her father.

"Well, it's officially a hurricane now, and it's turned in our direction. Not the biggest on the block, but you know how these things work. We could get clobbered, and a bad storm can spawn most anything. We're in emergency mode."

The telephone rang, and Wanda went to take the call. From the sound of things, it was one of her suppliers, who wanted to moan at length about how the storm was affecting his business, so Maggie knew she had her father to herself for a few minutes.

"What about you?" Ken asked her. "You going with your mom?"

"I haven't decided for sure," she said, although that wasn't exactly true. "I know you're in a hurry, but I need to pick your brain about something while you finish."

"Ask away."

Her father had already told her everything he could about the Dutta case from the perspective of the local cops, so now she cut right to the chase. "You know Felo and I are still looking into those murders in Miami."

"What I *know* is that you don't sound done with the job or the man, Maggie."

It was like her father to waste no time. Maggie didn't wince, but she came close. "I don't know about that, but I do know a few things are turning out to be interesting." In as few words as possible, she caught her dad up on everything she and Felo had just learned, including the possible connection to Blake Armstrong.

"And there's something more," she went on. "I sent myself a copy of Harit Dutta's novel. He was a talented writer. In fact, he had some important grant to help him finish up the book, and —"

"You sent yourself a copy?"

She explained briefly. "But here's the thing. I was looking through it last night. I'm pretty sure the police must have checked his computer, but not closely, since they're sure he was the murderer. I doubt they wanted to go through the novel page by page, and I more or less have started to. I haven't gotten all the way through it yet, but I discovered he made notes to himself at the end of each chapter. Some of them are ideas for the next one, but some are a kind of diary. What he did that day, what it made him think about. And there was a long conversation I found this morning that he described in detail. It was with one of his customers. The guy asked him about his marriage. I guess barbers get that, just like hairdressers do. Nothing else to do but chat, and it can get personal."

"So what did you find?"

"Harit was surprised to find himself, as

unhappy as he was, announcing he would do anything to protect his own marriage, because his vow to his wife was sacred. The customer asked if he would feel the same way if his wife treated him badly, or was unfaithful or abusive, and Harit said he would forgive and move on." She paused. "Those aren't the words of a killer."

"You don't know that, Maggie."

"Dad, it was important enough that he put it in his book, as notes to think about. And the whole book is about forgoing violence, learning to tap into the peace inside."

"Could be he wrote about the subject because he was struggling with his own anger. Maybe it got the best of him."

She had thought of that herself, but it just didn't jibe with Rishi and Janya's assessment of the man.

"There seems to be a picture forming, but I just can't figure out how any of it goes together," she admitted. "What if Blake Armstrong is involved in some way?"

"Why would a man like this Armstrong fellow want his barber dead? Plus, want it so badly, he came up with an elaborate plan to make it happen?"

"I'm just guessing, but let's say Harit found something to blackmail Blake or somebody else with. Even though that doesn't seem in character, either, for our purposes, let's say he did. Now, how and why did he and his wife end up dead in a Miami hotel room?"

"If there's something to your theory? Maybe whoever killed them knew how loyal Harit was to his wife, even though the couple had problems, so they kidnapped her, then lured Harit to the motel. They could have forced the wife to phone and tell him she had gone there with another man, knowing Harit would come after her. What better way to get rid of him than to make their deaths look like a murder-suicide?"

Maggie had been thinking along similar lines. If she was right about other things, this was the only explanation that made sense. She was glad her father concurred.

"And it's possible, isn't it, that the customer he had that conversation with was involved, because who would know better than that *particular* man how strongly Harit felt about keeping his marriage intact."

"You're thinking it might have been this Blake Armstrong fellow."

"I don't know for sure Blake was a customer, but those toys say he could have been. It's possible he never went to the shop but had Harit come to his house."

"That's a whole lot of speculation. Way too many maybes." Her father pushed his plate away. "I'm getting a bad feeling here. You have a lot of theories and no evidence. The next step is to get proof, but you're not a cop anymore, and even a cop would have to go through channels. You go into this Armstrong's house or office to look for connections, you're breaking and entering, plain and simple. And I don't want to be called out to arrest my own daughter."

She grimaced. "You would, too, if it was called for."

"You think so?"

"*I* would, and I got that from you."

He thought about that for a moment; then he shook his head. "I don't think so, honey. I'd find a way around an arrest if I could. Truth is, you're a lot bigger fan of the letter of the law than I ever was. I see shades of gray, and I'm not sure you ever do. I'm not even sure you want to, because you might need help interpreting."

She was about to ask what he meant, when her mother finished her call and came back. He checked his watch, then stood, said goodbye and headed outside, discussing evacuation plans with Wanda as he went.

Maggie was cleaning off the counter, when her mother rejoined her.

Wanda went straight to the point. "Your dad's worried you're going to go off half-cocked and do something you shouldn't on this investigation. And as usual, you're not listening to anyone else. Tell me he's wrong."

Maggie didn't respond, but Wanda didn't drop the subject. Far from it. Instead, her next words came rushing out.

481

"You know what? You think I don't see what's going on with you, Maggie, that I've never understood you. But I do. You're too impatient to let things unfold in their own time, to wait and see, because that's not your way. Back in Miami you thought you were right, and you lost just about everything that mattered to you. So what did you learn? You still don't trust anybody else to know better. You were sure of yourself as a kid, but it got worse after you became a cop. I don't exactly know what happened to you. I know it's not easy being a woman in a man's world —"

"Look, I don't think —"

"I know what you don't think," Wanda said. "You don't think I have any right to say this. But you're wrong."

Maggie knew she had made a mistake in Miami, everyone did, but her mother's assessment went deeper. Wanda wasn't talking about the secrets that had been kept from Maggie about Paul Smythe, or decisions she had made without having all the information. She was talking about a fundamental flaw in the person her daughter had become.

"Wow," she said after a moment of silence. "This is pretty much an indictment of everything about me."

"Nobody loves you better." Wanda raised a finger as if ticking off points in a lecture. "But you're here to rethink your life. That's just a little grist for the mill."

"More like a hundred-pound sack."

"You're a tough woman, but not as tough as you think. Something happened to you those first few years in the sheriff's department. I saw it, knew it, but you kept me at arm's length, the way you always did. Your dad saw it, too, but you wouldn't let us help. You were warned not to take that job, but you did anyway, because you were sure it was the right thing to do. And whatever happened there . . . ? It's still eating at you."

Anger shot through Maggie, and it showed in her voice. "Nothing happened to me that didn't teach me something important. I learned to stand up for myself. I learned to count on myself, because nobody else was going to be there to count on. That's something every cop has to learn."

"Most cops know they have their friends behind them."

"Well, I didn't, okay?" That was as much as she wanted to say — more, in fact. "But I'm stronger because of it," she finished.

"You won't admit you made a bad decision, and you won't face it because you're not over being *wrong*. Mistakes bother most of us, some more than others. Lord knows I'd know about that, since I make more than most people. But all your life nobody ever worked harder at being right than you did. You miscalculated a little, actually screwed up? Didn't matter how small an error it was, it haunted you like you'd just run over your best friend."

"That's an exaggeration."

"Not much of one. And this next part isn't one at all. It's time to start trusting somebody besides yourself again. Past time, for your own happiness. Start right here and now with this Dutta family. Don't go off half-cocked —"

"Half-cocked? This is not a small error we're talking about. In this instance," Maggie said stiffly, "nobody else seems interested in finding out what happened to the Dutta family. And there are two little kids who are going to grow up believing their father killed their mother unless I prove that's not true."

"Do you think so? If you're right and there *was* someone else involved, they'll still be involved in a week or two, or even a year. Let Felo help you since his department's handling it."

Maggie was saved from having to answer by the tinkle of the bell. Two older women came in and headed right for the pie case. Maggie used the opportunity to escape.

Back in the kitchen again, she finished what little there was left to do, but she was haunted by her mother's analysis, an analysis spurred on, she imagined, by private, worried conversations her parents had engaged in at home for years. Their analysis matched that of her own police chief, who had kept vital information from her. But hadn't that been the real problem? That she hadn't been fully informed? And wasn't the way around that to become more so, not to back off? To get all the information she could so she never made the same mistake again?

Right now the missing piece seemed to have Blake Armstrong's photograph plastered across it. She just had to figure out how to fit it into the Dutta puzzle. She took out her cell phone and found Blake's number, but she didn't risk using it, since she saw the battery was low again and now even her car charger had given up on the phone and refused to recharge it. She used the kitchen phone instead and leaned against the wall while it rang. When he answered, she kept her voice low, since her mother was still chatting with her customers, who couldn't choose which pies they wanted most.

"Blake? Maggie here."

"Hey, where are you calling from?" He sounded genuinely pleased to hear her voice.

"The shop. We're cleaning up and getting ready to close. Where are you?"

"Packing the car. I hope you are, too."

"Soon. I wanted to thank you for last night and make sure everything's okay. You were obviously worried."

"I'm really sorry I had to cut our date short. We'll make sure that doesn't happen again."

She was sure it wouldn't, since she had no intention of going out with him in the future, but she injected warmth into her voice. "It was no problem. I was just concerned about you."

"Everything's fine. Just some logistical complications. I think I have a lifetime of those ahead of me. I need to figure out which ones really demand my attention, and which are false alarms."

"Never easy," she said. "Anyway, I'm glad all's well. Where are you heading?"

"One of our partners has a house near Sarasota. I'll go there. We'll make a party out of it. You say you're leaving?"

"I'm planning to, if things get any worse."

"You could come with us. We'd have fun."

"Unfortunately I promised my mother I'd go to a friend's house with her. She hates storms, and my father'll be busy here. I'll hold her hand and help her pack." Maggie heard a sniff from the doorway and turned to see Wanda glaring at her.

"You stay safe then," Blake said. "Maybe I'll see you out on the highway."

"I hope the traffic's not *that* bad."

He laughed, and they exchanged a few more sentences before Maggie hung up and faced her mother.

"That was a lie," Wanda said. "You made me sound like some fragile old lady."

"I'm sorry." Maggie sifted through possible

responses. "I was just using you as an excuse, Mom. When I'm done here, I'm meeting Felo at Alvaro's camp and staying with him a couple of days. I didn't want to get into that with Blake. A little hard to explain, don't you think?"

"Why, because you're dating him? Or trying to finger him for the murders?"

Maggie had gained a new respect for her mother. She realized she didn't want to deny the truth. She owed her that much. "Either way, I'd like to keep him hanging on for a while."

Wanda looked as if she was debating her answer, but in the end she just shrugged. "About time you and Felo spent some real time together. Maybe you'll actually talk for a change."

"I'm just going there to get away from the storm. But I'll talk to him about the case. I'll consult him, the way you said I should."

Wanda didn't look convinced. "Well, if you're going to do that, don't you think you ought to go back home, load your car and get that cat of yours? You've got a long drive ahead."

"You'll be okay here without me for a few days?"

The shop door tinkled again, and Wanda shrugged. "I'll close soon enough. No point in pushing things. Hardly ever is."

Maggie wondered if that was true. Was

there a point in pushing this? Did she really have the right, or the duty, to go to Blake's house and see what she could find? Because she would never have a better opportunity. If she wanted to find a connection between Harit and Blake, this was the afternoon to do it.

She was still asking herself that question when she gathered up her purse. Wanda was alone again when Maggie came out of the kitchen. Her mother looked tired, as if she had used up a day's energy. Despite her own turmoil, Maggie felt such a surge of love for her that she didn't know what to say.

"Maybe it wasn't a good idea for you to come here and help me, after all," Wanda said. "I just don't seem to be able to keep my mouth shut, though I sure have tried."

Maggie put her arms around her mother and gave her a long hug. Wanda hesitated, then hugged her back. They stood that way for most of a minute.

"I'm glad I came," Maggie said at last. "Maybe we see each other clearer now, good and bad. But I like what I see when I look at you, Mom. I'm proud to be your kid."

"You're not making that up?"

Maggie finally stepped away. "Nope, I'm just like you in that way. I could never tell a lie just to be nice."

Wanda laughed a little. "You'll be careful out on the road? Traffic's bound to be awful.

And don't pack anything that's not important. It will still be there when you get back."

Outside a minute later, as her umbrella
turned inside out from the force of the wind,
Maggie questioned her own decision. But the
question was window dressing. She already
knew her answer.

CHAPTER TWENTY-FOUR

Tracy had grown up with mud slides, with earthquakes and fires that incinerated entire Southern California neighborhoods. Hurricanes and tropical storms were not nearly as familiar but seemed normal enough. Natural disasters might differ in warning time and duration, but coping with them was deeply ingrained in her DNA. The moment she first realized the buck stopped with her when it came to protecting the cottages and tenants at Happiness Key, she'd drawn up a hurricane plan and found people to help implement it.

This was the first time since her arrival in Florida that she'd had reason to put her plan in action, but so far everything had worked. The plywood twins had secured everybody's windows. She had called all her neighbors to make sure they planned to go inland and remind them to pick up loose objects around their houses and move furniture or decorations inside. Her plan seemed to be working, since as she'd passed the Kapurs' house on her way to the center, Tracy had seen Janya hauling her many potted plants inside with Rishi's help.

Her own evacuation plan hadn't been nearly as well thought out. But the moment she had arrived at the center this morning with some of her more treasured belongings, Gladys had invited her to stay at the Woodley residence. One guest room was still available, and she was touched to discover Gladys and Woody had earmarked it for her. The house was new, built to the highest standards, and just far enough away from the Gulf that the Woodleys were confident they would sustain little damage. Tracy had said a grateful yes.

While the rec center, too, was built to hurricane specifications, Tracy's office was on the bottom floor, and the only thing between her and the outdoor pool were the shuffleboard courts. The pool, of course, was equipped with overflows to ensure drainage of excess water, and the maintenance staff was draining a foot of water anyway, just to minimize problems. Still, Gladys had suggested that Tracy might want to move anything valuable or particularly vulnerable upstairs to a storage closet. So now she was sorting and choosing, and a couple of teenage boys were carrying boxes upstairs as she filled them. Equipment could be replaced, but notes and schedules and plans for next year's youth camp were irreplaceable. Her computer had already made its way up, and the boys were now carrying boxes of files.

She was on the floor filling the final box with photographs and youth campers' drawings when she heard footsteps. She looked up and found Marsh looking down at her.

"You aren't answering your cell phone."

She tilted her chin so she could see him better. Faded jeans, rusty-colored Wild Florida T-shirt, inscrutable expression. "You can see why, right? I'm on the floor packing. You're not taking it personally?"

"You weren't answering last night, either."

That part was true. After the ultrasound yesterday, she had remained at the doctor's office for her monthly exam. Marsh had volunteered to stay, as well, but she'd sent him away. She had been feeling too vulnerable to have him there asking questions and ingratiating himself with her obstetrician. Even worse, she hadn't wanted a real conversation after they had both seen their baby cavorting on the monitor, their own little space alien with the funny-shaped head and the visibly beating heart. She hadn't wanted to talk about names or visitation rights or how it had felt to have Marsh there at that extraordinarily intimate moment. Had he asked her to move in with him again, she might well have been too weak to say no.

So, okay, she had turned off her cell phone

and ignored her landline when her caller ID showed his number.

"You may have noticed," she said, "that a hurricane's thinking about a little trip to Palmetto Grove. I've been a wee bit busy getting everything protected on Happiness Key."

"As if that's really possible."

"Trying," she amended. "And those cottages have remained standing through worse storms. Anyway, it's not exactly a good time for chitchat."

"Chitchat?"

"Did you have something important on your mind?" She glanced at her watch as a visual clue.

"Among other things, I wanted to be sure you had plans in case you needed to evacuate."

"Thanks. Once I finish here I'm heading home to make sure everything's secured and to finish getting my stuff. Then I'll be staying with Gladys and Woody." She paused, and when he didn't comment or ask her to reconsider and hunker down at the old Cracker house that had withstood centuries of storms, she asked, "What about you? I assume you're staying home and battening down the hatches?"

"Wild Florida's decided to make a party of it. We'll be at the offices camping with whatever staff wants to be there."

"Oh, what fun," she said in a tone that

contradicted her words. "Toast a marshmallow for me."

"You know, Trace, I'm not stupid. It's absolutely clear you're avoiding me. The hurricane's a good excuse, but it's pretty transparent. I've tried to be patient, to wait this craziness out, but I think it's obvious that's not going to help anybody. You've written me out of your life, and you don't want me to have any say at all in what happens to our child. You throw crumbs at me, like inviting me to the ultrasound, so I won't protest too loudly, but you'd better realize one thing. Crumbs aren't going to do it. I am going to be a part of this baby's life, just the way you are, and if I have to go to court to establish my right, I will. Don't imagine I'll give up claim to my child, even if I have to give up claim to you."

She was so incensed she didn't know which part of his speech to address first. "What claim did you *ever* have on me? Offering to let me move in with you was damage control. You weren't establishing claim, you were mopping up after yourself. You think I can't see the difference?"

"I was trying to improve things, to make your life a little easier. If you didn't like my solution, you could have volunteered one of your own."

"I don't need my life easier! I'm a big girl. I don't need any man taking care of me, even

494

if I used to think I did. I don't need to shack up with you or anybody else so you can feel like you've done your two bits. I am so much better than that. Look at me, Marsh. When you walk out of this room, I'll still be sitting here. I won't disappear, even if you're not here to see me."

He was angry now, not coldly controlled but visibly furious. "What is your problem? This baby didn't come out of nowhere. We were happy together, happy with the way things were. I don't see any damage I need to control, or at least I didn't until you started slamming the door in my face."

"Happy with the way things *were,* Marsh? Guess what! Things are not that way anymore. And as for this child of ours? I know you're a good father. I expect you'll be a good father to our child, too, but don't you dare start issuing ultimatums! Because the moment you do, I'll fight you tooth and nail. You get it? We can work out visitation and everything else once we're both calmer, but the moment you try to legislate, I'll go after you, in court, out of court and everywhere in between. Don't you ever, *ever,* threaten me or this baby again."

"I did not threaten you. I'm just letting you know you can't cut me out of your life no mat—"

She cut him off with a sharp chop of her hand, afraid that if she didn't, she would leap to her feet and strangle him. "Oh, I can and I *will*. The baby's life? That's a different issue, but you'd sure better learn the difference before we have another conversation. This one's finished. I have a million things to worry about right now, and I don't need this on top of them."

He looked angry enough to shake her. "You know, I think you're right. I'd better get out of here. We can't do this face-to-face. I should have figured that out."

"Good, we agree about one thing. I *am* right."

He strode across the room, but he turned in the doorway. "Just give this a little thought while the winds blow tonight, Trace. If we can't settle this in a quiet conversation, the only way to settle it will be in court. That won't be my first choice. You'd better think about yours."

On the way to her car, Maggie debated calling Felo. Like her father, he had already warned her against dangerous or illegal snooping, and of course, technically, they were both right. But she saw clearly, even if they couldn't, that her chance to discover Blake's connection to Harit Dutta had arrived. Blake and his partners were on their way out of town, and most likely their house was already empty. Judging by the morning's traffic many people had already abandoned

Palmetto Grove Key, so it was unlikely anyone would notice her slipping into his house to sift through papers.

Of course, if Blake had anything to hide, he was smart enough to have disposed of any evidence or at least have taken it with him, in case the storm exposed his secrets to the four winds. But she wasn't looking for a canceled check from Blake's favorite hit man or a blackmail note from Harit Dutta. She simply wanted evidence the two men had been acquainted. A calendar notation. A receipt. Anything that would tell her she was on the right trail. Anything that might indicate a reason why Blake could have been involved in the Duttas' deaths.

The internal debate ended with Maggie slipping into her car, then pulling out her cell phone to use up the last of the battery. This wasn't a call she could have made from Wanda's Wonderful Pies.

She fumed as the phone rang and Felo didn't pick up right away. The hurry-up-and-wait aspects of police work had always been hardest for her, but when she was almost to the point where she needed to compose a voice mail, he answered.

"Hey, where are you?" she asked.

"About twenty miles from camp. Where are you?"

"I'm going home to get Rumba and my

stuff, then I'm going to drive over and meet you."

There was a long pause, and by the end of it, she was sure their relationship was well and truly over, and he was trying to find a way to tell her not to bother. But his voice when he spoke was low and indefinably sexy.

"Shall I prepare one bedroom or two?"

"Does my welcome there depend on my answer?"

"I'll take you any way I can get you."

She relaxed, and unaccountably she felt herself choking up. "You're sure? I know I'm not the easiest person to have around." It was as close to an apology as she'd come so far.

"Insightful, though."

She knew this wasn't the time to go into the issues that had separated them. Her cell phone was liable to cut off any moment. "I'll be there just as soon as I finish up a few things here. Can't say when, though. It will depend on . . . things. And traffic."

He was no fool. "What kind of things? I thought you were loading the car and getting on the road?"

She hesitated just a second too long.

"This isn't the time to go looking for answers in the Dutta case," Felo said before she could configure a response. "You know a hurricane's nothing to fool with. Katrina was only a category three, and look what happened to New Orleans."

"Phyllis is a one, and likely to swerve up the coast and miss us altogether. And Blake's on his way out of town, and his house is empty. I'm just going to see if there's anything there to help me figure out what's going on. I —"

"Mags, forget that for now! If there's anything to the Armstrong connection we'll find it without risking your safety. And don't even think about breaking into his house. You don't have an ounce of authority. All you have is a theory and no real evidence to support it."

"That's what I'll be looking for."

"You know you won't be able to use anything you obtain. What's wrong with you? This is crazy."

"I'm not going to obtain anything illegally. I'm just going to satisfy my curiosity and see if I can make some connections. Come on, you know that's how this works."

"Get your stuff and Rumba, then get back in your car. It's going to be a long, slow trip in heavy traffic, and the storm's getting closer every minute. Forget the case and hit the road. I'll be here waiting. We can talk about what to do next."

"I know what to do next, Felo. I'll do it, then I'll meet you there. And don't worry. I can take care of myself. I won't do anything stupid."

"Maggie —"

She cut him off before he could finish. She figured she was simply saving him the effort, since she already knew what he would say. The phone beeped weakly, and she saw that the battery was either dead or taking its last breaths. Disgusted, she turned it off and vowed to buy herself a new phone with her next paycheck.

She started the engine and backed out of her parking place. Hampered by wind and rain, the drive through town was slow, but even now the roads were less crowded than she'd expected. People had either evacuated earlier or were battening down the hatches at their own homes, flashlights with fresh batteries, canned goods and camping stoves at the ready, gallons of water neatly stored in closets. She imagined that the highway out of town was congested with all the people who were leaving, and she reconsidered her decision. If she was driving to Felo's camp, she should gather her things, pick up Rumba and leave right now. He was right about that. She had a full tank of gas, and she was a trained driver who performed well under the worst conditions. But along with expertise came an understanding that taking unnecessary chances was foolish.

"One hour," she said out loud. "One-thirty, no later." She would give herself an hour and not a minute more before she crossed the bridge back to Palmetto Key. She would stop at Blake's house first, do a quick, efficient search — if she could find a way inside — then leave in time to collect her cat and suitcases and get back on the road.

No matter what others thought about her, she was not above taking advice. But neither was she willing to compromise her own good judgment. Even though rooting around in the wind and rain wasn't an appealing prospect, she felt sure that this was the only chance she would ever have to safely look for a connection between Blake Armstrong and Harit Dutta.

How could she abandon the young man who had written so eloquently and sincerely about making peace? How could she abandon his children, who would someday deserve the real truth about the deaths of their parents?

No one else was going to do this if she didn't.

As she crossed the bridge to the key — much easier than it had been in the other direction — she decided that she would follow her own best instincts. Then she would do a bit of peacemaking with the man who had warned her against it.

Chapter Twenty-Five

Rain was sluicing across the windshield in sheets by the time Maggie pulled behind a crape myrtle hedge about twenty yards beyond Blake's house. She had driven slowly as she passed and seen no lights, cars or people.

Between the rain and the hedge, she would be well hidden from view for the short time she spent here. She had already resigned herself to being soaked to the bone, and even if her umbrella hadn't already thrown up its spokes, she wouldn't have bothered with it. She took a waterproof windbreaker she used when she hiked or kayaked out of the backseat and pulled it on, zipping it to the top and pulling the hood over her hair. She was careful to tie it so it didn't interfere with her peripheral vision. At least the windbreaker would keep the rain out for a while.

She had given back her gun and her badge, but her lock-picking kit had been purchased at her own expense, and now she took it out of the glove compartment and slipped it into her pocket. She was fairly adept at using it, but she hadn't practiced in months, and even at her best she wasn't successful with the newest locks, with their rotating pin tumblers, false slots and sidebar mechanisms. She was simply hopeful that this, a beach house on a sparsely occupied barrier island, would not be rigged out like Fort Knox.

She pocketed her cell phone, although she knew that was probably pointless. Then she put her keys under the seat, quietly opened the car door and stepped into the downpour.

The rain was cold, and immediately her feet sank into the saturated sand. She hoped that when she was ready to leave, she wouldn't need a tow truck, but parking in a safer spot would mean possible detection. On the remote chance there was someone left at the house, she didn't want to be visible from a window. And she didn't want to be spotted from the road, in case her mother or someone else from Happiness Key noticed her car. She just had to take her chances.

She slogged along behind the hedge, glad on one level that the rain was falling hard enough to provide some cover. She positioned herself where she could see the house without being seen and watched for ten full minutes, looking for lights or movement. When she was satisfied, she dashed across the road to crouch in a tightly clustered grove of podocarpus trees. The stiff branches scratched at her wrists and legs, but she stayed perfectly still. This time she waited only five minutes.

Finally she straightened and started toward the house. She had a plan in place but hoped she wouldn't need it. After hiding and slinking, it felt bold and unbearably foolish to dash up to the front porch and ring the doorbell, but that was exactly what she did. Once, twice, three times.

As she waited, she examined the lock and knew immediately that this one would not give over easily. The doorknob was egg-shaped and solid brass. It looked new and expensive, with what was obviously a complex key slot. The sleek new knob was joined by an equally intimidating dead bolt, and all the windows on the bottom floor had elaborate grillwork across the lower panes that both adorned them and kept them inviolate. The house was also used as an office, which could legitimately rate a more advanced security system, but she was glad there were no signs near the door warning of alarms. Still, someone had carefully secured this door, most likely in the last few weeks, if the shining brass was any indication.

No one answered her summons, which delighted her. She had been prepared, if necessary, to ask for Blake. If he'd been here, or answered the door himself, she would have presented him with the two pies in her car that were otherwise earmarked for Felo and any other residents of Alvaro's camp. She would have told Blake the pies were her contribution to his party, wished him well on his journey to Sarasota like a lovesick groupie and disappeared back into the rain.

Since, as cover stories went, that one was weak and suspicious, she was glad she wasn't going to be forced to use it.

Five minutes of picking the lock proved she was right about its complexity and the futility of trying harder. She rounded the house, carefully climbed the stairs to the deck off Blake's bedroom and examined the doorknob and the dead bolt above it. This time she didn't even pull out her kit. Perhaps with enough time and patience, she might breach this one, which was minimally less high tech, but there was little shelter here, and she had been in hotel showers with less water pressure. She abandoned the deck and the waterfall, and slipped around toward the garage.

A car passed on the road, but as she flattened herself against the side of the house, it continued toward the point. She wondered if the passenger was one of her neighbors, making a final trip to get her belongings before abandoning the island for good. When the car didn't turn around, and the road as far as she could see was empty, she finished her trip around the house and stood under the garage overhang.

The lock-picking kit was in her pocket now,

since she knew from watching Blake last night that access was via a keypad. Her only chance of getting into the garage was correctly guessing the code. If she was lucky and Blake himself had programmed it, then he might have used a familiar number. And she had some of those numbers on the fax in her pocket, thanks to the friend who had come through for her just as she left the house that morning.

Maggie pulled the sheet out of her pocket, glad that here, at least, she was protected from the worst of the elements. She had circled the most obvious numbers to try, and now she punched them in. The first four digits of Blake's social security number. The last four. When neither worked, she methodically started deleting a digit at the beginning and adding one at the end until all were exhausted.

Next she tried Blake's birth date. The month and year abbreviated. The year alone. The month and day, day and last two digits of the year. After every combination she could think of, she gave up on that and progressed to his driver's license.

Ten minutes later, she was frazzled and pessimistic. She had tried everything that seemed possible and much that seemed unlikely. She had even tried the most basic. The house number. Variations of the house phone number. Blake's cell-phone number. Nothing had worked.

She was beginning to question her own sanity. Two veteran cops who knew her well, her father and Felo, had warned her not to do this. Perhaps the fates were telling her the same. Yes, wouldn't it have been nice to get inside and prove to everybody that she was still good at her job, that with nothing to go on except intuition and guts she had found a link between Blake Armstrong and Harit Dutta that no one could ignore? But to whom did she need to prove herself? Who was questioning her skills? She was the one who had sacrificed her beloved job on the altar of her own ego.

It was time to pack and get out of town.

She folded the fax and slipped it in her pocket. As she did, her fingers touched the other piece of paper she had put there. She debated, but only for a moment. She slipped out the email attachment Felo had sent her and unfolded it. The record he had sent of Blake's connection to the Atlantis Casino, including the photograph of his player's card, stared back at her. She fingered the paper, then shrugged. Stepping back to the keypad, she punched in the first four numbers of the ID card.

The door slid open.

For a moment Maggie just stood there, stunned that she'd been successful. Then she stepped into the garage and let her eyes adjust to the deeper gloom. The room was large enough for two cars, but neither side was occupied. The walls held metal shelves and the usual garage paraphernalia, a ladder, a Peg-Board with tools hanging from hooks. A shovel and rake in one corner, a lawn mower in the opposite one. The door leading into the house was on her left. She debated pressing the button on the wall and closing the garage door, but instead she climbed the two steps to the inside door and examined the knob.

This was the door she had hoped for. The knob had probably been installed when the house was built decades before, well before technology complicated the lives of burglars. Whoever had so carefully secured the front and back doors and windows had counted on the garage door itself to ward off intruders. In only a little more than a minute she had closed the garage door and opened the one leading into the house.

She had given herself an hour to accomplish her search, and now she was down to twenty-five minutes. She would need more than that, of course, but she planned to keep her little treasure hunt as close to that time frame as possible. With luck she could investigate, then pack, grab her cat and be on the road by two-thirty.

She stepped inside and let her eyes adjust

again. No lights shone, and even though it was early afternoon, the skies were so dark outside it could be evening. She moved cautiously through what turned out to be the kitchen, then into the dining area. With no suspicion that Blake was anything more than an affable man interested in a casual date, she hadn't paid much attention to the floor plan or anything else about the house. She refreshed what memories she had as she tiptoed through, still listening carefully.

Vaguely she remembered a wing that housed an office where the housemates conducted business. She moved through the living room and found a hallway close to a freestanding metal fireplace. She listened, then followed it to find two rooms directly across from each other, both furnished with desks and bookshelves, as well as tall file cabinets.

She chose the one on the left and set to work. She didn't need much time to ascertain that the place had been well and truly cleaned out. The file drawers were empty except for some debris: empty folders, unimportant papers and, in one drawer, a stash of Hershey bars. All the drawers had been ajar, and she left them that way, stifling an urge to swipe one of the candy bars, since she hadn't yet had lunch.

The desk was unlocked, and a search showed nothing inside. Although the wall had half a dozen empty spaces with picture hangers intact, a framed commendation remained for Ned Bournes, and she remembered the older housemate from Blake's party, a gangly balding man in a shirt with long sleeves that still exposed his wrists.

Nothing on the shelves looked interesting. Clearly anything of value or importance had been hauled away in case Phyllis did her worst.

Maggie abandoned Ned's office and crossed to the next one. Nothing remained on these walls to hint at the occupant's identity, but a brass nameplate sat askew on the desktop.

"Blake Armstrong," she read out loud. "Gotcha."

She began in one corner, moving slowly and carefully around the perimeter of the room, lifting and examining anything of interest. There wasn't much. There were shelves here, too, with a few books, but she found nothing inside them or under them. Blake was apparently a fan of thrillers, and these had all been read and left to their fate.

When she'd checked the entire circumference, she went to the desk and began a systematic search like the one she had conducted across the hall. Here she didn't even find candy. The desk had been completely cleared out, and when she pulled out the drawers to look beneath them, she found nothing there, either.

She located an empty wastebasket. No help. A closet turned up nothing except the scent of cedar and four expensive wooden hangers. A bug — she didn't look too closely — scurried up one corner. She left the closet door half open, the way she had found it.

Although she hoped to have better luck upstairs, twenty minutes later a thorough search of Blake's bedroom had turned up nothing of interest. Except for furniture and heavy items, the house had been thoroughly cleaned out. She had hoped the safer second story would have received a less exhaustive overhaul, but it, like the first, had been emptied of everything personal.

Maggie was sorry she hadn't listened to Felo and her father. She had wasted more than an hour, broken the law she had once sworn to uphold and set herself up for a harder, longer drive to Alvaro's camp. Blake Armstrong was not a fool. If he was involved in the Duttas' murders, then he had probably gotten rid of all evidence weeks ago. Her hope, that he had missed something that would lead her in the right direction, had been foolish.

She did a cursory exam of the other upstairs rooms, even sorted through the remaining toiletries in the bathroom to see if Blake had anything with a label or tag from the barbershop where Harit had worked, but if he had ever possessed anything like that, he had it with him or had discarded it.

Downstairs again, she circled the living room, lifting abandoned newspapers and magazines to check beneath them, although by now she had more or less given up. She stopped at the wall holding the photographs she had admired on the day of the party and officially gave up the search.

The time had come to go back to her rental house, throw everything of value — mostly sentimental — into her car, put Rumba in her carrier and head out of town. She had hoped to flaunt her success in Felo's face, but instead she would have to acknowledge he had been right.

And what else would she say to him? How much of this dangerous side excursion had been to find something that would derail a conversation about their relationship, at least for a little while? How much had been a hope that they could avoid discussing their problems, and how and whether to try to address them?

Outside, the wind was wailing louder, and the house creaked in response. She was staring at the wall, her thoughts spinning away from this house and onto a crowded highway, when something else vied for her attention. Pulled back to the wall of photographs, she looked closer, but nothing jumped out at her. She was tired and discouraged, and hadn't

she already decided there was nothing here?
And yet . . .

Maggie moved a little closer. What exactly, besides the howling wind, had disturbed her train of thought? She examined the photographs one by one. Bridges were prominent, of course — the reason, she supposed, for this artistically wrought display. These men built bridges, repaired bridges and naturally their handiwork deserved center stage. Not all the photographs contained bridges, though. Several featured roads, one climbing a mountain straight into the clouds, another skimming a cliff. They looked to be a set of sorts, similar sizes, identical frames, matted much the same. She moved closer and saw the photographer's name in small print in the right-hand bottom corner of one, then another.

She stepped back and viewed them as a whole once again. About to give up, she turned away when the answer hit her. Whirling, she stared at the wall. And yes, one of the photographs did not belong here, was framed similarly but not exactly like the others, did not have a road or a bridge featured prominently. She stepped forward to view the mountain pool with a waterfall cascading into it, a lovely and, at first glance, compatible nature scene. There was no photographer's name in the corner.

The photograph looked familiar, but she

couldn't remember why. She tried to let her mind go blank. She had not seen it on a wall, and she didn't think she had seen it here during her one and only visit. She imagined it in a frame on a table, and that didn't seem right, either. In a gallery bin. No.

And then she remembered. Pages. Lots of pages. She had seen this photograph in a catalog. But why and where?

Stuck, she moved restlessly back and forth, staring at it until the answer appeared. The photograph had been in a catalog of security essentials. More than a year ago she had thumbed through it to find an appropriate gun safe for her service revolver. The photograph hid a small safe, and she had been intrigued by the graceful efficiency of such a thing. Two for the price of one, a pleasant photograph to adorn her living room, and a place to keep her gun.

Except that the price for the unit had reflected its dual purpose, and instead, since she and Felo lived on cops' salaries, she had purchased a cheaper, utilitarian vault that she and Felo could share.

She moved toward it to be sure she was right. The safe jutted out just enough to set it apart. She thought she remembered that this model worked with a remote the owner could program with his own code. If the safe had been installed by Blake himself, she might be in business. He might well have used the same numbers that had gotten her into the house.

Excitement was building. She told herself that this, like everything else of importance in the house, had probably been emptied and the contents carted away. But she owed herself a chance to find out. She just had to find the remote.

She turned to begin.

Blake Armstrong, his expression murderous, was standing just a yard away, a table lamp in his hand.

Her eyes widened, and she took a step backward, but not quickly enough. Before she could lift a hand to protect herself, he smashed the lamp against the side of her head. The last thing Maggie heard as she fell to the floor was the wailing of the wind that had so thoroughly hidden his approach.

CHAPTER TWENTY-SIX

Wanda figured there were signs, then there were *signs*. Phyllis turning into a real hurricane wasn't much of one, not by itself, but when Wanda noticed she was down to just three pies and both hands of her wall clock were sitting squarely on three, she pondered the coincidence. Then, when a man sporting a T-shirt with a picture of the late Dale Earnhart and his car — number three — arrived to put her three hurricane shutters in place, she knew it was time to head home to get Chase and her remaining boxes. She called Ken to tell him that his man had arrived and she was leaving, but the line crackled so badly she wasn't sure he caught more than the gist.

She made it to her car without incident, although trash was skipping across the street, followed by heavier objects that hadn't been properly secured. To avoid the worst of the rain she was wearing a bright orange slicker and vinyl boots with leopard spots, and she'd covered her hair with a rain scarf tied so tight she could feel the pulse pounding in her throat, like a bird beating its wings against a cage.

It took her two minutes just to get a break so she could pull into traffic. She wondered why all these morons had waited this long to go home or leave town. Of course, she was one of those morons, but what kind of excuse was that? By the time she got into the line heading across the bridge, all her patience was used up. There was no call for all these people to be heading to Palmetto Grove Key. She couldn't see very far ahead, but judging from the snail's pace of the traffic, everybody in southwest Florida had decided to sightsee. Maybe they all wanted a good look at the waves. Maybe they wanted to have a run at the surf.

By the time she was actually on the bridge, which almost felt as if it were swaying in the wind, she was no longer silently fuming. She had reverted to childhood, when she had constructed her own one-of-a-kind expletives to escape the wrath of her mother, who'd been all too handy with a bar of soap.

"Fiddling fraternizing frivolous flounders!" She gripped the steering wheel harder. "Seriously stupid simple-minded sheepsheads!"

She was working on "k's" — one of the hardest, if memory served — when a bright light cut through the rain-fogged gloom to her left. She squinted and peered across three lanes of traffic.

She abandoned her strings of adjectives and went straight for the real thing. "Well, damn!"

There was activity on the pedestrian walkway, lights blinking, people moving back and forth. Nobody had to explain to her what was going on.

The man in charge had already explained.

She closed her eyes, which had no consequences, since traffic was now at a dead halt. She realized that there weren't really that many cars on the bridge. But the ones that were had almost stopped moving right at this spot so they could watch Derek Forbes and his band of merry men setting up to film the scene he had warned her about.

She realized more. One, that she should have warned Ken and asked him to talk Derek out of this latest escapade. Two, that she should have tried to talk him out of it herself. Three, that, as usual, she'd been so overwhelmed by the man, she hadn't thought about the ramifications of anything he'd told her. Four, that a man who lived that close to the edge was always in danger of tumbling over it. And in addition to that possibility, this time, by slowing traffic when people needed to evacuate, he was endangering the lives of Palmetto Grove's citizens.

There was nothing she could do now. She couldn't talk him out of doing the shoot. The most anyone could hope for was that Derek would realize he was causing a traffic jam and abandon his plan. When the car in front of her began to move again, she stepped on the gas and followed suit. The best thing she could do was get off the bridge, so others could cross behind her.

Once she passed through the traffic light, the trip to Happiness Key went quickly. Randall's was closed, and the store's parking lot nearly empty of cars. She passed a couple of SUVs towing boats toward the bridge, most likely hoping to find higher ground and safer storage. She knew Alice and Olivia were already battened down at Shell Horizon with Roger Goldsworthy, because Alice had called to tell her not to worry. Now she wondered about the rest of her friends.

She slowed as she passed Janya's house and saw, with some surprise, that lights were on inside and Janya's old sedan was still parked in front. She passed Tracy's house and saw neither lights nor a car, and figured her landlady had done all she could to secure the cottages and was on her way to higher ground. On a whim she drove to the end of the tiny development to Maggie's house and saw that here, too, the place looked abandoned. She hoped Maggie was halfway to the camp and more than halfway to a real reunion.

The packing went quickly. She'd already stuffed boxes with important memorabilia, and in less than twenty minutes she managed to get them all tightly squeezed into the trunk of her car, sheltered now under the carport, which helped, at least a little, to keep her dry as she worked. The phone rang once, but by the time she picked it up, the caller had hung up.

Chase, who had been cooped up too long, scrambled outside as she made her final trip to carry his bed and supplies to the car. Without asking permission, the dog took off down the road. She wasn't worried that he wouldn't return. Chase was a greyhound, after all, and running was what he did best. But she *was* worried that with the rain falling harder, an approaching car might not see him in time to brake. She called to him, but he was already long gone, in the direction of Janya's house. She decided she would lock up the house, then follow in her car and hope she could coax him into the backseat so they could leave for town.

When she got near Janya's, she saw her friend, but not the dog. Janya was trudging toward Wanda's, no children in sight.

Wanda slammed on her brakes and put down the passenger-side window as Janya approached the car, spray pelting her face. "What are you doing out here?"

"I phoned you."

"I couldn't get to it in time. What's wrong?"

"We were preparing to leave." Janya was

half shouting, because thunder was booming in the background now. "Rishi took his car and most of our possessions. I was to follow with the children when they woke from their naps. But I tried to back the car closer to the door to load it, and it will not start. The battery, I think. It has been slow to start all week. I have been watching now for almost an hour for someone to come by and help."

Wanda leaned over to open the door. "Did you call Rishi?"

"I cannot get him to answer. He is not good about remembering to turn on his cell phone, and the phone at his office just rings and rings. I doubt that he is yet worried about us."

Janya slid inside as Wanda asked, "Where are the kids?"

"Still napping, but I have to get right back. They are due to wake soon."

"Have you seen that fool dog of mine?" Wanda asked.

"He is on my porch."

"We'll get him, the kids and your stuff, and go. It'll be tight, but we'll do our best."

"I should not leave my car at the house."

"We can't jump it in this weather. We'll drown. And the way it's parked, I can't get behind you to push it with mine."

"Perhaps the key will not flood."

"It'll be fine. Phyllis won't amount to much." Wanda didn't know if that was true.

She just knew they had no choice.

"Thank you for stopping. No one else came by."

Wanda was in the act of nodding when she realized what Janya had said. "In the past hour? You didn't see Tracy or Maggie?"

"No, and I was watching carefully."

Wanda thought that was strange. "You didn't notice Maggie earlier? Of course, why would you? You were busy packing."

"I was carrying things to the car. I looked up the road but saw no one at home."

Wanda supposed her friend had just missed the others, that they had passed as she was tending the children or packing boxes. But would either woman leave without checking to be sure Janya was on her way to safety? It seemed unlikely. They were all too close for that. The possibility that Maggie hadn't come home began to nag at her. If Maggie hadn't been home yet, where was she?

"We'll keep an eye out for them while we get your stuff moved to my car," Wanda said. "They'll probably pass right by us."

"I would feel better just knowing," Janya said.

Wanda was afraid that sentiment was mutual.

Tracy was used to heavy traffic. In California she'd been stuck on the Ventura and Santa Monica freeways so frequently that she had routinely traveled with meditation tapes, rice cakes and bottled water in her car. Unfortunately, she had none of those with her this afternoon as she waited for traffic to start moving across the bridge to Palmetto Grove Key. Sunset Bridge, as Marsh had called it.

Marsh.

She flipped open her glove compartment in a futile search for something to eat. She had been so upset after their encounter that she had forgotten to eat the lunch she'd brought from home, and it was still sitting on her desk at the center.

Marsh.

The glove compartment yielded nothing but a packaged oatmeal-raisin cookie from a kid's meal that Bay hadn't wanted — stowed there more months ago than she cared to think about. Bay disliked raisins to the point of phobia, and felt the same way about mushrooms. Otherwise, food was his friend. Marsh had done a great job of introducing his son to different cuisines and flavors.

And there was that name again.

She opened the cookie and sniffed; then, too hungry to be fastidious, she nibbled at one edge. When the cookie yielded, she ate it in three bites.

No rice cakes and no meditation tapes, nothing to help set her mind free to float unimpeded by coarse human emotion. She couldn't remember feeling this sad, this pathetically dejected and *re*jected, in her entire life. Not even when she had discovered that the pampered life she'd lived in Bel-Air was over. And now, with nothing else to occupy her, she was forced to face the truth.

She had done this to herself.

She was in love with Marsh Egan, totally, devastatingly in love. And yes, that was clearly over the top, but there it was. She had been in love with him for months — before the pregnancy, before their reconciliation last summer — in love with a man who would never have caught her eye when she was still obsessed with money and celebrity, and incapable of noting the real worth of any human being. In love with a redneck attorney with a bratty son she also, unfortunately, adored. In love with the head of an environmental organization that was never going to change the world but might possibly change a tiny corner of it.

Of course, for most of her life she had thought she was better than tiny corners, that she was a woman destined to live large, destined for the best of what life had to offer. And now, because of her own inability to realize the truth, her inability to step forward and take a risk and tell Marsh she loved him, she had sacrificed all hope for happiness. Tiny-corner happiness. Big-picture happiness. Yes-we're-different-but-who-cares happiness.

She had pushed him away so fiercely that now he was talking family court and custody agreements. She had pushed him away so finally that the small things they'd shared, things on which they might have built a lasting relationship, were gone for good. Whatever Marsh had felt for her — and really, did she know what that had or hadn't been? — now he felt nothing but anger.

She understood much too clearly what had brought her to this place. A childhood where love was absent and values were something you picked up at the annual sale at your favorite Rodeo Drive boutique. Marriage to a man she had chosen because of his income and social standing. But that was then. And now?

Now she was a better person, but clearly she was scarred.

She had never learned to search her heart. She had never learned to speak the truth. She had taken baby steps in both directions since moving to Happiness Key, but maybe Marsh had come into her life too soon. Before she had made enough progress. Before she had learned to put aside pride, to take chances with a heart that had been too frequently wounded.

Sick of self-examination — which really was *not* her style or any kind of an upper — she edged to the left to see if she could spot whatever was holding up traffic. Despite the rain, she had a clear view of a line of cars stretching at least a city block, although after that, it seemed spottier. If she was right, that meant eventually traffic would move again. As she started to pull back into line, a door opened, maybe eight vehicles ahead of her, maybe more, and a man got out of what might be a pickup, since he appeared to hop down. He dashed across traffic to the pedestrian walkway and disappeared, not such a daring feat, since traffic in all lanes was, at best, crawling and, at a certain spot, had stopped entirely.

She leaned forward and wiped her windshield with her palm, peering harder at the road ahead. Nothing happened for a few minutes, and she wondered if she had imagined seeing someone. Then she saw the same man dash back across to his pickup.

Marsh.

Now she was seeing the guy everywhere. But hadn't that looked like him? Hadn't he been wearing a rust-colored T-shirt when he confronted her at the center? She pulled a little farther left for a clearer view. Couldn't that be his pickup? Same basic shape? Same nondescript blue?

As if to make sure she wouldn't know, the rain began to fall harder and wind rattled the car. The car ahead of her moved forward, and she pulled back to the right and did the same. It would make sense that Marsh would head over to Palmetto Grove Key. Perhaps he was doing exactly what she was, going back to load his car before his final evacuation. But why had he run for the pedestrian walkway? What could have possessed him? Was he warning somebody to get off before a gust of wind sent them sailing over the railing?

She inched forward again, several car lengths this time, until finally she could see what the fuss was about. Way ahead of her, but clear enough even in the rain, a film crew was set up on the walkway. Cars in the closest lanes were completely stopped and watching, although she heard honking behind them.

"Derek Forbes!" She slammed her palm against the steering wheel, sure she had her man. She'd spent too many years around notable actors. She had gone to school with their children, attended their parties, even dated a few B-list social climbers. The nicest of the lot still needed inflated egos to survive in their chosen profession.

Derek Forbes was a nice guy, but if he wanted to film during a hurricane, God help anybody who stood in his way. By virtue of his celebrity, he was undoubtedly sure he had the right. If he got in trouble for causing a traffic jam during an evacuation, who would dare do more than slap his wrist? He could pay any fine, charm his way out of jail time, even offer to do community service that would consist of him telling funny stories about his life to senior citizens or hospital patients. He could do magic tricks and sign copies of his DVDs on the pediatric ward, and the publicity would be perfect.

Suddenly she felt so tired she wanted to cry. In fact, she *was* crying. Tears were becoming a habit. Pregnancy was a veritable minefield. This baby had a lot to answer for. The whole world seemed intent on proving what a loser she was, and, of course, the baby was the reason she was reacting. Not Marsh. Not her own mistakes. Not Derek Forbes. Just the pregnancy.

Traffic had slowed again, and even though her wipers were on high, between the tears and the rain she could hardly see out the windshield. She put the car in park and rummaged through the glove compartment yet again, this time for tissues. She took out the owner's manual, her registration information, a small first-aid kit.

By now she was crying harder. If this kept up, she was going to need water wings just to stay afloat. Tissues were mandatory if she wasn't going to drive off the side of the bridge. She emptied the glove compartment, but there wasn't a tissue in sight. She felt around behind her for her purse and jerked it open. She hated Velcro. The ripping sound infuriated her, as did the lone shredded tissue caught in the sticky loops. When she tugged the tissue away, it fell apart in her hand.

She threw the purse back on the seat and settled for the hem of her T-shirt. She had no pride. Who cared if she wiped her nose and eyes on her shirt? Who would notice? Not Marsh, who was way ahead of her in line, probably cynically making notes on how to keep her from cutting him out of their baby's life.

She stopped short of blowing her nose and simply scrubbed at her eyes. Then she straightened, and when she peered through the windshield, she realized the car ahead of her was now way ahead. She glanced in her rearview mirror, sure she would see angry faces in the next car, but there was no one behind her. She was at the end of the line.

She jerked the gearshift into position and jammed her foot down on the accelerator to catch up. Except that the little Z3 roadster was either feeling ornery or poorly used. The engine whirred briefly, then something under the hood ground, and the car shuddered and died.

She had to get hold of herself. She'd owned this car since the day she got her license. She treated it with the same affection with which Wanda treated Chase. She wanted to pass the little Bimmer on to her son or daughter. By then it nearly would be a vintage model. She had to make sure it was still drivable in sixteen years.

This time she did everything slowly and carefully. When the engine was purring, she eased her foot down on the accelerator. But instead of the reassuring *whoosh* she expected, she heard a roar like an earthquake or an avalanche.

For a moment she was beyond confused. What had she done? She slammed her foot on the brakes just as the car began to move forward and it jerked to a halt. Her mind sped forward instead.

No car could imitate an avalanche. The sound hadn't come from her car. The car was behaving normally again, now that she was treating it gently. Nor was that terrifying sound the screeching of the wind or the torrential downfall. Only a second had passed, but that second felt like an eternity. Her eyes lifted to the rearview mirror to see the most frightening sight of her life. Behind her, just yards away, a gaping hole was opening in the bridge. And the chasm was moving inexorably and rapidly in the direction of her rear bumper.

CHAPTER TWENTY-SEVEN

By the time Wanda managed to wedge both Lily and Vijay's car seats where Chase's bed had been, she was well and truly soaked. Now the rain was coming down so hard she couldn't see anything beyond Janya's house. Her friend was inside waking the children and readying them to leave, but before that, she and Janya had managed to consolidate several boxes into one, including the three "books" Vijay had written since his parents' deaths. Then Wanda had substituted Janya's box for one of the least important of her own. Finally, they had lifted everything else up onto tables and the master bed, hoping that even if the house took water, it wouldn't rise that high.

Janya appeared beside her without the children. "They are cranky and frightened."

"How long before they're set?"

"Vijay refuses to dress. I will dress him myself." Janya was a gentle soul, but today poor little Vijay didn't stand a chance.

"You do that. I'm going to drive by Maggie's, just to be sure she got everything and got out of here. You not seeing her go by and all," Wanda added.

"That is a good plan. We will be ready."

Wanda had already tried Maggie's cell phone and gotten voice mail. Now, everything stowed as well as it could be, she slammed the doors and got behind the steering wheel. She suspected she would be bunking with the Kapurs tonight, who had reserved two rooms at an inland motel. After the drenching she'd received, she was in no shape to drive farther, and by now the traffic going out of town would be horrible.

She prayed Maggie had gotten away a long time ago.

Wanda swung her car around and headed back toward her daughter's cottage. She parked as close to the entrance as she could and pulled out the key Maggie had given her as she ran for the door. She jammed it in the doorknob, not content to peek through windows in the downpour.

All her fears were substantiated when a yowling Rumba greeted her.

Maggie would never, under any circumstances, leave the cat behind. Her daughter had not yet been home.

But why?

"You been abandoned, little one?" Wanda asked. She picked up the cat and moved inside. A pile of boxes greeted her. Maggie had brought a suitcase with her this morning, but here was the stuff she'd intended to come back for. All of it, sitting right here waiting for her.

Wanda debated her options. There was no way she could add any of her daughter's possessions to everything already squeezed in her car. The cat could come along in his carrier on Janya's lap. But that might be the extent of what Wanda could do. Surely Maggie was on her way home to get the rest. Wanda would leave her a note about Rumba.

Except that none of these plans relieved the fear building inside her.

She went to Maggie's phone, but when she lifted the receiver, she was greeted by static so loud, she instantly hung up and pulled out her cell phone. She hit speed dial for Ken.

He answered immediately, but he sounded as if he were overseas. In an underdeveloped country. Hanging from the coal car behind the locomotive of a steam train.

"Kenny!" she shouted. "I'm at Maggie's. She hasn't been here yet. She call you? You seen her since you left the shop?"

He replied, but she couldn't understand him. "Speak loud and slow," she said. "Real loud."

She listened carefully. She was pretty sure he said he'd seen Maggie heading toward the bridge just a little while after he left the shop.

He'd been checking an accident when she passed.

"She never made it!" Wanda shouted. "She's not here, Kenny! Cat's here, boxes are here. No Maggie."

There was silence. She didn't know if they'd been disconnected or if Ken was thinking. Ken was a great thinker. It drove her crazy.

". . . Calling Felo."

She nodded, as if he could see her. Whatever else he'd said, that part made sense. "You do that. See if he knows anything. Call me back."

Wanda hung up.

The minutes that passed were some of the longest she remembered. She spent them sifting through boxes to see if anything was both small and precious enough to warrant stuffing into a crevice in her car. She found a jewelry box that fit in her purse, scarves she knew Felo had given her daughter, Maggie's diplomas. She figured if she had to, once she was settled in the car, she could drive with the diplomas wedged between her seat and the door.

Her cell phone rang at last. Ken sounded even farther away, and she had to ask him to repeat himself several times before she got the basics of his report.

"She told Felo she was going to Blake Armstrong's house?" she shouted. "Why on earth would she go there?"

She thought Ken said yes, then something else she couldn't understand.

"He didn't tell her to forget that man and get moving?"

She listened, the phone jammed against her ear.

"Felo's on his way here?" she repeated, when she thought Ken had finished.

"On his way to Palmetto Grove. She's not answering —"

So Felo was worried, too, so worried that when he couldn't get Maggie again, he had set out from the camp in the swamps to drive straight into the storm to look for her.

"Wasn't he afraid he'd pass right by her?" she shouted, although it was just something to say, because who the heck gave a plugged nickel? He *hadn't* passed her because she hadn't left.

"Don't like this —"

She struggled to understand. "What, Kenny?"

"Don't like . . . Coming to look —"

A deep rumbling sound began somewhere not too far in the distance. She struggled harder to hear what Ken was saying, but the rumbling, like an immense roll of thunder, continued. The thunder was so intense, the floor seemed to shake along with it.

"Kenny! Kenny, are you there?"

She couldn't hear him at all now. The rumbling had finally stopped, but the only

535

sound on the phone was static, and even that was breaking up.

"Kenny!"

The phone went dead. She punched speed dial again, but nothing happened.

Wanda closed the phone. She wasn't surprised she'd lost the connection. Cell service on this end of the key was never top-notch, and she was a little surprised she'd gotten him at all. But what had he been trying to tell her? He was worried, and he was coming to investigate? She knew that meant he must be *seriously* worried, since every cop on the west coast of Florida had his or her hands full this afternoon with evacuations and accidents.

She grabbed the cat carrier and lowered Rumba inside, found a scrap of paper and scrawled a note to Maggie telling her what she'd taken with her and demanding Maggie call her the moment she got the note. Then she tucked the diplomas, jewelry and scarves in a shopping bag, and set out for her car.

Worry was rapidly mounting. Maybe Maggie was on her way, and maybe she had just run into some kind of roadblock, an accident, or someone in need of assistance. Maybe she had changed her mind and gone back into town first, before crossing the bridge. Blake Armstrong was leaving, but maybe Maggie had stopped by his house to help him pack boxes or move items to the top floor. She could be there right now, ingratiating herself to see what she could learn about him. Nothing like a crisis or a murder to make Maggie feel alive.

Of course, if Maggie *had* gone to Blake Armstrong's house, maybe the reason hadn't been to help him pack but to snoop through his belongings and search for information that might help her solve the Dutta murders.

Wanda had been worried before, but suddenly she was frantic. In the car, she set the cat carrier on the passenger seat, along with the diplomas; then she barreled back to Janya's house. There was nothing they could do with the children in the car, but the moment Janya and the children were safely across the bridge, Wanda was coming back to the key to look for her daughter, even if she drowned searching for her. Something wasn't right here. Ken had said as much, and Felo was on his way to Palmetto Grove. They were tough cops, not alarmists. But both men were obviously concerned enough to drop their other plans.

Wanda pulled as close to Janya's door as she could, and her friend stepped out with Lily cuddled against her chest. "Did you hear that noise?" Janya asked.

Wanda bolted out of the car to join her. "The thunder?"

"I have never heard thunder sound that way."

"I'm worried about Maggie. She hasn't been home. I have the cat with me, and just a few of her things. I hope she's on her way here now, but I'm going to get you across the bridge with Rishi, then come back to be sure she's all right."

Although Wanda had seen no reason to worry Janya unnecessarily, the other woman read between the lines. "You would not come back unless you thought there was a problem."

Wanda gave up the pretense. "Ken says she might have gone to Blake Armstrong's house." She paused. "Maybe to look around. Could be she suspects he's involved in the . . . you know." She nodded toward Lily. "I'm going over there, but not with you and the kids in the car. We'll get you across the bridge fir—"

"I hear a car." Janya turned away from Wanda and peered into the rain. Lily began to fuss, and Janya rocked and shushed her. "Listen. Do you hear it, too?"

Wanda didn't hear a thing except the sloshing of water as it tumbled in sheets from Janya's gutters. But she hoped her friend was right. It wouldn't be Felo, not this soon. It might be Ken, who could even have been on the bridge when she called him, in which case he could load Maggie's boxes into his car.

But even better, it might be Maggie.

A car materialized out of the rain, and

Wanda felt a stab of disappointment, although she knew that wasn't fair. She had been so worried about her daughter, she had forgotten to worry about Tracy's safety. In fact, since realizing that Maggie had not come straight home, she hadn't thought about Tracy at all. She hadn't even checked her landlady's house.

The BMW pulled into Janya's driveway, but Tracy didn't get out. Wanda leaned forward to see what was up and realized Tracy was sitting with her head in her hands. Her shoulders were shaking.

"Something's wrong," Wanda said. Again she thought of her own daughter and wondered if Tracy had already heard bad news. Her heart froze in her chest. For a moment she couldn't move. Then she was skirting the car, throwing open the driver's door.

"What's wrong?" She stooped, water seeping through the cheap vinyl of her boots. "What on earth is the matter?"

Tracy threw herself into Wanda's arms and almost sent them both sprawling in the mud.

"I . . . I almost died!"

"What?" Wanda hugged her hard, as much to stay at least partially erect as to comfort her friend. "What do you mean?"

"The bridge . . ." Tracy began to cry harder. "I . . . the bridge . . ."

"What about the bridge?"

"Collapsed."

For a moment Wanda couldn't absorb that. Bridges did not collapse. Some of them were built to open so ships could sail under them. Sometimes they were closed temporarily so repairs could be made. This bridge, *their* bridge, had already been repaired — by Blake Armstrong's company, in fact — but even when the work was going on, they had been able to use it to go back and forth to the mainland. One lane in each direction had stayed open. They had been assured it was safe, that the bridge would hold the weight of fewer cars, even in the midst of repairs. They had been *promised* it was safe.

"Collapsed?" She couldn't think of anything else to say.

Tracy began to cry harder.

"You were on it?" Wanda asked, holding Tracy away from her.

"It opened . . . right behind . . ." She began to wail.

"My God." Wanda squeezed her hard, then harder. Hard enough to squeeze all breath from the younger woman's body.

"What is it?" Janya shouted from the porch.

"The bridge went down," Wanda shouted back. "Tracy was on it when it went."

Janya looked stunned. She covered her mouth.

Suddenly Wanda wondered who else had been on the bridge.

"My God," she said again, feeling herself

go pale. She hugged Tracy harder, and she, too, began to cry.

Tracy felt numb, but if she was numb, then how could she be choking on her own tears? She wasn't even sure how she had gotten here. As the bridge had collapsed and the abyss, like a malevolent carpet unrolling behind her, had come closer and closer, she had shoved the car in gear again and jammed her foot on the accelerator. This time the little Bimmer didn't stall. It shot forward as only solid luxury engineering could guarantee, and she flew along the bridge, praying that now that the cars were past the film site, they had sped toward their destinations.

She was hurtling forward so fast, struggling to keep the Bimmer in her lane and avoid a collision ahead of her in the storm, that she couldn't even glance behind her again. Only when she was well and truly on Palmetto Grove Key did she finally know she was safe.

And then she was here. In front of Janya's house. Sobbing so hard she might turn inside out from the fury of it.

"I was sure . . . I was going to die! It . . . it was right behind me. It just . . . fell in. In pieces. Like dominoes."

Wanda pulled her out of the car. "Let's get you inside."

Headlights split the sheets of rain, and as Wanda hauled a shivering Tracy up to the porch overhang, a pickup pulled into sight.

"Marsh!" Tracy held the back of her hand over her eyes to shield them.

"How did he know you were here?" Wanda asked.

But Tracy didn't answer. She sprang forward and was in Marsh's arms before he could even close the door of the cab.

"Marsh!"

"Oh, God." He held her so tightly that she stopped trying to breathe. "I thought . . . I thought you were dead. Oh, Trace, I thought you'd had it."

"How did you know I was on the bridge?" she squeezed out.

"I saw your car way behind me when I got out to give Forbes a piece of my mind. I was on the key driving toward my house when I heard the bridge go. By the time I turned around and got back there, the intersection was a mob scene. I couldn't see your car —" His voice broke. "All I could think to do was drive over here, just in case. I thought I'd lost you."

"I'm fine." Although she wasn't. She wasn't sure she ever would be again. "The baby's fine."

"Baby . . ." His voice broke again, and he gave a terrible laugh. "I didn't even think. The baby! Our baby. It was you, just you, I was thinking about. I thought . . . I thought I'd lost you!"

"You didn't." She stepped back so she could see his face, although she had to wriggle free. "But almost. Marsh, before something else happens? I love you. I realized it when I was stuck on the bridge. That fight? That awful fight? I just . . . I just thought I needed more from you. But I'll take you the way you are, whatever you feel."

"What I feel?"

His words finally penetrated. "You were thinking about *me,* not the baby?"

"I know. That makes me a bad father. I'm sorry, but the baby is still a stranger. I couldn't imagine — I *can't* imagine — life without you." He stopped. "You love me? Did you just say that?"

Surely she had said the same words to CJ at some point in their marriage. Surely she'd said them on her wedding day. But she had never said them like this, with all the feeling she had refused to acknowledge for so long.

"I *love* you. I adore you, as exasperating as you are." Then she began to sob again.

"Ah, Trace . . ." He kissed her hair. "It's just . . . I've made so many mistakes. Look at us, you and me. We're so different. I thought . . ."

"That I didn't want you enough."

"Yeah, something like that." He turned her face up to his and kissed a tear, then another. "That's why I asked you to live with me. I thought maybe we could ease into being a

543

family, that one morning we'd wake up and realize it was going to be okay and the world wouldn't cave in on either of us again."

"It almost caved in on me today. Marsh, all those people!"

"We don't know how many went down with the bridge."

She wrapped her arms around him, and now the words tumbled out without restriction. "But *I* didn't. It's so selfish, but I am so, so glad I wasn't one of them. While I was trying to get off the bridge I kept thinking that I had to live, that I had to tell you I love you, that I'd finally realized how much, and I wasn't going to be cheated out of saying the words, no matter what you said back to me."

"I love you, too," he whispered, and she heard what saying it cost him. Still, she was sure, finally and for the first time, that he really did.

"I don't want to interrupt this touching display of affection," Wanda said, joining them, "not after all the time you two have wasted, but we got problems. More than either of you know. First off, we're stuck here on the key with two little kids. No way we can get across that bay to Palmetto Grove without a bridge. And the weather's only going to get worse and worse while we stand here trying to figure out when to schedule your wedding and what to name the baby. We got to get these kids to shelter, and I'm thinking your house, Marsh, is the place."

Marsh didn't release Tracy. They were both soaked now, hair plastered to their heads, clothes clinging, but he held on to her as if he was never going to release her. "Best choice," he agreed. "I've got a skiff, but it's not big enough to navigate waves this big or the debris in the water from the bridge collapse. What other problems?"

"Well, we lost people on that bridge." She cleared her throat. "But we can't think about that right now. Maggie didn't come home. Something's wrong there. Could be she's still in town, but Ken said she might have gone to Blake Armstrong's house, maybe to snoop around."

"Snoop?"

"She thought it was possible Blake had something to do with the Dutta murders," Tracy said.

"You got it," Wanda agreed.

"Blake?" Marsh sounded skeptical. "How does she figure that? Why?"

Tracy pulled away from him, horrified, as the truth hit her. "Marsh, Blake and his partners were in charge of the repairs, weren't they? Oh, God help us all, they were! Well, take it from me . . ." Her voice was shaking again. "Somebody didn't do his job!"

For a moment the only sound came from the rain and wind. Palm fronds were blowing across the street, and the rain on Marsh's windshield rattled like a drum tattoo.

Marsh took charge. "First we get everybody and everything to my house. Then we figure out what to do from there."

"Where's Bay?" Tracy asked, realizing for the first time that the boy was not with his father.

"He's at Adam's. I was supposed to pick him up there once I got back into town. He'll be safe. Their house is almost new and they're at least a mile from the water. They'll take care of him. But I have to get word to him that I'm all right. Once the bridge collapse makes the news, he'll be frantic."

"Good luck with your cell phone," Wanda said. "Mine stopped getting through, and the landlines are down and have been for a while. Can you get Maggie's stuff in your truck? And the rest of Janya's and mine? It's in the house."

"I have boxes, too," Tracy said. "I can fit those in my Bimmer."

"Janya's car won't start, but maybe we can jump it together," Wanda said.

In the flurry, Tracy was pulled one way, Marsh the other, but at the last minute, as she was climbing back into her car to drive to her house, he caught up with her and pulled her close one last time.

"We'll get through this," he promised. "My house has stood through a lot worse."

"You're darned right we will. Not losing

you again. Done with that."

He kissed her. Hard. Then he set her away. "Try your cell, then turn on your radio. See if you can get a station. I'll do the same. We need to find out what's going on out there. We have to know about the bridge. Then we'll go look for Maggie." He left to get his jumper cables.

Tracy wondered how she could feel this wonderful and this terrible all at the same time. And until they knew the fate of all the people they cared about, until the storm was well and truly over, nothing was about to change.

CHAPTER TWENTY-EIGHT

Maggie came awake gradually. At first she just felt uncomfortable, as if, in the midst of a nightmare, she had thrashed so violently that she had wrapped the sheet around herself. Then she became aware of a throbbing in her head, much worse than waking up in the morning after one too many of Felo's fabulous mojitos. Not even in the same universe.

Opening her eyes was difficult, and once she had managed it, the room was still black. Her eyes felt strange, too, as if something was just in front of them. She attempted to reach up and brush whatever it was away.

When her hands wouldn't move, she remembered.

Blake.

She was still too groggy to flat-out panic, but fear was immediate. She tried to piece together the puzzle of her recent waking moments. Information seeped in slowly. She remembered her realization that a photo on

548

the living room wall hid a safe. And that when she'd turned to find the remote that might open it, Blake had been waiting for her, lamp raised.

She had been taken down like an old tree in a new development. She remembered the look on Blake's face. He had been furious. She was surprised she was still alive.

How could she have been so foolish? She was a cop. How could she have allowed him to sneak up on her? At first she had been so careful to watch and listen. But then, close to the end of her own illegal activity, she had grown careless. She'd been busy trying to remember where she had seen the photograph. The shrieking wind had hidden the rest.

Up to speed on the past, she started on the present. Although her head was fogged with pain, self-loathing and fear, she tried to piece together her situation. Her hands were bound behind her, and all attempts to move her feet indicated that they, too, were tied together. The utter darkness was evidence of a blindfold, and the bad taste in her mouth, like somebody's dirty underwear, indicated a gag. Whoever had done this — and she had the perfect candidate in mind — hadn't taken any chances. She was not only slumped against a hard surface but fastened to it, so almost all movement was impossible. She wasn't going anywhere, that was for sure.

She retracted that. This was no time for hasty conclusions. There was lots of rope around her, and not all of it had necessarily been tied well. As if to encourage that line of thinking, when she wiggled her hands again she felt just the tiniest bit of give. There was space where her palms were supposed to meet, just a fraction of an inch, but enough to change her assessment from "impossible" to "dismal."

She realized quickly enough that the give in the rope was her best — in fact, her only — shot at escape. She tried moving her hands again. Rotating her right hand seemed like the best idea. Rotating and sliding. If she could slide her hand high enough and hook her thumb over the rope above it, quite possibly she could pull the rope down far enough that the rest of her hand could slip free. Then she would be in business.

Of course, figuring out the route to freedom was the easy part. Following it was another matter. She managed to slide her hand perhaps half an inch before she couldn't move it any farther. She began to rotate both hands again, over and over, until the rope seemed slacker. Then she inched her hand a fraction higher.

She was getting somewhere. Not quickly, and certainly not with any guarantees. But she was encouraged.

As she twisted her wrists back and forth,

and slid her hand another quarter of an inch, she listened to see if she could determine where she was. She could hear rain falling, although "falling" was an anemic term for rain at the edge of an approaching hurricane. Driving. Sluicing. Pounding. But even with all that water pelting the earth from the heavens, she wasn't getting a lot wetter. She was wet, yes, but a mist, not rain, was striking her face. After standing outside in the rain watching the house, she had been soaked by the time she got inside, and quite possibly the soggy condition of her clothing was due to that.

Wind howled loudly, but while she felt occasional gusts against her cheeks, she was sure the worst of it was blocked. She heard crashing, like small objects colliding, and something scraping back and forth not far from where she was bound.

She guessed she was somewhere not far removed from the outdoors. Not snug in a house like Blake's, where walls packed with insulation would shield some of the storm's racket and all the wind. The air felt wet here, not controlled and dehumidified by an air conditioner. She thought perhaps she'd been packed away like a piece of driftwood in a storage shed or a boathouse. She tried to remember what outbuildings the beach-house property included and couldn't. Perhaps she was in the same garage she'd broken into, but even that seemed too carefully cloistered, too comfortable.

She worked her hands as she listened. The wind was so loud, she wasn't sure she would hear whispering, or even the soft approach of footsteps. She thought she was alone, but she couldn't be sure. After all, she had thought she was alone in Blake's house. Despite not knowing, she kept working her hands, trying desperately to inch her right hand higher and higher. Her thumb still couldn't touch the rope, but she had to believe she was getting closer.

Minutes passed. She listened, her hand creeping higher; the wind growing louder. At last her thumb brushed the rope that bound her wrists. Foolishly, hope filled her. Of course there was no guarantee that hooking her thumb over the rope would accomplish anything, but it was something. A thumb could probe a knot. A thumb could, eventually, untie one, or loosen it enough to provide access for a finger. Opposable thumbs. The very thing that separated man from his brethren in the animal kingdom.

A hand suddenly ripped off her blindfold. She gasped, sucking the gag farther into her mouth. She began to cough.

The gag came off next, and the man who'd removed it stepped back. "Woke up with a magnificent headache, did we?"

Still coughing, she stared up at Blake, her

heartbeats coming so fast she couldn't have counted each one. She let her eyes adjust. He was a shadow at first, but then his features began to emerge.

"I *have* to get the wax cleaned out of my ears," she said when the coughing fit passed.

"Save the bucks. Not much point anymore."

"That lamp looked brand new. Your landlord won't be pleased."

"What, no begging, no pleading?"

"I don't think you'll believe me if I promise this'll stay our little secret."

"I kind of liked you. Why did you have to keep poking around?"

She kept up the patter, sure that showing fear would just make him feel more powerful. "In my genes. My father'll continue the tradition if I suddenly disappear, by the way. As will my boyfriend. I told him I was on my way here."

"There's a hurricane coming. Think they'll find anything?"

"Depends on your plans."

Another man materialized out of the gloom. Lankier, older, what hair he had plastered by water to a glistening scalp. Maggie recognized Ned Bournes. Ned of the framed commendation and the abandoned bag of Hershey bars. Now she wished she'd nabbed one.

"You look like a pretty sane guy to me, Ned," she said. "Surely you know kidnapping me is only going to make things worse."

"Can't get much worse," Blake said.

"Why did you take off the blindfold and gag?" Ned asked Blake.

"Gag's going back on. She was choking. Blindfold isn't. She's going to walk to the boat."

Maggie was listening, but she was also cataloging her surroundings as the men talked to each other. This was not a tidy boat or storage shed. The building, whatever it was, was sprawling and dilapidated. Not too far away she saw rain pouring in through a hole in the roof and the filthy broken windows. Cobwebs hung from the driest part of the ceiling, which consisted of nothing more than crossbeams under a peaked roof. A broken table lay on its side maybe fifteen yards away, and several tipped chairs lay much closer.

They couldn't have taken her far. She searched her memory for abandoned buildings in the immediate area of Blake's house.

The fish camp.

She'd passed the deserted camp every time she'd driven to the bridge, although she'd rarely paid much attention. Now she pictured a ramshackle half-burned-out building that had once housed a bar and bait shop on a shallow, narrow inlet to the Gulf. Guides had picked up tourists for a day of deep-sea fishing there, or driven them across the key to the bay side for quieter fishing among mangrove islands along the shore. She thought the land was protected now that somebody — maybe Wild Florida or even the state — had bought out the owners several years ago, but not yet cleared away the debris.

"You're going to let her walk? You don't think she'll try to run away?" Ned asked, his tone incredulous.

"She can try. It could be fun to stop her."

"Somebody might see us. Put the gag back in, and let's leave her. This place will flood. It's guaranteed."

"Right, and when Miss Maggie dies here, all trussed up like a pig at a barbecue, you don't think somebody will think that's a little strange? If they find her body, I mean? And we can't untie her, because she's a resourceful little thing, and the moment we leave, she'll find her way to help faster than our bridge went down."

"There has to be another alternative."

"I could finish her off right here, but why me? *You* need to get your hands dirty. Break something else over her head. Bash it in good this time." He raised a brow at the pained expression on Ned's long face.

"But before you do," Blake added when Ned didn't respond, "see if you can think of a good reason why she would have been here, one that preferably doesn't involve us. If you *can* think of a good one, maybe we'll be lucky and the cops will come up with the same explanation if they find her in these ruins, skull fractured and not a drop of water in her lungs. If not, I'd say killing her here and now is *not* a good plan."

"I don't think killing me at *all* is a good plan," Maggie said. "I suspect you boys are already in a lot of trouble, and despite your obvious misconception, the more bodies linked to you, the quicker your date with Old Sparky."

"How about *no* bodies linked to us?" Blake asked. "I kind of like the sound of that one."

"What about the Duttas? It's only a matter of time until somebody follows up my leads, even if it's not me."

"Shut up."

"And did you say something about a bridge?" she asked.

"Shut up!" Blake stepped forward and slapped her so fast that she didn't even have time to close her eyes.

Maggie inhaled sharply, but she didn't cry out. She had learned one important thing in the sheriff's department. Not to give bullies satisfaction. When she could speak, she looked straight at Ned.

"You really want to link yourself to this guy?" she asked.

Blake raised his hand again, but Ned grabbed his arm. "Cut it out! We don't have time for this. We have to get out of here while we can."

"Then we have to take her with us."

"Nobody I know can afford a ransom payment," Maggie said.

Blake glowered at her. "Nobody has to."

"She's right, Blake. We have to rethink this," Ned said. "It's just a matter of time until we'll be held accountable. For everything. And she's right, killing her's only going to make things that much worse. The bridge, the barber —"

"You shut up!" Blake shoved his partner in the chest, and Ned nearly fell backward, awkwardly catching himself just in time. "Either you help me get her in the boat or you aren't getting a ride to the mainland. You understand? You can stay here and take the consequences, whatever they are. All by yourself. I'll be long gone."

"Don't let him do this," Maggie said. "Use your good sense, Ned."

But Ned, clearly frightened, just shook his head. "We're in too deep."

"Exactly where you're going to be before long," Blake told Maggie. "As deep as we can get you."

He stooped and started untying the rope that held her feet. She waited until he was nearly done, then she kicked out at him, striking his chest, but not with the force she had hoped for. At the same time she screamed, although she knew that unless someone was standing right outside, it wasn't going to do any good.

"Hold her knees," Blake told Ned when he regained his balance and his breath.

Ned held back for a moment, and Maggie prayed he was reconsidering Blake's plan, but in the end he grabbed her legs and held them tight as Blake finished what he'd started. And he didn't apologize.

Getting everyone settled at Marsh's house was accomplished as efficiently as possible, which still meant precious time went by when they couldn't figure out how to notify anyone they were safe, or find out how many people, or who, had gone down when the bridge collapsed. They didn't even know how much of the structure had fallen into the water. Worse, they couldn't search for Maggie.

Nobody's cell phones were working, and neither Marsh nor Tracy's car radios had picked up strong enough signals to make out more than snatches of the news reports. The words *Phyllis, bridge* and *Derek Forbes* had all been audible. As had *deaths.* No amount of tuning and switching of stations had helped. The only one that came in clearly was playing easy-listening music without news breaks, as if someone at the station had set up endless hours of Barry Manilow and Anne Murray, then locked the door behind them to head for higher ground.

Janya took the children up to Bay's room to

work out sleeping arrangements. Tracy moved her things into Marsh's room, and Wanda took a guest room, as Marsh turned the electricity and gas back on.

Once everything was out of the car and stowed away, they met in the living area and received assignments. Tracy filled the two bathtubs and every available container with water for the inevitable moment when the electricity failed and the pump stopped working. Wanda made coffee, then boiled eggs and potatoes and threw frozen chicken parts in the oven to defrost and bake. They could finish making dinner on charcoal in the fireplace if necessary. Marsh gathered all lanterns, flashlights and emergency supplies. Even Vijay helped by bringing kindling for the fireplace from its storage bin near the door, while Janya, with Lily in tow, changed sheets and put out towels.

They reconvened in the living room when everyone was finished.

"I know there are things left to do here," Wanda said, "but I'm going to look for my daughter. And I'm going to start at that Blake Armstrong's house."

Tracy hadn't had a moment to talk to Marsh privately. She doubted he believed Blake Armstrong had anything to do with Maggie's disappearance. Blake was such an unlikely villain, and there could be a dozen reasons why Maggie hadn't come back to

Happiness Key. Right now she could be in Palmetto Grove saying prayers for all of them or worse, she could have been on the bridge, although the timing didn't seem right.

Instead, Marsh surprised her. "If Cardrake Brothers had done what they were supposed to, the bridge wouldn't have gone down. I think it's pretty clear they used inferior materials, or didn't follow the plans they submitted and took shortcuts. They wanted to come in under budget so they'd get the contract for the new bridge, and whatever they did worked, as far as it went. But they gambled that the old bridge would stand until the new one went up, and they lost. It's possible Maggie uncovered something, and they found out."

Tracy was relieved she wasn't going to have to plead Maggie's case. "Where do we look for her, and how do we go about it?"

"I can start over at Armstrong's house," Marsh said. "There's no reason for all of us to go."

"Dead wrong," Wanda said. "You couldn't stop me with a truck."

"I'm going, too," Tracy said. "We can spread out."

"It's getting wild out there," Marsh warned.

"And I'm physically fit, and perfectly capable of figuring out what I can and can't do," Tracy reminded him.

He smiled just enough to let her know he

heard the message. "Got it. Janya, will you go through my cupboards and see what food you can find that won't need heating? Maybe set that stuff on the counter by the microwave so it's easy to find when the power goes off. Cook anything that appeals to you and the kids while you still can. I have a generator, but we're going to have to conserve fuel. We don't know how long we'll be here until the bay is quiet or clear enough for my skiff or any rescue craft."

They donned the rain gear they'd removed on arrival and took Marsh's truck. Tracy sat beside him, with Wanda in the rear seat of the cab.

"I think we should break into Blake's house," Tracy said. "What if she's in there?"

Marsh didn't sound enthused. "Let's just look around and see first, okay? And if it comes to that, will you let me go in by myself, please? If this guy's done something to Maggie, then he's not somebody we want you to encounter."

She heard his concern, and despite everything else, it warmed her. Wanda was punching in numbers on her cell phone, still unsuccessfully trying to get through to Ken or somebody on the mainland. Tracy leaned closer to Marsh and rested her fingers on his arm. "My hero."

He smiled at her, but sobered as he pulled into the driveway of Blake Armstrong's house. "Let's make a plan before we get out."

"Think we should march right up there and ask if Maggie's in the house?"

"What are the chances anybody's there? But I think that's the way we ought to start."

Wanda snapped her phone shut. "I can't get through to anybody anywhere. Now they're saying all circuits are busy. When I get anything at all."

"Unlikely we'll be able to get through until the storm's passed. But when we're done looking, I know an old guy not far from the bridge with a ham radio."

"Awesome. How fifties," Tracy said.

"Still lots of amateur radio around, although nowadays the equipment can be really high-tech. That stuff was invaluable during Katrina. He's kind of a recluse, so it's unlikely he evacuated. We'll head there and see what we can find out. He might already be in touch with the cops."

Tracy opened her door, but Marsh put his hand on her arm. "Listen, you and Wanda be careful. Don't take any unnecessary chances. That won't help anybody."

She nodded. "Let's see what we can find out."

Tracy hadn't gone more than ten steps before she realized just how difficult their mission was. While the rain had lessened, at least temporarily, the wind was blowing so hard she found it difficult to keep her balance. She, Marsh and Wanda held on to each other as they struggled toward the door. Just as bad, the skies were growing dark enough to pass for night. On the stoop, Marsh rang the bell; then he pounded on the door with both fists. As all of them expected, nobody answered.

"She could still be in there!" Wanda shouted.

Tracy tried the door, but of course it was locked.

"It's going to be hard to break a window. They all have bars over them. I'm going around back and see what I can find," Marsh said.

Wanda nodded in agreement. "I'm going up the road. If Maggie was snooping, she wouldn't have parked where her car could be seen."

"Why don't you wait until we're done here, then we'll drive a little way and look for it together," Marsh said.

Wanda considered. "Got nothing better to do while I wait."

"I'm going with Wanda," Tracy told him. "Easier for two to stay upright."

They separated, and Tracy and Wanda headed down the driveway as Marsh went around back.

"Didn't see anything driving in, let's go the other way," Wanda said.

They walked into the wind, leaning forward

and making slow progress.

"I know something's wrong," Wanda said after a minute of forging their way against the wind. "A mother knows."

"A mother worries, but that doesn't mean she's right."

Their progress was slow, but it was progress nonetheless. Both women were avidly searching the roadside as they lurched forward, but so far there was nothing to see except trees swaying in the wind. Tracy was tired almost immediately, but she kept moving.

One minute they were safe, far enough from the trees to limit their risk. The next a six-foot section of sheet metal came flying from the direction of the beach and missed them by mere feet as it finally caught, at least temporarily, against the trunk of a crape myrtle, one of a small grove at the roadside.

"This isn't a good idea," Tracy said, heart in her mouth. "We shouldn't be out on the road unprotected. Marsh was right. We'd better go back and do this in the pickup."

"She was going to park out of sight, she'd have driven a ways," Wanda said. "A good long ways, then doubled back. Not somewhere where it'd be easy to spot her car."

"We'll get Marsh to drive this way before we turn around." Gazing toward the sheet metal to figure out where it might have come from, Tracy caught another glint just behind the crape myrtles, their segmented blossoms whirling madly in the air as the wind stripped them from the branches. She halted and pulled Wanda to a stop beside her.

She pointed, and Wanda shielded her eyes to see what Tracy had spotted.

Beyond the copse of bending, twisting limbs, the trunk of Maggie's sedan was just visible. Hidden there by Wanda's daughter or, worse, by someone else who had not wanted the car to be discovered.

CHAPTER TWENTY-NINE

Maggie didn't need years as a police detective and a degree in criminology to figure out what was going to happen next. The men had a boat, and they were taking it and her toward the mainland — only there would be three passengers on departure and two on arrival. They would untie her hands and remove the gag just before they shoved her out of the boat somewhere in the middle of the bay. Now the only question was whether they would depend on the fury of Mother Nature to take care of the final step or help the Good Mother along.

Despite the futility, she was hoping for the first. At least if they threw her in the water in a conscious state, she had a fighting chance. She was a strong swimmer, which, unfortunately, Blake might remember from their "getting to know you" conversations. In waves kicked up by an approaching hurricane, being a good swimmer wouldn't be enough, of course. She would only survive if she stayed afloat long enough to be washed ashore. But it was a chance. And she needed a chance.

Maggie fought the two men as they tried to lift her to her feet, and kicked out at Blake, who slapped her again. "Keep that up and we *will* drag you to the boat," he snarled. "By your hair!"

She didn't doubt he meant it, or that he would get some kind of perverse enjoyment out of doing it.

Every part of her ached from being bound, but her head hurt the worst. She knew she had to forget the pain, even welcome it. Pain meant she was alive, and that was good — a condition not guaranteed to last. She tried to welcome the blood rushing back into her limbs, and the stabbing ache in her back, where her bound hands had been shoved against her body while she was tied to one of the posts holding up her fish camp prison.

Upright at last, nausea threatened to overwhelm her, and she was almost sorry it didn't. She would have loved to spew everything she'd eaten that day over Blake's expensive topsiders.

"What . . . makes you think you can make it to Palmetto Grove in the storm?" she asked. "Your plan is full of holes."

"Stuff the gag back in her mouth," Blake told Ned.

Ned released her arm to rummage on the

ground for the gag. As he did, Maggie's bound wrist brushed against the pocket of her windbreaker, and she felt just the slightest bulge. She was sure the men must have searched her, but they had missed something zipped into her inside pocket. The familiar bulge of her cell phone in her jeans was gone. She couldn't remember what this smaller bulge was. Certainly not her car keys. She remembered leaving them under the front seat before heading up Blake's driveway.

How long ago had that been? The skies were now dark, so dark it could already be night. These days the sun set around six-thirty. Could it be that late, or even later? She had no idea how long she had been unconscious. Judging from the stiffness of her body, the numbness in her limbs, a long time. The dark skies could simply be the storm blotting out all remaining sunlight, or the hour could be advanced enough that the sun had disappeared on its own. Whichever scenario was true, one thing was certain. The storm had picked up intensity. Maggie guessed it was quickly bearing down on them.

She tried again to remember what was zipped inside her windbreaker pocket and couldn't. Ned grabbed her arm again; then, when she struggled, he clamped his fingers on the rope still tying her wrists. As he did, she felt the rope give just a little more.

But was it enough?

"Give me that," Blake said, and Ned handed him the gag. Blake wrapped it around Maggie's mouth as she fought him, kicking her hard in the shin when she attempted to bite him.

She used the kick as an excuse to collapse to the ground, where he kicked her again.

"Cut it out!" Ned shrieked above her. "You want to leave proof she was beaten before she died?"

"You don't think a corpse drifting on the tides gets knocked around?"

"I watch cop shows. Maybe you ought to watch a few. The coroner can tell if somebody was killed before or after they were injured."

"You think this is, what, an episode of *Palmetto Grove CSI*?"

"I think you ought to concentrate on the task at hand."

"Me, huh? This isn't about *me*. It's about *us*. It's about saving our necks. We have one chance here. We kill her. We make sure nothing — *nothing* — connects us to that barber and his wife. We plead ignorance about the bridge, tell them the fault was the contractors' and we did everything we were supposed to. The guys cheated us. They lied to us. The only way we disappointed anybody was not uncovering their plans."

"Like they're going to go along with that! The guys who did the labor worked for

Cardrake, too. Nobody's going to believe any of this."

"Then you come up with a better plan, Ned."

On the ground, Maggie was breathing raggedly, afraid Blake might have cracked a rib. She prayed Ned *would* come up with a better plan, and that it wouldn't involve killing her. But then she saw the man's shoulders slump.

"Let's just get this over with," Ned said. "Just see if you can manage to do it without enjoying yourself so much."

Blake launched into a profane tirade that Maggie might have found funny once upon a time. Now it was clear that the man was simply at the end of his rope. If she pushed him too hard, he might well kill her now just for the brief moments of release her death would afford him.

Ned bent over and grabbed one arm, and Blake, his clasped hands like a vise, raised her to her feet again.

"Don't push me!" he shouted at her, as if the gag had somehow affected her hearing, too.

She longed to tell Blake where she would like to push him, but communication time was over. She just stared at him, her gaze steady, until he shoved to get her moving again.

She dragged her feet as much as she could, and she stumbled over every obstacle in the way, buying herself seconds each time. Once they were out of their dubious shelter she was instantly drenched again, and the wind was a living creature clawing and moaning as it wrapped itself around her, nearly lifting her off her feet.

She had no idea how far they still had to go. Praying someone would happen upon them, she continued to stumble, to drag her feet, to fall to her knees once again when the men missed a piece of driftwood and she tripped, this time without planning to. There was a sliver of silver along the horizon, and now she guessed that sunset was just ending. She suspected the men had carefully waited until this moment, the hurricane not yet here, the sun just down, the bay still navigable, if only just.

Ned hauled her back to her feet by the rope tying her wrists. She felt it give a little more and prayed he wouldn't notice. They pushed her on, and she stumbled again, but between them, they held her upright.

The men had stopped talking. No one would hear them over the storm, but she supposed they really had nothing to say to each other, anyway. She wished that, while she had the chance to talk to Ned, she had pointed out that if Blake was willing to kill her for what she knew, he would be just as willing to kill his partner. The boat and the storm might yield the obvious ringleader a twofer.

When lightning flashed, which it did intermittently and distantly, she attempted to
gauge her whereabouts. She had expected to
be thrown into a car to cross the key to a
boat on the bayside. But now that she was
oriented, she saw they were moving in the
general direction of Happiness Key, and then
she saw why. Lightning sizzled again, and
when it did she saw, opening up before her,
the small silted-up channel where guides had
once brought boats to ferry customers out
into the Gulf. She saw a craft anchored in
the water near the mouth. A cabin cruiser,
from the look of it.

They weren't yet close enough for her to
guess the boat's size, but she knew it had to
be large, because Blake was willing to risk
taking it to safety somewhere. Leaving from
here meant that he would have to negotiate
the Gulf waters, then, most likely, one of the
saltwater canals that cut across the island at
the tip nearest the bridge. Or perhaps, even
more hazardous, skirt the island, giving it
wide berth to avoid sandbars and treacher-
ous shallow water, then round the point to
head into the bay toward town.

Exactly where would Blake shove her over?
She tried to imagine the worst place, the one
she was least likely to escape from. At the
same time, she knew it probably didn't matter, because Blake would make sure she
wasn't conscious wherever she went into the

water. Gulf or bay, halfway to Palmetto Grove or only a hundred yards out to sea. She would be just as dead in one place as another.

She felt tears welling in her eyes and blinked them away. She had to stay focused. She had to stay alive.

Her arm brushed the slight bulge in her pocket again. Whatever was there wasn't worth the time she was spending trying to identify it. She had to concentrate on getting away from the men, breaking free and running. She couldn't let them put her in that boat.

As if they knew what she was thinking, both men tightened their grip on her arms. They were half dragging, half propelling her forward against the wind now. She dug her feet into the sand, but she was no match for the two of them, especially since they were motivated by their own desire to escape while they could. They finally reached the water's edge, despite her every attempt to delay them.

The tide was as high as she had ever seen it, and the waves were rougher, not good news on either count. The boat was moored out from the shore in deeper water, and the men waded in, pulling Maggie along behind them. The water was cold, the waves already spraying as high as her chest. She shuddered, but the shock seemed to clear her head a little, and when Ned stumbled as the shore fell away near the ladder to the boat, she took advantage of the moment. She yanked her arm away and angled toward Blake, using her body as a battering ram to knock him into the waves. The attempt was futile; he didn't even stumble. He shoved back, and Ned, who had recovered his balance, caught and gripped her arm again.

"I'll go up and haul her in once I'm on board!" Blake shouted to Ned. "You push her up the ladder."

Maggie hoped this might be the moment to escape. Ned alone would be clutching her while Blake climbed, giving her precious seconds to get away from the partner who was at least partially ambivalent about what they were doing.

"And, Ned," Blake said, "you lose her now, I take off without you. It's a guarantee."

Blake dropped Maggie's arm and started up the ladder, but before she could do anything, Ned shoved her hard against the bottom rung and pinned her there with his body. She tried to wriggle free, but clearly Ned had taken Blake's threat as gospel. She felt hands reaching down, then Ned lifting her. She struggled, but with no success.

"You pin her into that seat over there," Blake told Ned once they'd hoisted her flailing body on board. "I'll get this thing going."

She had been afraid the men might tie her to the seat, but this wasn't much better. Ned was lanky, but wide in the hips. He pinned her between himself and the sidewall, and Blake went to the steering console. In moments they were moving out into the high waves, the boat rocking crazily beneath them. Ned tried to snag a life jacket on a seat from the other side of the aisle, but it was tantalizingly out of reach. Maggie watched carefully. If he stood to get it, she might have seconds to launch herself past him and into the water. But Ned quickly gave up.

She wedged herself in the corner of the seat and began to work her hands. Ned was clearly anxious, and seemed less worried about *her* than about being out on the water with a hurricane descending. The rope was definitely looser now. She could touch it with both thumbs and managed to turn it an inch, then another, until the knot was within reach, but after long minutes of struggle she despaired of inserting a thumb into the knot itself. Blake had obviously trained as a sailor, probably at his local yacht club. But her struggles had loosened the bond enough that she thought she might actually be able to slip one hand free.

The maneuver required room, and she doubted Ned would give it to her without question, or ignore what she was doing. When he leaned forward to shout something to Blake, she used the opportunity and yanked one hand as high as it would go. She made progress, but the rope caught on the heel of her hand and held.

One more try. She just needed one more chance and she might be able to free herself.

"Listen, I'm sorry," Ned said, settling back against the seat. "This wasn't my idea."

She was gagged and couldn't answer, which was just as well. Carefully, as the boat rocked violently, she tried to slide her hand higher, to free her palm from the grip of the rope. Again she brushed whatever was in her pocket and was distracted for a moment.

She didn't need distractions, but the bulge continued to occupy some portion of her mind anyway, as if it was a living presence that would not be so easily set aside. Furious at herself, she tried harder to concentrate, to pay attention, so if Ned leaned forward again, or gave up and reached for the life jacket, she could give her hand one more jerk to freedom.

And then she remembered.

The GPS unit that Felo had given her, in case she got lost on one of her solo adventures. She had slipped the little unit into this windbreaker during her canoe trip on the morning before she and Janya had searched the Duttas' apartment. She hadn't thought of it since.

She struggled to remember what the GPS required to set off its alarm. Was it as easy as pushing a button? She had accidentally set off the locator after moving to Palmetto

Grove Key. That's how Felo had tracked her there. But she knew there was also an SOS button. Unlatching and pushing the button in a crisis sent a signal that was tracked by an international rescue center. Her coordinates would continue to be tracked and logged and all information sent to local rescue personnel, as well as to her designated personal contact.

Felo.

Had he continued to pay the service fees? They hadn't been together for months now. She wouldn't blame him for canceling. A cop's pay allowed few luxuries, and these days Felo was paying the mortgage alone.

One thing was certain: there was no point in worrying now. The unit was in her pocket, and her hands were still tied. Getting to it was as distant a hope as a Coast Guard patrol boat suddenly showing up.

As if her thoughts had somehow spurred the action, Ned edged along the seat and tried to reach the life jacket again. Maggie gave a hard jerk as soon as he turned his back, and this time the rope gave enough that her hand shot free.

Ned, life jacket in hand, sat back. Maggie, heart pounding faster, looked beyond them. Land was no longer visible through the rain. She knew now that Blake had chosen to go out into the Gulf, then around the tip of the key. The closer they got to Palmetto Grove or

577

another port, the better her chances. Her hands were free now, and she could swim. Her chances of survival were remote, but they were better than before. She debated whether to surprise Ned, pushing past him the next time his concentration faltered, and diving over the side. But he was watching carefully, his body squeezed against hers, and the life jacket was now blocking her exit as he fumbled with the straps.

The boat was ferociously slapping the waves, diving as it rode the downside of a wave, climbing as it faced the next. Ned moaned a little, and she drew hope from the sound. If he got sick, he might turn away to toss his Hershey bars. She could use that opportunity to escape.

She didn't know how far they'd gone. She was disoriented by the motion and the darkness, not sure any longer if they were traveling around the point or out deeper into the Gulf. Clearly, Blake wasn't aiming for one of the inland canals. Wherever he was going, he didn't want to be seen.

Ned moaned intermittently, and once he lifted his hand to his mouth as if he was going to be sick. The boat rocked fiercely beneath them, fiercely enough that now she was being jolted against him, which seemed to make him feel worse. Just as she tensed and readied herself for the inevitable bout of seasickness, Blake cut the engine.

Suddenly they were sliding up and down in the waves, and water was splashing freely into the boat. Blake stood and came toward them.

He was carrying an oar.

"Move," he told Ned. "We're going to get this over with."

Ned moaned again and covered his mouth. "Move!"

Ned threw himself off the seat and toward the stern, and just in time, because he was already retching as he went. But Maggie wasn't paying attention to Ned. Blake was moving toward her. She had one chance, and she knew it. He raised the oar to strike her, and as it came down, her hands shot out from behind her and she grabbed the blade.

Blake, thrown off balance, stumbled, but he managed to find his feet. They struggled over the oar while Ned ignored them, too caught up in his own misery to help his partner.

Blake shouted something, and she shoved the oar back toward him, catching him in the stomach. He stumbled backward, gripping the end of the handle to protect himself, and she shoved again, aware her window of opportunity was closing as the retching noises behind her ceased. Blake was at the side now, trying desperately to wrench the oar out of her hands but still off balance. With every bit of strength she had, she tried to push him overboard, but he wrested the oar from her grasp, threw it to one side and leaped at her.

At the side herself now, she saw her chance. He jumped, and she threw her arms around him in a parody of a lover's hug. Then she used her own momentum to carry them both overboard.

After spotting Maggie's car and finding it unlocked with the keys under the seat, Tracy and Wanda had headed back into the wind toward Blake's beach house. Marsh, who had broken a window off the deck, let them inside. That victory was moot, since a thorough search of the house turned up nothing to indicate Maggie had ever been there. They left the way they had come and drove slowly out to Happiness Key, in case Maggie's car simply hadn't started and she had been forced to walk home. But she wasn't there, nor did they see anyplace along the way where she might have stopped for shelter. Happiness Key itself was deserted, and the beach closest to the houses was already flooded.

When Marsh and the two women finally arrived at the ham radio operator's house, they found it abandoned. To Tracy's mind, the house resembled a fortress, thick unpainted concrete-block walls, narrow windows and a steel door guaranteed to discourage everything from mosquitoes to battering rams. A huge antenna sprouted from the chimney side of the house. Despite the man's absence, Marsh wasn't convinced his friend had evacuated. The house was certainly locked, but the porch hadn't been cleared of plants or furniture.

"I hope he wasn't on his way back here to the key when . . . you know," Wanda said.

All of them knew exactly what she meant.

Marsh left a note, asking the old man to radio the police when he returned, and to tell them that Maggie was missing, and her mother and friends were afraid of foul play. The cops were to detain Blake Armstrong for questioning, since her car had been found at his house.

The last part seemed unnecessary, since if Blake showed his face in Palmetto Grove, the bridge collapse would be enough reason for anyone in authority to detain him. But Marsh wanted everyone, particularly Ken, to know that Blake might be involved in Maggie's disappearance, as well.

Now back at Marsh's house, they discovered that the power had gone off, and Janya and Vijay were setting the table by the light of a kerosene lantern.

"Let me help," Wanda told her.

Janya began to protest; then she took a careful look at her friend's expression.

"I would like that," she said instead. "And you will know what to do with your chicken."

Wanda nodded. Tracy could only imagine how she was feeling.

The children chattered as they ate. Vijay, who had, in the past weeks, begun to smile now and then, seemed particularly excited about what Janya referred to as their special camping adventure. He talked about sleeping on a mattress on the floor with Lily beside him, and how Janya had promised they could toast marshmallows over the fire. Tracy was glad someone was talking, since there was nothing the grown-ups could say to each other that any of them wanted to hear.

Outside, the wind was howling with increasing force. Thunder and lightning were intermittent, but when the thunder rolled, the old Cracker house shook with the rumble. They tried to guess when the storm might pass over, but they had too little information to go on.

Marsh used one lull in the conversation to make an announcement. "I have an emergency radio, the kind that has to be cranked to provide power. I'll get it out after dinner. It has a shortwave channel."

"Why didn't you say something before?" Wanda asked.

"Because the other one was working until the power went off. I doubt we'll hear anything if we didn't hear news on that one. But you know how these things go. I think we ought to take turns cranking and listening tonight. Just in case we can catch something. And the shortwave channels aren't good, but they could be better than nothing."

Wanda pushed her plate away, her food hardly touched. "I'll go get it. Where did you say it was?"

The meal ended quickly. Janya took Vijay and Lily to roast marshmallows with Marsh's help, and Tracy cleaned up, filling the sink with water from their supply and rinsing with careful economy. Tomorrow she would suggest paper plates to conserve water, if conservationist Marsh had any in the house. Or maybe by then rescue personnel would have been dispatched to the key.

Wanda was in the living room, sitting on the sofa cranking the radio, when Tracy finished and went looking for her.

"Hear anything?"

Wanda shook her head. "Static. Buzzing. Not worth the fleas on a bluetick hound."

"You're still cranking."

"Have to do something."

Tracy lowered herself to the sofa beside her friend. "I don't know what to say, Wanda. It's still possible Maggie got off safely or she's holed up with somebody here on the key. It's even possible Blake's not the bad guy we all think he is. Maybe he took her somewhere safe, and they're waiting out the storm together playing gin rummy."

"She would have gone back for the cat."

Tracy couldn't think of anything to say to that, because of course she would have.

"Where *is* Rumba?"

"Curled up with Chase in my room. I took Chase out a little while ago while you were cleaning up. I couldn't get him off the porch. This is some storm, considering the official hurricane season ends in a day or two."

"Last gasp I guess."

Wanda stopped cranking and tried to tune in a station, any station. She jerked her hand as if she'd been burned when a voice began to speak, audible over the crackling and screeching.

"Marsh!" Tracy shouted. "News."

Marsh came out of the back of the house and joined them. He lifted an eyebrow in question, but Tracy was too focused on the report to answer.

The eye was expected to pass north of Palmetto Grove around midnight. They would not get a direct hit. Relieved, she concentrated on every sound, trying to decipher what she could.

"Bridge," Wanda mouthed, pointing at the radio.

They all listened intently. Three sections of the bridge had gone into the bay. Emergency personnel were on the scene. "Derek Forbes . . ."

"Deke," Wanda said, resting her forehead on her fingertips.

"Shh . . ." Tracy put her head closer to see if she could catch more.

"Hero. Saved a woman . . . two . . . dived . . . water . . ."

"I'll be damned," Marsh said when the crackling began again and drowned out the announcer.

Tracy looked at him questioningly. "Did they say if he was okay? Could you tell?"

"Darn fool," Wanda said, but her eyes filled with tears.

"I think they did," Marsh said. "Talk about publicity for his movie . . ."

"That's not why he did it," Wanda said. "Deke's a real-life action hero. If he was about to die, that's the way he'd want to go."

They listened for another hour, but the signal came and went, and never stayed long enough to give them hard information. The house creaked in the wind, but the roof didn't leak and the hurricane shutters held.

Janya was the first to go to bed, settling the children on their mattress on the floor, then pulling her own beside them so they could join her and cuddle if they got frightened. Wanda was still trying to get more information on the radio when Tracy and Marsh finally went up to his bedroom.

Tracy used stored water to wash up and flush the toilet; then Marsh went into the bathroom to do the same. By the time he came back she had rifled through his dresser and slipped into one of his Wild Florida T-shirts as a nightgown.

He got into bed beside her and put his hand on her belly. The baby bump was now unmistakable, and an alligator on the T-shirt stretched tightly across it, as if the gator was sunning itself on a hill.

"I don't even know what to say about this day." Marsh made slow, steady circles with his palm, as if giving her and their baby a loving massage. "You're here. You're going to sleep with me tonight. I'm still having trouble believing it."

"Everything's been so awful, but being here? A miracle, in all kinds of ways." Tears filled her eyes. "We came so close, Marsh. To losing it all. And Maggie may have done just that."

"Shh . . ." He put a finger against her lips. "We're not going there. We don't know enough, okay? Let's just wait and see what we find out."

She turned so she could see his face. "Tell me, why was it so hard to admit you love me? You so obviously do."

"It's not that complicated. You married the wrong guy. I married the wrong woman, encouraged her to have my kid, and look where it got me? Sylvia and I couldn't have made worse choices. And I didn't trust myself not to put you and me through the same thing."

"We're a pair, toting lots of baggage. Do you think we really have a chance?"

586

"You just said it."

"What?"

"We're a pair." He squeezed her hand; then he raised her palm to his lips and kissed it. "Let's stay that way, okay? No more dancing around it. We're good together. Let's just trust it. Let's never have another day like this one."

She sniffed back the tears trying to fall. "Do I have to go camping in the Everglades every time you have a vacation?"

"Not if I don't have to join the country club."

"I actually might like canoe camping, once I'm not pregnant."

"I will never like the country club. You can live with that, right?"

"Nice restaurants once in a while. Deal?"

"Just as long as the food's good."

"I'll need validation occasionally. Once a year or so, you'll need to tell me you love me."

"I'd much rather show you."

"Tell me now, okay?"

He must have heard the plea in her voice, because he leaned over and stroked her hair back from her forehead. "I love you, Trace. Probably have since our first confrontation. I'm never going to stop."

She reached down and pulled him close. "Now we'll do things your way."

"Do what my way?"

"Now it's time to show me."

Chapter Thirty

Maggie went under twice, the first time struggling to the surface with enormous difficulty, only to let herself slip back under when she realized she couldn't avoid Blake's boat, which was inches from her head. If Blake was anywhere nearby, her brief seconds on the surface hadn't revealed his whereabouts. She descended as deep as she could, using long, sure strokes to take her to what she hoped would be the other side of the boat, but when she tried to surface again, she knocked her head on something solid.

Starting to panic, she managed to swim underwater again. Once more, when she tried to surface, her head grazed something hard. Instinctively she pushed away from it, and this time the mass moved. Encouraged, she swam just beyond it, and when she finally shot out of the water, gasping for air, she realized she had come up beside what looked to be the partially shattered hull of a rowboat.

She grabbed it and held on, riding the

waves to their crest, then sliding back down, scrambling to clutch what boards she could until she discovered an oarlock she could wrap her fingers around. Whatever view she might normally have had was completely obscured by rain. She listened for Blake's boat, but the storm hid all sound. The Gulf was even rougher than she'd realized. There was no hope of making progress, of making her own way back to land. The best she could do was hang on and hope that what was left of the rowboat would be washed to a safe haven.

After a period of trying to gauge her surroundings, she realized that Blake and Ned were no longer a threat. She thought Blake might have hit his head on the edge of the ladder as they pitched over the side. He had cried out and released her when he crashed against something on the way down, and she had instinctively pushed away from the boat and him, a reflex that had probably saved her from the same fate. If Blake had managed to reboard, she doubted he would be looking for her. He and Ned were undoubtedly long gone, leaving her to her fate.

And what would that be, exactly?

What remained of the rowboat wouldn't stay together long in a sea this rough. It might well have been intact when it was washed out on a high tide, and now it was little more than a skeleton. She had no hope of climbing on board because there was no on board. She had been fortunate to find the oarlock, but at any moment the boards attached to it could split apart and she would be left in the open water with nothing to cling to.

She was shivering now, her body's vain attempt to control its temperature. She had swallowed mouthfuls of salt water each time she surfaced, inevitable but dangerous. She was exhausted, her side ached where Blake had kicked her, and the brief spurt of adrenaline that had taken her this far was quickly draining away. She didn't know how far from shore she was or what shore, at that. She guessed that Blake hadn't been willing to head too far out to dump her, since that would have meant traveling farther back to port. He had counted on knocking her unconscious so she would drown quickly. He had probably traveled just far enough that her body wouldn't wash back too soon, if ever.

That gave her hope. She was past gauging how long they had been in the boat, how fast they had traveled, how much the rough surf had slowed their progress. Now false optimism appealed to her. She preferred believing she still had a chance versus facing a more difficult truth. She would hang on until the rowboat fell apart; then, if she could, she would swim until she found something else to carry her to the beach.

The GPS unit was still in her pocket, the windbreaker still zipped and tight against her body. She was grateful it hadn't ballooned when she hit the water. She debated trying to unzip the pocket and remove the unit, but the chances she would lose it in the water were so good, she knew she didn't dare. If she reached a more stable place or situation, then she could try. But she couldn't chance it now, nor could she hold the device aloft, so that it had a chance of establishing a signal. Unfortunately, in this storm, even if she was standing on a beach with the GPS held above her head, she wasn't sure she had a prayer of being found.

By now her mother, her father and yes, Felo, would have realized she was missing. She was glad she had called him before going to Blake's house. At least if she didn't survive, he knew where she'd been heading before she disappeared. Neither Felo nor her father would stop at anything to bring Blake and Ned, and any other employees who were guilty, to justice. Had Blake not been such a sociopath, he would have realized he could never get away with another murder, not when the latest victim was the ex-cop who had been trying to pin the first ones on him. With any sense at all, he would have headed for life outside the country and a new identity. But Blake had believed himself beyond reproach, beyond conviction. Lucky to a fault.

Blake had been wrong.

That knowledge gave her a little satisfaction as the rowboat's carcass soared with the waves and she held on for all she was worth. Her fingers quickly grew so cold she couldn't feel them, but she was still attached to the wreckage, and that had to be good. She thought she was moving. The tide plus the waves were propelling her somewhere. Of course, "somewhere" could be out to sea, but that was too horrifying to consider.

Felo. She wondered what he had done after she hung up from their phone call. Had he called her father right away? Or had he washed his hands of her, thoroughly and finally disenchanted with the woman who refused to listen to anybody? He had given advice, something Maggie didn't take well, and once again she had ignored him. Felo wasn't a controlling man. He had always trusted her to shoulder her own burdens. But even with a long history of respect and understanding between them, she had gone off the deep end the moment he questioned her judgment. She had gone off the deep end the moment he asked her to trust him the way he had always trusted her.

The deep end. And here she was, submerged in it.

Out of pride she had given up everything that meant anything to her. Her job. Felo and the family they might have had together. Life

593

in Little Havana. The friends she had made. She'd sacrificed everything because she had been so sure that she, and only she, was right. And still Felo had hung in with her, given her the space she needed, even supported her quest to discover who had murdered Harit and Kanira Dutta. He had gone out on a limb, but it hadn't been enough. When he'd asked her not to go to Blake Armstrong's house today, but to travel to the safety of Alvaro's camp where they could figure out what to do together, she had ignored him.

She supposed there was nothing like a passionate affair with the Grim Reaper to clarify everything. But now, for the first time, she could see exactly what she had thrown away. The fact that Felo had been absolutely right was all around her and indisputable. The fact that she had been wrong over and over, and still he had waited for her to come to her senses . . . ?

Equally indisputable.

Felo loved her the way no other man ever had, with the commitment, the unswerving devotion, that every woman claimed to want. She had loved him in return, but not with the same single-mindedness. Her pride, and what was left of her fragile sense of self after those unbearable years in the sheriff's department, had been most important to her, and both had stood in their way. Not because Felo had assailed either, but simply because, once upon a time, others had. And she, fool that she was, had not understood the difference.

Maggie wished with all her heart that she had told Felo how much she loved him, that she had asked for space to deal with her real problems, then found someone to help her do so. He would have waited. She would have gone back to him, cleansed and ready to try again.

Now the chances were all too good that she could never go back.

She knew better than to cry. She swallowed hard and tried to concentrate on just surviving each wave, each bolt of lightning, each frightening creak of the hull supporting her. She was shuddering harder, and she could no longer feel her feet. She closed her eyes and willed herself to hang on. If nothing else, she could delay the inevitable. Every second counted now. Every wave was one more wave she never had to ride again.

She didn't know how long she gave herself up to the rise and fall, how long she struggled not to swallow water and to grip the oarlock that now seemed a permanent extension of her body. There were perhaps a hundred roller-coaster waves beyond the boat — perhaps an infinity. Her thoughts were drifting, too formless and too fleeting to hang on to. She still kicked her feet when she could, trying to return circulation, but so much time had passed, and the effort seemed less worthwhile. The waves seemed higher, the lightning closer, and the thunder became an unceasing drumroll. Once, she lost consciousness for seconds, perhaps longer. Her hand slipped, and that jolted her awake, scaring her enough that she gripped harder. For a time she was alert again.

That spurt of awareness wasn't destined to last. Time continued to blur, no longer a linear progression of minutes but stops and starts, moments when she was perfectly lucid and aware, along with an increasing number of them when a part of her wondered if hanging on was worth the supreme effort it demanded. Her chances of survival were almost zero. What was left of the rowboat would disintegrate before the storm ended — long before, she imagined. She was merely delaying the inevitable, and she was growing so tired. If she simply let go she would quickly drown, and the pain and exhaustion would end. She was beyond debating how much worse that would be. Soon she would be beyond thought at all. Then whether to let go or not would be a moot point.

She hung on anyway. Some part of her found it funny that the same stubbornness that had brought her to this was the only thing keeping her alive. Of course, she would lose her grip at some point and that would be that. But apparently she was unable to give in before she had to.

She kicked her feet halfheartedly, then again, but now the water felt spongy, and the waves seemed to be breaking ahead of her, spraying in all directions. She couldn't think why. She was incapable of the needed logic.

Suddenly the rowboat splintered so quickly, so thoroughly, that she was left holding the oarlock and nothing else, and in a moment that, too, was gone. The crash shattered her stupor, but she couldn't summon the strength to respond in any meaningful way. She was too exhausted to swim, and it was too dark to see where she was or what had happened. She managed to tread water, staying just on top of the waves.

And then she was scraping against something. Flailing, she reached for purchase, anything she could hang on to, and her hand brushed something that felt like rock. The waves pulled her away, then threw her back against it. Again she tried to grab hold, but there was nothing to grab. The waves began to draw her back, but this time she knew she was drifting away and thrashed in the water to slow her departure. She managed to make contact again.

The surface was rough, as if it might be covered with barnacles. A pier? A seawall? Desperately she spread her arms, trying to embrace it. Whatever she was touching was jagged, but just as she began to wash away one final time, she grabbed something, a rod or a stiffened rope, perhaps, that was solid enough to cling to. As she held tight, the water threw her against the rough surface, once more scraping her exposed skin. The pain was almost welcome. She was still alive. She was almost surprised that, as exhausted and chilled as she was, she could still feel.

She couldn't stay like this. Eventually she would lose her grip and be washed away. She struggled to pull herself up the bar. She was fairly sure now that the object she clung to was metal, and it seemed firmly attached to whatever structure she had encountered. She only had to put one hand above the other and lift herself higher, perhaps even, if she was lucky, out of the water. But did she have the strength? It would have been fairly simple earlier in the day, but now she doubted she could lift her own weight more than an inch.

She tried anyway, summoning every molecule of energy left inside her. One hand, then the other. She made five agonizing attempts to drag herself upward before her feet found purchase. The surface wasn't vertical. She was climbing at an angle. Half out of the water now, she was still in danger from the waves slapping angrily against her legs. She lost her balance once and nearly let go, but as she hung there, she managed to find her footing once again. She climbed higher, rested, higher. Now the water was only up to her knees, although the waves were still threatening. The rod ended, and she was forced to stop. She twisted so she could hold it with one hand and lower herself to sit on the surface beside it.

She tried to make sense of where she was. No lights shone. She could be in the middle of the Gulf or nearly home. The structure beneath her was the only clue she could muster. She thought she was sitting on concrete. But where and what? She turned to look to each side of her, careful not to turn too far and risk losing her grip. She could see water splashing, but little else. She turned her gaze to the rod that had brought her this far and leaned closer, willing her eyes to focus in the darkness.

Rebar. A reinforcement used when pouring concrete. For a road.

Or a bridge.

She'll find her way to help faster than our bridge went down.

Blake's words surfaced as sluggishly as she had, but now they danced in her head. He had been furious when she'd asked what he meant.

Our bridge went down.

The bridge to Palmetto Grove Key, the one she had traveled back and forth every day, the one her mother, father and friends had traveled. The bridge that Cardrake Brothers had repaired. Blake's own handiwork.

Down?

Could she be sitting on the wreckage even now? If so, how long would her perch remain? And how long before anyone found her here? Under any circumstances but these, the wreckage of a bridge would be swarming with rescue personnel and local officials surveying the damage. Helicopters would be flying overhead, and tugs, even barges, would be moored nearby. But not in a hurricane. Not even one that, by hurricane standards, was mild. The work would only begin after the worst of the storm had passed.

She could be wrong, of course. She could be somewhere else, perhaps on the wreckage of a seawall. She needed to rest and continue her exploration when she could.

Only Maggie knew that a brief rest wasn't going to be enough to help her. She had used up every internal resource getting this far. She could no more climb higher and negotiate what would surely be a precarious path than she could sprout wings and fly to safety. One misstep and she would be in the water again, washing away to who knows where.

The fact that she was still alive was extraordinary. She had gotten herself to this place using her own strength and determination. But the only way she would survive this night was to summon help. With her free hand she managed to unzip her windbreaker, then the inside pocket. With trembling fingers she fished out the GPS unit. The chances it would still work were small. It was supposed to be waterproof, but it had been submerged a long time, not briefly dunked or rained on. And even if it *was* working, she didn't know if she could get a signal in this weather.

With her fingernail, she dislodged the casing over the SOS button and held it down. She thought a light was supposed to blink, but for five long seconds, nothing happened. Despair filled her, then the faintest tinge of green appeared.

For a moment she couldn't believe it. Could this really mean that the signal had been sent? That her coordinates could be mapped? That rescue personnel might be dispatched to find her?

She examined the unit again, looking for the button that provided a direct link to Felo. If she pushed this one, her SOS would also be sent to him, along with her coordinates. She didn't hesitate. If nothing else, if he received a message saying that she had tried to reach him, at least he would know she had thought of him. There was no hope of a personal message, not in this downpour, but at least she could let him know she had trusted him to try to help her.

She held the button down and raised the unit above her head for as long as she could, so the satellite would have a chance to find her coordinates.

And finally, waves still crashing against her

legs, she cradled the GPS in her hands and murmured a prayer.

Awareness came slowly. She was lying on something hard and rough. Wind howled all around her, and water was sloshing all the way to her waist now. Her arm seemed to be tethered, and at first she thought she was back at the fish camp, hands tied to a post, with Blake taunting her. She heard voices, but she was too exhausted to open her eyes.

"Maggie!"

She didn't want to answer. She wouldn't give Blake the satisfaction of a reply.

But this voice was not Blake's.

Startled, she tried to sit up, but something was holding her down. Memory returned in bits and pieces. The boat. The water. The oarlock that had saved her life. Then . . .

"Maggie!"

She realized that somehow she had managed to slip her arm under the rod in the concrete, the rebar that had once been part of some collapsed structure.

The bridge.

She had passed out, but before she did, she had slipped her arm under the rod, effectively pinning herself in place. The GPS seemed to be gone. Or perhaps she had zipped it back in her pocket.

But someone was calling her name.

"Here," she rasped. "Here."

She could hardly hear herself over the roaring of the wind.

"Here!"

A light shone in the darkness, and she heard men's voices.

"Here," she said again, a little louder; then she began to cough.

In frustration, she saw that the light was too far to her left. Shouting was futile. She had almost no voice. She couldn't stand so she could be seen more easily without risking everything. She could only wave her hand, then wave it again.

"Got her!"

She closed her eyes against the sudden brightness, wondering if this was a dream, or if she was dying and this was the white light people claimed to see. But she wasn't floating above her body. She was tethered to concrete, and even if this was only a dream, it was better than her reality had been.

She heard scraping above her and managed to open her eyes. Something seemed to be dangling in front of her; then she realized the something was legs. A body materialized part by part out of the darkness as it was lowered toward her, strapped inside a harness.

"We've got you," a man's voice said. "We're going to haul you up. Can you hang on to me while I get you into this?" He held up another harness.

"No."

"You've got to try."

"Can't," she said. "Want to . . ."

"Pull that thing up and let me get her. I'll hold her," said a voice from above. "Maggie, hang in there. You're safe now."

She knew that voice. Had she been able to, she would have smiled.

She tried to answer, and the man swung a little closer. "What'd you say?"

"I know," she said.

"Know what?"

"Tell Felo. He's here. I'm safe. I know." And finally she let herself cry.

CHAPTER THIRTY-ONE

Wanda wasn't sure what the mattress in Marsh's guest room felt like, hard, soft or Goldilocks in-between. It didn't matter to her, because she hadn't once stretched out on it. She hadn't even changed out of her clothes. She had made a spot for herself and the emergency radio in the den, and that where she was now.

She wasn't sure how much sleep her house-mates got, either. Flashlights flickered through the night as people made trips to the bathroom or got up to peer outside the few windows too small or otherwise protected to rate hurricane shutters. She hadn't tried to talk to them, because what could she say? She had listened to the storm slowly dying, and by the time dawn fought its way through the clouds and rain and waved from the horizon, she was almost certain the worst of the hurricane had missed them. No eye had passed overhead, and she'd been awake all night to confirm that. There had been no silent lull, not five minutes, not twenty-five. The storm had peaked before midnight, and since then, everything had been over but the shouting.

Phyllis had done her share of damage, though. Maybe she hadn't hit the key full force, but at about eleven the winds had sounded like a jet plane coming in for a landing. The house had rattled as if a toddler giant had picked it up and shaken it to see what fell out. A minute later Wanda had heard a crash nearby, and she'd been afraid one of the red cedar trees in a thicket up near the road had succumbed to the wind. Either that or the massive bay oak in the middle of the yard that Marsh was particularly fond of because of its name. Tracy had told her he called it Bay's oak, and there was a tree house nestled in the branches.

If Marsh's house had belonged to *her,* the tree would have been long gone, on account of it being within striking distance of the house. But Marsh had been willing to take chances. If it had toppled last night, at least it had toppled in the right direction.

She heard footsteps and turned to see Tracy, in a terry-cloth robe that was too big for her, approaching with a cup of coffee, which she held out. "Strong and black and sweet. The way you like it."

Wanda took it, although she wasn't sure her stomach would cooperate. "How long you

606

been up?"

Tracy crossed her arms over her belly. "About as long as you. Who could sleep? At least the worst of it seems to be over."

"No, the worst of it comes today, when we find out what happened . . . to everybody else."

Tracy moved closer and put her hand on Wanda's shoulder. She didn't say anything.

Wanda did. "I keep telling myself Maggie's strong and smart. When she was a kid, nobody could ever get the jump on her. She always seemed to know what was going to happen next. Once Kenny and I decided to take the kids to a beach motel for the weekend right before school was going to start. Summer's last hurrah. A surprise, if you know what I mean."

"I do."

"I went in to tell Maggie what we were doing, and she was already packed and waiting."

Tracy nodded, but she didn't smile. "Maggie also knows how to be careful."

"Yeah, she had to learn, that's for sure. Those are the good things about her, the things that might keep her safe. Then there's the bad part. The part where she doesn't listen to advice. The part where she's sure she's right and just plows in when she shouldn't."

"I wonder where she learned that?"

607

Wanda had thought about that a lot. She'd had all night. Everybody said that Maggie was just like her father, while Junior was like Wanda. But Wanda knew Maggie wasn't a hundred percent Ken. Her stubbornness, her commitment to doing whatever she thought best? Wanda could take credit for that, too, something she would surely do every day of her life if the news today was as bad as she feared it might be.

"You know how else she's like me?" she said. "Kenny would come home at night, and if I could get him to talk about what he'd done, I'd feel this stab of envy. Right here." She put her fist to her chest. "See, there I was, waiting tables and changing diapers and making supper. Not that Kenny didn't do his part, but let's face it, he's a cop. He never worked anything as normal as a forty-hour week in his life. More like a forty-hour shift and then another, one on top of the other. He was gone too much, and there I was, holding us together, helping with homework and making Halloween costumes. You know how many times I wished I was the one out there trying to figure out what some bad guy had done and why?"

"So you understood why Maggie became a police officer?"

"Understood, but I never approved. You worry, you know." She cleared her throat. "And now, maybe I've lost them both. Right before the bridge collapsed, Kenny said he was coming over to look for Maggie. I don't know where he was when he told me that. Maybe on the bridge . . ."

"No, he wasn't behind me in either lane," Tracy said. "Not that I saw, and I'd have noticed him. I looked behind me a couple of times. And if he wasn't behind me, then he's okay."

Wanda thought about that; then she nodded, a little pressure lifting from her heart. "Maybe you're right."

"Oh, I am. Count on that. And since he knew about Maggie and her interest in Blake, then you can bet he's spent the night checking everywhere Blake might have gone if he evacuated. That's what he's been doing since the bridge fell. He's been looking for Maggie, checking all the options over in Palmetto Grove. For all we know, she's with him right now."

Marsh came in, coffeepot in hand. "Ready to warm that cup?"

Wanda shook her head. "How'd you make coffee with no electricity?"

"Camp stove. I could make eggs and bacon, but I'm guessing nobody's that hungry."

"Sun comes up a little more, I'm going out to see what I can discover."

"Power lines will be down all over the key. It's going to be touch-and-go out there."

"I'll take my chances. You haven't been out

to check anything?"

"It's still pretty dark, and I couldn't see anything from the porch. I thought I'd have coffee first."

"We ought to go see how much damage we got at Happiness Key," Tracy said.

"Palmetto Grove didn't get a direct hit," Marsh said, confirming Wanda's guess "Phyllis probably went up the coast and came in north of us somewhere."

Janya descended the stairs, a smiling Lily in her arms. Wanda was glad one of their little group could smile.

"Vijay is still sleeping. We slept together on one mattress, but at least the children slept."

"Those kids landed in the right place, that's for sure. You're good to them," Wanda said.

Good or not, Janya still looked beat. "No news?"

Marsh started to answer, but he was interrupted by a loud pounding at the front door. Everyone froze; then he set the coffeepot on the closest table and took off to answer. Tracy followed, then Wanda and Janya with Lily.

Marsh threw the door open wide enough that Wanda immediately got a good look at a grizzled man sporting a beard that probably hadn't been trimmed since the day he'd decided not shaving was some kind of good idea. The beard was snow white and fanned out over his collarbone.

"Earl," Marsh said, sticking out his hand.

The two men shook.

Rain was still falling, but the wind had diminished to a weak imitation of itself, and in an hour it would probably be down to a strong breeze. Patches of lighter sky were visible between dark clouds, and Wanda could see the shadow of Bay's oak, still standing tall.

Earl followed Marsh inside. He wore a dress shirt as wrinkled as his face, and knit workout pants that had been hacked off midcalf. He'd solved the problem of shoes by wearing flip-flops, which he kicked off at the door.

"Got your note last night," he said. "Friend got his car stuck on the way over to stay at my place. Had to tow him half the way back."

Marsh bypassed pleasantries. "Have you got news?"

"Which do you want first?" Earl paused. "I guess you'll want to hear about the woman before the rest of it. You don't need to worry about anybody finding her anymore. She's in the hospital in town. They rescued her last night. Got dumped in the water by some maniac, but she made it as far as that damn bridge. Boyfriend and father rescued her."

He looked at Wanda when she cried out.

"I'm not making this up," the old man said, narrowing his eyes. "You don't believe me?"

Tracy and Janya closed in on Wanda, putting their arms around her as if they knew she needed to be held up.

611

"She will be okay?" Janya asked Earl, but she was looking at Wanda. "The woman? Maggie?"

Like all men, Earl wasn't immune to Janya's considerable charms. He forgot Wanda entirely. "She will, though the guy who dumped her in the water probably wasn't as lucky. They think he drowned."

Wanda couldn't think of a thing to say, which was, she figured, the first time in her whole life. Everyone else was asking questions, but her friends' arms tightened around her, as if they knew what she must be feeling.

"A lot of damage," Earl said, "but most of it minor. They say the hurricane spawned a few tornadoes here and there. They're still looking into that. Power's off in town, just like here. I hope you have a generator, because it'll be a while before any of us can get across the bay for supplies. They'll have their hands full over there for a while, so we'll be fending for ourselves. They asked me to get a group together to go house to house to see if anybody's injured or in serious need of assistance. We'll see what we can set up here until the authorities can take over."

"I'll help," Marsh said.

"Looks like you have your hands full here. But as soon as it's light, I'll get some people together, then we'll figure out what you can do."

"Derek Forbes," Wanda said. "And the

612

bridge. We thought we heard —"

Earl looked happy to tell that story and cut her off. "He and somebody on the camera crew got two women out of a car that went into the water when the bridge collapsed. Not too many people would have done something like that. They risked their lives for real, not just for entertainment."

"They're okay?" Marsh asked.

"Yeah, everybody made it, but the press is going to descend on Palmetto Grove like barnacles on a shipwreck. They thought another car went in, too, but it looks like that wasn't true. Lucky for everybody the bridge wasn't crowded at the time. Not right where it split open, anyway."

Marsh clapped him on the shoulder. "Can you get messages out for us, telling people we're okay? My son's in town worrying. Janya's husband, too." He nodded in her direction.

"That's all I'll be doing the next few days, I figure. Seems like nobody much understands that all them cell towers and phone wires can go down in a storm. But some of us, we stay prepared."

Marsh wrote down names, phone numbers and messages, and Earl promised to make sure all the information got to the right people. Then he left, cautioning them to drive carefully when they went out, because there were trees and wires down all over.

Marsh closed the door behind him just at the moment when Wanda began to sob.

"If there's a lot of damage, I don't know how I'll pay to fix it all," Tracy told Marsh as they waited on the porch for Janya and Wanda to get the children ready for a trip across the key. "My deductible's sky high, and you know all the insurance caveats about hurricanes and how many different companies get involved. This one won't pay for this, that one won't pay for that. By the time they're done 'won't paying,' I'll get a twenty-dollar bill and a pat on the back for my time and effort."

"Don't borrow trouble." Marsh put his arm around her. "So far our luck's been good."

Tracy gazed at the cedar tree blocking a portion of Marsh's driveway out by the road. Fortunately none of their cars had been in its path, and the rest of Marsh's yard looked okay, though some branches were down, the door of Bay's tree house was half off, and shingles from the tree-house roof were scattered nearby. A piece of tin from Marsh's roof hung over one side of his porch, but once the tree was sawed up and hauled away, the rest could be repaired with a short day's work.

"We *have* been lucky," she said. "Me and Maggie most of all. I'm alive to wrangle with the insurance company, and she's alive to figure out the rest of her life."

"You have yours all figured out?"

"I have part of it figured out."

"Which part is that?"

"The part about who to spend it with."

He kissed her. "Funny thing. I have that part figured out, too."

"We ought to get together sometime and compare notes."

The door opened, and Wanda came out with Lily. "We're leaving Chase and the cat here to guard the house. Hope that's okay."

"Good idea." Marsh went down the steps to pull his car up to the porch. His hybrid had all-wheel drive, and they had agreed to go in one car. With little or no traffic on the roads, it seemed silly to take two just to accommodate the kids' car seats, and also more risky.

"If everything's okay, we'll move back into our houses this afternoon," Wanda told Tracy. "Leave you lovebirds alone."

Tracy gave a shake of her head. "No, I think we ought to stay together until things are at least a bit more normal. Ferry to the mainland, electricity. No sense in everybody fending for themselves when we can work together here and make it easier."

"Will you be staying here from now on? You moving in with Marsh?"

Tracy wondered the same thing. She knew that was what Marsh wanted, and she loved the old Cracker house, *and* the man and boy in residence. Living there made complete sense. Yet she was torn. If she lived with Marsh, she would no longer be part of life on Happiness Key.

"I don't know what I'm going to do," she said.

"Sure you do. This is where you belong now. You and the baby."

Janya came out with Vijay. "We are ready. Vijay says this is a new adventure. He has started a story about a big wind that takes a little boy to a brand-new land."

"Better read him the *Wizard of Oz* before he gets too far along," Wanda said.

Tracy wondered if Vijay and Lily would soon be transported to a brand-new land of their own, one with the grandparents who had never acknowledged them. If Janya and Rishi were allowed to keep the children, they would all travel back to India whenever they could to see Janya's family, perhaps even the children's relatives if fences were mended. Staying here with the Kapurs would not be a rejection of the past, but a new chapter. She hoped the families and authorities on both sides of the ocean would realize that.

Wanda and Janya squeezed the children between them on the backseat, and everybody fastened their seat belts. At the end of the driveway Marsh maneuvered carefully around the fallen tree. The road ahead was clear.

They watched the unfolding scenery without much conversation. Even the children were quiet, although Lily insisted on climbing up on Janya's lap, and Wanda scooped up Vijay so he could see better. Marsh was driving slowly, watching for fallen limbs and other obstructions, and they saw only two cars, the first one parked and abandoned by the local Indian mound where the land was higher. Someone had undoubtedly hoped to protect it in case of flooding. The second car passed them, and Tracy recognized the owner of Randall's, who had probably gotten up early to see how his store had fared. From the road, it looked fine.

"If he opens up, we can restock our supplies," Marsh said.

"Look at that old fish camp." Wanda pointed out her window. "I guess that'll save the state from having to tear it down. Nothing much left of it now."

Tracy peered beyond Marsh and saw that Wanda was right. What little had been left of the dilapidated structure was gone now — blown out into the Gulf, most likely.

"And there's Blake's house," she said a minute later, pointing down the driveway that led to it. "It looks okay. I wonder . . ."

They all wondered but didn't voice their suspicions with the children in the car. They only knew that someone had tried to kill Maggie, not his identity. But Blake himself was their top candidate.

"That's a story I'm all ears to hear," Wanda said, "now that I've heard the happy ending first."

"Things are looking pretty good so far." Marsh had dodged felled trees, and once a downed pole and all the wires strung from it. There was debris on the road, uprooted bushes, pieces of tin and what looked like siding from somebody's house or fishing shack. Tracy was encouraged. An osprey nest that she had passed every day on her way to the bridge was still in place on the top of a telephone pole, and as they passed, an osprey was circling, as if checking the nest's status, just the way they were about to check Happiness Key.

"That's a good sign," she said, pointing to the bird. "If a nest made it, our houses probably made it, too."

"Maybe we'll be sorry we worked so hard to get all our important stuff out," Wanda said. "Maybe we wasted a lot of time yesterday."

But Marsh had slowed again, and Tracy immediately saw why. The road curved here and swung a little closer to the water. They were almost at Happiness Key now, where her property began. Even with some familiar landmarks changed or gone, she knew she should be able to see the houses ahead.

Except that now, a hundred yards in front of them and plainly visible from where she sat, was a pile of rubble blocking the road.

She put her hand to her mouth and stared. Marsh leaned over and put his hand on her knee. "Take a deep breath."

"What?" Wanda asked, unable to see from the backseat.

"Please. Stop," Tracy told Marsh.

"I can get us closer."

"No, stop. Please."

He did, not a difficult job, since he had already slowed after his first glimpse of the sight ahead.

Tracy unsnapped her seat belt and opened the door. She turned around, blinking back tears. "It's not good news," she told the women behind her. But she could tell that now they realized the situation, as well.

"How bad do you think it is?" Wanda asked, unsnapping her belt to get out.

Tracy shook her head, although she was afraid the answer was all too clear, even from here.

"A twister," Marsh said, getting out, too. "Earl told us they'd tracked some that were spawned by the hurricane. It looks like one of them came right across here."

Tracy was out of the car now, staring ahead. Not all the rubble was manmade. Something, most likely a tornado, had cleared a path from the bay to the gulfside. Trees lay on their sides. Shrubbery was gone, and so was the road. Erased. Or nearly so, as if nothing had ever occupied this ground.

She began to walk slowly toward what had once been a small beachfront community with the absurd and still completely suitable name of Happiness Key.

"You don't have to do this," Marsh said, coming up beside her and taking her hand.

"It was mine." She heard the past tense, and tears filled her eyes again.

"You made it yours," he agreed. "In all the right ways. You brought it to life."

She started to say, "For what? Look where it got me." But she stopped herself. Because she knew the answer.

Wanda and Janya, each with a child in her arms, joined them, and they walked as close as they dared. There were too many downed wires for them to venture very far. Instead, they stopped and stared.

Wanda's house had been hit the worst. Where it had stood there was nothing but a foundation and, incongruously, a row of hibiscus that, except for blossoms stripped by the wind, looked almost unscathed. Enough of Janya's cottage remained to mark the spot where it had been. A wall, holes where windows had adorned it. The roof lay just beyond it, as if it had blown off in one piece.

Tracy's house was still marked by portions of two walls, but even from here, she could see that everything she had left inside was gone. Somewhere in the Gulf a school of fish

620

was enjoying her take on budget interior design.

Alice's house was missing its roof, as if someone had reached down and carefully pried it away. There was no sign of the roof itself, but for the most part, the walls were standing. And finally Maggie's house — the same house where Dana and Lizzie had also lived, the house that had originally been home to Herb Krause, the old man who had left all the women a unique legacy — was just a heap of crumbled concrete.

"Well, damn," Wanda said. "There's no place like home."

"No place at all." Tracy closed her eyes. "Nothing like home anymore."

"At least our insurance companies won't fiddle around. They'll have to pay up." The quaver in Wanda's voice belied the pep talk.

Janya spoke from behind them. "We saved the things that were important. There was nothing you could have done that you didn't do."

It was just like Janya to try to console her friends. Tracy took a deep breath, trying to quell the turmoil inside her, and stared at the ruins of the first happy home she had ever known. Marsh slipped his arm around her waist and lightly rested his fingers on her belly, where his child was cocooned from all life's disappointments.

"My house is big enough for all of us," he

said. "Everyone is welcome there as long as you need to stay."

Tracy felt a strange sensation. Not turmoil after all. Not sorrow welling from deep inside her, although there was plenty of that. But movement. A vague fluttering where Marsh's hand rested.

"Marsh . . ."

He kissed her hair. "You okay? Do you need to go back to the car?"

"I think the baby moved. Did you feel it?"

He pressed his hand tighter against her belly. Then he laughed. "That's what it is. She's making herself known. And what a moment to do it."

Tracy wasn't sure whether to laugh or cry. She was choking on both, and inside, from its place of safety and sustenance, the baby was offering comfort. She had waited for this moment, and it could not have come at a more emotional time.

Then she realized exactly what Marsh had said. She turned to him. "She?"

He looked instantly guilty. "I just think of the baby as a girl, that's all."

"You know, don't you? You asked the technician when I left the room to see the doctor. You found out the sex without me!"

"Trace, there are bigger things to think about today, okay?"

She pressed his fingers harder against her belly, hoping the baby, their daughter, would

622

flutter again. Suddenly she knew she was going to be all right. All of them were going to be all right. "Are there? You're sure?"

"Doesn't matter where we live," Wanda said, setting Vijay on the ground at her feet, then draping her arm over Tracy's shoulder, and pulling Janya and Lily into line beside them. "You just remember that in the days to come, okay?"

CHAPTER THIRTY-TWO

February in Palmetto Grove was high tourist season. If they weren't part of the service industry, residents hunkered down and took cover. If they *were,* they hoarded their tips and smiled brightly. Nobody with any sense planned a major event in February.

Nobody except Tracy and the women of Happiness Key.

"The next ferry's about to dock," Wanda said, coming into the bedroom at the old Cracker house where Janya and Alice were helping Tracy dress for her wedding. "Kenny's on it, and good thing, too. If he'd missed all the hoopla here, he'd of had to get his nookie somewhere else for the next few months."

"I'm sure he must have known," Alice said as she took out the pearls she had worn on her own wedding day. They were to be Tracy's "old" and "borrowed" all in one. "He is . . . a bright man."

Tracy was just taking her dress off the

hanger. The dress, unlike her sadly clinging slip, was designed to take the emphasis off her expanded middle and prominent baby bump. It was strapless, white chiffon over ivory silk, and fell from a satin sash positioned right below her breasts to midcalf. Okay, she was still clearly pregnant, but at least she was going to look good. She figured she deserved that, since for the next and final three months of her pregnancy, she was pretty sure she would be mistaken for the Goodyear Blimp.

"Maggie and Felo are with him?" she asked, because Wanda hadn't said, and Tracy hated to think what kind of punishment Felo would endure from Wanda if he missed Tracy's wedding.

"Present and accounted for."

"Relax, dear," Alice said. "Everything is set."

There was a knock at the door, and before anyone could answer, Olivia stepped inside. "It's crazy out there!"

"You look beautiful," Wanda told the girl. "And am I right? I hear you and Lily match?"

The two girls were sharing the position of flower girl. Lily, who was now toddling everywhere on her own, was to go first; then, when she inevitably wandered off to do something else, Olivia would scoop her up, and together they would finish the job. Olivia's dress was floor-length and a deep violet color; Lily's was the same, although hers was a shorter version so she couldn't trip over the hem.

Olivia did look beautiful. Before too many years passed she would graduate to bridesmaid, then maybe a bride herself. Tracy was glad she would be watching the transformation up close. After the destruction of Happiness Key, Olivia had moved in with Tracy and Marsh and never moved out again. After much conversation and thought, everyone concerned had decided that letting the girl live there permanently was the right thing.

Olivia still spent part of each weekend and one school night a week with Alice and Roger at Shell Horizon, but her home was now on Palmetto Grove Key, in a former guest room that sported posters of Justin Bieber and Daniel Radcliffe on freshly painted lavender walls. Alice could do what she was best suited to do, enjoy being Olivia's proud and adoring grandmother, while Marsh and Tracy fulfilled the day-to-day role of parents.

Tracy thought that once Roger and Alice worked out all the details of merging their separate lives and incomes, there would be another wedding for all of them to enjoy. Olivia had already announced that when the time came, she planned to be the one to give her grandmother away.

"Now that everybody's together, are you finally going to tell us the baby's name?" Olivia asked.

"Maggie's not here yet," Wanda pointed out before Tracy could answer. "And I heard tell from Kenny there's a surprise guest coming over on that ferry. You just have to wait."

"This is *so* not fair. She's practically *my* little sister."

Tracy smiled sympathetically; then she held out her arms, and Janya, who had taken the dress, slipped it over her head.

Olivia perked up suddenly. "Are Lizzie and Dana the surprise?"

There were secrets the girl didn't know, and none they could share with her now about Dana's reasons for leaving Happiness Key. Instead, Tracy shared some good news, because Dana, who was finally beginning to feel safe again, had written to tell her that she could. "No, they can't be here. But I got a beautiful card from both of them, and Pete, too. And you want to know where it's from?"

Olivia screwed up her face in thought. "The way they move, it could be anywhere."

"Australia," Tracy said, then waited a moment for the surprised murmur to die down. "Dana said they've bought a little cattle ranch there, and they're very happy. And . . ." She smiled. "They want all of us to come and visit. They'll buy the tickets when we're ready."

Tracy saw understanding on the faces of the women. Better than anyone, they knew this was a gift Dana could afford and generously offer them.

"Wow! I bet I'm not supposed to tell anybody, right?" Olivia asked.

"You are one smart cookie," Wanda said.

Janya changed the subject before more questions ensued. "Olivia, was Vijay still clean when you saw him?"

"Rishi is making sure of it."

"Vijay has taken a particular liking to mud pies," Janya said. "I am sure he is looking for a source today."

"A boy can't start too young on making pies," Wanda said. "We'll get him making the real ones soon enough."

She didn't add "if the children stay with you." All news so far had been good. The second set of grandparents had been located and, like the first, seemed unwilling to become guardians. These days none of the women mentioned the possibility that Vijay and Lily could still be moved elsewhere, for fear of jinxing the children's future.

To accommodate their new family and make the possibility of an adoption more likely, Janya and Rishi had just closed on a comfortable house in a family neighborhood near the bridge, where the children would have plenty of friends, Janya would be close enough to visit hers, and Rishi would have a shorter commute. The Kapurs were moving out of their temporary rental next week, and Janya had been hard at work painting murals based on Hindu folktales on the children's new bedroom walls.

Wanda and Ken weren't far away, either. While they debated whether to buy or rent, they had moved into a pet-friendly condo overlooking the Gulf, complete with an Olympic-size swimming pool to entertain their grandchildren and friends, a dog park where Chase could run and a kitchen that satisfied even Wanda's requirements.

Tracy drew a deep breath so Janya could zip the dress. "Everything has changed so fast! Sometimes I feel like I can't keep up."

"Just wait till that baby comes," Wanda said. "Then we'll talk about keeping up."

"I can have her with me at the center. I told you that, right? It's all set. She can stay in the nursery with our attendant."

"And when that does not suit, then I will have her with me," Janya said.

"Her?" Olivia asked. "Who?"

Tracy knew what the girl was up to, but she played along. "The baby."

"Which baby?"

Tracy winked at her. "You mean . . . Waverly?"

"Waverly!" Olivia clapped her hands. "Wow, that's cool."

"You let Ms. Olivia here twist you around those skinny fingers of yours," Wanda said, "you'll deserve everything she gives you in adolescence."

"You wanted to know, too," Olivia said. "You *know* you did."

"Waverly?" Wanda asked, ignoring what was obviously the truth. "How'd you come up with that?"

"Do you like it?"

"I think so. Yeah, I do. Of course you'll shorten it to . . . ?"

"Way," Tracy said.

"It is a beautiful name," Janya said.

Alice, who was fastening the pearls around Tracy's neck, agreed.

"It's better than Olive Tree. That's what Marsh calls *me,*" Olivia said. "That's so dorky." But she didn't look as if she minded.

Wanda took down the rhinestone-and-pearl comb that Tracy planned to wear, and carefully blew off a spot of dust. "When I talked to him just now, Ken said the word's come down that the bridge will probably open again next week, now that the repairs are about finished."

No one said anything for a moment. Tracy wasn't sure if she would ever cross the present bridge comfortably, and she was looking forward to the new one going up next to it. The new bridge would be the most carefully built, state-of-the-art bridge in Florida. In penance, every official remotely involved was making certain of it.

"He also said they've reached a plea bargain with that Bournes guy. Life in prison for murder and attempted murder instead of the death penalty, and he rats on everybody who was part of the scam. They'll clean out Cardrake Brothers real fast."

"The scam . . ." Tracy thought how anemically the word described everything that had occurred.

Everyone now knew that the "scam" had started as just that, before it morphed into something darker and murderous. The elite group of engineers under Blake Armstrong's leadership had convinced themselves that they could skimp on materials for repairs for the old bridge. Assured of the lucrative contract for the new one if they brought the repairs in under budget, they had seen their plan as foolproof. Odds that the repairs wouldn't hold up were small, so small that in the mind of Blake Armstrong, avid gambler, the scheme was worth the risk. If necessary, bridge inspectors could be paid off, and so could contractors. Nobody would have discovered the plan, except that on a routine maintenance run, one of the Cardrake team had spotted a crack, a substantial crack that considerably changed the odds of not being discovered.

By then the team had earned reputations as golden-haired boys, the best and the brightest young engineers in the business. Their choices were limited. Do nothing and hope the crack didn't widen and wasn't discovered.

Make minor repairs without admitting the extent of the problem and hope they could explain things in such a way that their previous actions weren't unduly questioned. Or confess that they'd made errors, close down the bridge for several weeks, and completely redo what they had done so poorly the first time.

When Harit Dutta arrived at the beach house to cut Blake's hair two afternoons before he died, several of the men had been in a heated discussion about which avenue to follow. Blake, who had forgotten about his appointment, looked up and found Harit standing in the doorway, and from the expression on Harit's face, he couldn't tell exactly what or how much the man had heard. Blake paid him and sent him away, and then the men discussed what to do. Most felt Harit was not an engineer and therefore would not understand what they'd been saying, even if he had overheard some of it. But Blake, who had engaged in several in-depth conversations with the intelligent, well-educated barber, was sure his partners were wrong. He felt certain that when Harit considered what he'd learned, not only would he understand, he would feel obliged to report it.

Overnight Blake brooded about the barber's involvement, aware that while he himself was trying to figure out what to do, Harit might well be discussing the matter with his wife.

By the next morning, he knew he couldn't sit back any longer. Well connected to the gambling underworld in his native Miami, he arranged to have Kanira abducted when she left home to do her grocery shopping the next morning, then brought to Miami, where she was forced at gunpoint to call Harit. He was sure from a former conversation that the frantic husband would drive straight to Miami once he knew his wife's location. The Duttas were immigrants with few ties. They were, in Blake's opinion, easy targets. He just hadn't counted on the Kapurs' insistence that Harit would never commit murder, nor Maggie's diligence in proving that her neighbors were right.

Blake's body had never washed ashore, but Ned claimed to have seen his partner floating facedown in the waves after Blake and Maggie went overboard. A skeptical Maggie believed an alternate scenario. She thought that Ned, suddenly rid of both Blake and Maggie, had probably started the engine and taken off for port before Blake could climb back on board. Whichever way it had happened, there was no doubt in anybody's mind that Blake Armstrong was gone for good.

"Let's forget scams and bridges and anything that's not part of this wedding," Wanda said. "It's almost time, and you've just got this one thing left." She moved closer to position the comb.

Tracy had decided not to wear a veil. A white dress was probably a bit much, under the circumstances, but she had let herself be persuaded by her friends. Her college roommate, Sherrie, who was in China while her husband consulted at a hospital there, had sent the comb as Tracy's "something new" and promised she would come for a week in May to help when the baby was born.

Now Tracy sat while Wanda carefully set the comb into the curls at the back of her head. She was wearing her hair half up and half down, and the comb gave the style the right festive touch.

She stood, straightening her skirt and leaning forward to make sure her makeup was perfect. Then she held out her hand for her flowers, a bright tropical bouquet, heavy on gardenias, that was Florida all the way.

"So what do you think?" She turned so everyone could see her. "Will he run screaming into the night?"

"You look just like a movie star. I want to be *you* when I grow up," Olivia said, and they all laughed. Everyone kissed Tracy's cheek and gave her a hug, then followed her to the door.

Olivia peeked into the hallway; then she motioned them forward. Tracy could hear a buzz of voices over the music of fiddles and a banjo. She and Marsh had debated where to have the wedding, or even whether to simply elope right after the hurricane, but now she was glad they had chosen to wait and have a real celebration here, on the front lawn of the house where they were already sharing their lives.

She had invited the rec center staff and the members she worked most closely with; he had invited Wild Florida's employees and board, as well as their most ardent supporters. Friends from the community had come, as well, and important people from far away, some extended family of Marsh's, a few old friends of Tracy's from California. Phillip Callander and the staff of the newly reopened Dancing Shrimp had prepared an elaborate finger-food reception, and the flower arranging club at the rec center had created all the floral displays. A bluegrass band that often played at Wild Florida rallies was providing the music.

Of course, there was no cake. Wanda's Wonderful Pies had made dozens of Wanda's newest creation, the Key to Happiness Pie, which was a ramped-up version of her signature Key lime, with a coconut crust and coconut meringue. Wanda's new assistant had worked tirelessly. She was a young woman who liked baking nearly as much as Wanda did and promised to be the permanent addition Wanda needed.

"Okay," Wanda told Olivia. "You know what to do."

The girl nodded and took off through the screened porch, straight down the steps to Rishi, who was standing close by with Lily and Vijay. She consulted with him, then waved at Wanda in the doorway. Wanda, who'd already gotten the band's attention, gave the signal. They quickly finished up an old-fashioned fiddle tune, paused to prepare, then launched into the song that would begin the ceremony.

"All set?" Wanda asked. "The kids are lining up."

"Never Ending Song of Love." Tracy looked out, and saw Marsh and Bay waiting at the end of the grassy aisle leading down from the porch. "Marsh picked this one. He said the lyrics are true. From the first time we met, he knew. Of course, it took him a while to figure that out."

"Not just him, dear," Alice said.

Tracy stared out at all the people she had come to love. Then she looked at the women surrounding her. "Thank you. All of you."

"We're out of here," said a misty-eyed Wanda. "There go Lily and Olivia. And Vijay. He's protecting that ring with his life. I'll be surprised if he lets Bay have it to hold for his dad."

Tracy kissed each of them as they started across the porch. Since no one from her family was present, the women had decided to give her away themselves. There had been no question of dressing alike, but each woman wore a dress she had chosen in a jewel tone that suited her. They walked up the aisle after the children, Janya first, then Wanda, then Alice. After a moment Tracy came down the steps and walked slowly behind them as people stood.

At the front, Alice's minister waited to begin the ceremony. He was a good-natured man who hadn't balked at any of Tracy's unusual requests. The women parted, and Marsh stepped over to take Tracy's hand. He was wearing a dark suit and a warm smile. Without waiting until the ceremony was over, he turned, pulled her close and kissed her, to the applause of all those who had gathered. Bay stepped forward and gave her a hug.

"Dearly beloved," the minister began when the applause died, and Tracy and Marsh were facing him again.

Tracy, who had never expected to be this happy, thought no words had ever suited an occasion more than those.

After photos of the bridal party had been taken, Janya looked for her husband to relieve him of some of the burden of two little ones. Rishi was a good father, but together the children were a handful. Nowadays, when Vijay got going, he was hard to stop.

She found Rishi balancing plates of vegetables and dip, and a squirming Lily. She took the little girl and kissed her hair before she straightened the lopsided bow perched on top. From the corner of her eye she watched Vijay picking through the food on the children's table. Tracy had told her not to worry. She had asked Phillip Callander to make the children's table vegetarian.

"Lily was a star," Rishi said. "And so was our Vijay."

Janya liked the sound of "our." For a moment she felt a lump deep in her throat.

"I could not tell the others," she said. "So don't expect to be congratulated. They will know soon enough. But today was Tracy's day. I didn't want to steal her spotlight."

"Janya, they would have been thrilled."

"They will still be thrilled tomorrow, or when Tracy and Marsh come home from their honeymoon."

"Then we will have a celebration. In our new home. With our children."

This time the word *our* brought tears to her eyes.

Last week the second set of grandparents had finally turned down the agency's offer of custody. Yesterday the social worker, Miss Crede, had made a surprise visit to say that once the families in India had seen enough information about the Kapurs, both sets had agreed that the children should stay where they were and grow up in the United States, the country of their birth, and had signed papers to that effect. Both sides had expressed a hope that someday the children would be brought to India to meet their extended family. Perhaps losing Harit and Kanira had softened their outlook. Janya and Rishi intended to honor that request.

Now the adoption itself was merely a formality to be accomplished when all the paperwork was finished. The children were as good as theirs.

"Some might say the families were heartless to abandon their grandchildren," Rishi said. "But I think they knew this was best for them."

Janya stood on tiptoe and kissed her husband, a rare public display of affection that made him blush. Since the day of their marriage they had gone from strangers to friends, and now they were parents. Along the way, she thought, she and Rishi had become lovers, as well. She couldn't imagine sharing her life with anyone else.

"Rishi, I am good at keeping secrets. I kept this one, but there is another I have kept, as well."

He looked as if a year of guessing would not provide an answer. She relieved him of the burden.

"My mother is coming to meet her new grandchildren, and to give us advice on how to be parents. She will be here next month. As yet, there is no return date on her ticket."

"She is coming . . . here?"

"I will do what I can to prepare."

"In a million years you could not do enough."

They gazed at each other, and then they began to laugh.

Wanda wasn't much for crowds anymore. Fighting her way to go anywhere had no appeal, but this crowd parted just ahead of her, and she was suddenly staring at Derek Forbes, who left his enthusiastic audience to come to her side, grab her and swing her around.

"Put me down, you foolish man," she said, hoping he would ignore her.

He did ignore her long enough to give her a big hug before he released her.

She put her hands on his shoulders and examined him closely. She'd known he was coming, but she hadn't been sure how he would look. "You don't look that much the worse for wear. You being a real-life hero now and all."

Derek's bold dive into the bay had been an amazing feat, but it hadn't been without repercussions. He had been badly bruised during the rescue, and he'd injured his back. As soon as the hurricane passed, he had flown back to California, where he had been ever since, recovering and working on the film. Wanda had evaded his phone calls, but there was no evading the man himself.

He put his arm around her shoulder and pulled her off to one side. People were staring and pointing, but nobody in the awestruck assembly approached them.

"Quite a day," he said. "The bride looks glorious."

Wanda thought so, too. "That darn storm brought a few good things along with it."

"I'm sorry about your house."

"I hate to say it, but it was time for all of us to move on. Nobody wanted to be the first, and I guess Phyllis took care of that. But it hasn't changed anything important. We still get together on Thursday nights at somebody's house. Tracy's the only one left on the key, but once that new bridge goes up, nobody'll be more than ten minutes from anybody else."

"And what about you?"

"Me? Well, Ken and I are living in a rental condo for now. We kind of like it. Might stay —"

He laughed and shook her shoulder playfully. "You know what I'm asking. What have you decided to do about the *franchise?*"

The jig was up, and Wanda knew it. She tried to think of a nice way to let him know her decision, but Derek saw the answer in her eyes. "You're not going to do it, are you?"

"I keep telling myself I'm crazy. It's the chance of a lifetime."

"Well, maybe not. If it's not what you want."

She tried to come up with the right words.

Derek's offer had forced her to think about some unpleasant facts. As a girl she had avoided higher education, despite her guidance counselor's urgings, married young, chosen a good, stable man, given birth to one son and one daughter and avoided any job she would have to take home at night. She had made friends with women like herself, the wives of other cops, servers at her restaurants, who had a similar outlook on life. Not until she'd gone to live at Happiness Key had she gotten to know women who were substantially different.

Somehow, through all that, and with the support of family and friends, she'd gained the confidence she needed to open her own shop. Then Derek had come along and offered to make her a Betty Crocker–style icon, and he'd turned her head for a little while, that was for sure. But there was no fool like an old fool. If that hadn't been a cliché, she would have coined it herself.

"See, here's what I figured out," she said. "Some part of me wanted this whole thing with you to be a big honking success. I wanted to wake up in the morning, look in the mirror and know I could be real proud of myself 'cause all of a sudden I was somebody special."

"Wanda —"

She held up her hand so she could finish. "The thing is, Deke, I realized I already *am* proud, and I already *am* special. See, I guess I just don't need to be famous, too. It was tempting, kind of an ace in the hole on the proud-of-myself front, but it comes with too much attached. I don't want to fly around the country and give interviews and show up at pie shop openings. I don't want to work any harder than I already do. In fact, I want to work less, not more. I want to bake pies, come up with new recipes and still have time to chew the fat with my customers. That's all. Then I want to go home and hang out with Kenny. I want to spend time with my kids and grandkids. I want to help Janya and Tracy raise their families."

"You want a life."

That just about said it all. She nodded.

"You think I don't understand?"

She supposed maybe he did. Who would understand better?

"How about just selling me your recipes, then?" he said. "Could you do that? I bet you could use the income. Those grandkids have to go to college. You could hire more help at your shop and not work as hard as you do."

"You would do that? You would buy them?" She considered for a moment. Then her eyes narrowed in speculation. "Maybe give me royalties?"

He laughed. "You would have been good to have in the business. But yes, your pies are the best. Maybe you could do a little training at the first shop I open, just to get things rolling. But all on your own terms."

"I'll think about that." She gave him a huge smile. "But I won't take too long. I think we have a deal."

They were six dances into the reception and two away from cutting the pies before Tracy could get Maggie off to one side. Alice was dancing with Roger, who looked wonderful in a suit that actually fit. Felo, in a lavender linen shirt that looked as if it was straight from Havana, was dancing with Wanda, who looked as happy as Tracy felt. Tracy figured she and Wanda had a long conversation coming. She'd seen her friend talking to Derek Forbes.

Now she grabbed and embraced Maggie, who looked gorgeous in a cocoa-brown silk suit over a black lace camisole.

"I knew you were coming, but I was starting to worry," Tracy said.

"It'll be a lot easier to see you once the bridge is repaired. Your wedding guests took up the ferries for almost two hours."

They embraced once more, just because they could. After the rescue, Tracy had visited Maggie in the Palmetto Grove hospital, and once Maggie was recovering at home, Tracy

644

and Marsh had driven to Miami for a night of Cuban food and a tour of the city. Still, every time she saw her friend she remembered how close they had come to losing her. Only Felo and Ken's dogged determination and savvy had convinced a rescue team to go into the heart of the storm to find Maggie. Despite all odds against locating her, they had already been out searching when the GPS coordinates were relayed to them.

"It was a beautiful wedding," Maggie said. "I want one just like it."

"Are you making an announcement here?"

Maggie held out her hand, where a single diamond solitaire looked perfectly at home. "Maybe as soon as this summer."

Tracy gave her a warm hug. "Then you've worked things out! I'm so glad."

"We got some help doing it," Maggie said, hugging her back. "I'm still working on some stuff, but at least I'm finally dealing now. Mom doesn't know yet, but I'm going to tell her in a little while. I want to have the ceremony when she and I have time to plan it together. Before school starts in the fall."

"I'm so happy for you!" Tracy hesitated. "School?"

"Law school. I've been accepted at UM. I still want to put away the bad guys and make sure it's done right. But I belong in the prosecutor's office more than I belong in a cop's uniform."

"It all worked out for you. I'm so glad."

"And for you," Maggie said. "Wild Florida's buying Happiness Key? Mom says it's almost final?"

"They're going to use the land as an outdoor classroom for schoolkids. They'll have one small building for administration and a lab, probably where the old office used to be, then they'll put in platforms to house the kids in tents so they can camp overnight. They'll be studying all kinds of things. Flora, fauna, tides, weather patterns, water quality."

"You're okay with it?"

Tracy looked up, and saw both Felo and Marsh bearing down on them. "I am. Once it's finally up and running, I may even join the staff. Who knows the place better? And I've been promised by the man in charge that our whole Happiness Key gang can still use our favorite beach whenever we're together."

Marsh put his arm around Tracy's waist and pulled her close. "I hear we're supposed to cut the pies in a minute. Then you and I have a plane to catch."

Tracy greeted Felo, who kissed her soundly in congratulations.

"Plane?" Maggie asked.

"Costa Rica. For a week. Alice and Roger are staying with the kids," Marsh said.

"An eco-resort with a spa," Tracy said. "We're learning to compromise."

The band struck up something particularly

raucous, and Tracy and Marsh were herded to the dessert table. She cut the first pie and fed a bite to him; then he reciprocated. Everyone swarmed around the table as the Dancing Shrimp staff cut and served the rest.

Marsh took Tracy's hand and led her through their well-wishers to the edge of the crowd. But their departure wasn't complete. When they got past their guests, her former neighbors were waiting.

"We got you something," Wanda said. "You should open it now."

Maggie went up to the porch and came down with a wide, flat package that was half as tall as she was.

"You might say we had to dig deep . . . to give you this," Alice said.

Tracy couldn't imagine what kind of gift this could be. A painting? Something expensive they'd had to dig deep into their pockets for? She was surprised, because somehow that just didn't fit with the kind of friendship they had.

The package was wrapped in plain brown paper, likely one of the few things large enough to enfold it. A bright red ribbon was tied in a fancy bow.

"Janya, I bet you tied this," Tracy said.

"It will be easy to untie," Janya said. "Just pull the end."

Marsh had stepped away, and he gestured for her to do the honors. Tracy, who still held her bouquet, took one look at it, then tossed it to Maggie, who laughed and caught it easily.

"Something I ought to know?" Wanda asked.

Maggie put her arm around her mother. "Let's watch her unwrap. Then I have a lot I want to tell you. We'll find a quiet spot."

The bow came undone as easily as Janya had promised. The paper, which had only been folded around the gift, came loose when the ribbon fell away.

Tracy stared at the sign that had reposed, faceup and neglected, at the border of her property since the day she moved to Florida. It had been cleaned and polished by her friends, but it was still a wreck.

"Happiness Key," she read out loud, choking on the words. Letters that were too faded to read had announced the future development of a condominium complex and marina, but now the only part she could make out was the name. It was enough.

"Do you need us to explain why we dug it out of the rubble? Took three of us to find it and do it. But it was just lying there waiting," Wanda said.

Tracy didn't need an explanation. Once she returned from her honeymoon and consulted with her new husband, the sign would find a place of honor somewhere in the yard of the Cracker house. But wherever it stood, this was one message that was perfectly clear.

"We took Happiness Key with us," she said, leaning the sign against her hip and opening her arms to hug them in thanks. "All of us did. Here's the proof."

"One thing about you we can always count on, Mrs. Marshall Egan," Wanda said. "Sooner or later, you do figure things out."

The employees of Thorndike Press hope you have enjoyed this Large Print book. All our Thorndike, Wheeler, and Kennebec Large Print titles are designed for easy reading, and all our books are made to last. Other Thorndike Press Large Print books are available at your library, through selected bookstores, or directly from us.

For information about titles, please call:

(800) 223-1244

or visit our Web site at:

http://gale.cengage.com/thorndike

To share your comments, please write:

Publisher
Thorndike Press
10 Water St., Suite 310
Waterville, ME 04901